Within se
and the s   road
tail. Its outer skin was burning and flaking off with the friction of a half-controlled descent and it was heading straight for the Palace. It passed narrowly over the icebreaker and clipped the uppermost bulge in the ice where the beacon was located, shearing it off completely and peppering the surface over a half-mile radius with sharp hail. The unhelmeted men on the ice had to cover their heads against the dangerous rain as the shuttle skipped upward from the impact, sailing flatly over their heads with a wash of hot air that set the rough snow crackling.

Also by Stephen Couper in Sphere Books:

DYING OF PARADISE

The Ice Belt

STEPHEN COUPER

SPHERE BOOKS LIMITED
30-32 Gray's Inn Road, London WC1X 8JL

First published in Great Britain by
Sphere Books Ltd 1983

TRADE
MARK

Set in Linotron Baskerville

Printed and bound in Great Britain by
Cox & Wyman Ltd, Reading

One

It was a little less than a thousand miles to the north of the city, and Alex Peters was cold and miserable.

Although he was young, he was on the scrapheap, condemned through a court-martial for gross insubordination to this dismal icebreaker run for an unspecified period. Which meant, as far as Peters was concerned, forever. He was lucky still to be in the service at all; whilst the navy was rapidly shrinking as the old ships simply fell apart at the seams the recruiting office was regularly pestered by hopeful young citizens desperate for the opportunity of something to do. Add to this the fact that a navy is something of an anachronistic luxury on a world with only one landbound state and no enemies, and one is led to the inescapable conclusion that Peters would be fortunate to be anywhere at all outside the city's limits.

Such philosophical comfort was worthless in the face of Peters' unformed, as yet undirected ambition; all he could respond to was the ache in his gut that he felt about twice an hour when he thought about the heights that he *could* be reaching if he weren't here. Previously the daily routine of service had given him enough satisfaction at least to dab the blood from this deep wound in his soul; but now it had all the open empty days to torture and taunt him, and above all there was no preoccupation to come between him and the nagging suspicion that perhaps, when tested, he might find that he had no real talent to back up his ambition. In reaction to this unvoiced self-criticism he fumed all the more at the impotence of his situation, and through the days of his trial and his first week on the icebreaker he had grown noticeably thin and hollow-eyed.

It was no good. There were two full hours to go until his watch, but he couldn't get back to sleep. Keeping the blanket around his shoulders he swung his legs out of the narrow bunk, feeling the cold air wash over them; and then he missed his trousers and boots in the dark, and his foot touched bare metal for a moment.

That brought him upright faster than he had intended, and his head banged into the wire of the empty bunk above. The springing shook and sang in its metal frame and Peters mumbled something obscene.

He didn't put the light on when he'd struggled into his two-part cold weather suit because he found the unshielded bulb too bright so shortly after waking. Instead he opened the door and stepped over the low threshold into the outer corridor with its permanent emergency lights. At that moment there was a chopping sound from the engines deep down in the icebreaker, and on hearing this he grabbed the doorframe and waited. After only a few seconds there was a bass rumble from somewhere below and the deck began a slow tilt, holding a shallow angle for a few seconds before subsiding. Peters guessed that they were close to the main body of the polar icecap now, perhaps forcing their way up an open lead; the rough stuff would come later as the ice barrier before them became thicker and more uneven.

Peters let go of the bulkhead before the floor had fully dropped to level so that it was falling beneath him as he made his way uphill. He passed five empty bunkrooms identical to his own and swung on to the cast-iron stairway which led via a gallery to the messroom. This was a low-ceilinged hall which ran the full width of the ship, installed for the crew that had run her before the installation of the automatics. Now there were vague crusty shapes under the paintwork where tables and chairs had been bolted, and most of the access doors had been spot-welded shut as the spaces beyond were converted for machine use. The ship was a confusing maze of corridors that led nowhere and the blank open spaces of former living areas; a floating metropolis built for hundreds and peopled by two.

The only piece of equipment in the messroom still intact was the dispenser. For the past week Peters had been trying to work out the ordering procedure, but as most of the labels were illegible or or had completely peeled away, it was still very much a case of trial and error. He punched the sequence which he always knew preceded a drinks order and then touched two more buttons at random. Behind a scratched plastic window three cups dropped into place side by side and were filled by three simultaneous jets, accompanied by the whirring of a pump somewhere inside the machine, As the jets died, the compartment lit up and the plastic window slid aside.

There was no way of telling what he'd ordered. It looked like vegetable soup but it smelled sweet. He shrugged and, after dropping one of the full cups down a disposal chute, took the other two and moved back towards the stairway.

He passed by his bunkroom and carried on towards the bridge. There was no direct access through the ship – installation of the central pump for the stabilizing gear had blocked that off – so the converting engineers had added a shielded walkway across what had been open deck. Loss of a couple of the side-plates on that walkway had turned it into a freezing wind-tunnel, a kind of gauntlet that had to be run several times during each period of duty. Encumbered with the cups he was fortunate in that he could elbow the big levers on the outer doors without much difficulty, but he found the walkway banked up with snow on either side and slippery underfoot. A bitter wind pulled at him and hurt his eyes, and when he finally got to the bridge door he almost fell inward with it.

If the captain had been using a pencil he would have thrown it down in annoyance. Unfortunately pressing the 'cancel' button on a calculator is nowhere near as flamboyant a gesture, so Peters was robbed of the drama.

'What the hell do you think you're doing?' the captain demanded, watching and waiting for a reply as his first (and only) officer used his back to push the outer door closed against the wind that had swung it in so violently.

'Sorry,' Peters apologized, 'it's rougher than when I was last out.' He held out the plastic cup as a peace-offering. 'I brought you a drink of something.'

The captain looked down as the anonymous brew was placed under his nose. It was by now almost cold, and half of it had been left behind in the walkway. A thin film of grease floated on the surface of what was left. 'Thanks,' he said, without sounding too convinced, and then he put it to one side and recommenced his calculations.

Peters knew better than to interrupt again, so he dropped down a folding seat in the rear wall and waited. Like everything else on the icebreaker the bridge covered a much larger area than was now necessary. It had once been a semicircular chamber with windows that gave 180° of forward view, but now it was shuttered and dark with the only light coming from a couple of gooseneck lamps twisted around to bear on the console where the captain worked. All he was actually doing was transferring the data received from navigation beacons into the ship's computer, where the real work of course-plotting and execution would be carried out.

The radar warning on the far left of the captain's console began to warble, and within a couple of seconds Peters felt a vibration through the wall behind him as the stabilizer pump came into action. The captain did no more than glance up at the radar readout, but Peters felt a small knot of tension begin to wind itself around somewhere behind his breastbone.

They hit ice on the port side. Ballast oozed through into the port stabilizer tanks to bear down heavy and give purchase to the cutting blades which ran the length of the ship, but still the deck rode up beneath them. Gears shifted and the note of the engine changed as more power was pushed through to the blades. They bit and gripped, and then there was a distant grinding and tearing as the channelside sheared and broke away from the main pack ice. The deck dropped and the captain's soup did a flip in the air and emptied itself over the floor on the other side of the console.

For a while it was quiet, and the captain worked on. He finished tapping the figures into the computer and then had them read back while he checked his own work. Only then did he push his chair back on its short track and swung it around.

'You're over an hour early,' he said. 'Couldn't you sleep?'

'I woke up cold. Couldn't get off again.'

The captain inclined his head in agreement, and then turned back slightly so that he could keep an eye on one of the dull red screens on his console. He was a short, round man; Peters guessed that he had survived for too many years on the junk food from the dispenser, and wondered what kind of offence he had committed to earn this posting. He seemed well settled into his job and to have no eagerness to do anything else; he'd grown a beard and his hair was in a ragged, almost shoulder-length cut which looked out of place on a middle-aged man.

'It's cold everywhere,' he said. 'Going to get colder. You'll have to start sleeping in your weather suit.' This, apparently, was what the captain did all the time, for his own suit was creased and stained like the lining from a dog's basket.

Peters asked, 'Do you want me to take over yet?'

The captain continued to stare at the unwavering dot on his red screen. He said nothing, and Peters wondered if he'd heard. Perhaps he couldn't raise the enthusiasm to answer; or, more likely, it was a hamfisted psychological ploy, an inadequate man's assertion that he was in charge and don't you forget it. Peters stayed put on his fold-down seat and felt his face slowly flushing.

'Does that mean yes or no?' he blurted, and then regretted it immediately.

The captain turned back, slowly. 'It means no,' he said. 'You don't come on this console until you're due to come on. This may be shit run as far as you're concerned but I'm still ship's captain and I expect to be treated like one. Understand?'

Peters nodded. It wasn't enough. 'Do you understand, sailor?'

'Yes, sir.'

The captain pointed to where the spilled soup was spreading on the deck, now visible beyond the edge of the console. It was creeping, glacierlike, towards the door. 'While you're here,' the captain said, 'check the angle of inclination. Looks like we might have a slight list.'

Grateful for the change of topic, Peters stood up and went forward to the inclinometer. It was a dial on one of a series of grey boxes and interlinked tubing fixed to the forward bulkhead. The needle was five degrees off and as he reported this he added, 'but won't the ship's computer compensate?'

'Not if it's a fault in the stabilizers,' the captain said, pulling his seat back towards the console. 'If it's not that, the cargo may have shifted. You'll have to go below and check.'

Peters went below, covering his face with his sleeve as he passed the gaps in the walkway and feeling ice needles stab at his knuckles. The stabilizer tanks ran the full length of the ship and access to the telltale dials wasn't standardized. It was an hour before he got around them all, and his last visit was to the Number Four hold where the Ice Palace cargo was tied down.

It seemed ridiculous, but these few miserable crates were the only justification for the icebreaker's existence. Peters had never even heard of the Ice Palace until he'd begun this assignment, and then they'd told him very little. The Palace was, it seemed, a prison without guards, security guaranteed by the most hostile conditions in the world; the icebreaker and its supplies were the only link between the Palace and the city, and it would be part of Peters's job to stand in the hold with a rifle during the unloading to make sure they didn't return with more crew than they set out with. An attack had been tried some years before, and only this measure along with the icebreaker's shielding had prevented its success.

Peters wasn't looking forward to the next few hours, nor was he particularly delighted at the prospect of the next few years to be spent shunting back and forth between city and pole in search of the Ice Palace beacon, never in the same place twice as the Palace drifted with the cap. The cargo consisted mainly of long, flat crates; pipe cladding and insulation, from what he'd been told, and virtually nothing else. He couldn't understand how the prisoners could be fed, since the sea had supposedly been sterilized over a two hundred mile radius and there was nothing on the ice that could live without the fish as prey. Surely, they didn't eat the pipe cladding – but why should they need so much of it, and nothing else?

He didn't go too close to the upright crate at the far end of the hold. It was bigger and heavier than all the others, as he'd noticed when he'd helped to load it; now, for some reason, it made him feel uneasy when he turned his back on it to check off the stabilizer dial.

The tank was a little below pressure, but hardly enough on its own to cause the list. He considered switching in the regulator to bring the tank up to its full poundage but decided against it. With his luck he'd probably split the damn thing right open and get them stranded.

He forced himself to check the automatic winches and the unloading platform before he left, all the time uncomfortably aware of the wooden shape which bulked in the darkness behind him. He was relieved to get back to the bridge and take over on the navigation console.

Two

It was four o'clock in the morning at the Ice Palace, but there was no way that any of the men under the ice could know this. Their only timekeeping was by the regular blips of the radio beacon, and a careful count of these told them when to work and when to eat. Even this method varied in its reliability as the men on counting detail skipped a few pulses to bring the end of their shift a little nearer, but then nobody could challenge their measurements; for most of the year the light outside on the ice was a uniform iron-grey without day or night, and the men of the Palace contrived to see as little of it as they could possibly get away with.

Four o'clock, and there was an echo on the beacon, a double-pulse which indicated the approach of the supply ship. The man by the equipment hesitated as he transferred the wooden counting-chips from one bowl to another, crouching close to the speaker to be sure that the sound was genuine and not just an imagined echo in his own head; and then, as soon as he was certain, he put the bowls aside and squeezed out through the narrow doorway. The procedure when this happened was long-established.

Go tell the Worm.

Minutes later a small man in an oversized snow-suit was trotting towards the bunkrooms. The corridor down which he moved was a rough oval carved straight through the pack-ice, its slick walls made translucent by the glow of buried lights at intervals beneath its surface. The man's gait was uneven as he hopped across the half-buried slats that formed the floor, and as he panted slightly with the effort his breath feathered condensation into the cold, still air.

After a while the corridor forked. The light was poorer but the footing was better, because here there was a slight incline to the floor which carried away any meltwater from the walls before it could form a crust over the wood. Rumbling sounds echoed up towards him now, the hard, desperate beat of the Ice Palace over the distant throb of the generators.

Now he was on Main Street, the circular tunnel which was the heart of the Ice Palace. The bunkroom doors along here were all numbered in black charcoal, solid metal structures set deep into the walls, and the man counted them off as he passed. At the fifth one he came to he stopped and pulled a piece of curled grey paper out of the front pocket in his snow suit, checking its information against the smeary number before him. He raised a hand to knock, thought better of it, and opened the door to slip inside.

It was dark and steamy in the bunkroom; not exactly warm, but a distinct contrast to the still coolness of the corridor. He left the door open a crack in preference to switching on the light, for all around him figures were starting to heave and turn under blankets in sleepy irritation as the outer chill began to penetrate.

The small man crouched by one of the shapeless heaps in a lower bunk and gave it a tentative prod. 'Willis!' he whispered urgently. 'Willis! Wake up, Willis!'

Willis squirmed to escape the prodding, and his voice came muffled from underneath. 'What's the matter? What's going on?'

'A ship, Willis! I just got the word from the beacon. The supply ship's tracking us across the ice!'

Willis risked a suspicious eye out in the open. He could see the silhouette of the small man against the slit of light from the door, and caught the glint from the single remaining lens in his spectacles. 'What are you playing at, Worm?' he demanded, and there was a groan from somewhere above. 'Why should I want to know that?'

'You know why, Willis,' the Worm said, sounding almost hurt.

'Will you cut the noise?' a voice demanded out of the darkness above. 'I got to be out on the ice in about three hours!'

'Sorry I woke you, Berg,' the Worm said, forgetting to whisper and causing more of the anonymous shapes to stir and mumble. 'I came to tell Willis about the ship.'

'I'm not interested in any ship,' Willis insisted.

'Go play with yourself, Worm,' Berg added.

The Worm dropped his voice back to a whisper and said, 'Willis, it's your turn to take an unloading duty.'

'It can't be my turn.'

'It *is*. I've checked. You and Lobo.'

'With *Lobo*? Forget it, Worm.'

Willis turned over decisively and tried to pull the blanket back over his head as another voice came from across the room, 'What's going on down there?'

'The Worm's kidnapping Willis,' replied the voice from the darkness immediately over their heads.

'For Christ's sake!'

The Worm stood up and addressed himself in the general direction of this latest speaker. 'Look,' he said, 'I'm sorry you're awake, but it's definitely Willis's turn. I mean, what's the point of me working these rosters out if you won't follow them?'

'He's right, Willis.' The speaker across the room said, having to raise his voice over the groans and complaints of those who had been newly awakened by the Worm's latest declaration. 'Get dressed and get lost.'

'Go on, Willis,' Berg added. 'Give us some peace.'

Willis sensed that the antagonism of the bunkroom was beginning to focus not upon the Worm but on him, and he demanded, 'Whose side are you on?'

'If we didn't cooperate and follow my rosters, where would we all be?' the Worm asked of nobody in particular, pleased to find that for once he was not the sole object of the general enmity.

'We'd all be asleep,' somebody said.

Willis still showed no sign of cooperation, but instead demanded, 'What do you mean, if *we* didn't cooperate? I've never seen your name on that roster, Worm.'

'And I don't see you working any rosters out yourself, Willis.'

'What?'

The Worm saw Willis's hand reaching for him and skipped backwards with a startled yelp, banging into the wooden support of the bunks behind him. Somebody said, 'Stop picking on the Worm and get down to the unloading bay, Willis.'

'Go down with Lobo and treat yourself to some scintillating conversation.'

To enforce the point, Berg reached down from his own bunk and jerked Willis's blanket away. Willis began to protest, and was told, 'You can have it back when you get back from the bay.'

Willis gave in, although not particularly gracefully. The Worm hovered a respectable distance away as Willis zipped into his snow suit and connected up the battery pack that had hung at the end of his bunk, and then he followed out into Main Street.

Willis paused outside the door and rubbed at his eyes in an attempt to bring himself fully awake. The Worm said, 'You got everything?'

'I've never had any complaints. You'll regret this, Worm.'

'I think I'm regretting it already. But, please, Willis, I've got to do my job. You know I'm not well enough to take a shift on the ice.'

No observer could hesitate to agree. The one called the Worm didn't, in fact, seem fit for anything much; he was a full head shorter than Willis, and he'd had to roll up the arms and legs on his snow suit to make it fit, the result of this being that the rest of the suit hung slack. His spectacles didn't only have a lens missing, they also lacked an arm and seemed in constant danger of throwing themselves on to the floor.

Willis moved off down Main Street towards the cavernous bay areas, and the Worm followed. The carved-out corridor was no longer empty. Men were starting to appear walking towards them, their snow suits glittering crystal in the twilight with a crust of unmelted hail from the surface outside. They seemed exhausted, heads bowed and with no intention other than to get to their bunkrooms. Four men passed without any sign of recognition but to the fifth Willis called, 'Hey, Spook.'

The man named Spook stopped by the open door to his bunkroom and waited until they drew level. 'Hi, Willis,' he said, ignoring the Worm.

'Want to do a shift for me? Trade you the next one back.'

'Sorry Willis, I'm beat. Any other time but now. We had a pipeline fracture and the power levels dropped almost to danger. Anyway, you already owe me two. What's the big problem?'

'Forget it. I'm sorry I reminded you.'

'The icebreaker's coming in,' the Worm said, as Willis started to move away.

'What does that mean?' Spook demanded bitterly. 'Another shipment of lousy second-rate pipe-cladding? The cold breaks it down and the wind strips it off. Those sadistic crumbs designed it that way to keep us working.'

'It's the secret of a happy life,' Willis said, and moved on.

They walked on in silence for a while, leaving Main Street and stepping through a less well-finished linking tunnel into a parallel passage. They went down this for a short distance and then took the next turn, which led directly towards the bay areas.

'You know,' the Worm said reproachfully after a while, 'you really shouldn't take it all out on me.'

'Why not?' replied Willis, unconcerned. 'If I've got to take it out on somebody, a skinny little runt like you seems a good choice.'

'But if that's the reason, why make fun of Lobo? He's almost twice your size.'

'You're a shrimp; he's stupid. It all evens out.'

A pause and then; 'I wouldn't depend on that, Willis. Appearances can mislead.'

'Come off it, Worm. You wouldn't even make a presentable frog.'

'I'm talking about Lobo. Just because he's big and slow, don't assume he's stupid. I've come to terms with all this contempt because I don't have the choice. Lobo won't be the same.'

'Quiet, Worm. You'll have me crying down my snow suit next. Where is he?'

The Worm pointed ahead. 'Down there in the loading bay. He got up and went there early, without being told.'

Willis laughed, not very pleasantly. 'And that's your idea of untapped intellect? I don't even think we should be trusting you to do the rosters any more.'

By now they were at the outer door to the loading bay. It took all Willis's weight to swing it open, and he walked off as the Worm struggled to get it closed. 'That's typical,' the Worm said. 'None of you understand how complicated those rosters are. We've got over fifty men here, and if we don't work at full efficiency we all die. That's how it was designed. And you think it's easy to keep all that going?'

'Shove it, Worm,' Willis's voice drifted back, strangely amplified under the high ceiling of the cargo store which led through to the loading bay. 'I don't do any thinking before breakfast.'

As the Worm had said, Lobo was already there when they rounded the corner into the loading bay, sitting on an empty crate next to the cargo chute and the massive iron outer door. He wasn't by any means twice the size of Willis, but he was certainly taller and broader. The impressiveness of this was increased by what somebody had called 'the Robinson Crusoe look', a shaggy beard and haircut that was the only style available to the Ice Palace detainees. Lobo looked up as they approached.

'Hi, Willis,' he said, his tone surprisingly gentle.

'You talk too much, Lobo,' Willis replied. 'Try to restrict yourself to the essentials.'

Lobo turned to the Worm. 'What did I say?'

'Willis doesn't feel too good this morning.'

Willis adjusted the power pack slung at his hip to compensate for the lower temperature in the bay, and said, 'Stop apologizing for me, Worm. Where's the ship?'

Lobo shook his head. 'I rolled up the hatch a couple of inches and had a look. You can barely see past the end of the ramp, but there's nothing there.'

'Check again, and this time there'd better be. Or else I'm liable to step on something . . .' With this, he reached out and grabbed the Worm by the ear. The Worm howled and tried to pull away, and Willis started to laugh.

'Let go of his ear, Willis.'

'What?'

'I said let go of his ear.'

The Worm was still protesting on the other end of the grip. Willis held it for a moment, but Lobo didn't move or look away, and after a couple more seconds Willis said, 'To hell with it. I'll get a helmet and look myself.'

The Worm got his ear back, and Willis stamped off back to the cargo bay where the racks of helmets were kept. The Worm said, 'Thanks, Lobo. Willis doesn't like me, you know.'

'Forget it, Worm,' Lobo replied. 'I don't like you either.'

Willis came back with a couple of the brightly coloured helmets. Countless generations of use had bleached the material of the snow suits into varied light pastel shades, but the helmets had kept their original brilliance. He offered one to Lobo, who had already collected one on his way, so in the end it was given to the Worm.

The outer door rolled upward, moved by a set of gears which concentrated a few feet of pulling on a chain into inches of advance. They were badly maintained and squealed horribly as the rusted surfaces ground together, Lobo dragging the chain with all his strength as Willis climbed to the top of the loading chute and spread himself to peer under the rising edge. Light slanted in, and Willis was enveloped by a swirl of hard snow that was forced in through the gap, so it was difficult to see when he raised his hand for Lobo to stop and release the door.

Willis got up and walked back down the chute to floor level, leaving a Willis-shaped outline in new snow at the top. 'Thought I saw some lights,' he said, and jumped the last couple of feet, 'but nothing near enough to get excited about.'

So they sat around for a while and if Willis felt like complaining any more about lost sleep he kept it to himself. In the end the icebreaker announced its own arrival, with a jarring thump that set the chains rattling. Lobo started to haul on the chain again, and as the bay door crept upward it disclosed the bright square of the open ship's hold sliding finally into line some distance beyond.

The blizzard effectively ensured that there was nothing more visible of the icebreaker as it lifted and subsided in the oily frozen slush that was the only form of open water to be found in these latitudes. The hold was a disembodied gateway ringed by a yellow haze, and Willis could see that there was somebody waiting in the gateway, dressed not in a powered snowsuit but a totally inadequate wrap-around jacket over ordinary cold weather wear. He was shivering, and the gun in his hands was waving everywhere. His voice drifted across the gap, thin and reedy without suit amplification, 'Is this the Ice Palace?'

'Cut the jokes, clown,' Willis projected back. 'Where the hell do you think it is?'

'Got a cargo for you. You ready to receive?'

'Stop waving that popgun at me and get on with it. You're making us lose heat.'

'Captain says I've got to have this. He told me to watch you.'

'Shove it, kid. I'm not dancing today.' Willis was getting impatient. Direct exposure to the wind fairly sucked power out of the suit's compact unit, and the time spent on recharge would be added to his next shift.

The gun – a rifled blaster with no recoil – stabbed warily in his direction. 'I had to watch you in case...'

'I know all about that! Will you just put the crates on the ramp and get on with it!'

'Don't you even want to hear the news?' Now the kid sounded hurt!

'Shove your news. I don't want to be well informed, I want to be warm!'

The young man on the icebreaker shrugged. 'Have it your way,' he shouted, and leaned over to thumb a button to one side of the open hatch. The first crate – a familiar shape, a set of quarter-section pipe cladding – swung out over the gap on an extending arm which was directed across by a joystick mechanism in the hold. As the crate swung close, Willis grabbed it and pulled it in on to the cargo ramp, steadying it and using his free hand to disengage the hook at the top.

Lobo had lifted a great armful of chain to knot it over on itself and hold the bay door three-quarters open and now he came forward to help with the unloading. They handled the crates carefully, laying each on its flattest side before letting it roll down the chute, for the wooden framework would be as valuable to them as the contents. The Worm had taken a green cargo manifest which had been nailed to the first crate and was making a great show of checking each one off as it came in. When congestion threatened at the bottom of the ramp Lobo left Willis and came down to move the boxes across to the harness-drawn cargo train that ran along narrow rails to the adjacent bay, stacking them on the low wagons so that they would be easily accessible for the outgoing surface teams.

It was a paltry load, all pipe-cladding with one unexpected bonus, a box of replacement lightbulbs. The Worm scrambled up the ramp, dodging a crate as it slithered towards him, and pulled at Willis's sleeve, shouting, 'That's the last one, according to my manifest.'

Willis shook his head, a motion that was barely broadcast

by his helmet, and indicated another crate which was in the process of being hooked up for transfer.

'But it can't be right,' the Worm insisted, waving his piece of green paper, 'There's nothing listed.'

Willis pushed the manifest aside and reached out to guide the cargo in. The Worm skipped back when he saw that it would almost fill the chute, scrambling to get out of the way before it could knock him aside; and then Willis had trouble getting it unhooked, for it was taller than himself and considerably heavier than any of the other crates.

Lobo came back to help, for it took both of them to get the box flat on the chute and down to the bottom whilst the Worm protested that it wasn't on his paper and it shouldn't be here. Willis swore at him and pushed him out of the way a couple of times, and then went back up the incline to the open door. The hook was back in the ship's hold and empty.

'That's everything,' the armed youth shouted. 'See you on the next run.'

'Up yours, kid,' Willis replied, and then, to Lobo, 'Let's get this hatch closed.'

Lobo unlooped the chain and let the weight of the door drag it down as the gears spun and shrieked. It closed at the bottom with a solid smack as a last handful of snow puffed in and settled. The silence after the scouring of the wind was unsettling, and the clicks and rasps of metal and plastic as they removed their helmets and set them down were somehow sharpened and magnified.

'I bet you even hate your own mother,' said the Worm.

'Damn right,' Willis replied, his eyes on the last, oversized crate. 'She sold me out and collected the reward when they put me here.'

Lobo shook some of the crystals from his arms and shoulders. The temperature in the bay had dropped considerably, and they lay like a handful of discarded diamond dust on the floor. 'What about this last crate, Worm?' he said. 'It's too big to stack with the others.'

The Worm consulted his piece of green paper yet again. He seemed to resent the fact that the crate was there at all, as if it challenged some fundamental law of his universe. 'I don't know, Lobo,' he said. 'I think it must have been a mistake. It isn't listed.'

'That's no mistake,' Willis said quietly. 'Look again, Worm.'

The Worm misunderstood, and went back to an inspection of the manifest. Lobo walked around to the other side of the crate and, putting his fingers under a narrow cross-brace, said, 'It isn't cladding. It's heavy.'

Willis glanced at the Worm, and then back to the crate. 'You ought to recognize it. They've changed the design, but the size is right.'

The Worm's head came up, and he frowned. 'Wait a minute. It can't be a man.'

'Why can't it?'

'Because . . . because it's the wrong kind of box. Because there's no paperwork to back it up. Besides which, the Palace is running over capacity anyway! They *can't* send us any more!'

''Fraid it looks like they have, Worm,' Lobo said, straightening after an attempt to see the contents of the box through a slight gap in the rough timber.

'Better get him up to the Doc and have him revived,' Willis added, 'or else he'll be beyond bringing back.'

The Worm brightened. 'That might be for the best. The rosters are hellish complicated as it is.'

He squawked as Willis's gloved fingers slipped into the round collar of his snow suit and hauled him up so that the material strained under his arms and Willis's knuckles pushed up against his nose. The Worm flapped his arms and gurgled, but this time Lobo made no move to interfere.

'Do me a favour, Worm,' Willis said. 'Any time I should happen to make a big mistake and be tempted to start liking you, remind me of what you just said. Shove your rosters. You can slot him in place of one of the men that disappeared on the ice last month.'

The Worm descended to his more usual elevation, grabbing at his glasses as they threatened to slide sideways off his nose. Lobo said, 'Do we open the crate?'

'No, we drag the whole thing along to somewhere warm. There's a place up near the Worm's office that we used to use, but I think one of the empty bunkrooms might be better.'

'That's a long way,' Lobo said doubtfully, 'and this is heavy.'

'And where's the paperwork?' the Worm said, making sure he was out of Willis's reach.

'How the hell should I know? Maybe it's "Torment-The-Worm" week back at the city. Get the other side, Lobo.'

Lobo got the other side, and it did them no good at all. The crate and its contents were too heavy, and even if they'd been able to slide it across the floors of the two adjacent bays they'd never be able to cope with the rough incline that led through to the Main Street passage and the bunkrooms. Willis sent the Worm off to find the man called Doc, and then he and Lobo cleared one of the cargo wagons and lifted it from its rails as a makeshift transport. Lobo worked slowly and patiently, taking Willis's directions without complaint or comment; and for Willis's part, he spent the next twenty minutes concentrating on a task without taking time out to abuse anybody. For that alone it was one of the Ice Palace's more remarkable days.

The metal wheels broke a good number of the slats on the corridor floor, but they were at least able to get as far as the passage which ran parallel to Main Street. This was where they hit a problem, because the crate itself was too wide to pass through the linking tunnel. As they tried to devise a way through the Worm arrived with Doc, who said it might be dangerous to tip the crate on its side, so in the end they had to forget about the bunkrooms and settle instead for the unheated chamber up the corridor which led to the Worm's office. It differed from the bunkrooms farther on in that it had bare ice walls and no lining or insulation, but at least it was less cold than the cavernous bays.

Under Doc's supervision they broke the seals and raised the lid. There were a number of gas tanks and liquid drips to be lifted out of the way and disconnected in a certain sequence, and only then could the wadding be pulled out to disclose the body underneath.

There he lay, huddled like a frog squashed into a matchbox. Nobody spoke for what seemed like a long time.

'Now why the hell,' said Willis at last, 'have they sent us a citizen?'

Three

No doubt about it, a citizen was bad news, and this one was an unmistakable specimen. He had all the patrician marks of the city's specialized breeding programme; the limbs that were a little too long for elegance, the regular features, the dark hair. A sculptured behaviour unit, ideal fodder for a rigidifying computer culture.

The Worm wanted to pull all the plugs and slide him into the crap tanks straight away. In that he was voicing Willis's private thoughts, which of course prompted Willis to react in the opposite extreme and insist that the newcomer at least be given a chance to explain himself. Lobo stood at the back of the room and said nothing, and Doc changed over the drips to start the revival procedure.

It was a slow process, seeming to consist of nothing other than standing around watching the citizen not waking up. After a while the Worm mumbled something about paperwork and edged out of the room. Lobo watched him disappear and then said, 'I'd better go. I'm due on shift. Coming, Willis?'

'I'll follow you down,' Willis replied. 'Tell the others I'm coming.'

Lobo nodded. 'See you later. See you, Doc.'

Doc gave a little wave, without taking his eyes off his 'patient'. The sleeper was almost up to temperature, and his heartbeat was normal; he'd be out of it within minutes, and it would hurt.

They pulled a fistful of needles from the crook of his arm and sat him upright. His eyes were beginning to twitch behind the lids, and the Doc had an idea.

'Better get him some yeast, Willis,' he said. 'He won't have eaten in more than a week.'

When Willis got back from the tanks a few minutes later the newcomer was awake and starting to get over the terrible cramps that were the immediate consequence of his confinement. He took the bowl of yeast that was offered to him, but choked on the first mouthful of the scummy warm liquid. At least it gave him enough moisture to manage his first words in the Ice Palace.

'It's foul,' he said. 'What is it?'

'Yeast,' the Doc replied. 'We grow it ourselves on waste. It may be foul, but it's all we've got.'

The newcomer turned his head with painful slowness to look at the Doc. He saw a shaggy-haired old man, a padded playsuit draped around a skeleton. Then back for a closer look at Willis; younger and better-fitted, but equally unkempt.

'I'm afraid you've got some re-orientation ahead of you,' the Doc went on. 'What's the last thing you remember?'

He frowned. You could almost hear the parts moving. 'Last night. Somebody came into my cell and threw a blanket over my head.'

'That was over a week ago. You've been in cold storage ever since, and that's literal. This is the Ice Palace.'

For a moment there seemed to be a flash of understanding in the newcomer's eyes, but it faded. 'The what?'

Willis moved around to stand by the Doc. 'The city's own private and secret social scrap-heap, designed and authorized by the Central Command computer. Fifty men fighting for their lives in a hole on top of two hundred miles of sterile sea. I doubt whether you've heard of it before.'

'Maybe I have, I don't know. I've got a killing headache. How long have I been here?'

'Hardly more than an hour,' the Doc said. 'The icebreaker dropped you off with the supplies. Try to drink some of the yeast.'

He tried, and didn't succeed. 'Does it all taste like this?'

'There's not much we can do with it, apart from dry it out and press it into blocks. We'll explain all this as we go along. It's essential you understand the system here.'

'What system? Who runs the place?'

'Wait a minute,' Willis put in quickly. 'We don't know anything about you yet. Who are you?'

'My name's Randall.'

'Randall what?'

'Randall nothing. Just Randall.'

'And what's a citizen done to be sent here?'

This brought a faster reaction than Willis had expected. 'I'm no citizen.'

'We're not stupid. Randall,' Doc interposed gently. 'Anybody can see you're a citizen. You've got Central Command stamped all over you.'

'There is no Central any more.' The information was received with polite disbelief. 'The Central Command computer. It's gone. A man named Rorvik broke into the computer building and managed to avoid the security systems. He interfered with the programme and wiped the memory.'

'I don't believe it,' Willis said.

'You don't have to. But you asked.'

Doc decided it was time Randall tried to walk. At first he couldn't straighten his legs, much less support his own weight on them; but with the attempt at use sensation began to speed back. Steadying himself against the cold, gritty wall Randall explained how the city they had known no longer existed; the computer defunct, the over-privileged community of citizens disbanded, the outsiders of the underbelly now forming the main strength of the provisional government.

'Is Avery Sim still leading?' Doc asked.

'Avery Sim died. There's a joint leadership of the two traders, Marius and Morden, and Chandler's running the Élite.'

From the corridor outside came noises, distant echoes of men on the move somewhere far down the passageway. Willis seemed not to hear them, but mused, 'Chandler. He was the agent hunter. If all this is true, why haven't we been taken home?'

The Doc shrugged. 'The underbelly doesn't want us, any more than Central did.'

'So what happened to honour among thieves?'

'You don't get honour among thieves, just a better class of dishonesty. It doesn't matter a damn who's holding the whip – we still get the worst of it.'

Doc and Willis took an arm each and walked Randall around. By the Ice Palace's own peculiar standards it would have been bad manners to ask Randall directly what he had done to be sent to them, but all the same Willis was obviously fishing for information. As they paced the irregular walls of the Recovery Room Randall explained that he'd been distantly associated with Rorvik and the plot against the Central installation, and that as the only survivor of the conspiracy the newly-appointed council had been unsure what to do with him; should they make him a national hero, or punish him to appease the citizens? Now it was obvious which way the toss of the credit chip had gone.

Willis had to be satisfied with this thin explanation, punctuated as it was by small yelps of pain and pauses as Randall bent to massage his protesting leg muscles, for a warning glance from the Doc told him that he was treading perilously close to the boundary of prisoner etiquette. Randall limped over to his transport box and lowered himself on to the edge, stretching his legs out to help the circulation.

'As long as I'm here,' he said, 'you'd better tell me the setup.'

'This is it, Randall,' Willis replied. 'Your world for the rest of your life, until we boil you down and filter you through into the yeast tanks.'

'What do you mean, "we"?'

'That's point number one,' Doc said. 'If it gives you any satisfaction, Randall, you're a free man.'

'Free to work or die,' Willis put in.

'There are no warders in the Ice Palace. We make the rules and enforce them ourselves, or we die. It's so simple that everybody understands it. The Palace is dug out around a fission power plant. It's automated and sealed, and we can't interfere with it. The power from that plant heats a network of pipes on the surface of the ice pack.'

Randall felt that something was expected of him at this point. 'To what purpose?'

Willis smirked, although it really wasn't funny. 'Tell him, Doc,' he said.

'None. The heat leaks off into the atmosphere, and we get the worst storms in the world because of it. But the power supply for the Palace itself is operated on an automatic cutout, and if that useless pipe network isn't kept together the Palace freezes up. Worse still, if the temperature in the yeast tanks drops below a certain level the yeast will die off and we won't be able to regenerate it without a live sample to start from. We'd be finished either way.'

'The pipe network's rotten,' Willis said. 'It was made that way and it's kept that way by the lousy repair materials the supply ship brings. We have to spend a hundred and fifty per cent of our time running around to forestall the cutouts. It happened, once. We had to burn some of the pipe-cladding to keep a sample of the yeast alive, and it took over a month to grow half a tankful from what we had left.'

When Randall was fit enough to walk unaided they took him to the Worm's 'office'. His first sight of the Ice Palace outside the Recovery Room was of a mis-shapen passageway with broken-glass walls lit from deep inside. The Main Street tunnel was close enough at this point to be seen as a soft, distant glow through the ice, rippling with the dark shapes of passing men like life growing in a translucent egg.

'Ever have an escape?' Randall asked as they moved away from Main Street towards a less well illuminated stretch.

'Never,' Doc replied. 'But I assure you, everything's been tried. It's over a thousand miles to the nearest settlement, and the yeast breaks down in the cold. Even tried using the protein direct instead of feeding people into the tanks, but nobody could digest it. Something about the essential bacteria in your gut – some of it must die off on an all-yeast diet.'

'So we have to work to soak up an over-production of power, just to ensure there's enough left for us to live?'

'That's it exactly. Willis, I thought you were due on shift?'

'I'm going,' Willis said as they arrived at a rough-looking wooden door set well back in the ice wall. He banged on it with the heel of his hand. 'Otherwise I'll have the Worm on my back.'

'The Worm?'

'You're going to meet him now. An obnoxious individual with too many teeth and not much forehead. We let him prepare all the work rosters because he's not fit for anything else.'

The door creaked open a suspicious crack, and a single spectacle lens glinted in it. 'What you saying about me, Willis?' a shrill voice demanded.

Willis gave the door a hard shove that sent the Worm tottering back into the room. 'I'm telling Randall what a nice fellow you are deep inside, and that he shouldn't be misled by your rotten nature.' They followed him in.

'Thanks, Willis,' the Worm said. 'You're all armpit.'

Doc glanced nervously at Willis, but he seemed to be respecting the fact that, alone in all the Ice Palace, this room was Worm territory.

'Watch it, Worm,' was all he said. 'Lobo isn't here now.'

'Sorry, Willis,' the Worm said, making no effort to seem sincere.

Randall looked around. There was less space than in the Recovery Room, but when your walls were solid ice you wouldn't want the luxury of unheated palatial grandeur. The floor was wooden slats raised on loose blocks, wet slush glinting beneath, and there was a coarse blanket and a bundle of wadding like that from his transport crate rolled up in the far corner, just visible beyond the upended box that the Worm seemed to use as a desk.

He caught the word 'citizen', and realized that they were talking to or about him. He dragged his attention away from the scraps of grey, mis-shapen paper that had been affixed to one wet wall with slivers of wood, and tried to focus back on the conversation.

'All that's behind you now,' the Worm was saying. 'You're going to find out what work is.'

'What would you know about it, Worm?' Willis demanded, unwilling to miss any opportunity.

'Aren't you supposed to be on shift, Willis?' the Worm asked with exaggerated polite concern. Willis, who had been getting ready to go, now found it necessary to stay a little longer.

'I'll go in my own time,' he growled.

'Okay, okay, I just thought I'd mention it.' The Worm turned back to Randall, revelling in his momentary importance. 'We had three men die last month. I thought it would be simplest to put you in one of their places on the roster.' This with a sideways glance at Willis, who had originally suggested the idea in the loading bay, but no reaction. 'You'll take over his shift, his bunk and his snowsuit.'

'I hope it fits,' said Randall, observing the comic-opera appearance of the Worm's pants and sleeves.

'None of them do,' said the Worm defensively, 'but that's your problem. I've been working out the details for the rostering, so now I'll show you where you'll be sleeping. You'll be sharing a bunkroom with Lobo.'

Willis suppressed a snort, and Doc said, 'Don't worry, Randall. You could do much worse. Do you feel fit enough to go?'

'You're the Doctor. You tell me.'

Doc smiled and shook his head. 'Only a nickname,' he said.

Randall thought about it for a moment, trying to assess the feedback from his body. It sang with all the energy of wet string. 'Not too bad,' he said at length. 'Just that I might be sick.'

'That's the yeast. It takes a while to get used to it, and after that you won't be able to eat anything else.'

The Worm was by the door, holding it open and looking pointedly from one to another. 'If you don't mind,' he said, 'I'd like to be getting along. I want to have your paperwork ready for the next shift.'

Randall stepped out first into the corridor. The Worm stayed where he was, holding the door and blinking expectantly at Doc and Willis. They followed Randall without comment, so that the Worm was the last to leave.

The Worm led Randall off towards Main Street, whilst Doc and Willis dawdled behind. Neither was heading for anything pleasant or enjoyable; if Willis's team were already out on the ice, which they probably were, he would have to grope his way out along the guide-wire until he caught up with them. Doc, in deference to his age, could look forward to a joyous ten hours' stirring in the crap tanks.

'What's the matter, Willis?' he said after a while. 'You've gone very quiet.'

Willis looked up to be sure that Randall had moved on out of earshot. 'I said it before, Doc. Something's wrong. Why send us a citizen?'

'If what he says is true, and there's no more Central Command, then the citizens will be technically of the same status as anyone else. Probably lower, if the underbelly council's in charge. Why shouldn't one of them wind up here?'

Willis dismissed it with a gesture. 'I don't believe that, either. If the computer's fallen, and the underbelly *has* taken over, why haven't they brought us home?'

'I can think of at least fifty reasons, Willis. Whatever made us dangerous to Central Command makes us equally dangerous to any government replacing it.'

'Clever talk, Doc, but these are our own kind. They wouldn't let us down. This Randall's something else.'

They were at the gap where the subsidiary tunnel and Main Street joined. They should have split to go on in different directions, but instead they stopped. 'What do you mean?' Doc asked.

'I watched him. The way he listened and took it all in. Accepted it straight away and without any self-pity. He may have the breeding stamp of a citizen, but his mind's something else.'

'I don't know. I never had much contact with them.'

'I stole from them. They were easy. Drop a citizen in here and he'd stick his head between his knees and bleat to go back to the herd. Randall didn't. And you know what Central did with that kind of failure.'

Doc's eyes grew large and round as he considered the prospect. 'The Élite?'

'Exactly. Randall was – or *is* – police.'

Doc considered it for a moment. 'Well . . . so what?'

'This is where you and I part company, Doc. There's no place for an Élite here. Maybe the Worm was right, and we should have lost him on the way up to the Recovery Room.'

'He'd be dead. You don't mean that.'

'Don't I? All that crap about some jerk closing down the main computer. The underbelly council wanting to re-open the space trade. This planet's been off the spaceways so long it's got nothing to offer. The story's so transparent, you could keep fish in it. Randall's a spy, and he's been placed here by Central Command. I don't know what for, but I'm sure of one thing. It's bad for all of us.'

The Doc sighed. 'Maybe you're right, Willis. Who's to say?'

'That's the trouble, we've no way of knowing. But as long as Randall's around there's an extra danger we can do without.'

'I hope you're not considering anything rash,' Doc frowned.

'Me?' Willis was a picture of wounded innocence. 'As if I would. I've got to go, I'm way overdue on the ice. See you around, Doc.'

'Be seeing you, Willis.' Doc waited a moment as Willis went off down the corridor towards the bays, and then turned and stepped through into Main Street, heading to where the crap tanks belched and beckoned.

Four

Randall wasn't fit for the grand tour that the Worm seemed to want to give him. He continually tripped and stumbled on the uneven flooring, and the cold air that eased down the passages in a barely noticeable breeze began to make him feel numb and sick. The Worm had to compromise in the end, leading him around the longer loop of Main Street and pointing out the branching tunnels on either side as they passed. What he called the 'Cantina' was, it seemed, in the centre of the loop, reached by openings at each corner, whilst the outside of the curve had the bunkrooms to the South and the crap tanks to the North. This tight little complex was boxed in by two massive chambers in the form of the loading bays and cargo store to the West and the generators to the South, but this relatively simple schematic plan was then confused by a rambling maze of hand-hewn corridors and tunnels, some of which led to sub-complexes of small chambers but many of which led nowhere at all.

Nobody knew the age of the Palace or its original purpose. The conjecture was that it had originally been some kind of long-term research base, remembered and converted by Central Command in a spasm of imaginative economics. Only surface meltwater was used for drinking, for the sea had been sterilized of life with a dumping of some exceptionally dirty radioactive material, perhaps from the Palace's own automated reactors.

Then the Worm began to talk about the pipe network and the need to maintain it at a set level of heat loss, and Randall mentally switched off. He'd heard this already, and he needed most of his concentration for the simple effort of keeping upright. The shallow curve of Main Street before and behind gave the impression that it had no real end which, of course, as a loop it didn't. He began to suspect that the Worm might be leading him around twice or more in order to make the most of his captive audience.

Randall stopped, and subsided against a wall. He felt the ice against his back begin to melt and soak into his clothes. The Worm returned and waited for him, looking a little disappointed.

'Only a couple of doors down,' he said, 'and you'll be there.'

'I think I can manage that,' Randall replied, and then added, 'I'm sorry, what do I call you?'

'Call me Worm. All these crumbs do. It stopped hurting long ago.'

Randall pushed himself upright, and his hands came away wet. They moved on more slowly than before.

'Is it as cold as this everywhere in the Palace?' Randall asked.

'Keep it too warm and the walls would melt. It's better in the bunkrooms – they're lined with the wood from the packing cases. They say it can get really cosy.'

'Where do *you* sleep, then?'

The Worm scowled. 'Think I'd bunk with any of those lousy crumbs? I wouldn't, even if they let me. I sleep in the office.' Randall remembered the bundle of blanket and wadding behind the Worm's 'desk'. 'None of the crumbs would even panel it for me. Lobo said he might get around to it, but he never has. They're all the same. Lousy crumbs. You'll be just like them, given time.'

'Why will I?'

'Stands to reason. Place like this, everybody needs somebody to pick on. Start too many fights and the whole thing breaks down – before you know it, we're all dead. Me, I'd rather be picked on than dead. As long as they're spitting on me, they're leaving each other alone.'

Randall was surprised. 'That's very philosophical,' he said.

'But I never said I liked it,' the Worm replied sharply. 'Don't get that idea.'

'I won't.'

'They don't appreciate what I do for them. What with the rosters, and all – they'd be *dead* without me to organize them. They've got no respect for the intellect.'

'No?' said Randall, mainly to keep the conversation going so that the Worm wouldn't go skipping ahead again at top speed. 'What about the one called Doc?'

'He doesn't count, him and his friends. They never did a roster in their lives. Just because they're called dissidents and not crooks like the rest of us, it's like they were priests or something. Me, I was a credit accountant – got a life term for grand computer fraud. I'd like to see any lousy dissident match *that*. This is where you bunk.'

They'd arrived at one of the heavy doors set back in the ice, and the Worm twisted the handle and pushed it inwards. A light flicked on, and Randall followed him into the room.

It was larger than he'd expected and contained six wooden-frame bunk-beds stacked in vertical twos. The walls were, as the Worm had said, lined with an uneven patchwork of raw wood. All of the bunks except for one had shapeless folded stacks of material on them and Randall recognized the dull pastel colours of snow suits.

'It's no warmer,' he said.

'Hard luck. It's better when it's full of people and the door's closed. Your bunk's up top, and you'll find a snowsuit and blanket on it. There's a charged power pack as well. If it doesn't fit too well, try one of those on one of the other bunks.'

'Whose were they?'

'It doesn't matter. That one, his name's off the rosters and he's gone. Took off his suit and walked out into a blizzard. Nobody would stop him, but I still think the lousy crumb could have left us his body for the tanks. Keep off that bunk.'

Randall had been moving to sit down on the nearest lower bunk, but the Worm grabbed his sleeve and pulled him away, reaching in to smooth the crease on the blanket where Randall's hand had rested momentarily.

'Lobo doesn't like anybody messing with his bunk,' the Worm explained.

Randall sat on the other side of the room, this time without raising a complaint. 'Anything else I ought to know about him?' he asked.

The Worm thought for a moment. 'He's slow, but he's decent. They leave him alone because he's big, except when there are a lot of them together and then they know that he's not dumb enough to cause trouble. He's a creep. Keep on the right side of him.'

'I'll try,' Randall said, wanting nothing more than to sink back on to the hard mattress but knowing that this might be his last chance to learn by any way other than painful experience. 'I don't seem to have a choice.'

'And another thing. Don't play on the citizen angle. It won't hold any sway in here.'

'I wasn't thinking of it.'

'Good.' The Worm moved towards the door. 'Your shift's not due back for a few hours yet. Ask Lobo to show you the routine and where you eat. You go out with them next trip. Bulstrode's the team leader, watch out for him. And Berg. He's as mean as Bulstrode but he's only got half a brain, so he's more dangerous. I'm going now. Sink or swim, Randall.'

Randall was framing a reply, but the door had already closed. The ice walls of the room were an effective deadener of sound, so that with the echoes of distant activity from the corridor cut off all he could hear was a faint, steady drip somewhere.

The top bunk he'd been allocated seemed impossibly far away. He reached behind him for the spare blanket on the bunk where he sat and about ten seconds later he was asleep, still grasping the half-unfolded material across his chest.

Five

There was no way of telling how much later he woke up, but it didn't feel like long. He was cold and bent, and his head ached fiercely around some impossible point centred between his eyes. He was damp from his own perspiration in the cold humidity of the bunkroom, the hard light from the single naked bulb hazed by the suspended moisture of his breath.

He lay for a while without moving, but the discomfort only intensified. He tried to spread the blanket out with a minimum of effort, but discovered he was lying on half of it. In resignation he pulled himself up and reached around to free it, but his hand landed on the padded bulk of the snow suit.

The material of the suit was warm to the touch, and when he unrolled the bundle it fell out into two complete layers, an inner suit lined and tracked with the tiny veins of heating elements, and the outer weatherproof layer. Moving as quickly as possible he removed his rough prison wear and pulled on the first garment; it showed no sign at all of its several generations of use, and it carried no stain or odour of any kind. The second layer was similarly clean but it betrayed its age by its faded condition – the lining was a deep flame red, in contrast to the pale orange outer surface. It was belted and the pants legs ended in light, cleated snowboots, whilst the upper arms and shoulders had an extra layer of ribbed padding. A long narrow plate lay along the outside of the right thigh, and here a set of terminals dangled free, along with an open clip.

The power unit was, as the Worm had said, with the suit and blanket on the upper bunk.

The pack snapped easily into its fastening on his hip and the terminals attached without any problem. Nothing happened.

Under normal circumstances he would have spotted the trouble straight away but he was cold, dazed, and still trying to process the long-sleep poisons out of his system. Minutes passed as he stared, tried to think, messed around with the connections, stared again. Then with what seemed like a terrific burst of inspiration he stripped down to the inner layer and found the point where the heating network had to be connected to the input from the outer suit.

This time the flat package against his leg came to life immediately, glugging a little inside its casing. His feet and chest began to warm first, and in a pocket he found gloves which linked into the heating circuit and locked on to the suit at the wrist. After hardly more than a minute the entire outfit was working, dissolving the pain in his joints and muscles. Before lying back on the bunk he switched off the light, and then he stretched out with the blanket pulled over his head to take the hard edge off the air.

When he awoke for the second time he knew that it was several hours later. The knot of pain in his head had fallen slack and unwound, and whilst he didn't exactly feel strong he was confident that he would be able to stand upright without needing a wall within arm's length.

And, of course, he was hungry. A week of intravenous feeding had left his stomach feeling like a loose bag of acid. Wait for Lobo, the Worm had said; he'll show you the routine and where to eat. Randall tried to remember how the Worm had pointed out the tunnels running inwards from Main Street to the Cantina, but the details of the whole progress from the Recovery Room to the bunkroom eluded him. He pushed the blanket away and sat upright on the bunk, waiting for Lobo.

The return of the shift from the ice was announced by nothing more than a muted shuffling filtered through the heavy door. The sound subsided, and then the darkness of the bunkroom split wide open as light and noise spilled in from the corridor.

The man who moved forward in this bright flood almost filled the doorway. He stepped into the room and began to swing the door shut but then he stopped in the sudden realization that something was wrong. He turned slowly and faced the middle of the room.

'Who's there?' he demanded. 'Stand up so I can see you.'

Randall wasn't sure what to say. He'd been sitting full in the shaft of light that had fallen from the open door, obvious to anybody entering the room. 'Don't panic,' he said, rising cautiously to his feet, 'I'm supposed to be here.'

The man in the doorway, a black silhouette against the opening, had his arm raised protectively in front of him. Not a cowardly stance, but certainly a defensive one. 'Over here,' he said with a sharp beckoning motion. 'I still can't see you.'

Randall moved as indicated. 'Why?' he said cautiously. 'What's the matter?'

'I'm ice blind, that's what's the matter. But don't try anything. Lay a hand on me and I'll break your fingers.'

'I wasn't thinking of trying anything. That – the Worm put me here and told me to wait.'

'The Worm?' The big man relaxed a little as understanding began to form. 'He says you're bunking in here?'

'That's right.'

'You're the new creep? Came in the coffin this morning?'

'That's what I'm told. I didn't know much about it.'

'I helped carry you. Later on, Willis brings the story out on to the ice. Says you're a citizen, and more. That true?'

Randall saw dangerous ground. 'Some of it. Maybe I'll tell you the full story some time.'

'Don't want to know it.' Lobo snapped on the bunkroom light and kicked the door closed with a backward flip; as an escape route it seemed he no longer considered it necessary.

Randall could see his eyes now that the light was on; they were red-rimmed and sore, the pupils contracted to tiny points. Otherwise he was big, his hair and beard in the same shaggy cut as Willis and the Doc. 'I can see you now,' he said. 'Willis was right.'

'What else did Willis say?'

'Never mind. Which bunk did the Worm give you?'

Randall pointed. 'Over there. The top one.'

Lobo didn't even look at it. He was watching Randall closely. 'He tell you it's a dead man's bunk?'

'He told me.'

'And the one below it, and the one next to that? It's just you, me and three dead men. Gets pretty cold at night.' If Lobo was joking, he wasn't smiling.

'If there are bunks free, why do they make the Worm sleep in his office?'

Lobo stripped off his gloves and stuffed them into the side pocket of his snow suit, then sat carefully on his neatly-arranged bunk. 'The Worm told you that? What do you think of him?'

'I didn't take any liking to him, if that's what you mean, but I think he's a miserable case. Nobody deserves the amount of contempt he seems to get.'

Lobo shook his head slowly. 'Brother, you're soft. I'll give you a piece of advice, free and for nothing. You get any kind thoughts like that, shove 'em. Otherwise you'll find the Worm's forgotten and you're getting his share. That's a hell of a thing to get rid of – I've had it, and I know. You—' he flicked a sideways glance at Randall, who was still standing—'you aren't even half my size, you got no chance. Any time you get any warm ideas about the Worm, just remember that he wanted to leave you dead to make his paperwork easier.'

'What?'

'It's a tough world. Give a guy your hand and all he'll do is steal your rings. That's the Worm, that's me, that's Willis. Welcome to the Ice Palace, Randall.'

'Thanks.' Randall dropped back on to the bunk where he'd slept. 'I'll remember.'

'The Worm say you're following my shift?'

'That's right. He said I should ask you to show me the routine.'

The tension that Lobo had carried in from the ice snapped

back at full strength. 'He's got no right. I don't want you owing me anything.'

Randall shrugged. 'Well, I'm sorry. What else can I do?'

Lobo considered it for a moment, and then wound down a little. 'Nothing. Just follow me round and watch. I'm doing nothing special for you.'

'I'm not asking for it.'

Lobo nodded. If he wasn't satisfied with the arrangement, at least he was resigned to it. 'That's all right, then,' he said. 'When the blindness is gone, we go and eat.'

The distance to the Cantina was much less than Randall had expected; obviously carved out with one original main entrance it was now serviced by irregular additional tunnels which connected to all parts of the Main Street passage encircling it. They emerged into a long, low-ceilinged cave; there was solid ice underfoot, but Randall found that his boots gripped on it with no problem. At the far end of the cave about a dozen men sat on rough benches at equally rough trestle tables, crouched forward over wooden bowls and looking like shipwrecked sailors in worn-out spacesuits. A similar number were in line, waiting as a man about the Doc's age spooned the sick-like liquid that Randall recognized as yeast from a wheeled metal drum. As he followed Lobo towards the end of the line, Randall heard the beginnings of an argument. He glanced up, interested but trying not to appear so.

'You call this food?' The man was about Lobo's size, perhaps even bigger. His snow suit was stretched to the limit of its elasticity.

'What's the matter with it?' the elderly chef demanded. 'It's the same as you had yesterday.'

'That's what I mean. It was crap yesterday as well.'

Hardly surprising, Randall thought, considering what it had fed on. One of the men at a table looked up. 'What's the matter, Berg?'

'Nothing's the matter. I'm just talking to the guy about the yeast.'

The man at the table wasn't to be put off. 'What about the yeast?'

'I think it's off.'

The seated man pantomimed astonishment. 'You mean you can *tell*?'

Nearly every head in the room was turned towards Berg

now, obviously as he wanted it. 'Look, Berg,' said the old man serving him, 'what do you think this is? The stuff's either fresh or it's dead. When it's dead it just slushes around.'

Berg shook his bowl experimentally. 'It's doing that now.'

'Well, what do you expect? You've been waving it around for ten minutes instead of eating.'

'What do you mean, ten minutes? I only just walked in!'

'Come on, Berg,' the next man in the line said, and Randall recognized him as Willis. 'Everybody's waiting.'

The man at the table looked up again. 'Get some fresh and sit down, Berg.'

'Up yours, Bulstrode,' Berg replied, and emptied his bowl back into the metal drum. 'Gimme some fresh.'

The line moved forward, and Randall collected an empty bowl from the stack, as Lobo had done. Lobo didn't turn or speak, which was fine for Randall; he wanted to concentrate on the two men in his team that the Worm had given him warning about. Berg took his bowl and went over to Bulstrode's table.

Randall tried to hear what they were saying, but was distracted by the closer conversation between Willis and the man with the spoon.

'What's the matter with him?' the old man said.

'He gets sick of talking about the weather. What do you think's the matter?'

'Listen,' the old man said earnestly to the line in general, 'if we could do anything with this stuff, don't you think we would? Anything you try to add just kills it off. I even left a drumload inside the shields near the fission plant to see if it would mutate into something more exciting.'

Somebody asked, 'What happened?'

'It started eating the drum,' the old man said mournfully.

Willis followed Berg, and the line moved on again. A couple of men came in behind Randall, but he didn't turn; he tried to concentrate his hearing towards Bulstrode's table. He heard Bulstrode say, 'What's with you, Berg?' and Berg reply, 'You know damn well. I'm two hours short on sleep from last night. What are you going to do about it, Willis?'

Willis was coming around the end of the table. 'Do about what?'

'Berg's sore because you woke him up this morning,' Bulstrode said, and Berg nodded in morose agreement.

'And what about me?' Willis demanded as he sat down. 'I had to go and freeze in the loading bay for those two hours.'

Berg was unimpressed. 'Who cares what you had to do? I'm talking about me.'

Willis hunched over his bowl. 'Don't blame me for it. Blame the Worm.'

'What you saying about me, Willis?' came a shrill voice from behind Randall, and everybody on Bulstrode's table gave an exaggerated groan.

'Get lost, Worm,' Berg said loudly. 'You're even less popular than usual right now.'

'Up yours, Berg,' piped the Worm with unusual bravado.

Berg's head snapped up and around. Randall looked away, hoping Berg's attention wouldn't focus on him yet. 'Say that again!'

'Cheers, Berg,' the Worm replied, a little less enthusiastically.

Berg turned his back, muttering, 'Is that shrimp trying to take a rise out of me?' and the line moved on again. Lobo moved away, and Randall found he was next.

The old man with the spoon faltered when he saw Randall, but he said nothing as he dropped a ladleful of grey scum into his bowl. Randall thought with regret that his short hair and stubble would ensure that he stayed conspicuous for some time.

Lobo set his bowl down on Bulstrode's table, and Willis said, 'Where've you been, Lobo? We've missed the thrill of your conversation.'

'Had to do a few things,' Lobo said quietly, meeting nobody's eyes.

'Give me a pencil, somebody,' Bulstrode said with energy. 'I've just *got* to write that down.'

Randall tried to get a final measure of these men as he approached the table. He passed other places he might sit, but he was bound to be noticed eventually and it might as well be now. As far as he could tell Bulstrode wasn't the giant that Berg was, but his smaller frame was thick-set with compact slabs of muscle. By contrast Berg was apelike, with a rounded head and a wide mouth like a slash in a basketball.

'Can I sit here?' Randall said, addressing himself directly to Bulstrode on the suspicion that his status as team leader might have forced a modification of the aggression in his personality.

Bulstrode didn't look up straight away. 'Did something speak?'

'My name's Randall. I arrived today. The Worm says I'm to join your shift.'

Dark eyes lifted, flicked up and down him. 'Sit where you like.'

The coiled spring of apprehension in Randall's belly loosed off a notch. 'Thanks. Hello, Willis.'

Willis continued to stare into his yeast and said nothing. Randall saw his cheeks starting to flush red behind the hanging loops of hair.

'Your friend says hello, Willis,' said Berg, grinning broadly. 'What do you say to that?'

'You talk too much, Berg.'

If Berg's grin had spread any more the back of his head might have fallen off. 'That's great coming from you, Willis. Especially after all the talking *you've* been doing today.' He looked down the table, and the grin wiped away like a raindrop from a windscreen. 'He's told us all about you, Randall. I didn't hear much that I liked.'

'I'm sorry about that.'

'Forget it, Berg,' Bulstrode interrupted, and indicated the remainder of the yeast line with a short movement of his head. 'Go take it out on the Worm.'

But Berg wasn't to be diverted. 'Why should I,' he said, 'when we've got a lower form of life right here?'

Randall sat down and looked across the table. 'What have you been saying, Willis?'

Willis went on studying his yeast, and Berg said, 'Willis has done enough talking for one day. He doesn't feel like doing any more.'

'I think I've got a right to know what's been said about me.'

Berg was on his feet. All the stored venom of his rotten prison existence came to bear on Randall. 'A *right*? You've got as many rights as we say you've got!'

'Sit down, Berg,' Bulstrode said.

'No, I don't think I will. I want to know what this citizen's about.'

'Is that what's bothering you?' Randall said, feigning surprise.

'That, and a few other things,' Berg replied, moving around the table towards him. 'Get up, Randall.'

Randall knew it had to come, and it might as well be now. Willis's head was still down, Lobo was watching without expression. 'Is this what you want?' Randall said, standing up and stepping around the bench. 'A quick standoff to show that you're superior?'

'You've got it wrong, Randall. All I want to know about is this.'

Berg's fist was the shape of a cured ham and the texture of a boulder, and he threw it with accuracy if with no great style. Randall was lifted several inches into the air from the blow, folding about the middle as he went and dropping into a tangled heap on the floor only a moment later. The padding of his suit took the force of the fall but his cheekbone banged hard on the ice and knocked his eyes way out of focus.

Berg was walking away, his suit a pale yellow blur. Bulstrode's voice seemed to come from the bottom of a hole as he said, 'You satisfied now, Berg?'

'Hell, Willis,' Berg was saying, and the landscape undulated as he turned and came back, 'this guy's no more from the Police Élite than I am. What are you trying to pull?'

'I only said what I thought.'

'You should tell us your thoughts more often, make it nice and peaceful. I'm sorry, Randall.' Randall felt an oversized hand slip under his arm, and he was hauled to his feet. 'I didn't break anything. Help him back to his bunk, Worm.'

The horizon was all wrong, the Worm a shapeless blob sliding uphill across it. 'Shall I take him some food?' the blob said, getting its shoulders under Randall's other arm as Berg let go.

'I don't think he's hungry.' Berg's voice, fading off into the distance. I *am*, screamed a voice at the back of Randall's head, I haven't *eaten* for a sodding *week*, but it somehow didn't make it to the outside world.

The universe began to rotate, and Randall realized they were moving. 'What's the idea, Berg?' Bulstrode was saying.

'You saw the way he folded.' Berg's voice was slipping away to one side as they moved, and Randall tried to hang back and listen. 'The Police Élite have these trained reactions. He should have turned my hand and wiped the floor with me. I gave him enough warning.'

Bulstrode: 'What do you think of that, Willis?'

Willis: something incomprehensible, along the lines of 'I can only say what I think, and that stands.'

A derisive laugh from Berg, a long way away.

Something else from Berg.

Nothing from Lobo.

Six

The Worm chattered all the way back to the bunkroom, but Randall took very little of it in. By the time that they arrived at the door he was at least breathing normally and seeing straight, even if he couldn't stand fully upright. The Worm unshouldered him and propped him against a wall as he opened the door.

'You took a bad one there, Randall,' he was saying. 'Remember I warned you about Berg – half the brains and twice the meanness. You'll have to be more careful if you want to survive in here.'

'I appreciate the support, but I can do without the philosophy.'

The Worm switched on the light. Randall saw the nearest flat surface and lurched towards it. 'Not there!' the Worm yelped, grabbing a loose handful of Randall's suit and hauling on it. 'That's Lobo's bunk!' He tried to propel Randall up to his allocated berth, but Randall wasn't going. He ducked under the Worm's arm and crash-landed on the lower bunk he'd used earlier.

'*He* won't give you any arguments,' the Worm observed. 'We recycled him last week.'

'Get out of here, Worm,' Lobo said.

Light flashed on the single lens in the Worm's glasses as he spun round to face the doorway. 'We didn't touch your bunk, Lobo,' he stammered. 'He was going to, but I stopped him.'

'Out.'

'Sure, Lobo.' The Worm scuttled past and out the doorway, turning as he went for a parting shot. 'You can't say I didn't warn you, Randall.'

Lobo shut the door so hard that dust shook off the frames of the beds. His eyes were narrow slits, and he was furious.

'What's the matter, Lobo?' Randall said. 'Didn't I drop fast enough for you?'

'Shove the comedy, Randall. I want some answers. What's with you?'

Randall shook his head. 'I'm sorry, I don't understand.'

Lobo moved closer. His fists were clenched hard, the knuckles white. 'You know damn well the rumours Willis has been spreading on the ice today. Who do you think you're taking in?'

'Taking in with what?'

'We've never had a citizen here, and then we get you with a half-assed story about the Central computer being shut down. It stinks, Randall. Within an hour the whole Palace knew we had a Police Élite spy on board. Berg just decided to test the idea and see what your reactions are like.'

Randall pulled his knees up closer to his chest to cradle his ache. 'Well, I hope the Palace is satisfied now.'

'The Palace may be, but I'm not. Most people watch faces – I watch hands. They give more away. I watched yours.'

'Didn't do me a lot of good, did they?'

Lobo took a step nearer and Randall saw that he was more than angry; he was hurt, and Randall couldn't understand why. 'Don't give me that. It took maybe a fraction of a second for Berg's fist to travel. You reached out, put both your own hands around it, changed your mind before they touched and pulled them back again. If I'd blinked I wouldn't have seen any of it. Nobody in the underbelly can move that fast, and I'm damn sure no citizen could. So how can you?'

'You tell me.'

'Because you've had that biofeedback response training, that's why. You let Berg floor you on purpose. You didn't even move with the blow, so Berg couldn't tell you were faking. Now give me a good reason why I shouldn't tear you open right now.'

Randall allowed himself to straighten out a little. 'Because with feedback training I could probably stop you from doing it.'

'I'd take a chance, but you lose either way. Beat me and you'll give yourself away to the others. So?'

No point pretending. Randall swung up into a sitting position. Lobo didn't move back. 'What am I supposed to say? You've already decided it's true.'

'Damn right it's true. I want to know what Central's doing, trying to put a spy in here.'

'I'm not a spy,' Randall insisted, 'I'm a prisoner like the rest of you. And I told you, Central's out of action. Doesn't it make sense? With the underbelly in charge, they're bound to start hammering the Élite. I'm only being careful when I cover my background.'

'Won't wash. Élite or not, you're still citizen. Crime's been bred out of you.'

'The Worm was right. There's nothing stupid about you.'

'I'm not asking you for a reference,' Lobo exploded, 'I want the truth!'

Randall was on his feet and matching volume. 'The truth is that Central's been wiped and there's no computer government any more. I told Willis and Doc that I'd been involved in some way, but I didn't tell them all the truth.'

Lobo nodded. 'Keep talking.' Randall didn't know if he was being given the chance to justify or damn himself.

'There was a man called Rorvik who'd worked out a way to cheat the computer's security systems and get into the unmanned areas. Incidentally, he was a citizen, so bang goes your idea about breeding. I was the Élite officer assigned to track Rorvik down and stop him. I followed him into the computer.'

Lobo had calmed considerably as the story was told, but he was not obviously convinced. 'So how,' he said, 'did he manage to wipe Central?'

Randall took a deep breath. 'He didn't. He was dead before he reached the deprogramming console. I did the wiping.'

There was a pause. Then: 'You're asking me to believe a lot, Randall.'

'Right,' Randall said emphatically. 'Now can you imagine me trying to convince all fifty of you with that story?'

'You'd be slung straight into the yeast tanks for a liar.'

Sensing that Lobo's tide of fury was well receded, Randall sat down on the bunk again. 'So I let Berg make his demonstration, everybody gets some entertainment and they stop wondering about me. Except you. What are my hands telling you now?'

Lobo frowned, saw the joke, and relaxed a little more. 'How the hell should I know?' he said. 'You're sitting on them. Maybe I'm stupid after all, Randall. Maybe I believe you. But I'm going to watch you.' And he dragged the blanket off his bunk and reached for the lightswitch.

'Watch all you like, Lobo,' Randall said as the room snapped into darkness. 'All I want is the time to work out a way out of here and back to the city.'

'Isn't that what everybody wants? Forget it, Randall. It can't be done.'

'They said that about the Central defences and look what happened.'

'Slow down,' Lobo cut across him. 'I didn't say I'd swallowed that one. I'm just reserving an opinion.'

'Thanks, anyway.'

'And don't thank me!' A flash of Lobo's earlier anger erupted in the darkness. 'I don't want any lousy crumb thinking he owes me anything. In a place like this it goes against survival. Maybe I'll wind up thinking that you took on Berg to get my sympathy. You think I can go bursting into tears every time he bops some guy?'

The shadow in the room wasn't absolute. The door was a close fit, but there was a faint glow along its upper edge that was caught and reflected by minute droplets of frozen condensation held in the surface fibres of the ceiling insulation. Randall could almost see it as a night sky overhead. 'All right, Lobo,' he said, 'so you stay independent. You've seen through me, and I've seen through you.'

Immediate suspicion across the bunkroom. 'What's that supposed to mean?'

'I mean that under all that hair and gristle there's a human being trying *not* to get out. But don't worry. The secret's safe with me.'

There was silence, and Randall wondered if he'd gone too far. Then: 'Any time you get a sentimental idea like that, remember I killed a guy to be here. Then see how you feel about it.' And he rolled over noisily, as if to indicate a definite end to the conversation.

'Sure, Lobo.'

'And get some sleep.' There was suddenly something

missing from the room, and Randall guessed that Lobo had switched off his power pack, thinking that it must give off some tone barely on the threshold of hearing. 'You're out on the ice in nine hours.'

Seven

Randall didn't sleep. He was sore from Berg's blow, but far less troubled by it now than he had allowed everybody to think. After a week's enforced sleep and several hours of natural recovery the last thing he wanted to do was switch off the machinery again so soon. After an hour or so he left the bunkroom to see if he could find any of the repellent yeast in the Cantina, but when he traced his way back through empty corridors he found nothing but deserted tables and a stack of rinsed wooden bowls. He was tempted to look for the place where the yeast grew but decided against it – so much of the Palace was the same, ice upon ice, that without a guide he might never find his way back. Instead he stayed with Main Street, following it in a complete circuit until he recognized his starting point.

If he felt anger or despair it didn't show – he had the State and his conditioning to thank for that. Any such unproductive or wasteful reaction would be suppressed and retained, charcoal burning to give a continuous and controlled delivery of energy directed to one purpose. Randall wanted out, back to the city he didn't know how not to love.

Until the opportunity came he would be the model prisoner. Berg's demonstration had already defused some of the controversy of his appearance, and all that now remained was to slide quietly into Ice Palace routine. At the same time he would watch, store the data, and wait.

He went back and lay on his bunk, waiting for something to happen. Lobo breathed slowly and evenly on the other side of the room, turning every now and again but making no other sound. Randall hoped that he had Lobo judged correctly, a gentle man in an ogre's ill-fitting clothes.

It seemed a long time later when a handbell rang out in Main Street. Lobo came awake instantly, swinging his legs out of the bed and clipping his power pack on as a matter of conditioned routine.

Randall followed down to the Cantina. Apparently they would have to eat and clear out of the way before the incoming shift arrived. He joined the line and took his yeast, this time served by a different oldster, and observed that all the men were heading for the same tables they had occupied for the last feed.

Bulstrode noticed him but didn't react. Berg gave him a wide grin that was neither threatening nor pleasant. Lobo looked at nobody, and Willis was turned slightly away, lost in some preoccupation of his own.

To eat was agony, but he couldn't let it show. The yeast was like a cold fondue of mouldy cheese, sticking to the roof of his mouth and coating the inside of his throat so that it threatened to choke him, making it impossible to take a quick swallow and get it over with. He managed to half-empty the bowl and decided to leave it at that – already it was a thick, greasy pool in his stomach. He assumed that he would get used to the diet; nobody else was showing any sign of revulsion, and Berg actually seemed to be enjoying it.

Conversation was minimal and when the majority of men started to move towards an exit Randall got up to follow them. Lobo caught his eye, and Randall joined him without being too obvious about it.

'Stick with me,' Lobo said almost in a whisper, glancing to one side as if in fear of observation. 'Couple of things you'll have to know.'

Randall tried not to let his pleasure show. Lobo was becoming a reluctant ally, propelled by his nature in the face of reason. Randall followed him out into Main Street, and when Lobo hung back from the moving crowd Randall did likewise.

When the last pastel-suited figure disappeared around the bend towards the loading bays leaving only long shadows on the ice wall and a distant shuffling, Lobo gestured Randall to follow and went off up a side branch. The flooring slats were laid lengthwise instead of across.

They emerged on to an iron gallery halfway up a large chamber. An open metal stairway led down to the lower level and up to another gallery above, where Randall could see two large riveted tanks and a lacing of pipework which ran down the wall behind them to the yeast pools below.

The purpose of the tanks was clear. They were neatly lettered 'Crap Tanks'. As Randall looked a man appeared from behind one of them and began to descend the iron stairs, closing the fastenings on his suit as he approached.

They climbed to the upper gallery and Lobo pointed out the cubicles around the back where Randall would go when he had to go. He also showed him a device called a sonic hose, part of the microwave generator which killed the bacteria in the raw material before piping it down to the yeast pools. It could also, Lobo explained, be used with care to sterilize the skin and clothes – this accounted for the mysterious freshness of Randall's aged suit and the absence of the odour that generally accompanies any area where men live and work together. They were all taking sonic showers – you wouldn't even have to take your suit off. Oh, and another thing, Lobo added. Use it often enough and it'll make you sterile for good – as if that mattered.

Lobo disappeared for a couple of minutes, and as Randall waited he looked down over the guard rail. On the gallery below – the one on to which they had entered – the oldster from the Cantina wheeled an empty yeast drum to the brink and snapped a hook on to it, then unwound a rope from the rail and pulled to swing the drum up and out over the drop to the bottom level, letting its own weight take it down against the resistance of the pulleys.

There were three pools containing yeast in various stages of maturity, none of which Randall found remotely appealing. They were being stirred by long poles like oars, a man to each tank. One of them broke away from his stirring and reached to receive the empty drum. After a couple of minutes, Lobo came back and they moved on.

On the way back to Main Street there was a squeak and rumble in the tunnel behind them. Randall looked around and saw a full drum riding on its castors, bumping along the lengthwise planks which served as rails. The man was putting all his meagre strength into keeping the drum moving, veins and tendons bulging under his sallow skin and white hair, and all for the sake of the poorest nourishment Randall had ever known.

Lobo walked ahead, ignoring Randall again. When they arrived in the loading bay Bulstrode's team was fitted out and almost ready to go.

The stark floodlighting of the bay dazzled him for a moment but then he readjusted to the crisp shadows and sharp outlines, finding them somehow unreal after the muted glow of the ice tunnels.

Bulstrode's team numbered about a dozen, and they were in the middle of the bay finishing the loading of a man-harnessed sled. All the men were helmeted, and from a distance none was recognizable.

'We've got a load,' Bulstrode's voice echoed, amplified by his helmet and clipped in the bass range for clarity. 'Let's make the line and clip together. Who's pulling the sled?'

'Berg's on first turn,' somebody said at lower amplification.

'So where is he?'

One of the figures around the sled came upright, and Randall found that by size alone Berg was unmistakable. 'Where the hell else would I be?' he demanded, and pushed through the crowd to take the sled harness.

Randall hurried after Lobo to the helmet rack. Lobo might be grudgingly cooperative elsewhere, but in public view Randall was on his own. Fortunately the helmet catch was a simple snap-lock, and the sound and voice channels engaged automatically.

They went over to join the team, falling in last in line because of their lateness. A couple of helmets turned and gave blank looks which Randall imagined to be of disapproval, but there was really no way of telling. Lobo showed no reaction, and the helmets turned forward to face the direction of the line.

A thin, grimy looking cord with loops at intervals was handed back. Randall didn't know what to do with it, and with everybody's back towards him there was no way he could observe and work it out. Hesitantly, he tapped Lobo's arm.

Lobo didn't turn at first. The line wasn't yet moving – the lead figure whom Randall assumed to be Bulstrode was consulting with Berg over a something written on a weather-proof plastic sheet. Then Lobo turned, and Randall held up the cord and shrugged as eloquently as the suit would let him.

Lobo held up his own section of the line, showing where it attached to a simple spring clip at the waist of the suit. It wouldn't be adequate as a safety line in case of a fall or avalanche, but it would at least keep the party together.

'This is only a token,' Lobo said, keeping his voice low. 'Stay close and don't let it get stretched. Sometimes the visibility gets below ten feet – slow down too much and you could lose the group.'

'But how does Bulstrode find his way at the front?'

'There's a wire staked along the surface of the ice. If you *do* get lost, try to find it and follow it back. They radiate out from the Ice Palace. He's got a report from the men at the reactors on where the danger areas are. The cladding rots pretty fast, and if we don't get out to replace it the power plant goes into shutdown and we lose the Palace supply.'

Bulstrode was shouting, 'Everybody clipped up?'

Lobo half-turned to wave his hand in the air, and Randall did the same. Gears clanked and the outer door began to rise. Bright snow light forced in under its lower edge and began to spread.

Randall touched Lobo's arm again. 'Where's Willis in the line?'

'In front of me. Watch him, Randall. He still doesn't trust you.'

It was unlikely that Willis heard any of this. Randall could barely make it out over the rising howl that was streaming in through the open bay door. He felt the line pull; the three men immediately behind Berg's sled threw their weight against it to overcome the drag of the floor, and the team moved out.

They emerged from the cargo bay door rather than the loading bay – they wouldn't be able to make any tight turns with the sled, and the lip of ice between the loading bay and the open lead of frozen soup to the North would be too narrow to negotiate. Consequently they came out in a deep trench, the snow on its gently rising floor trodden into particles of mushy grey ice and then scattered over with a layer of fresh white. Presumably one of the teams' rostered duties would be to keep the trench clear; the leading men had already kicked through a two-foot high mound of fresh snow that had piled against the door, and a steady drift was starting into the bay itself.

They emerged from the trench on to a plain of snow. It seemed impossible that it could reflect so brightly when the sky overhead was a featureless iron grey, but even as Randall took it in the wind gusted hard and his helmet visor was suddenly crazed over with ice crystals. The line pulled taut and he staggered after it, rubbing at the clear plastic with the back of his glove. No sooner had he opened a patch of visibility in the middle and glimpsed the procession of stooped figures ahead than another wave of scouring hail washed over him, dragging him aside and almost making him fall.

The temperature in his suit was dropping. What had been adequate for the chill of the Ice Palace was barely effective in this bitter, freezing wind. He boosted the level on his power pack and felt the unit hum against his leg, but there was no immediately noticeable effect.

A glance back, but the Palace was already lost; even the deep slash of the trench, only yards behind them, had been swallowed by an impenetrable grainy swirl. Randall looked for Bulstrode's guidewire, but couldn't even see that.

The team waded on, knee-high in soft, crusty snow. As the last in line Randall was following a man-trodden ditch, the marks of the sled-runners slewed to either side and already filling in. The wind continually tried to push him aside, fooling him by slackening off and then slapping at him with a sudden hard dash of ice needles.

This continuous uncertainty was even more wearing than the numbness which was starting to spread as the blood cooled in his hands and feet. He reached to turn the power pack to its maximum output and almost ripped it away from its connections as he unexpectedly pitched forward, his leg thrusting down into uncompacted snow almost up to his hip. He scrambled up and staggered on, thankful at least for the inexorable guided progress of the line.

Apart from where they walked, the snow seemed even and pure. If the previous shift had followed this wire their passage was by now completely obliterated. Randall could make out in detail perhaps four or five of the suited figures ahead, leaning forward to keep their balance against the wind. The sled was no more than a blurred grey bulk, imagined as much as seen, the men ahead of it merged into its dim shape.

Far off to the right something was taking on regular form in the swirling murk. It angled to meet them, becoming more distinct as its line and theirs converged.

When they met the pipeline they stopped for a moment,

presumably as Bulstrode checked his diagram to find the first specified danger area. The pipe was about three feet in diameter, raised above the snow at a level of about four feet, supported every ten yards or so by an ice-crusted pylon. Randall could now see what the long-standing Ice Palace residents meant when they complained about the quality of the cladding – it was nothing more than processed rags or something similar, four quarter-sections to every five-foot length clamped into place by two sliding metal belts. The air above the pipeline was filled with a furiously dancing pattern of snowflakes, stirred into a frenzy by escaping heat; and even as Randall watched a strip of soaked rag detached itself, hung as a streamer in the wind for a few seconds and then whirled away.

A signal, and the line moved on, following the pipeline and enjoying the rare pleasure of being battered from two directions at once as they marched in the strong eddy caused by the fixture. A few hundred yards and they came to a junction, a nowhere crossroads; they ducked under the pipe, one after another, and went on.

A different signal passed back along the line, left hand out sideways. Randall cursed his inattention, realizing that communication was being carried along by some kind of code. If he didn't watch it he'd never learn it, and in these conditions such ignorance could prove fatal.

Left hand outstretched meant arrival. They'd been moving, Randall guessed, for an hour or more, but they probably weren't much further than half a mile from the buried Palace. Everybody was unclipping from the line and moving towards the sled, and Randall followed, gathering in the loose cord as he went.

The damage was obvious. The cladding was hanging off the pipeline on one side, and each gust of wind tore and exposed a little more metal. Bulstrode pointed first at one man, then at Randall, who had no idea what he was supposed to do next. But the first man was already being boosted up to straddle the pipe by two of the suited figures, so Randall moved to the other end of the damaged section and climbed up in the same way.

An almost imperceptible flash of light – it could have been the glint of the faceplate on a turning helmet. Then, as Randall struggled to undo the simple catch on the binding hoop, a rippling crack of thunder and another hard sideways buffet from the wind. He almost toppled, but somebody grabbed his ankle and hauled him back. A layer of ice broke loose from the catch and the hoop opened. As he slid it back the four sections of cladding fell away and others were manhandled into their place.

The pipeline was bright metal, jointed in a flexible coil so that it could snake and absorb any shifting in the ice-cap as the supporting pylons moved out of line. The under-sections went on without any problem but the cladding to be fitted over the pipe tried to lift in the wind. Somebody shouted, indistinct above the tearing of the blizzard, and the two largest figures – obviously Berg and Lobo – moved in on either side of the pipe. As soon as he saw the opportunity Randall slid the hoop forward and clamped the cladding down. He looked up towards his opposite number as the man's silhouette flashed white against the landscape and another eruption of thunder followed almost immediately.

They were arguing around the sled as Randall dropped from the pipeline and floundered up to his waist in the loose powder of the drift. Brief, indistinct snatches of amplified conversation, and Bulstrode was shaking his head. Berg came around and joined in, pointing at the sled and at the newly-completed job, and Randall caught what sounded like, 'more harm than good', and 'Worm', and 'nearly screwed up'. Bulstrode's voice cut through with 'got the most critical section, but . . . ' and the rest was drowned in another thundering rumble. Bulstrode looked up, and then all visibility went for a few seconds as a belt of airborne snow whipped through the party. When Randall could see again the line was re-forming and the sled was being turned around.

Lobo was buckling into the sled harness. Obviously the roster was being discarded with the onset of the storm, and Lobo was taking over from Berg to get the sled and the line back to the Palace as fast as possible. As Randall waded out of the drift to join the group the last anonymous figure in the line handed him the linking-cord. The line was moving even as Randall clipped on.

The journey out seemed easy in comparison with the return. As before they tracked the pipe for some way but it was a blind, heads-down progress, stumbling and pushing ahead on shifting ground. Randall didn't even see when they veered away from the pipeline; one time he looked up and it had gone, that was all.

The wind was coming from all directions now, and the signs of their earlier passage had been wiped out. The earlier brilliance of the ice pack was now little more than twilight, lit by the occasional lightning flash which threw the line ahead into sharp relief before the darkness fell again and the thunder rolled over them.

Randall's foot sank into a pocket of soft snow, and he pitched into the man ahead. The man stumbled and grabbed Randall's arm, the two steadying each other; and at that moment lightning forked and the man's blank faceplate became momentarily clear. Willis looked out.

A hard push against his chest, a snatch at his waist, and Randall fell backwards. He hit the snow spread out and it gave way under him, swallowing him to a depth of a couple of feet and then breaking up and falling in. He reached for the linc, and it wasn't there.

He tried to roll over and push himself up, but his arm sank up to the elbow. Every second he wasted took the team further away; he put his weight on both hands to reduce the concentration of pressure, and this time made it to his knees. There was nothing to see but a wall of snow, nothing to hear but the wind that drove it.

He shouted once, and then abandoned the effort; he could barely hear it himself. He floundered forward, hoping to fall into the trodden snow-ditch before it could fill in, and he covered several yards before realizing that in this direction was nothing but plain, crisp white. He turned, and saw that his own tracks were starting to fill, and at the limit of visibility were almost gone completely; he followed them back, tried to judge how far to go.

There's a wire staked along the surface of the ice. If you do *get lost, try to find it and follow it back.* Good advice, but where *was* the wire? What did it look like? Was it buried?

Perhaps he hadn't gone far enough to cross it, perhaps he'd overshot it. The wind was switching directions continually, giving no basis for a bearing. It sucked the heat from his suit, and the little unit on his leg was pumping determinedly to compensate. How long could the power pack take this excessive drain? He hadn't the experience to know.

He dropped to his knees and thrust his glove deep into the

snow, scooping out as much of a narrow trench as he could. He moved on this way for several yards until he could be sure that he would have hit the wire had it been there and then reversed, tracking the already indistinct furrow back to his starting-point. He was trying to cover the area from one central spot, afraid that without any reference to the ground around him he might stagger in a blind circle and miss the wire completely.

On his third attempt he found it, striking it with his forearm beneath the surface of the snow. He got his hand around it and pulled, and it came up and broke free for several yards on either side.

Randall's power pack gave a little bleep and died.

He looped the wire over his arm and reached for the pack. The tiny red indicator light was out completely, and the unit on his leg had stopped pumping. He twisted the switch to 'off', left it a couple of seconds, switched it on again. The light glowed feebly and the heating unit glugged a couple of times, but the whole system died again when he tried to raise the level to anything above the absolute minimum.

There was also another problem. Which way was the Ice Palace?

Eight

The door to the cargo bay was down when the team arrived back at the Palace, and they had to lift the sled and use it as a ram before they could make themselves heard inside. The door lifted and they fell in as soon as there was enough space to duck under the rising edge.

Several suit units were bleeping continuously, the final sign of total depletion in spite of conservation. The men were milling around and unbuckling their helmets even though the outer door was still open, and the man on the chain was shouting for the team leader.

Somebody told Bulstrode, and Bulstrode went over. 'What do you want, Palmer?'

'I want to know if your men are all inside so I can drop the hatch.'

Bulstrode glanced around. The bay door was still open, and the storm outside was rapidly becoming a storm inside. 'How the hell should I know?' he demanded. 'You think I'm going to *count* them? Get the hatch closed, Palmer.'

There was a chorus of agreement and somebody said, 'Get off your backside and pull the chains before we all freeze.'

'I only asked a civil question,' Palmer protested indignantly.

'Up yours, Palmer,' Berg shouted from over by the helmet racks, and he moved over to join Bulstrode.

Palmer turned and unhitched the chain. As the door began to rattle down he said, 'All right, but don't blame me if one of you freezes to death sometime.'

There were a few unenthusiastic 'up yours Palmers', but the entire team was now headed for the bay exit. One man came from the back, elbowing through until he reached Bulstrode and calling to him from behind. Bulstrode didn't look up, but Berg, who was walking next to him, turned.

'Leave it, Lobo,' he said. 'Can't you see he's beat?'

'Then you tell me, Berg. Have you seen Randall? You know, the new guy?'

'I know who he is, but I don't know where he is. Who cares, anyway?'

'He was clipped behind me in the line going out,' Lobo explained, 'but I didn't see him after I took over on the sled.'

Berg thought for a moment, a rare and spectacular effort. 'I think he may have been behind Willis. But I'm not sure.'

Lobo frowned. 'Have you seen Willis, then?'

'No, I haven't seen Willis, and with his popularity rating at zero I don't want to. What is this, Lobo? Does Randall owe you, or something?'

'Forget it, Berg,' Lobo said, moving away.

'Speak to the Worm,' Berg called after him in a moment of inspiration. 'Find out where he's got Randall rostered next.'

'I'll try it,' Lobo said, and disappeared up a side tunnel.

The group spread out and split, but most of the men carried on towards the generator room to get their exhausted power packs recharged. Berg said nothing for a while, and then:

'Hell, Bulstrode, Lobo may be right. We could lose a couple in that storm and never know it.'

Bulstrode nodded. 'You don't have to tell me. It's lucky that *any* of us got back.'

'What if he's right? We couldn't organize a search in this weather.'

'No chance,' Bulstrode agreed. 'Best we can do is go out when it dies down and try to find the suits. Even if the suits are ruined we can maybe use the heating units for spares.'

They turned the sharp corner into the generator room. 'Right now I'm more concerned about the Palace holding together,' Bulstrode went on. 'If the storm rips up the pipe network too much we'll get the generators going into shutdown, and you know what that means.'

Berg knew what it meant. They would have to live in their suits without being able to recharge the power packs, whilst in the unheated pools below the yeast would get cold and die.

Bulstrode was worried about the pipe network. There were three more weak spots that they hadn't reached, and he was beginning to regret turning back so early. But had that been the case it would have meant that the men who had staggered through the bay door with totally depleted units might now be dead, and he couldn't regret being persuaded. Hell, he was no engineer. Maybe the network would be all right. And, after all, they'd covered the worst spot first. He hoped that would prove to be enough.

In the tunnel outside the Worm's office Lobo stopped a man on his way down from counting in the beacon. Until the storm was over, the Palace had no need of him. Lobo asked if he'd seen the Worm, but the man hadn't, and seemed surprised that anybody should actually want to look for him.

'I think we've got people out on the ice,' Lobo explained.

'What are you trying to do? Organise a requiem?'

Lobo wasn't laughing. 'It may not be too late to get a search going,' he insisted.

'In *this*? Don't joke, friend. The dials on the beacon say the Ice Palace is on emergency standby as of now. They'll be transferring a yeast sample in case the tank heaters close down.'

When Lobo arrived on the gallery he saw the Worm's familiar baggy yellow suit below. He was 'helping' with the transfer of a yeast sample to a lined container, which basically meant that he was watching and keeping out of the way. Doc was actually carrying out the transfer.

The yeast was difficult to handle. It wouldn't pour like water but it wasn't solid enough to scoop out. If the tanks' heating was withdrawn as part of the automatic shutdown procedure this sample would have to be kept alive to be the base for a complete new yeast culture; Doc had a theory that spores in the air might eventually get into the wastes and grow, but their development would take far too long to be of any use.

'Please be careful, Doc,' Lobo heard the Worm saying as he descended the iron stairway. 'I don't want to die.'

'Amen to that, Worm,' said the Doc.

'Worm,' Lobo called, 'I've been looking for you.'

'Quiet, Lobo,' the Worm replied, 'can't you see I'm busy?'

'Busy watching somebody else, as usual. I want to get a search organized.'

The Worm lost interest in the yeast. 'What do you mean?'

'I think we've got a couple of men still out on the ice.'

The Worm thought for a moment. 'Any team leaders?'

Lobo was puzzled. 'No, Willis and the new guy. What difference does it make?'

'Team leaders are hell to replace. You almost have to rewrite the entire roster.'

Lobo stifled an impulse to grab the Worm and insert him headfirst into the tank. 'Who *cares* about the roster?' he demanded.

The Worm tut-tutted sanctimoniously. 'You're talking about the guiding-plan of an entire community. It's no less important than this yeast, here.' Doc almost had the container filled.

'It couldn't be less important than you, Worm,' Lobo said ominously.

'There's no need to get personal.'

'I'll get personal with your neck in a minute. What about a search?'

'Out of the question,' the Worm said, stepping aside as Doc pushed the container over towards the pulley. 'The Ice Palace is on emergency standby already. Nobody goes out apart from volunteers for unavoidable repairs. Rules are rules.'

'He's right, you know, Lobo,' the Doc called over. 'Anybody going out in conditions like these won't be coming back.'

'So what are we supposed to do? Write them off?'

'You've got it,' the Worm said. 'The order's gone out to bolt down all the hatches against the wind. Lose too much heat and we could tip the generator cutout anyway.'

'I'm sorry, Lobo,' the Doc said. 'We'll all miss Willis.'

'To hell with Willis,' Lobo spat, and turned abruptly to go.

The Worm didn't wait long enough. Lobo was still within earshot when he said, 'That's a surprise. Lobo getting sentimental over the citizen.'

'I heard that, Worm,' Lobo called down, and the Worm jumped. 'One day soon I'll make you pay for it.'

'I was only joking,' the Worm shouted anxiously. 'Wasn't I, Doc?'

The Doc wasn't interested. He called up to Lobo, who was now on the middle gallery, 'Will you give me a hand to get the yeast to the generator room? It'll stay warm longer if it's left outside the shields.'

'Sorry, Doc, I've got to see this through. The Worm can help you carry.'

The Worm started to rub his arm, like a dog limping for sympathy. 'Come on, Lobo,' he protested. 'You know my problems.'

'Damn right.' The voice echoed from the tunnel across an empty gallery. 'You're an obnoxious weed and nobody likes you. Outside that you've no excuses. Help the Doc.'

The men crowded into the Cantina, because there wasn't enough room for them all to stand and watch the dials on the generators. Even those who had been on the previous shift emerged from their bunkrooms early and waited with Bulstrode and his returnees. Despite the grimness of the situation there was a certain undercurrent of cheer, a camaraderie rarely felt in the Palace; danger or not, something unusual was happening, and the threat of disaster wasn't enough to detract completely from the interest of a break in routine.

Berg asked a few questions. The last anybody had seen of Willis was in the cargo bay, and they weren't sure it was him because he didn't take his helmet off. He was near the open door and when they looked again he wasn't there. Nobody could remember seeing Randall at all.

'That's Willis all over,' Berg told Bulstrode. 'His spy theories get pulled to pieces so he has to take it out on Randall. I bet he left him out there and went back to finish him off.'

'The idiot,' Bulstrode agreed. 'Now he's done for himself, as well.'

Berg wondered if Lobo would succeed in getting a search together, but Bulstrode said it was against the survival rules during a standby. He'd given up trying to understand Lobo. He knew when he was wasting his time.

Lobo arrived a couple of minutes later, and Bulstrode beckoned for him to join them. 'We were just saying it seems you're right,' he said, 'about Randall and Willis on the ice.'

'Willis was always the same,' Berg added. 'Can't let go of an idea when he thinks he's in the right.'

It took Lobo a moment to force himself to readjust. They were neither rejecting nor mocking him, and he wasn't used to it. 'I've just seen the Worm,' he said. 'It seems a search isn't allowed under the shutdown procedure.'

'It's going to take everything we've got to keep the rest of us alive,' Bulstrode agreed. 'When the storm's over we can go out and look for the suits, get the bodies for recycling.'

Lobo still wasn't satisfied. 'What if one of them finds his own way back along the guide wires? He'll die on the doorstep with the hatches bolted down.'

'So what are we supposed to do?' Berg said. 'Leave him a flask of coffee and a sandwich to sit it out until the storm's over? Be realistic, Lobo.'

'All of a sudden it's being realistic to leave a man to die without lifting a finger?'

'Two men,' Berg said for the sake of accuracy.

They all three looked around at the sound of some disturbance at the far end of the cave. Palmer had just appeared, and he was carrying one of the Worm's home-made paper mis-shapes. 'Listen,' he was saying, 'Listen everybody. The Worm's given me this list for the allocation of duties for the emergency standby.' Which, in effect, meant that you were to be told where you could go and sit while waiting to see if you were going to freeze to death or not.

Somebody said, 'All of a sudden the Worm's running the place.'

'You got any better ideas?' Palmer demanded.

'You think I'm enough of a creep to bother with those lousy rosters?'

'Well, shove it if you've got nothing to say.' Palmer moved across to the ice wall and began to chip out a small hole to wedge the sliver which would pin the list in place. 'You can come over and look for your own names.'

Objector included, the men shuffled forward to read the list or have it read to them. There was an animated discussion going on at the back, rising in volume.

'We've got to keep one hatchway open,' Lobo was saying.

'That's impossible,' Bulstrode told him. 'We'd lose heat and tip off the generator shutdown.'

'Not if it was the loading bay door that was kept open. It isn't heated, and you could close the door through to the cargo bay. You have the outer hatch open and the inner one sealed, a kind of rescue chamber.'

'You'd need two people. You couldn't hold the hatch open and look out at the same time. The chains would keep slipping.'

'That's right,' Lobo said, growing excited as the idea became more feasible. He looked round at his newly-acquired audience. 'Any offers?'

The audience promptly became a set of backs. Lobo looked at Bulstrode.

'Not me,' Bulstrode said. 'I'm not going to risk freezing for dead men.'

'That goes for me too,' said Berg.

Palmer had detached himself from the crowd around the notice, and now he came over. He was well-known in the Palace for his undisguised terror of the ice cap – any duty or service that he could trade against shift cover, he would.

Lobo had never traded with him for anything, but even so Palmer stood well back as if in fear of a physical rebuff.

'You interested in a bargain, Lobo?' he asked.

Bulstrode said, 'Crawl off, Palmer,' and Berg rumbled, 'Get back into your crack.'

Lobo said doubtfully, 'I don't like to owe anybody.'

'Nice ethics,' Palmer said, 'but what good are they going to do you?'

'Don't take him on, Lobo,' Bulstrode urged.

Palmer turned to him. 'You going to suggest some other kind of currency?'

Bulstrode reddened, and Berg stepped in closer. 'Sure,' he said. 'You leave us alone, and I don't break your arm.'

Palmer stood his ground, although he was more than a little nervous. Lobo hesitated, then seemed to make up his mind. He looked from Berg to Bulstrode. 'Either one of you crumbs going to give me a hand?' Neither spoke. 'Then it's a deal, Palmer. Meet me in the loading bay in five minutes.'

Lobo turned to go, and Berg said, 'What's going on, Lobo? This Randall owe you, or something?'

'Nothing, and it's the same both ways. What of it?'

Berg shrugged, surprised at the sudden burst of aggression from the usually placid Lobo. 'Who said anything? I only asked.'

'Well don't try thinking, Berg. It doesn't suit you.' And he went off through one of the minor tunnels.

When he'd gone, Berg looked at Bulstrode. 'You thinking what I'm thinking?'

Bulstrode frowned. 'I don't believe Lobo's gone fairy, if that's what you mean,' he said.

'No,' Berg said earnestly, 'but I reckon he knows something about this Randall. Maybe Willis was right and he *is* a spy. Maybe –' he began to get excited by his logic – 'maybe he's doing Willis in right now, and he's made some kind of deal with Lobo to get his help!'

Bulstrode was watching him with a pained expression. 'Lobo was right,' he said. 'Thinking doesn't suit you. It's like watching a one-legged man trying to tap dance. Go check the list.'

When Lobo arrived at the bays, Palmer was already there. If Lobo could have managed his vigil alone, he would; but the chain which held the outer door up was notoriously insecure, and whilst he could mangle it into a loose knot which would probably hold for a few minutes until it slipped, he couldn't trust it. He didn't find much entertainment in the idea of the door dropping on his head as he looked out, unhearing through the double barriers of wind and helmet.

The cargo bay was heated whereas the loading bay was not. There was a door across the short passage which connected the two, but it was hardly ever closed. Lobo closed it now, stooping first to clear the dirt and debris from the shallow rail it ran along, and effectively sealing the loading bay off from the rest of the Palace. Now they could open the outer hatch without fear of tripping any thermostats and affecting the delicate balance of the generators.

Lobo knew the idea was impossible, inadequate. He cursed himself for giving in to his impulses, cursed Randall for making it all happen in the first place, cursed the whole mismatched, unjust world for simply being there. And still he hauled with determination on the chain to bring the bay door to its fullest open position where the light would spill out on to the ice and glow in the storm, the only point of welcome anywhere on the ice cap.

There was a danger, Lobo knew, that Randall might find his way back along the guidewire and still miss the light or, seeing it, might stumble off the narrow lip and into a freezing slush of open water. It was a waste of time, a waste of effort, he was going to look a monumental fool. The hatch squealed over the last couple of feet and reached its limit with a crash.

'Get helmeted and stand with me in the doorway,' he said to Palmer as he lifted the chain over on to itself. 'I look out, you look in. This knot starts to move, you slap me on the arm fast and we both get out of the way before the door comes down. Okay?'

Palmer nodded briefly, and his eyes strayed over to the open hatch. He shuddered, and not from the cold.

'If it scares you so much,' Lobo said, 'Why don't you try for one of the inside jobs, like the yeast tanks?'

'Don't think I haven't tried. Bulstrode heard about it and came to my bunkroom. He said there was nothing wrong with me and he'd tear me up for a coward if I didn't pull my weight.'

'That's Bulstrode,' Lobo said as he clipped his helmet into place. 'He's subtle.'

'And he doesn't forget. Come to that, neither do I. Willis owes me three shifts, and if he doesn't come back I can't collect.'

They stepped on to the ramp and climbed to the doorway. Lobo said grimly, 'If Willis comes back alone, you may not get to collect anyway. I'll want to know why he set the citizen up to die out there.'

Palmer started to frame a question, but was distracted as the bay's lights dipped for a few seconds before coming back up to their usual brightness. They both knew the sign; a section of the pipeline had become exposed, and the Palace cutout had come very close to firing.

Lobo looked out. The snowstorm boiled on, the light from the open bay diffusing out on to the swirl of crystals. Lightning forked, throwing a still frame of the landscape into sharp relief and then blanking out again as the rip of thunder followed. Ahead was the open water, to his left the open plain and the pipeline; behind him, he knew, was the smooth, rising mound of the Ice Palace which would obscure the bay lights to anyone approaching from that direction.

At least he now had some sense of distance, even though his imagination had instantly interpreted every mound and shadow on the plain as an army of crawling, moving figures. He wouldn't have to watch for long. His own power pack was low on charge, but it was almost half-an-hour since he had come in off the ice; anybody still out there would almost certainly be carrying a weak or discharged pack, and the chances of survival with suit insulation alone were probably nil.

A double flash, two brilliant bursts that lit the plain in machine gun succession; and in the bellying rumble that followed, an urgent tug on his arm from Palmer. Distracted, Lobo fell back on to the ramp as the leading edge of the door came down, almost clipping his visor. He nearly lost his balance on the incline as he hurried down to pull back on the chain and raise the door. Two pictures were etched in his mind, bright exposures close together and they weren't the same. Already the twin images were fading but the certainty remained; something out there had moved between the flashes.

Gears moved and the door rose again with painful slowness. Of course, it might have been an eddy of snow, raised by the wind into a brief illusion of solidity and dropped again as quickly. Or a section of cladding, stripped away and bouncing along towards the sea. Lobo bunched the chain, trying to make a more secure knot. Palmer was in the doorway, but he wouldn't turn and look out. The lightning was firing off irregularly, an aerial inferno backed by thunder which was overlapping into a continuous roll.

Out on the plain, a snow suit was blundering, taking a straight course for the edge of the floe and the sea. Lobo scrambled out on to the glassy lip outside the bay and tried to run towards the figure, but on the third step he left solid ice and plunged waist-deep into snow. Within seconds his power pack was setting up a bleeping protest, but he waded on.

The man was blinded, rubbing at a crust of ice on his unheated visor as he stumbled towards a short drop and the bitter sea only yards ahead. The more that Lobo tried to hurry to intercept, the deeper he thrust himself into the piling drifts. Then the ground gave completely, and when he came up his own visor was a blank mass of granules.

He dashed them away before they could freeze and cling. The man was no more than a couple of feet from the edge of the floe, and he had stopped; perhaps the lack of deep snow on the hard rim had made him suspicious. He was scrubbing hard at his faceplate, and when he took his hands away he saw the grey, heaving soup of the sea filling his horizon. Then he began uncertainly to turn, and he saw Lobo.

It could be Randall, it could be Willis. There were only four basic colours in the Palace's range of snow suits, and both men chanced to wear pale orange. But the helmets were random, the same basic colours but pulled from the rack when needed – this figure was in a bright yellow helmet, fine for Randall but what had Willis picked up?

Lobo couldn't remember. He tried to picture the scene in the bay as they'd prepared to go out, but it wouldn't come. His heating unit was dead and the cold was climbing into the suit with him in an unwelcome but irresistible possession.

Blue! Bright blue. He remembered it in the line ahead of him on the way out to the pipeline, slogging along in the tracks of the sled. Randall struggled towards him, and together they headed back to the angled shaft of light from the bay.

Abruptly, the shaft was chopped by one-third. Lobo grabbed a handful of Randall's suit and pulled him on faster – the knotted chain was slipping, and the door had dropped. Lobo knew that Palmer could manage the chains in the cargo bay – he'd opened the hatch at the beginning of their shift – but the gears in the loading bay were stiffer, and their ratio was different. Randall was flagging, falling on every third or fourth step. Lobo doubted that Palmer even had the weight to get the door open once it had closed.

It was no more than a three-foot slot, a long letterbox. Randall was slung through without ceremony and Lobo rolled after. Palmer had the remnants of the knotted chain gathered in his arms, trying to stop it from slipping any further, but when he saw Lobo safe he let go and the gap slammed closed.

Randall had tumbled all the way down the ramp to the bottom, and he was trying to sit up. Lobo called over to Palmer, 'Your power pack, fast. Him first.'

Palmer disconnected Randall's pack – now so exhausted it couldn't even bleep – and snapped his own into its place. Randall started to shake his head from side to side, and when Lobo came down and removed his helmet he was gasping as the heat began to penetrate his senseless tissues.

'It'll hurt a while,' Lobo told him, 'then it gets easier.'

'Open the hatch,' Randall managed to say. 'There's somebody else out there.'

'Shove Willis. I'm not putting myself out for him.'

'Not Willis.' Randall shook his head emphatically. 'Somebody else. He led me back this far until I saw the light from the bay.'

'You getting religious on me?' Lobo asked with suspicion.

'I'm telling you, there's another man out there! He can't be more than a few feet away from the top of the ramp!'

Lobo glanced up at Palmer. 'Take a look,' he said.

Palmer began to back away. 'Not me, Lobo. Please.'

Lobo rose and took a step towards him. 'Take a look or I'll bust your head and fry your brains. I'll hold the hatch.'

Surprisingly, Palmer was close to tears. 'You're as bad as Bulstrode, Lobo,' he said accusingly. 'I had you figured for better.'

'I'm worse than Bulstrode,' Lobo snarled, feeling mean and guilty as he said it. 'Move yourself and you'll find out by how much.'

'You're lousy company, as well,' came Palmer's parting shot, and Lobo felt better.

When the door was open and a miserable Palmer was tentatively sticking his head out Lobo came back. 'Now, what is this?' he said. 'Willis is the only other man outside the Palace, and he stranded you there in the first place.'

'I told you, it definitely wasn't Willis. Whoever it was, he called my name and I followed him until I came within sight of the bay lights. Then my faceplate froze over again and the next thing I saw was the sea.'

'He called your *name*?' Lobo was incredulous. 'There can't

be more than about twenty people in this place even *know* your name.'

'I'm not pretending I understand it.' And Randall went on to explain.

He told of how he'd floundered around, and how he'd managed eventually to find the guidewire, only to realize that with his sense of direction completely confused there would be no way of being sure that he was heading towards the Ice Palace and not away from it. He'd taken a chance, and he'd been wrong.

He realized his mistake when there was a momentary clearance of the blizzard and the pipeline appeared briefly ahead of him. In surprise he'd dropped his grip on the wire – he'd barely been able to feel it through the gloves – and had stooped to rummage in the snow for it, knowing that without it he'd have no chance of retracing his route. The feeble output of his power pack, stopped down as it was to minimal operation, had robbed his hands of feeling, and he could have grasped the wire a dozen times and never known it.

That was when he'd heard his name being called. Turning, he had seen a figure through the blizzard waving him back; when he followed, it moved away, and stayed ahead of him all the time.

Randall had found the sloping trench and hammered on the cargo bay door without effect. Then, hearing his name again, he had come up out of the trench and seen for the first time the light from the loading bay.

'It wasn't Willis, Lobo,' he concluded. 'I couldn't tell for sure, but it didn't even look like he was wearing a snow suit.'

'That's too much,' Lobo said. 'Nobody goes out there without a snow suit and lives.'

'All right, I'll concede that. But I know it wasn't Willis.'

Palmer's helmet-amplified voice quavered from the open doorway, 'There's nobody, Lobo. Can't I come in, now?'

Lobo realized that he'd been standing there with no power pack, and beckoned him in. Randall unclipped the pack and offered it with his thanks.

'You're welcome,' Palmer replied unsteadily. 'I'll work out what you owe me and let you know.'

As Palmer walked away, Randall asked, 'What's he talking about?'

'He deals in shift cover. He'll do anything to avoid taking his turns on the ice. I had to bargain for you.' Lobo gathered their two dead power packs together.

'Thanks,' Randall said. 'I suppose I owe you, as well.'

'No, we're even. Now I don't have to feel bad for not standing up for you against Berg.'

Randall hadn't seen the generator room, and didn't know what to expect. In relation to the Palace it was symmetrically opposite to the crap tanks, with Main Street and the Cantina in between the two.

They came out on to a catwalk, with a sheer concrete wall to one side and the natural ice wall on the other. Lobo explained that the generators themselves were the other side of the concrete, and the only part of them which was exposed was at the far end of the catwalk. Randall wondered what was at the bottom of the drop beneath them, but didn't ask.

The catwalk ended in an open area with an arch in the concrete which made way for a console and some racks of contacts and switches. There were three men on the other side of the console, and their argument could be heard from some distance away.

One of them was the Doc. He'd put a lot of effort into manhandling his containerload of yeast to the generators, and now the other two were trying to persuade him to take it away. Doc's idea had been that the yeast would live longer in the working temperature of the generator room and would be safe from contamination as long as it was kept on the right side of the shields. A man about Doc's age but with much less hair was trying patiently to explain that yes, radiation *does* travel in straight lines but the shielding wasn't too tight, and contaminated air tends to move in whatever direction it damn well pleases. At this Doc began to look dubious, and the other man, who Lobo murmured was called the Weasel for obvious physical reasons, offered to help the Doc carry his container back to get a fresh, uncontaminated sample.

The two of them moved off, still arguing over the container, and Lobo introduced Randall to Cohn.

Cohn nodded agreeably. 'You set for the shutdown?' he asked.

'If it happens,' Lobo replied, and held up the power packs. 'Need a couple of recharges while we've still got the generator.'

Cohn reached for them. 'Better get them hooked up fast,' he said. 'We've no spares.' He went around the console and fixed the packs onto terminals set in a bank on one wall of the archway.

Randall said, 'How long does recharging take?'

'Few minutes.' Cohn left the packs in place. 'Don't believe we've met.'

'This is Randall,' Lobo said. 'Been here a couple of days. We just pulled him in off the ice.'

Cohn gave a whistle, and gestured at the dials on his console. 'You were out in *that*? You're lucky to be alive, Randall.'

'I know it. I'm glad it's warm in here.'

'The warmth isn't for our benefit. It's optimum working temperature for the machinery. All these dials and indicators are linked to the surface network and the cutout trigger. That's what I'm monitoring. I gave the alarm.'

Lobo bent to study the dials, his puzzled frown showing that he understood none of them. 'How're we doing?'

'Holding on, but only just.' Cohn pointed to one part of the board. 'There's one hell of a leak to the Southwest. The cladding must have been ripped clean away. I've got all the bunkroom lights down to try and keep some kind of balance. It's not much, but it helps.'

Randall had wandered around to the archway. It had been blocked off in a rough-and-ready way, obviously at a much later date than its original construction. Now it was being used as a noticeboard, and was covered in charts, lists and measurements. All were on the same grey, rough paper he'd seen elsewhere in the Palace. He turned to Cohn and said, 'Are you in here all the time?'

'Only when I'm rostered. We have a few regulars, and anybody who's ill or injured. The Worm takes care of it.'

Randall would have snapped his fingers, but they felt too brittle. 'That reminds me. Lobo, I want to see the Worm when the packs are charged.'

'For what?'

'I want to know who else was out on the ice with me. I want to know who led me back.'

'Forget it, Randall,' Lobo said. 'There was nobody.'

'You can't say that. You didn't see him.'

'We're on the point of a shutdown. That means we'll be needed any time now.'

'It's quiet at the moment,' Cohn pointed out helpfully, but Lobo dismissed the fact.

'That's now, but what if there's a call for an emergency ice party?'

Randall asked, 'What happens? Do they ask for volunteers?'

'Like hell. They pull your name out of a hat and boot you through the door with a sled. Who'd be stupid enough to volunteer for a job like that?'

'Look at the chart behind you,' Cohn said to Randall. 'Those dips show the power loss spread over a number of shifts. They're getting deeper and closer together. With all the heat we pour out, it's no wonder we get freak weather.' He was right; extrapolated to its logical conclusion, the chart offered a frightening prospect for the Ice Palace.

When the packs had taken a full charge Randall plugged into his and went off to look for the Worm. Lobo objected, but followed him anyway. They found plenty of places the Worm had been, but nowhere that he actually was. In the early stages of the crisis he'd gone around 'supervising' every group and been chased off by each in turn, so in the end it came down to the most obvious place.

Randall knocked politely on the door of the Worm's office.

'Go away,' was the muffled shout from the other side.

'I need to speak to you,' Randall called.

'I'm busy.'

'You're using the wrong approach,' Lobo whispered. Shouldering past Randall he hammered on the door and yelled, 'Worm? If you don't come out I'm going to break down the door and stamp on your fingers!'

'There's no need for that!' Randall hissed.

Lobo winked. 'Stick with the system.'

The door opened and the Worm peered out. 'Hi, guys,' he said. 'Something you need?'

'You can start by letting us in.'

The Worm let the door swing open, and backed towards his desk. 'This is my office, Lobo,' he said anxiously. 'I hope you'll respect my office.'

'It's me that wants you,' Randall said. 'I want to know who else was left out on the ice at the same time as me.'

The Worm put his head on one side to bring his single lens to bear on Randall, and gave a start of surprise when he recognized him. 'That's easy,' he stammered. 'Willis.'

'Besides Willis.'

'That's easy, too. Nobody.'

'Is there any way you can check?'

Lobo gave a deep, here-we-go-again sigh, and the Worm said 'Why should I have to?'

'Just do it,' Randall insisted.

'Look, I already did. At the first warning of a possible shutdown I went all over the Palace. I took the register so I wouldn't miss anybody, and the only people I didn't see were all on Bulstrode's team. He's accounted for them since.'

'Happy now?' Lobo asked.

'No, I'm not. I saw somebody and I heard him call my name, and I know it wasn't Willis.'

'Now, listen,' Lobo said carefully. 'The ice can have a strange effect on a man's mind.'

'That's right,' the Worm added helpfully.

Lobo frowned, and turned to the Worm. 'When were you ever out on the ice?' he demanded.

'I had a look, once.'

'Keep quiet, or you'll be having another.'

'I know what I saw,' Randall insisted.

'But don't go round broadcasting it. You've seen what they can be like if they think they spot a weakness.'

'Yeah,' the Worm joined in, and for once didn't get an instant rebuff. 'Lousy isn't the word for it. I know.'

Lobo added, 'For once, the Worm's right. It doesn't matter what you believe as long as you keep it quiet.'

Randall wasn't happy with his answer, but it seemed to be the best he was going to get. He and Lobo went down to the Cantina and heard, as they approached Main Street, the ring of the shift handbell.

'It's the all-clear,' Lobo explained. 'We didn't tip over into shutdown, and the weather must be easing off. If it goes according to pattern we'll have a lull and then another bad one. A repair team should be on its way now.'

There was still some of the emetic yeast to be had in the Cantina, and Randall strangled some down. A drum of it had been wheeled in as a parody of a buffet for the waiting men, but now most of them had either gone off to their bunkrooms or had joined the rostered shift on the ice. The floor was wet and slushy from the unaccustomed crowding.

Back in the bunkroom Randall watched the star-patterns form overhead. It seemed almost a lifetime since he'd last done this, and more than a lifetime since he'd left the city. Already the city was like a dream to him, and the Ice Palace was becoming his only true reality.

It could have been worse. At least the Palace had a settled society, one based on a careful code of threat and bluster and abuse dictated by the harsh necessities of survival. True conflict was avoided by the institution of an elaborate pecking-order, with the unhappy Worm at the end of the line; all Randall knew for sure so far was that he himself came somewhere above the Worm and below Berg, and only the oldsters were allowed to stand apart from the system.

'Lobo,' he said quietly into the dark, 'are you asleep yet?'

A pause. 'What does it sound like?'

'Sounds like you're not very pleased.'

'You've got it. Go to sleep.'

'But there are some things that don't hang together. Like the man on the ice . . .'

Lobo groaned, and mumbled something into his blanket.

'Other things as well. I don't understand the power setup here.'

'I already explained it to you.'

'I know *how*, but not *why*.'

The bunk on the other side of the room creaked in the dark as Lobo turned over. 'So we'll work and work to keep alive, and always know it's futile. That's why.'

'But I can't grasp the idea of power going nowhere. I can't see it not being *used*.'

Lobo's grasp of practical physics was probably even better than Randall's. 'It gets wasted as heat,' he said. 'That's the whole idea.' And then he yawned, noisily and pointedly.

'According to Cohn's chart, we have to produce about twice as much power as the Ice Palace needs to prevent the cutout operating.'

'We don't have to produce *any* power. That's all automatic. All we have to do is conserve it.'

Randall thought about it. 'All the same . . . I saw a stranger out on the ice – ' muted howl of agony from Lobo – 'and there's enough power being fed out there to run another Ice Palace. Don't you find that interesting?'

'Tomorrow. I'll find it interesting tomorrow.'

'It's *got* to be,' Randall said, more to himself than to Lobo. Then, out loud, 'What's the furthest anybody's ever strayed from here?'

'End of the guidewire.' Lobo was nearly asleep, probably hardly aware that he was answering. 'Further than that, they don't come back.'

Damn it, Randall thought as Lobo's breathing became deep and regular, there's something out there. In the Worm's office a chart had caught his eye, and he'd assumed it to be a copy of Cohn's power record. But a closer inspection had shown it wasn't; it was a log of the Ice Palace's manning levels. And yet the curve was the same! Every big storm, and there was a massive power drain, a near shutdown and a man disappeared. Willis had never come back.

In a few hours the normal shifts would start again, blind agony out on the ice, eat, a break for sleep and out again. No wonder nobody had time to think, to plan, to draw conclusions. A few weeks of the killing routine and perhaps he would become as stubborn and short-sighted as the rest of them – and then how could he ever hope to see the city again? Let alone the corrupt bunch of thieves that the underbelly council had turned out to be, a dream of democracy gone sour.

The weather was improving, and he had a fully-charged power pack. And he wanted to know what was on the other end of the guidewire.

Nine

In the time that had passed since the fall of Central, little had changed in the city. A rigged election had, as predicted, put the underbelly council in overall power. It was business as usual, then, with the exception that the old-time crooks became the new-style business powers, and they continued their activities unhindered by the Police Élite.

The embarrassing problem of what to do with Randall had been solved in true underbelly fashion by making him disappear. After a couple of days nobody even thought to ask about him, with the exception of his former assistant and now replacement. Killoran asked loud and public questions, prodding and testing all the appeals and enquiry procedures of the city's archaic legal system. It was taking a lot of effort on Marius's part to anticipate and forestall him, and he wished that Killoran would lose interest and give up.

Marius was working harder than anybody to make the new democracy successful. He publicly raised and examined difficult issues, pointed fingers of accusation, promised that the space trade would be resumed and the city put back into the mainstream of history; whilst privately he stalled, threatened, manipulated and blackmailed, and all to the eventual good of Marius.

Morden was worried about Marius and in particular the massive deal that he'd hinted at with an offworld interest. Morden paced his blind man's castle on the rooftops, his hand reaching out occasionally in the darkness to brush some familiar fixed object in passing. Any attempt to analyse his own feelings only brought him further confusion; whilst he couldn't deny that legitimacy had robbed most of his enterprises of their enjoyment, he wondered if the moral repulsion that Marius inspired in him was based on some fundamental touchstone of right behaviour that transcended law and crime, or whether it was a simple re-focussing of his energies through ennui. Whatever the cause, he decided that he was thoroughly opposed to what Marius was planning, whatever it might turn out to be.

Meanwhile, Marius grew in power and influence. He was neither more dishonest nor more wily than any of the other underbelly leaders, but whereas they quickly grew tired of the dry processes of government he saw them as an infinite avenue of dodges and angles, a hall of mirrors where his opportunities magnified and multiplied. Whilst promising his public the space trade again – well, yes, but in a *little* while, when we've sorted out the intricacies and complications that you simply can't see on the surface – he was quietly arranging with the offworlders to sell that public out.

He needed another vote to side with his on the council, and he obviously considered blind Morden to be the most compliant and least controversial of allies. Avery Sim was dead and with Chandler ('doesn't even like me') happy running the Police Élite it left Morden as the single uncommitted voice.

The idea of a deal with offworlders seemed pretty fantastic. When Morden found out the truth, it made his early speculations appear mundane.

The story came out in scraps and hints. Marius had been contacted by an agent, some time before when the controversy over Randall was at its height. The offworlders were in a ship some distance away, and they were prepared to wait until conditions were right for them to move in; they weren't interested in food, or artefacts, or technology of any kind. They wanted processed raw materials – metals, plastics, rubber, paper, glass – as much as the total industrial production of the city could manage until existing resources were worked out. They had nothing to offer in exchange and were prepared to make no restitution, in view of which they were preparing a small force with Marius's essential cooperation to supervise the exploitation.

One other thing emerged. The offworlders weren't human.

Alien contact had been a long-cherished and finally abandoned hope of every settled system. For a while the colonized worlds had competed for prestige in hunting through their neighbour-planets for the aggressive signals of intelligence; but then, as the realities of non-productive expense were felt, that interest had dwindled. Now, after all man's talk, a maverick had taken the trouble to seek him out.

Marius's policy was to give Morden as little information as possible, calling on him privately to get his thumbprint on some document or other whenever the need arose. He rarely explained the nature of the papers and if he had there would be no way that Morden could ensure he was telling the truth. They mainly seemed to relate to the streamlining and expanding of the city's meagre factory facilities into units which were in line with an expectation of economic growth; and who, in such circumstances, would publicly accuse Marius of *anything*?

The morning was typical of its kind. Marius left the city centre where he now lived in a suite comprising an entire floor of citizens' apartments knocked into one, and set off to cross the river back towards his old home. He travelled in one of the Élite's armoured vans, not because he really needed the protection but because he liked the idea of frivolous consumption that their oil-burning engines displayed. If he'd had more nerve and even less sensitivity he'd have travelled by one of the helicopters. Those machines positively drank the stuff.

He sat in the dark in Morden's main room, waiting for his eyes to adjust. In spite of that he was already talking. It seemed that Killoran had found yet another appeal procedure to set in motion, this one relating to internal Élite discipline.

'We'll have to see this Killoran,' Marius said, 'and buy him off.'

'You can't buy off the Élite,' Morden told him, knowing he wouldn't really believe it. 'They're all fanatics for honesty. Central bred them that way.'

'Well, we'll have to silence him somehow. Find something to appease him. It doesn't matter what – as long as it's not the truth.'

Morden sighed and settled back in his chair. Marius barely made out the shadow of a movement. 'I don't like what was done to Randall,' Morden said in a voice filled with as much self-pity as distaste.

'It's the only significant contribution you've made to our partnership so far, and there's a long way to go yet. Any time you get worried, think of the rewards.'

'Rewards? Or empty promises to collaborators?'

'Look, the off-worlders couldn't hope to pull this one without our cooperation. We're safe, Morden. Probably the only two people in the city who are. With the power they've got available they could wipe us out and leave us burning. By selling them our compliance we're making sure they act with moderation.'

Morden had heard Marius give this argument before. It was so plausible he was almost tempted to believe it. 'But the price for that compliance could never be high enough. What use is wealth on a burned-out world?'

Marius wondered if his eyes had fully adjusted to Morden's dark yet. He thought he could see the dim outline of the table between them, and with this target fixed in his mind he reached for the folder of papers he'd brought. 'Central Command's already ruined what was left of this world. It killed off progress generations back when it tried to make a perfect city full of average men and women. Look at the citizens! They've never had an original idea between them, with the exception of Rorvik. Can you honestly say they're not a sign of a degenerate trend?' He slapped his papers down on the table to make his point, but the table wasn't there. The folder opened as it fell and the sheets poured on to the floor.

Morden permitted himself a thin smile, but tried to keep it out of his voice. 'Does it matter what I say?'

'You couldn't alter the fact.' Marius was on the floor now, his documents no more than dim grey shapes before him. 'When the offworlders have got what they want we'll be rich enough to move to another system and live like kings.'

'It's thirty years' subjective travel to the nearest system. How do you propose surviving it?'

Marius was back on his seat, rustling as he settled. 'Trust me, Morden, and leave the details to them.'

'Can *you* trust *them* not to take what they've learned from us and move on to the next system? Not to be content before they've cleaned out the entire sphere of human settlement?'

'I've got their word, Morden. They're an honourable race.'

'At least as honourable as men.'

'That's the idea.' Marius wasn't fooling, he was totally insensitive to the irony. 'They want to hold a strategy meeting on their own territory.'

Morden was thinking that he would have the table moved back before Marius's next visit when this new and unexpected information suddenly pushed everything else aside. 'What do you mean?' was all he could say.

'On board their ship,' Marius went on. 'We'll have to rendezvous with their shuttle at the established landing point.'

'But I've never been off the surface before!' Morden had ridden in a helicopter on the day of the first council meeting in the city, and it had made him sick.

'It's easy. Just like riding the mono.'

'You mean you've already *been*?' Perhaps Marius found pleasure in Morden's discomposure, a small revenge for the trick with the table.

'Of course,' he said smoothly, as if such travel were an everyday matter. 'They've even fitted me out with my own chambers. They'll even do the same for you – just tell them what you'd like. They're really pleased about you joining us.'

The conversation seemed all wrong, as if some fundamental block of rationality had been removed. Morden had been able to entertain the incredulity of the notion at second hand, but now it had been brought close he felt his own sense of reality backing off defensively.

'I suppose I have no choice,' he said weakly.

'You've got the choice between surviving and going under. What else did we ever have?'

Marius promised to make the arrangements through the agent and bring the details on his next visit, and the conversation moved on to other subjects. Rorvik, for example; Louann had requested the release of his remains, at present packaged in a deep-freeze at Élite headquarters awaiting the final decision on what portion of guilt or credit he should be accorded. She had, it seemed, taken up with one of the newly-established religions, a racket that Marius would be interested in getting into if he only had the time for it. Public opinion, carefully moulded by the council, had come down firmly on Rorvik's side; he was the creator of a new dawn for the city, liberator of the people, and several other equally trite kinds of hero. Randall, on the other hand, was pure dog's mess.

'A dead hero,' Morden phrased it, 'and a live scapegoat. How much more humane to arrange it the other way around.'

'Humane, but dumb. Dead heroes can't lead opinion against you. Randall's best off where he is.'

Morden thumbed some papers and they talked a little more, but the main topic of the meeting had come and gone. Marius made his excuses and said he was expected across the river in less than an hour, but that the discussion, as always, had been 'really meaningful'. Morden called somebody to lead Marius back to the outside world and the light.

When Marius was well clear one of the deeper shadows at the back of the room detached itself and moved forward, filling out to the shape of a man.

‘Is it true?’ the shade whispered. ‘Or have I been listening to some monstrous practical joke?’

‘It’s no joke, Chandler. Marius is attempting to sell out the city.’

‘But for what? Invasion?’

‘Exploitation. He expects to share in the spoils and then move to another system where he’s not known.’

Chandler laughed bitterly as he moved round, hand outstretched in the dark, guiding himself to Marius’s still-warm chair. ‘That’s him all over. A hundred per cent in favour of what’s good for Marius.’

Although he hadn’t believed Morden at first, Chandler had to accept his story now. He hurriedly tried to weigh the courses of action open to him but found he could think of none. He was the nominal head of the Élite, but they weren’t his own private army; he couldn’t use them to prepare any elaborate defence without Marius finding out before anything could be properly organized. And then there was the Élite itself; supertrained and superbly capable, they were woefully lacking in imagination. What would they make of this underbelly savage who raved about the raiders from outer space?

‘Hasty action won’t serve us at all,’ he told Morden. ‘We’ll need information. That’s up to you.’ He tried to make it sound as if it was a measured conclusion and not the stalling of desperation.

‘I’ll follow it through, Chandler,’ Morden said. He didn’t need the sinking feeling in his belly to tell him that Chandler’s presence hadn’t helped him to unload his problem in any way at all.

Ten

There was a team out on the ice for emergency repairs and everybody else, it seemed, was either in the generator room or by the crap tanks, or else they were asleep. Randall didn’t want to wake any more people than necessary. The man on the generators told him exactly where he’d find Palmer’s bunk.

The brief slice of light from the bunkroom door showed quite a different layout from the one he shared with Lobo. Being well-insulated, hardly ventilated and fully populated, it was stuffy, even hot. The men in here slept only in their inner suit linings, the outers hung on lines strung between the top bunks. Deep mumblings and guttural breathing sounded all around as he tried to remember where Palmer was supposed to be.

Randall gave a couple of experimental prods at one of the figures covered in a lower bunk. The man turned, came perilously close to the surface of sleep and then gracefully slid back again. It wasn't Palmer. Along a bunk, and try again.

Palmer rolled over, opened sticky eyes, tried to focus on him. 'Wake up,' Randall whispered. 'I want to talk business.'

'It can wait,' Palmer moaned, and tried to roll away. Randall took a fistful of blanket and jerked the whole thing off the bed.

There was cold air frosting in from the unclosed door. Palmer whipped upright, and banged his head on the slats of the bunk above. The occupant stiffened ominously. 'Give me that blanket back before I freeze!' Palmer hissed.

'Are you ready to talk now?'

'Yes! Give me the blanket!'

A voice from one of the other stacks came; 'Wha's going on?'

Another voice, which Randall identified as Cohn's; 'I don't want to break up a good argument, but do you mind if we sleep?'

The man in the upper bunk asked, 'Who is it?'

'It's Randall,' Cohn replied.

Groan from the upper bunk. 'Get lost, citizen.'

'Up yours, peabrain!' Randall snapped in the gutter talk of the Ice Palace.

Cohn chuckled in the dark. 'You're learning, Randall.'

Randall crouched, leaning close to Palmer and lowering his voice. He held up the blanket. 'Come on, Palmer. Time to trade.'

'Keep your voice down. What do you want?'

'I'm going back out on the ice . . . '

'At *this* time?'

'It has to be now or I'll miss the quiet time between the two storms. I need somebody to operate the chains for me.'

Palmer had pushed himself up into a sitting position, right

back in the angle of the bunk and the wall. The white of his suit lining betrayed his outline, and dull blue light glinted on the wet of his eyes. 'You're mad,' he said and then, with guarded interest, 'What are you offering?'

'Shift cover. What else is there?'

'And how in hell am I supposed to collect? I've never seen a dead man take a turn on the ice.'

'I've no intention of being killed. The weather's improved and I know the guidewire system now.'

'Forget it, Randall. I've got too much riding on you already. There's your own debt from last night and three shifts carried over from Willis . . . '

Randall interrupted him. 'How do you work that out?'

'Like I said, you can't collect off a dead man. I helped save you, so you take over what Willis owed me. That's only fair.'

There were silent, attentive forms on all sides of the bunkroom now. Randall gave an inward sigh, and prepared to take the irrevocable step. 'Like Cohn said, I'm learning. Pick a bone, Palmer.'

Palmer radiated confusion. 'What?'

'I'm being fair and giving you a choice. Pick a bone, and if you can't help me I'll break it.'

'Get lost, Randall. I may not like going on the ice, but I'm not the Worm and you're not exactly Bulstrode. You're a citizen, Randall. Anybody in the Palace could wipe the floor with you.'

Randall shifted his weight, balanced his crouch. 'Don't be misled by Berg's demonstration. I could reach out and close your eyes for you before you could even move to stop me.'

'Big talk's cheap, and –' there was a blur across Palmer's limited vision, a light pressure on his eyelids and his eyes were closed. 'Hell,' he said sharply, 'What did you do?'

'I told you. Want me to do it again?' He did it again. 'I barely touched the lids. I could have put your eyes out just as easily.'

'Damn you, Randall, Willis was right. No citizen moves that fast.' Wood creaked, above and behind. 'What do you want with us?'

'I want you to come down to the exit bay and operate the door for me. That's all.'

'Go with him, Palmer,' the bunk overhead rumbled. 'Sling the crumb on to the ice and lock the doors behind him.'

'I've got half a mind to do just that,' Palmer replied, a little louder than he'd intended.

'We know you've only got half a mind, Palmer. Get out and get rid of him. Maybe Willis will find him.'

'I should think Willis is dead,' Cohn said doubtfully. 'His suit unit would be drained hours ago.'

'And the sooner this crumb joins him, the better. Take him out.'

Everybody in the room seemed to be awake, and there was open hostility in the cooling air. 'Palmer's right, Randall,' Cohn said reasonably. 'Élite training won't stop you dying out there.'

'My choice, Cohn,' Randall replied. 'Do you think I'd survive if I stayed, now that you all know what I am?' He turned back to the bunk beside him. 'What about it, Palmer?'

Palmer was plaintive. 'Who's going to cover the shifts I lose?'

'Isn't that a little academic? Whether I stay or go, I'm still a dead man.'

'Go with him, Palmer,' somebody urged. 'We'll ask the Worm to work something out for you.'

'Or else I'll go myself and cancel a couple of the shifts I owe you,' came another voice which was far less sympathetic.

Palmer muttered something to himself and, swinging out of the bunk, reached to pull his suit off the line. Randall stepped back to give him room and came level with Cohn's bunk.

'Why are you doing this, Randall?' Cohn asked him. 'Everybody accepted you as a citizen. Why throw it away?'

Randall shrugged. 'I've got my reasons.'

'But there's nowhere to go outside. And nobody's going to let you back into the Palace now.'

'If I find what I'm looking for,' Randall replied, 'I won't be coming back.'

Palmer clipped his power pack on to his belt and stood by the door, shuddering a little as he waited for the heat from the unit to make its way around. Randall opened the door and they both stepped out into Main Street. 'Go freeze, cop,' somebody shouted as the door swung closed.

There was a silence, and then Cohn said, 'He's mad. He's got to be.'

The man above Palmer's empty bunk said, 'Who cares? Won't matter a damn when he's dead.'

Main Street was still empty. As they crossed into the tunnel leading to the bays Randall asked how long it was likely to be until the next bad phase of the storm. Palmer didn't answer at first, but then seemed to find the silence more embarrassing than the prospect of conversation. As they walked down the incline Palmer said that it would be unusually calm now, but that it would get much worse in a few hours.

'But how long exactly?' Randall pressed him.

Palmer shrugged. 'What do I care? It was never my problem.'

'It's your problem now. Make a guess.'

Palmer guessed about two hours, perhaps even less. When they reached the bay Randall went to pick a helmet from the racks as Palmer took up position by the chains. Then they both turned at the sound of somebody approaching down the tunnel, fast and breathless.

Lobo emerged into the bay. He was trying to blink off the stupor of interrupted sleep, but in spite of that he was plainly angry.

'Randall!' he shouted across the bay. 'What the hell do you think you're doing?'

'I've got to go out, Lobo,' Randall replied reasonably. 'You know why.'

Lobo seemed to want to come nearer, but was holding back, attempting to salvage the last shreds of his cherished reserve. 'What kind of idea do you call that? As soon as I woke up and saw your bunk was empty I knew what you were going to try. There's nothing out there!'

'Don't argue with him, Lobo. He's police.'

Lobo dismissed Palmer's revelation without even looking at him. 'I know,' he said, and continued to fix Randall with a glower that was half challenge, half plea.

Randall said, 'Open the hatch, Palmer.'

'Don't touch those chains.' Lobo seemed to be straining at the limit of a leash of his own making. 'I stuck my neck out for you last night just to get you in off the ice, made myself look a goddamn fool for a citizen nobody cared about. Is this how

I get thanked? At the first opportunity you throw yourself back outside?'

'There's good reason . . .' Randall began.

'I don't care about your lousy reasons. This is the Ice Palace. Randall. You don't get castles rising out of the mist just because you want them bad enough.'

'The waste power from the Ice Palace reactors has to go *somewhere*. The system can't be so irrational.'

'But it *is*!' Lobo was appalled at Randall's inability to grasp the Ice Palace's fundamental function. 'That's the whole idea! we survive, and we don't get any satisfaction from it. That's how Central designed the place.'

'It won't wash,' Randall argued. 'Look at the fittings, all those tunnels that double round and go nowhere. This place is older than Central.'

'But how could there be anything outside without us knowing?'

'Because anybody who strays beyond the guidewire never comes back.'

'*You* came back,' Lobo pointed out.

'And I was led all the way.'

Lobo didn't seem remotely convinced. 'That's just so much birdseed. You were probably ice blind.'

'Whether that's true or not, I no longer have any choice. Now that it's generally known that I'm Elite I'll be torn apart if I stay. I could fight off a small group, but never the whole Palace. So what else can I do?'

Lobo couldn't hold back his venom at what he saw as a personal betrayal. 'Damn you, then,' he spat. 'If you'd kept your head down you'd have survived like the rest of us. Whatever happens now is only what you deserve.' And he turned to leave.

'Can't you understand I'm not just looking for a novel way to do away with myself?' Randall called after him. 'This might mean escape for all of us.'

Lobo stopped, but didn't turn back. 'What does a lousy cop care for the likes of us?' he said.

'Whether I like it or not, you're my kind now. I can't go back to the city and be at home – *I'm* the trusted guardian who wrecked the system. The people I indirectly put into power sent me here by way of a reward. I want to see them again.'

Lobo looked back over his shoulder. His eyes shone with

tears of frustration. 'I'm sorry I wasted my time. Now the whole damn Palace knows what a fool I am. Go kill yourself, Randall. I'm doing nothing else for you.'

It was Palmer who broke the silence which followed Lobo's departure. 'He's not very pleased,' he said, rather unnecessarily.

Randall tried to fight down the guilt he felt rising at his rough treatment of Lobo's feelings. Until this moment he wasn't sure that he had even acknowledged that the quiet giant had any, except in a kind of manipulative, Machiavellian way. 'He thinks I'm paying him back badly,' he told Palmer.

Palmer nodded. 'That makes sense. Lobo never liked to owe or be owed. I'd never traded him a shift until you went missing.'

Randall closed the latches on his helmet, and Palmer hauled on the chains to raise the door. He said something as Randall walked out into the trench, but Randall didn't turn back to find out what it was.

There was still snow, but now it was falling as a silent curtain. The air was impossibly still, with no trace of the gales that had scoured the surface when last he had been out. Now the only sound was of his own breathing inside his helmet.

The tracks of the repair team were still faintly visible where the trench emerged on to the surface, although they were filling slowly. They had angled sharp left, down towards the opposite extreme of the pipe network from where Randall had decided he wanted to go.

Visibility was good compared to conditions earlier on. Much of the Palace itself was visible, a series of humps and mounds covered and made indistinct by thick ice. There were two obvious levels to the covering, as if at some time the cap had shattered along a line of weakness and split off a good section of the Palace. Perhaps this would explain the apparently purposeless tunnels that drove on towards the south-east and invariably ended in blank, smooth walls.

It was a night sky above, in sharp contrast with the eye-wrenching brilliance he had encountered on his first emergence. The white landscape reflected a perfectly adequate amount of light with a bluish tinge that he hadn't seen before. He seemed to remember hearing or reading somewhere that ice could be compacted to the extent that it would hold back a little of all but the blue light in the spectrum, but he'd thought it dubious. Any snow that fell in the city had always been slightly grey.

The guidewires started from a series of posts which spread in a buried arc from the trench. He kicked through the snow until he found the one he wanted and then lifted it so that it pulled free of the surface for a few yards. There seemed little danger of his becoming lost as long as the weather was so tranquil, but he didn't want to be caught out by any sudden change.

The steady effort of wading raised the temperature in his suit in the absence of any wind to draw it away, so he was able to conserve the power pack by turning it down to stay barely above the level of discomfort. He let the line run loosely through his fingers – it was tethered to the ground at intervals and here he would have to stop and transfer his grip from one side to the other before moving on.

When he reached the pipeline he dropped the wire altogether and began to follow the steady march of pylons. He had no idea what he expected to find at the other end, only the deep conviction that the constant outflow of power and the stranger on the ice had to add up to *something*. He felt apprehension but no real fear, as the grim and despairing existence that he was leaving behind held no more attraction for him than any danger that might lie ahead.

He tried to pace himself, conserve his energies for when the going turned bad. The pipeline seemed to go on for ever and he noticed that the further he moved from the Ice Palace the less common the cheap cladding seemed to be. Most of the pipe along here was covered with a much stronger and durable-looking material which even carried a crust of ice on the windward side, showing that there wasn't enough heat escaping to stop it forming.

But wait a minute. There hadn't been any wind. Without any exposed skin to sense the movement of air and his hearing inhibited by the helmet, Randall would have difficulty perceiving the first signs of a worsening in conditions out on the ice. But now, when he stopped and looked, the falling snowflakes were not simply dropping and settling as before but were being carried sideways.

Two hours, perhaps even less, Palmer had said. How long had he been moving? There was no way of telling. In the Palace a shift started when the Worm said so and ended when the work was done and that was the only kind of measurement needed.

He knew for sure that the weather was getting bad when the first spatter of hail swept across and crusted his faceplate. It began to loosen and slide almost immediately, but it was a sign; already he began to feel the cold through the suit and he boosted the power to compensate. A few more yards, and the wind was audible over his noisy breathing; his faceplate crazed again, and this time the ice stuck. And somebody called his name.

He rubbed frenziedly to clear his visor, afraid of losing the pipeline and of finding an empty landscape when vision returned. The ice fell away and the pipeline was still there – but nothing, and nobody, else.

His name was shouted again, distant and windborne, and Randall began to look in a wild circle for the caller. Back down the pipeline a suited figure was making its way forward in his tracks.

Confusion was replaced by realization as he saw that the suit was a shabby blue Ice Palace garment. Within a minute Lobo had reached him. They both stood for a moment, the rising wind pulling at them, neither sure of what to say.

Randall spoke first. 'Why did you follow me?'

Lobo considered the question as if for the first time. 'I got thinking,' he said. 'Damn me if the whole idea didn't make sense.'

'That the only reason?'

Lobo grinned sheepishly. 'Not really. I was so mad at you when I came down to the exit bay that I forgot to look surprised when Palmer said you were police. I remembered when I got back to the bunkroom and went round to do some threatening, but he'd already blabbed to Cohn and the Anteater.'

'The who?'

'Guy with a big nose in the top bunk. They'd already got you tagged as a spy and me as your contact.'

By unspoken consent they carried on following the pipeline. Lobo had made good time by walking along in the tracks that Randall had cleared, but now he had to slow down as they walked side by side in order to maintain the conversation. Randall asked, 'What did you do then?'

'Dragged Palmer out again and made him open the hatch

for me. He wasn't very keen so I had to bounce him in the corridor. Bastard tried to drop the hatch on my head.'

Randall smiled. 'You can't blame him. Twice in one night.'

'That's not the point. I think he'd got it worked out that the two of us would be covering his shifts for some time to come. He didn't like waving goodbye to his meal ticket.'

'You could have cleared it for yourself. You didn't have to follow me.'

Lobo made a dismissive gesture which set up an eddy of snow around his arm. 'Oh, what the hell,' he said. 'So I could have stayed in that place until I was too old to work. Put myself in line for a crack on the head and a swim in the crap tanks.'

'Is that how it is?' Randall was surprised by the brutality of it.

'It happens.'

It was Lobo who first noticed that the pipeline was starting to angle downwards. In a short distance it would disappear under the ice. Randall had hoped to be further along by now but he hadn't taken account of the slow, dragging progress that was necessary at the best of times in heavy snow. At the first rumble of returning thunder Lobo suggested that they reach the end of the pipeline and then dig into the snow. 'We can get away from the wind chill and save the units until we can move again,' he explained.

The digging was easy at first, more difficult as they went deeper. The first few inches of snow was like dry sand, but below that it had compressed to become hard and crystalline, and had to be broken out in fist-sized lumps. When they'd got a hole about four feet deep Lobo started to scoop out sideways, forming a temporary and fragile cave.

Once inside they carried on digging, breaking out the floor and back wall and passing the debris back to fill the entrance. It was hard work, but after only about an hour they were sealed against the wind and the worst of the storm. Lobo took his helmet off, and Randall did the same. Although the first lungful of cold air was a shock after the heated stream the suit had fed him he found that, after a few minutes, the foxhole was no more uncomfortable than the bunkroom had been.

There was enough room to stretch out and so avoid cramp. Randall asked. 'Did you mean what you said about . . . when you're too old to work?'

Lobo nodded grimly. 'I meant it. It's just like in the city, and just as unofficial.' Randall realized that Lobo was referring to Central's 'voluntary' euthanasia programme. 'When you get shaky they have a ballot, and one night you find yourself alone in your bunkroom. Then one of them comes in. I've never had to do it, and I'm glad. So I thought, what the hell? You're never too old to chase a good, eighteen-carat fairy castle. If there's only a chance in a hundred of it being there, it's still worth it.'

'It's there, Lobo,' Randall said with determination, as if he was willing it to be true. 'I know it. Soon as the storm cools down we'll find it.'

'Hah! I like that. If it cools down any more it'll freeze the goddamn sunlight.'

There was a peculiar feeling of security in the foxhole in spite of the fact that there were only a couple of bucketsful of crystallized water between them and the storm. Sound transmitted badly and it was impossible to judge the conditions above, but the grinding of the pylons as they shifted to take up the slightest flexing in the pipeline was clearly audible.

Randall was hungry, but he'd been learning to live with it. He wondered when he would next eat and what; Lobo would have special problems after a number of years on a yeast-only diet. Hadn't the Doc said something about losing certain intestinal flora?

Lobo seemed to have no difficulty in switching off from his surroundings and falling into a light doze, his helmet serving as an improbable pillow. He awoke quickly when Randall tugged urgently at his arm.

'I thought I heard a noise,' Randall explained, 'but I'm sure I was wrong.'

'What kind of noise?'

'It sounded like footsteps, but it couldn't be. I'd never hear them over that wind outside.'

'You might, if the snow's packed hard enough. Can you hear them now?'

They both listened for a moment, but heard nothing. 'Hell,' Lobo muttered, 'I wonder if they've come out after us.'

That would mean an ugly and pointless end to the expedition. 'I'm probably mistaken,' Randall said, trying to sound reassuring.

Lobo rolled over on to his knees, turning in the confines of the hole and pressing his helmet to the wall as an impromptu sounding-board. 'Mistaken or not, we'd be stupid to ignore it,' he said. 'I don't want to crawl out and see Berg bearing down on me waving a club.'

Randall tried the same trick with his helmet, and they listened in silence for a while. Then, as he was about to speak, he heard it again. A dry, steady crunch, granules being squeezed and compressed. There was no way to tell distance or direction.

'Doesn't sound like Berg,' Lobo said, dropping his voice to a whisper. 'Not heavy enough.'

'It isn't,' Randall said with growing confidence as it became obvious that the walker on the ice was alone. 'It's nobody from the Palace.'

'Then who?' Lobo asked, although he knew the answer before the words were out.

'I already told you. Where's the snow thinnest?'

'Why? What are you going to do?'

Randall located the entrance to the hole by its uneven texture. 'For the sake of my own sanity,' he said, 'I'm going to poke my head out and have a look.' The loose handfuls of snow had already frozen together, and he had to attack them with straight fingers to force a way through.

'Don't be stupid,' Lobo said, but he didn't move to stop him. 'You'll give us away. You can't hope for magic saviours in Hell.'

'Magic nothing. It's a man, and he came from the other end of the pipe network. I'll try to see where he goes.'

Lobo began another half-hearted objection, but Randall had cleared a space for his head and shoulders and had already started to worm his way through.

As soon as his head came clear of the surface he realized the folly of looking out without a helmet. The sudden wash of cold air filled his eyes with tears, and whilst they didn't actually freeze on contact it certainly felt that way. Blinking repeatedly, he opened his eyes to cautious slits and tried to scan around.

He saw the pipeline and the pipeline's end a short distance ahead. Beyond that a broad white plain with a mist that was starting to rise from it and a solitary figure who was watching the sky.

Randall dropped back into the hole and tried to rub warmth

back into his eyes. Frost broke and showered from his hair and eyebrows as he told Lobo what he'd seen, adding that the man outside was not from the Ice Palace.

'How do you know?' Lobo asked, reaching for his helmet. 'Recognize him?'

'Too far away. But he's not wearing the standard suit.'

Lobo paused, and gave Randall a look of pure doubt. 'That's a lot of crap, and you know it. Unless he's dead and frozen to the spot . . .'

'What's the matter, you dumb brute? Can't you let me finish?'

There was an awkward silence, then Lobo said quietly, 'Go on. Finish it.'

'I'm sorry, Lobo. I didn't mean it.'

'I said finish it.'

'All I was going to say was that he's wearing a decent suit that fits, not like Ice Palace rags. I can see the unit on his belt. Look, I'm sorry I was angry, but nobody believed me before.'

'I know what you thought.' Lobo snapped his helmet on and moved across to look for himself. 'Don't make it worse by pretending to apologize.'

Randall tried to frame a few more words of pacification, finding with faint surprise that he was fully aware of their insincerity, but Lobo was already halfway out of the foxhole. Randall pulled in a few more handfuls of snow and emerged next to him.

The figure was still there, far away and still looking expectantly upward. 'Okay,' Lobo whispered, 'So you're right and I'm a dumb brute. Who is he?'

'I don't know.'

Lobo frowned. 'And while you're puzzling that one out, maybe you'd like to tell me where all the light's coming from.'

'What do you mean?'

'Since when did the sun burn *under* the ice?'

Lobo was right. The plain was glowing, lit from beneath and creating the illusion of a mist on the falling snow. It was brighter now than when he had looked before, and the figure had become a black silhouette; the level of light was rising still, and the source of illumination became a distinct ring buried deep.

Could this be where the Ice Palace's power was drained off to at the height of every storm? Far from being any kind of solution, it only deepened Randall's confusion. He could see no immediate purpose to the buried light, and it rather tore to pieces his theory about a second Ice Palace at the end of the network.

Looking back on the event, Randall and Lobo would still not be able to agree on a definitive version of what happened next. Lobo would describe it as being 'like somebody reached over and put a lid on the sky'.

Randall would remember being startled by the loud roar that suddenly thundered out of nowhere overhead, and losing his grip on the edge of the hole so that he had to grab Lobo's arm to stop himself falling back. They both felt a shock, and the outline of Randall's glove burned on to Lobo's sleeve; and in that same moment there was a painful surge of heat around both their inner suits which lasted for a second or so until both the power packs blew.

And there were lights, bright lights, overhead where they had no right to be. A low roof on the world, studded with incomprehensible detail and slicing down and over them, its hard edge passing away and revealing the cool dark of the night sky.

When the almost physical wave of noise had swept over it left only the diminutive cries of the suit units, drained and empty. Randall tried to pull himself out and step on to the ice, but he moved the wrong way. He put his weight on to the thin roof of the foxhole and it collapsed in under him.

When he tried to rise Lobo had dropped alongside him and was pushing him back. 'Stay where you are, damn it!' he hissed urgently. 'That thing came down just beyond the pipeline!'

He did something to the two power packs, and the giveaway signals stopped. Now there was no sound but the wind overhead, and the distant crack of something cooling. Randall asked, 'How long can we survive without power?'

'How long does it take a fish to blink?'

That didn't sound very promising. 'We've got to move.'

'Brilliant, cop, but where?'

'I don't know!'

Lobo pushed himself upright and slapped the collapsed wall bitterly, sending a spray of ice particles everywhere. 'What the hell did you lead me into?' he said.

'I led you nowhere! you followed me!'

'You mean you left me a *choice*?'

They both knew it was futile to argue, but it provided a brief distraction from what was out on the plain. 'I'm sorry, Lobo,' Randall said, and was fairly sure he meant it.

'No, *I'm* sorry.' They couldn't even agree on that. 'May as well admit we're both scared. My suit's losing heat already.'

Cautiously, they levered themselves up to where they could see. A dark shape almost filled the plain, curving edges lit from underneath by the dying flares. A long column of light spilled out across the ice from somewhere around the far side; a searchlight, perhaps, or even an open doorway into the craft itself.

Randall said, 'We'll have to go down there, unless you can think of anything else.'

'We may be risking a reception.'

'But not necessarily a bad one. When I was in trouble I was helped.'

'You were led back to the Palace, that's all. He wasn't helping you, he was getting you out of his way.'

Randall had to admit the possibility. 'But like it or not, we're committed. If we try to go back they'll tear us up.'

Lobo started to scramble out of the hole. 'I don't care where I go,' he said, 'I'm *cold*.'

They ducked under the pipeline and circled the long way around the craft, keeping well back at first but then moving close to its side as they realized that it provided the only cover. Randall thought he had seen something like it before, out at the old spaceport where the hospitals were based. Of course, the one he had seen had been wrecked and broken open, and hadn't flown in over a hundred years whilst this one was fully operational. Which left a question – who was operating it?

There was a stubby wing which gave a degree of atmospheric control and they stopped under it, welcoming the slight shelter it offered. A curved section of the ship's side had dropped to make a ramp down to the ice. In the light it threw a similar section of the ice had lifted, breaking its frozen covering into plates and shedding them on either side as it tilted back.

Nothing was happening. There was no sign of the man on the ice.

It was obvious to Randall that the Ice Palace's original

function had been as one of the bases for the space trade. The generators, the beacon, the pipelines – even the suits were all relics unrecognized by their present users. Who could tell how far the port extended under the ice, how many of these landing points might still be usable? And then, back to the same question – who was using them now?

But, Randall decided, the academic stuff could wait until later. The main problem now was to get off the ice and get warm. He decided to try for the buried cargo bay first; of the two, the ship was likely to be the better-defended.

'That's a hell of a long way to run across open ice,' Lobo said doubtfully. 'The boots grip best when there's some snow cover.'

'What do you want to do? Stay here and become your own commemorative statue?'

Lobo shivered violently. 'What's one of those?'

'Forget it. You ready to go?'

'Jesus, Randall, I'm dying here. What's keeping you going?'

Randall could have explained that he was the best that Central could make; that he'd been selected at the baby farm and trained until he'd been unable to take anything else in; that he could outfight, outmove and out-think any non-Élite in the world. But instead he took Lobo's arm and they ran.

The wagon came up out of the cargo bay without any sound of warning, its mounted spotlight stabbing towards them. Randall swerved in mid-step and dragged Lobo with him, but the bigger of the two men wasn't expecting the change in course and his legs shot sideways from under him. Fortunately the ice was still slick from the shuttle's landing and as Randall kept pulling Lobo kept going. The wagon swept on by, the spread of its beam missing them completely.

Their skins tingled as the wash of charged air from the wagon's lift passed over them, but it was safely past and climbing the ramp into the shuttle's hull. The man from the ice was standing on the platform behind the light, and on the back of the wagon was some unidentifiable cargo.

The open bay was a disappointment. Far from being the first stage of some underground complex it was no more than a single large room, unheated and with no obvious exits. It was lit by one harsh beam mounted high on the back wall, and the shadows of various-sized crates and boxes pooled black on the floor and on to each other. Randall and Lobo hid themselves in one of the deeper shadows, making sure that they would still have a view of the entry ramp for when the wagon returned.

'So where the hell are we now?' Lobo demanded.

'Part of an old dockyard, at a guess. The rest is probably buried under the ice all around us. One hangar opened and that's it.'

'Opened for what? How can it help us?'

'I don't know, on both counts. The wagon was loading crates, but don't ask me what was in them.'

Lobo tried to turn and look, but it seemed the effort caused him pain. 'You want to go and find out?'

The box they were crouched under could have held a small car but it was old, brown and dirty. The fresh-looking wagon-sized crates were all in a stack at the far side of the hangar, about five of them.

'Risky,' Randall said dubiously. 'What if he comes back?'

'We steal his wagon.' Lobo ignored the pain and looked up. 'I can't do any more walking out there. We'll have to steal the wagon and take it back to the Ice Palace.'

Randall was surprised. 'You're joking. After the way we left?'

'All that's changed. Now we've got something to trade, something they can't turn down.' He indicated the entrance ramp and the ship beyond. 'A way out. Two of us would get picked off, but fifty or more could storm on board and take it.'

'So why wasn't that tried with the icebreaker?'

'It was, and it failed because the boat was shielded against attack. You reckon this ship's just a cargo freighter.'

The idea made sense, but Randall wanted to get the prospective difficulties out of the way while there was still time. 'So we've got something to offer them. But Berg tends to hit first and save the discussion for the long winter evenings.'

'Leave Berg to me. I know these people. And if I don't get some shelter in the next ten minutes I'll have had it.'

Light and noise announced the wagon's return. It came down the ramp much too fast, but air-jets hissed and brought it to a steady halt by the cargo. It bobbed on its air cushion as the driver stepped off the control platform on the far side.

Randall had time to notice and wonder that the driver wasn't wearing any kind of helmet and then they were moving.

The control platform – a flat plate behind the guidance mechanism and lamp housing at the front of the vehicle – was a little too high for an easy leap, and whereas Randall only just made it Lobo caught the edge square across his shins and nearly dived headfirst off the opposite side.

The wagon dipped beneath their weight, and extra jets immediately cut in to bring it up level; and the wagon's driver heard the change in pitch and stopped with his back to them, turning his head slightly to listen.

As Lobo struggled to keep himself aboard Randall looked for the controls. He expected something like a rheostat for speed and a directional handle, but there was nothing. The wagon was slowly turning around its own centre, sliding forward and aligning its nose with the ramp; and as the hangar rotated around them the rear jets cut in and they surged forward.

The driver was slow to react, and didn't even shout as the wagon took in the incline and coasted out on to the ice. It gathered speed, angling across the short distance to the open hold of the cargo shuttle. There was no sign of a buried wire under the ice, but Randall knew there had to be one. Their weight on the control platform had triggered the wagon into running over its programmed route – a route which didn't include the Ice Palace.

They were taken up the ramp and into the belly of the shuttle, a utilitarian chamber running the length of the ship. One side was a flat wall dividing them from the rest of the craft, whilst the opposite wall bulged outwards and was lined with the struts and braces that supported the ship's outer skin. The floor was ribbed metal and the walls were painted grey, scuffed and marked as if some sharp-edged object had floated free on a rough ride.

The wagon followed a yellow line to the end of the track and drew up alongside two crates, the wagon's previous load, chained side-by-side in a marked-off area.

Lobo gratefully released his numb grip on the control platform and slid off on to the floor. Randall dropped beside him and helped him to his feet, looking back down the hold as he did so.

The entrance was a black square, the hell of the ice-cap invisible beyond it. Within moments the man from the ice would have covered the distance between the hangar and the ship. Randall didn't feel too bad but there was no way that Lobo could be taken back on to the ice – already he'd limped to the nearest crate and had unzipped one of his gloves, flexing his white-tipped fingers in the meagre warmth of the hold.

There were bulkhead doors set in the inner wall, and the nearest was open. Low emergency-type lighting showed a ladder beyond. Randall left Lobo for a moment to step over the low threshold and check that it wasn't a dead end; looking up he could see access to three levels from the vertical tunnel, and there was nobody coming down. Like it or not, it had to be good enough.

Lobo had his helmet and gloves off, for the suits kept heat out with the same efficiency that they kept it in. They were on the floor, dropped carelessly as Lobo had bent to inspect the crate on which he was sitting. He looked up as Randall came back into the hold.

'It's split,' he said with vacant wonder, all danger apparently forgotten. 'I can see inside.'

'Worry about it later. I've found the way in.'

Lobo came obediently to his feet when Randall dragged him up, but wouldn't leave the crate. 'This is *important*,' he insisted.

'So's staying alive! Come on!'

'It's a transport coffin,' Lobo tried to explain as Randall pushed him through the door and on to the ladder. He began to climb automatically, and Randall turned to get his helmet and gloves. He felt a stab of horror as Lobo's voice echoed back down the ladder, loud enough for anybody on the upper levels to hear.

'Willis is in there,' he was saying. 'They're stealing *men*!'

Eleven

Killoran arrived early for his appointment with Marius but was told that the councillor had been delayed in a meeting for the past hour, and did he mind waiting? He was offered the option of a hard chair in a grimy corridor or the autumn chill of the roof garden; he saw the dim-witted psychology of dominance in both, and opted for the garden.

Split over two levels, the garden was no more than a thin crust of soil over a disused helicopter pad. Plants were dying in the borders whilst the lawns were determinedly drifting apart into their component squares. An ornamental fountain guttered and spat brackish water over in the far corner.

The council building was a hasty adaptation, this much was obvious. Marius had argued the need for an imposing headquarters for the new administration, but one suspected that the only real criterion would be that the building should be taller than the old Police Élite block. And so it was – by one storey. Formerly one of the many deserted towers that lined the city's boulevards, this one had been selected and broken open, the crawlers flushed out with gas flares and the top three floors painted and cleaned out for use as council offices.

There was a sad irony in it, paint on the face of a ruin to herald a new dawn for the city. Killoran turned on hearing a distant clatter to see an Élite helicopter pop out of one of the boulevards further up-river and head over towards the underbelly, passing over Central's old dome and making a quick loop around the first tall building just for the hell of it.

A citizen girl about his own age came over and asked if there was anything he needed. Marius believed in promoting a new understanding between the underbelly and the citizen. To this end he employed citizens in menial positions wherever he could.

The girl asked Killoran for details of his case so that she could withdraw the appropriate files. When he told her that he had come about the Randall appeal she gave a puzzled frown and went away again.

Killoran looked out at the grey sky, the empty city, the fat, sluggish river. Entropy, he thought; the universe is running down. How can we expect something as artificial as a roof garden to resist the process?

Morden ran his hands nervously over the objects on the table in front of him, trying to fix their relative positions in his mind so that he wouldn't have to fumble for anything. He was unhappy and insecure, as he always was when away from the familiar geography of his home.

'Is it essential I stay?' he asked Marius, who was noisily

turning papers over at the head of the table. 'I've nothing I can truthfully say to this man.'

'Say something untruthful, then. Just as long as he gets an impression of power in action and takes his cringing complaints elsewhere.'

'Then why are we bothering to see him at all?'

'You tell me,' Marius said wearily. 'You helped design this godawful democracy. It's a pain in the backside.'

Marius's citizen girl came in and left a file on the table. Marius opened it and flicked through a couple of sheets. He said to Morden, 'You want me to read you any of Killoran's file?'

'I'm familiar with it.'

'This isn't Chandler's information,' Marius said with a hint of evil glee, 'it's my own. I wanted to see if I could get some dirt together about the Élite. Never know when it may be useful.'

Morden tried to hide his distaste. He was as underhand and conniving as anybody, but he tried not to let it show; Marius, on the other hand, seemed to revel in it, like a fat child stealing sweets. Morden said, 'And have you got the kind of dirt you wanted?'

'No damn chance. Either they're more devious than I am or they're the most upright bunch of creeps in the city. I don't like anything I can't buy. The only people I can get to are the pilots – take them away from the 'copters and they're nervous wrecks after a week.'

'Central bred for specific strains,' Morden reminded him. 'You can't wipe that out as easily as the administration.'

'No, but the Élite were bred to respect and defend authority, right? Without Central that leaves you and me.'

'And Chandler.'

'Forget Chandler. I'll work something out for him.'

Marius decided that Killoran had been kept waiting for long enough, and sent for him to be brought down. Minutes later the young Élite Inspector was ushered in and Marius made the introductions, apologizing for Chandler's absence.

Although he wouldn't admit it out loud, Marius was worried by Killoran's persistence over Randall's appeal in the face of a State decree. The Élite were supposed to be loyal without question, programmed biological machines; it wouldn't do to have them trying to make moral judgments or question their orders. Marius couldn't put into effect any of the simpler solutions that came to mind for fear of Chandler finding out and further stalling would be difficult. Much better to lead Killoran by the nose for a little way and then let him wander on to his own destruction.

Killoran wanted to know where Randall was; why he'd not been released and reinstated.

'Simple questions demand direct answers,' Marius began, secretly taken aback by the directness of the challenge. 'Firstly, he's in a prison camp at a location I'm not at liberty to reveal. And secondly, he stays there because he was tried by the council and found guilty of treason. That verdict stands pending appeal, but I might as well warn you not to hold out any hopes of it being reversed.'

Killoran couldn't do much about the low seat he'd been given, but he leaned forward onto the table. 'With respect, councillor, I'm appalled. Randall carried through his duty right up to the end. There are no grounds for condemning him.'

Marius consulted a sheet of paper before him. It had no bearing on the case, but the action lent a certain authority. 'There are certain ambiguities about the whole affair which throw some doubt on to that.'

'Only doubts? No proof?'

'In a case as extreme as this we have to err on the side of safety if at all. Treason, Inspector Killoran! How does your Élite training react to that?'

'Not at all,' Killoran replied guardedly, 'if it's not proven.'

Marius dropped the stance of cold authority. It didn't seem to be working. Instead he decided to try an illusion of confidence-sharing. He noted with some annoyance that Morden didn't seem to be inclined to make any contribution, but no matter. His time would come later.

'Let me put it another way,' Marius said. 'No repeating of this, you understand, because the secrecy of the original proceedings still holds. We gave careful attention to the recording of your exchange with Randall when he was in communication with you from inside the Central computer building. The way it sounded, Randall was the only one alive in there when the computer started into its shutdown procedure.'

'Then he put you in power, councillor,' Killoran replied. 'What kind of treason do you call that?'

'You've missed the point,' Marius told him, his tone implying kindly indulgence for Killoran's slow-wittedness. 'Treason is an attempt against the State, and it doesn't really matter who's representing the State at the time of the act. Central held the power then, and the underbelly holds the power now. And a rebel is a rebel, equally dangerous in either case.'

'So what about Rorvik?'

'Rorvik's quite different. He happens to be dead, and the city needs a hero. Memories of the dead are much easier to control than the activities of the living. Morden, you must have some ideas on this. Do you want to add anything?'

'Nothing, Marius,' Morden replied drily. 'You seem to be doing perfectly well without me.'

'Obviously I'm not appreciating the politics behind your decision,' Killoran said, failing to disguise the sarcasm because he wasn't trying very hard. 'I thought I was here over a matter of simple justice.'

Marius's eyebrows went up. 'Whoever told you that justice was a simple matter, Inspector? I'll agree it's a pleasant ideal, but at this crucial stage in our history it's one we can hardly afford. These are times of change, and the city needs strength from its leaders above anything else. That means the strength to do what we know is right even when our feelings tell us it is wrong.' He gathered his papers together and slid them into a folder. He went on, 'You'll understand that there are more practical pressures on the council than would allow us to continue this hypothetical debate. Go back to your work, Inspector, and be grateful that, one way or another, your city holds together.' He turned to Morden, who was toying with an empty water glass. 'I have to go now. I'll see you later, Morden.'

Morden nodded, and, with a stateman's insincere smile, Marius said goodbye to Killoran and left the room. Killoran sat, his mouth hanging slightly open, incredulous at the speed and skill of the brush-off he'd been given. He'd expected a false display of polite concern, of mystified shock and the promise of a most strenuous enquiry; and whilst he'd known that the sentiments and the promise would have been equally empty there was still something deep inside that gave him an irrational faith that some fundamental universal law would come into play and the right results would come if only he could keep the wheels moving. Marius had disarmed him with an ornate and sweetened version of the truth; that it didn't matter a damn whether Randall was guilty or not, but it would be better for everybody if he stayed where he was.

At least it was more tangible than the polite uninterest that his fellow-Élite showed. It was a State decision. It *must* be all right.

So basic truths and ideals were not as inflexible as he'd always supposed. They could be altered and reshaped by self-interested men in little rooms like this. Success involved altering the world to the way *you* wanted it and then convincing lesser people that it was what they really wanted as well.

Killoran pushed his chair back and rose to go.

'Obviously you're not satisfied,' Morden said.

'Am I hiding it so badly?'

'You're not hiding it at all. That's dangerous, and you should be more careful.'

Probably this was some new angle to put one over on him, but what the hell. Morden sounded almost sympathetic and Killoran needed to talk to someone. 'If I'm reckless,' he said, 'it's because there are limits on the resilience of my loyalty. Before Central fell I served a rotten city without complaint. I didn't complain because I didn't even understand that things could be changed. Now I've seen progress. The city's more rotten than ever.'

Morden pushed the glass away and sat back in his chair. 'I told you to be careful. Remember I'm a councillor.'

Somehow, Morden's presence seemed to intimidate Killoran far less than that of Marius. 'I remember when you were the biggest crook we ever chased, Morden,' he said. 'We never could pin down any of your factories.'

Morden allowed himself the brief hint of a smile. 'Progress is only more of the same. Then it was crime, now we call it free enterprise. But listen to me and be warned about Marius. It's not beneath him to take your complaint personally and interfere in your career.'

Killoran couldn't resist the offered posture of sacrifice. 'I hardly care . . .'

'Shut up and listen.' Morden's manner had unexpectedly hardened. 'Right now he's probably speaking to Chandler about you. I'm not without influence myself, so I'll do my best to persuade Chandler not to take any action. But you've got to learn to keep your mouth shut.'

'You mean knuckle under.'

'I mean that a public show of bitterness works against your cause, not for it.'

'What else can I do? Whether I like it or not, I'm still loyal to the city.'

Morden raised his head, gave Killoran the full force of his dead eyes. Killoran looked into them and saw a frozen blue waste that drew and held him against his will. 'It's about time you learned otherwise,' Morden said. 'Blind loyalty's totally without value to anybody apart from a dictator, whether that's Central or the head of the council. At the moment the future of the city depends on an Élite force of fawning puppies, overtrained and under Marius.'

'Marius isn't the whole council.'

'Believe that if you must. Believing doesn't make it so.'

Killoran fought to pull himself away from Morden's hypnotic influence. 'All right,' he said, forcing himself to look at his hands, 'What is this? Some kind of test on my loyalty? See how far you can lead me and then turn me in? Well, hard luck.' For the second time he left his chair. 'I'm not staying to be set up and knocked over.'

Morden didn't try to persuade him. He waved his hand dismissively, and said in tones of bored disappointment, 'Go, then. Go and prop up your festering city. I overestimated your resources.'

Killoran hovered, halfway to the door. He couldn't leave on such a note, and he suspected Morden knew it. 'Listen, Morden,' he said, 'I may not be much more than a kid, but I'm the best Central could breed. I'm Élite, Morden! I don't have to listen to that kind of talk . . .'

'From underbelly scum?' Morden said quietly.

A pause. Then, with some sincerity, 'I'm sorry, Morden. I deserved that.'

'The polite thing would be to say forget it, Killoran. Don't ever forget it. The offence is just a small part of the load you will always carry if you don't work to wipe it out. You're the end result of an obscene experiment, and there is so much to avenge.'

'Why me? Why am I so special?'

'Because you're here. Because you didn't accept, you challenged.'

'So what?' Killoran said dejectedly. 'It's got me nowhere.' He wandered over to the window and stared out.

'Of course not,' Morden said, rising from his own seat. 'Now it's up to you.' He moved faultlessly around the table and joined Killoran at the window.

Killoran was confused, and his mind tried to reject the burden of lawless action that Morden seemed in an oblique way to be offering him. 'Surely there are legal processes . . .'

'Forget the legal processes. Marius has them in his pocket like everything else.'

'But you're bigger than Marius.'

Morden spoke with sadness. 'I used to be. Not any more. Now nobody's bigger than Marius. What do you want most out of life, Killoran?'

Killoran looked inward, tried to find some kind of evasion. But the anger at an action that had attacked the fabric of his understanding of the world blotted out everything else.

'I want justice for Randall,' he said.

'Justice for Randall consists at this moment of imprisonment in an unguarded base on the polar ice cap. He's living on the brink of survival, and the labour of the rest of his life will never put him more than an arm's length away from that brink. There's no way he could leave without help.'

Killoran took the information in, feeling triumph mixed with horror. He'd got what he wanted, but no longer could he restrict himself to the adoption of a crusading pose; now action was being demanded of him and his earlier confidence began to dissolve in a rush of uncertainty. But a little voice of ego shouting loud said, forget it, kid, now's the time to deliver. He held on to that one point of stability in his inner turmoil as Morden began to tell him about the icebreaker.

Twelve

When Killoran left Morden he didn't go straight back to the Police Élite building. He wanted to compose his thoughts and test his own uncertainty against the need for action and he had some vague idea of finding one of the newly-opened city cafés where he could sit in a cleaned-out basement with a cup of ersatz. An hour or more passed and he was still walking.

When he arrived at the Élite building he went up to the office that he had shared with Randall and now shared with a cheerless individual named Partington who seemed to spend most of his time shrivelling his brains with a nasal spray. There was a teleprinter flimsy on his desk, raggedly torn across the bottom, which carried his order for the afternoon.

Louann Roget had claimed Rorvik's remains, and the council had approved their release that morning. Killoran was to provide Élite presence at the Chapel of Rapt Contemplation during their disposal.

The C of RC was part of a multi-unit operation which had originally been a purely underbelly organization. With the fall of Central they had moved across the river and begun legitimate competition with the Hospitals and they had a quaint slogan which went, 'Your Dolour is Our Concern'. This was accompanied by their sign, an S with a slash through it that Killoran imagined was some ancient guild symbol.

The chapels complex was a converted building in the middle of some weedy parkland. The muzak was suitably pious as Killoran presented himself at the reception desk to ask for directions, but before he had the opportunity to announce his interest the watery-eyed man behind the desk had produced a list on a clipboard and was asking whether he was a registered relative or a professional. While Killoran was puzzling over this one, the man asked for his card.

'Which card?' said Killoran, by now totally bewildered.

'The Mutes' Union,' the man replied, regarding him with

increasing suspicion. 'I'm the branch steward and I have to watch out for my members' interests.'

'I'm not a professional mourner,' Killoran started to explain, but he was interrupted.

'An amateur? Beat it, slug. We don't want your kind here. Some of us have a living to make, without your morbid profiteering.'

Killoran finally managed to explain who he was and why he was there, but before he could be given directions to the relevant chapel there was a commotion behind them. Killoran turned to see five men of varying heights and widths trying to squeeze through a single doorway at the same time. There was some grunting and struggling and then a little fat man popped out of the middle as if he'd been greased. This loosened the pack for the others and they fell in behind.

The little fat man came over, breathless and panting. 'Sorry I'm late,' he gasped. 'That's what comes of depending on the slugging public transport in this city. What've you got for me?'

'About time, too,' the watery-eyed man said with obvious disapproval. 'Even the deceased's getting impatient. Those your bearers?'

The other four were dusting themselves down at the far side of the foyer. As bearers they were an ill-matched crew; Killoran was certain that the smallest of them would have no chance of reaching up to the coffin.

'Have a heart, sir,' they wailed when the receptionist pointed this fact out. 'We need the work, honest.'

'What about that little short one? He won't even be able to reach.'

'I'm taller than I look, sir,' the one in question promised.

Faced with such impeccable logic the receptionist shook his head sorrowfully. 'It's nothing to me,' he said, 'but if the client complains I'm throwing it straight back to you.'

'Who is the client, then?'

'Police Department.'

'Oh, slug. Straighten up, lads.'

The little fat man was, it seemed, the priest in charge of the ceremony. He went off to change into more solemn garb and Killoran followed the bearers to the Chapel of Rapt Contemplation.

The chapel was quite large, and two thirds of it was filled

with forward-facing benches. Before them and the focus of some well-placed lights, were a dais with a slide marked 'Loved One Here' and a raised pulpit.

The pulpit and the dais were empty, but the chapel was full.

Killoran got his first inkling of what was going on from the excessive brilliance of the lighting. Looking around he could see, just beyond the halo of the spotlights, at least three remote-controlled 3V emplacements. The cameras were motoring from side to side, testing their fields of view and lining up shots at the command of some distant operator, whilst below about forty people were being shepherded into place on the benches by a young man with an earpiece linked to a radio set on his belt. Three girls were moving amongst them, pausing to dab the shines off foreheads and noses with sponges and powder-puffs.

A dead hero. Marius was fixing to make the most of the occasion.

The young man with the earpiece spotted him and fought his way through the crowd. 'You're late,' he said with an air of practised harassment. 'You've already missed the tech. run and damn nearly the whole thing.' And then his attention switched off and his eyes unfocussed as he listened to the voice in his head. 'Yes,' he said, and then 'Yes, but . . .' and then he listened for a while longer as Killoran looked around and wondered who he was talking to.

'Police rep? Front row,' the young man snapped, and he gave Killoran a light push in the direction of the front row before turning his back and walking away. Killoran moved down the aisle, past a row of women who were rehearsing their weeping. 'No, dear,' one of them was insisting, 'four bars and *then* the sob. Otherwise it sounds contrived.'

He was, it seemed, to sit alone. There was a handwritten card with his name on it pinned to the bench and he removed it before he sat down. One of the makeup girls brought her case over to him and set it beside him as she worked on his face with pencils and tiny sponges. 'Make you look really miserable,' she explained with enthusiasm, 'for when they do the closeups.'

Killoran tried to sound politely grateful, but probably failed. He didn't really want any of this, but it was his job. All the same, he couldn't give it any more than the most superficial attention; his meeting with Morden was continually replaying itself in the back of his mind. The replay invariably came to a frightened halt when confronted with any future course of action, only to start promptly from the beginning again and move inexorably towards the same inconclusion.

The girl moved away. Somebody shouted for quiet, but was distracted halfway through and didn't finish the request. Killoran glanced around to see what was happening, and recognized Louann. She was across the aisle on the same row as he, and there was an older woman with her, sitting apart a little further down the bench. There seemed to be no immediate danger of anything happening, so Killoran left his seat and went over.

She didn't recognize him at first; it was a long time since she'd seen him and in addition to this she seemed to be trying to disassociate her mind from the mercenary bustle around her.

'I remember you,' she said after a moment. 'Don't you think you've done enough?'

'I have to be here, Ms Roget,' he explained. 'I'm the only available senior officer from Lee Rorvik's case.'

'That may be so. But I don't think we've got anything to talk about.'

'Perhaps not,' he pressed, 'but can I see you after the service?'

She was looking ahead, concentrating on the curtained wall of the chapel. 'I can't imagine why.'

'I need your help, Ms Roget. There's something I want to do, and I need to be sure I'm doing the right thing.'

'After the service. Please don't bother me before that.'

The older woman was giving him a look of warning. Killoran nodded and returned to his seat.

There was another shout for silence, which was ignored, and then another which was accompanied by a few choice threats. As the extras composed themselves the same voice called out, 'Rorvik funeral, production number one-oh-nine stroke four-five, take one.' Then ten seconds of silence and the lights over the pulpit blazed on.

The priest was thoroughly transformed. His glitter suit sparkled and dazzled as he stepped forward through the curtains on the first rumbling notes of the Moog. His grey hair had vanished under a glossy black wig and his belly had apparently vanished into the strictures of a corset.

The Moog pulsed almost erotically as he slunk across to the pulpit and draped himself over it. 'Friends,' he said, his voice picked up and amplified with a seductive echo, 'I welcome you to the Chapel of Rapt Contemplation. I hope you'll enjoy the programme we've set out for you and that you'll consider us for similar occasions in the future. Tissues are freely available from the box in front of your seat. The Chapel of Rapt Contemplation is run by the World Wide Worship Combine for your spiritual comfort.'

He bowed his head with perfect timing as the lights dropped and a single brilliant beam speared down to the back of the chapel. The music swelled into a loud and brassy fanfare as the coffin swayed up towards the dais, unevenly supported by the unfortunate bearers whom Killoran had followed up from the foyer. The extras showed the benefits of careful rehearsal with a loud and energetic howl of grief.

The Moog was joined by a hearty quartet singing a song about a new cloud in the sky and a tear in every eye and we know you want the best for them as you wave them goodbye. The Loved One was deposited in his appointed place with a decisive thump and as the bearers moved away the priest rippled and glinted across to stand by the plain wooden case, one hand resting lightly on its lid. As the song ended with an exhortation to turn your face to heaven and never say die he looked up and said, 'May I offer my commiseration on this saddest of days. The service will continue after a short message from our sponsors.'

He held the pose for a moment and then looked up expectantly. The young man with the earpiece called, 'Okay, that's a take.' Then there was another number and a countdown and the service proceeded.

It all went fairly smoothly except for the finale, which needed a retake. They slid the coffin back from behind the curtains and did it over and this time everybody seemed satisfied. The extras promptly dried their eyes and formed a line for their money and Killoran elbowed his way across the flow of the crowd to get outside to where the air wasn't choking with powder and sweat.

It was late afternoon, but still light. He waited on the dry lawn outside the building, and he turned when he heard the door swing and footsteps on the path. It was the woman who had been sitting a little further on from Louann, and she came across to him.

She explained, 'Louann Roget's in my care. It seems you want to talk to her.'

A nurse? How would a citizen afford a service like that? Then it fell into place; the council would be paying her fees. No chance of Louann becoming controversial over the fall of Central as long as she was kept under such close control.

He asked, 'Is there anything wrong in that?'

'Probably not. She's been improving steadily for some time. I wouldn't like to see all that good work undone by irresponsible talk of what's gone by.'

'That's not why I'm here,' Killoran reassured her. 'My official job's done, now. If anything I need her help.'

'Really? Now there's a change. I hope the novelty of being needed doesn't prove too much for her.'

'I'll be careful.'

The faintest suspicion of a threat came into her voice. 'You'd better. Being in the Élite doesn't mean what it used to under Central. I could raise a complaint with the council and have your rank.'

She left him to think about it as she returned to the foyer, where it seemed Louann had been obediently waiting for the ground to be prepared.

There was a wooden bench over by an ornate fountain, flanked by memorial litter bins. Killoran waited there until Louann emerged, and then stood up so she would see him.

She didn't come all the way, but stopped a few yards short of the bench. Killoran reflected that she was quite pretty in a conventional sort of way; she'd grown her hair longer than the standard citizens' crop, and that helped. Furthermore her face was marked with faint lines of intelligent concern, marks that she hadn't carried when filled and sustained by the continuous outflow of pap that Central's library had provided.

'I don't have long,' she said, raising her voice to cover the distance between them. 'I'm not even sure I want to be here. What is it you have to say?'

He knew what he wanted; he needed to talk to somebody who knew the facts about Central's fall, who would say to him, 'Of course, Neil. It's obvious what you have to do now. I don't know what you're so confused about.' But this opening display of antagonism unsettled him, threw him off completely.

'I'm not even sure how to start,' he admitted.

'You surprise me. I thought uncertainty was a feature confined to human beings.'

'What do you mean?'

She couldn't know he was fragile, but she needed to hurt him. All the pain and indignity of the travesty of a funeral that had just taken place came to bear on him. 'Why should I explain?' she said, meeting his eyes for the first time. 'You're the Élite. You don't have to care about our problems. Just chase us, pursue us, stamp on us, kill us. You're not men. You're machines designed and built by a machine. Designed for persecution.' And then she looked away.

Killoran thought, this is all wrong, this isn't what I came for. 'Suppose that's true,' he said, already unconvinced by his own defence. 'Suppose we rebuilt the city all over again and one man tried to pull it down. How else could we act other than the way we did?'

'If it's so frail and unbalanced that one man *can* pull it down, then it doesn't deserve to stand!'

He couldn't pretend to oppose her; and yet he was strangely pleased to find her so changed. 'I don't understand you,' he said.

'I'm surprised it bothers you.' By unspoken consent they both moved to the bench and sat down.

Killoran said, 'Last time we talked Lee Rorvik was on the loose and out in the underbelly somewhere. I remember you told us that you didn't care where he was or what he was doing, and furthermore you didn't want to know. All you wanted were your tapes and your dreams.'

'And now I have neither. You're wrong about the last time we talked. It was on the Library mezzanine.'

'That hardly counts . . .'

'Why?' she demanded, looking at him hard. 'Because I was hysterical? Because I got roaring, screaming drunk? You don't know anything. That was the most important day of my life.'

'Do you remember much of it?'

'Like crystal in cold water.' She stared ahead, seeing her memories re-forming in the fountain's spray. 'I remember leaving the computer terminals with an armload of tapes and going down into the foyer. I remember the outer doors bursting in and three men charging through the crowd. They weren't stopping for anything, pushing people aside and kicking things over. They went over the turnstiles, and then I recognized him and he recognized me. He slowed down and stopped. We were looking at each other – we were yards apart and there were hundreds of people between us – and his friends had stopped on the stairs and were calling to him. He seemed not to hear them at first, then he turned and ran with them. The next day they were all dead and the city was down.' She brightened a little, as if the sadness of the moment had become a separate experience in the telling that she could now push away from herself. 'There. Does that make your enquiry neat and complete? Is it what you wanted to hear?'

It was barbed, but it lacked the savagery of her earlier remarks. 'Randall didn't want to kill him, you know. He set himself up.'

A little shrug. 'And where's the real difference?'

'And who's the real rebel, Louann? Rorvik was a hunted killer. He had nothing to lose. Randall staked everything when he started the deprogramming sequence.'

'Lee's dead.' It was a flat statement, something you couldn't argue with; all the same, he tried.

'Randall may as well be. He's been stranded without a trial on the polar ice cap.'

'And how can *you* object? When the State decrees, the Élite obey.'

He glanced around. The nurse had wandered off some way into the park, well out of earshot. 'Not this one,' he said quietly.

'What?'

'I don't know where I'm up to and I can't talk to anyone. I hoped you might understand.'

'I don't. I think you're trying to trick me into saying something.'

He smiled sadly and mostly to himself. 'Of course. Isn't that what you expect of the diehard Élite, fanatically loyal to the State? Except that I no longer know what the State is. Once it was a machine, and the underbelly were a bunch of crooks to be held at arm's length. Now those same crooks are giving the orders and the machine's the worst evil in human history. I've watched the other officers around me – their loyalty's like a lightbulb, it's bred into them and they switch it on and off for whoever happens to be in charge. They follow any power, never the *right* to power. And after what I've seen, I can't.'

It was getting colder, and the light was beginning to soften and take on a pre-twilight glow. She tried not to shiver and said, 'What have you seen?'

'Randall and I were a team. I had to watch him and learn from him, so that I'd eventually be able to take on the same kind of authority. After all those years of training he was the most immediate and understandable example of what the Élite stood for – at least, he was to me. But then we weren't a common team. Randall tended to think for himself and I was picking up the habit. When he killed the governing programme I understood why; if it had been me there by the central console I'm sure I'd have done the same. He was serving the State as an abstract concept, not as a particular form of government. Both he and Rorvik had the same idea in the end – whose hand turned the key made no real difference.'

'That's not what the underbelly council say.'

'Don't you see?' he said, trying hard not to raise his voice in exasperation and barely succeeding. '*That's* where I get desperate. Before the council's decision came out I was ready to accept it as a good Élite officer. I knew that the State had been served and I expected Randall to be reinstated with honour. It didn't happen and I was lost. I still am.'

She tried to think of some comfort to offer him. She was surprised to find that she wanted to. But when she reached in towards her long-untapped reserves of sympathy, they eluded her. 'What do you think I can do about it?' she said, the guilt of helplessness beginning to stir her cold composure.

'I don't expect you to do anything. But I had to be here and you're the only person I could talk to who might understand what I was saying. Anybody else would call it sedition.'

'But I wouldn't?'

'You were *there*. You followed the whole story through and you know where it led. For everybody else it's been twisted and turned around by publicity as an exercise in manipulation by the council.' He indicated the chapel complex behind them. 'They're attempting to manufacture history to consolidate their own authority, to remove the precedent that such authority can be challenged. And it's working.'

She tried not to sigh. It would seem so trite. 'Congratulations,' she said. 'You're the last sane man in the world. What do you think you can do about it?'

He shook his head, and said with determination, 'I'm the last of three. One's dead, but the other can be reached. And I know how.'

'Such ambition and such ideals. The harder you push them, the harder the world pushes back. We've both seen it happen.'

Killoran didn't want consolation for his failure to act, although for a moment he was tempted to take it. It would be so much easier to follow the escape-route that was being offered to his conscience, to be able to say 'There I was, poised for any danger, but . . . ' Once he'd recognized it, the route was closed to him.

He told her about the Ice Palace and the icebreaker which made irregular supply runs to it; how he was going to exchange his credit for the untraceable money that the underbelly had introduced into the city and use it to bribe the ship's captain. He watched her for some hint of reaction – the ridicule that would add to his doubts, or some shadow of admiration or encouragement that might stir his residual adolescent sexuality for a new source of energy. All he saw was confusion as she struggled to separate her reactions, the ones she felt she ought to be having from the more sincere impulses beneath.

'You've got my sympathy,' she said carefully after a moment. 'Nothing else, because I've nothing else to give.' She was surprised to find that she wanted him to succeed, that she could draw no triumph from Randall's fate; he was another in the parade of victims in which she included herself and who stood in the shadow of a great amorphous oppressor whose shape might change but whose tactics never varied.

Killoran was thinking about this, uncertain as to whether he was encouraged or disappointed, when there was a rasping buzz from somewhere.

Louann drew back her sleeve to uncover what looked like a wafer-thin wristwatch with no display. 'My personal alarm,' she explained as she touched it to stop the noise. 'It's synchronized to the one the nurse carries. That means it's time for my medication.'

He glanced around and, sure enough, the nurse was heading purposefully towards them. Louann saw her as well, and said quickly, 'Goodbye, Mr Killoran. I believe in you, if that's what you want to hear. And if it isn't . . . well, I don't know what I can say. Except good luck.'

She was up and hurrying away before he could reply.

He stayed for a while, alone on the bench. Some of the 3V crew went past chattering, the vulgarities of the service forgotten. There was, he decided, no point in canvassing for opinions any further; they wouldn't make him any more right or wrong in what he was doing, nor would they substantially help or hinder him in any way. He might as well face it; he was on his own.

For Louann, the medication was beginning to reassert its hold. The unpleasant realities that Killoran had revived for her began to dissolve and percolate away to be replaced by a cotton-wool warmth that was all the more agreeable because it was meaningless. Killoran wasn't forgotten, but his troubles were – the drugs pushed them firmly away before they could reach the vulnerable interior of her sensibility. He'd been quite nice, really.

Thirteen

Lobo was in a bad way and Randall didn't feel much better. The consolations of their predicament did nothing to relieve the discomfort.

They'd made it up the ladder without meeting anyone, made it out on to the second level without meeting anyone, followed a corridor the entire length of the ship without meeting anyone – the inescapable conclusion was that there *wasn't* anyone, that the ship was being run by a more sophisticated version of the automatics that had guided the wagon into the hold and trapped them there.

It didn't seem right. Of all the available space, more than half was taken up with facilities for a large crew – the level on which they moved was lined with doors, some of them open to show the hanging webs of unusual but recognizable sleeping quarters. There were lockers with coveralls and uniforms and alcoves with drinks dispensers that had inexplicably ruptured and peppered their contents on to the walls opposite, freeze-dried and undecayed. And everywhere had grab-handles, even the ceilings.

Lobo had become more coherent as he'd warmed up. As the ship had revealed itself to be deserted he began to argue that they should return to the hold; the man from the ice was obviously alone and couldn't call upon the support of the crew as they'd feared and it was obvious he'd have no chance against the two of them. Randall was inclined to be more cautious. They hadn't seen all of the ship and if the man from the ice happened to be armed it wouldn't matter if they were two or twenty.

They had still been arguing when it had started. The metal around them seemed to shudder and there was a swimming feeling which told them the shuttle had lifted and was turning. Then an increasing, steady drag which pulled them first to their knees and then flat on the deck. It was bearable, but irresistible and frightening. Anybody walking the corridors could have found them then, spreadeagled and defenceless; but then, nobody could be moving under that pitiless and inexplicable drag.

It lasted about twenty minutes and when it stopped it got worse. Randall had seen the surprise on Lobo's face as his body detached from the floor all at once and began to rise, but the perception had been wiped away by sudden panic as he'd felt his own security go and the floor drop away from under him. It was a mistake to grab for it, because the result had been an upward sail and an uncomfortable impact on the ceiling – still, he'd got a grip on one of the handles, and it gave him a firm anchorage from which to assess his position.

Lobo was less fortunate. He was spinning in midair, out of reach of anything. He'd been sick and the droplets were slowly dispersing, undulating globes which spattered on to every surface they met.

Randall made a guess, took aim, launched himself. He tangled with Lobo but they kept some of the momentum and coasted on to within reach of another handle. Randall caught it and swung them both in to the wall.

'I closed my eyes,' Lobo explained miserably. 'I closed my eyes and everything disappeared.'

'Think of it as swimming,' Randall told him. 'No up, no down – you sink, you float.'

'I can't swim, either,' Lobo said.

They were now open to discovery by anyone who might decide to look for them, and being completely lacking in the skills of weightlessness they would be able to offer little resistance. Lobo's last meal was now a greasy film on the corridor walls, an instant giveaway if they hid nearby. He hung in midair like an unhappy sack as Randall towed him back towards the access ladder.

He'd intended to go down, but there was a faint 'upward' draught in the tunnel which made it easier simply to let go and rise with it. The air couldn't be moving by gravity, for its rules no longer seemed to have any relevance; it must be differing relative pressures, bleeding off in a flow from one to the other.

The third level was a copy of the second. Randall considered hiding in one of the rooms off to the side, but decided it would be too obvious; Lobo wondered if there was any point in hiding at all on an empty ship.

Randall was adapting to this environment a little more every time he moved. For Lobo the process was much slower and although his initial nausea was coming under his control they agreed that he should stay in one of the empty crew rooms whilst Randall carried out some cautious reconnaissance.

He didn't have to go very far. He was swinging into the access tunnel when he heard a sound and looked down its length. There was a suited figure about halfway, drifting towards him feet first.

He hauled himself back, tumbling a quick circle in midair and kicked off. He sailed straight down the centre of the corridor, managing to turn about his own centre and reach to swing himself in where Lobo waited.

'He's probably checking the level below,' Randall said. 'Both the helmets and your gloves are still floating around down there, so they should mislead him for a while. We've got to hide.'

There were a couple of lockers in the room, tethered at each corner to the bulkhead wall. They were man-sized and filled with coveralls, bunched and creased without any particular concern for the fabric. Randall and Lobo unloaded one of the lockers and stuffed most of its contents into the other, quickly getting the hang of the fact that there could be no effort without leverage in no-weight. They got inside the locker and pulled the door shut, but they had to open it again after less than a minute. Not only did the locker seem to be airtight, they also needed the orientation that the narrow slit of light provided.

When the man from the ice came he pushed the cabin door open and then moved on. They could hear him kicking along, the bang of the next cabin door, move on again. They listened as the noise receded, and then listened for a while longer to the even hiss of circulating air before they let the locker door swing back.

Randall looked out into the corridor. It was empty.

Even assuming he was alone – and this was by no means definite – Randall and Lobo would be poorly matched against somebody experienced in no-weight conditions. They couldn't be sure he'd be hostile, but all the signs were bad; they'd stumbled on a big, incomprehensible operation, a massive enterprise which seemed to dwarf its purpose in deep-freezing prisoners and carrying them off in secret. Somebody had gone to the trouble of patching up this wreck and uncovering part of the old Ice Palace dockyards. In itself this was sufficient to convince Randall that technology from outside the city was involved, for his home didn't even have the expertise to rebuild the Élite's helicopters. They were barely maintained, and every year saw one or more dropping out of service.

So these were offworlders, obviously men from one of the other settled systems and one of them was at this moment searching the ship. Sooner or later he'd go over it all again, and this time he wouldn't be giving each room a quick check – he'd find them.

'But there's only one of him,' Randall said. 'We'll have to force him to land us somewhere near to the city.'

'What if he's armed?' Lobo objected.

'What if he is? We've still got exactly the same range of choices. We go along with him or we make him take us back.'

'Sounds really easy,' agreed Lobo. 'You go ahead and I'll be here if I'm needed.'

They searched the cabins for anything that might be used as a weapon. Lobo found a toolkit and produced a bolt-spanner the size of his forearm. Although it had no weight it still had mass, and would deliver a devastating blow if swung from an anchored point. They practised a manoeuvre in which they hid just inside one of the cabins and imagined their pursuer being almost level with the door, at which Randall would propel himself out, spanner aloft and Lobo would catch his legs at the last moment, his own grip on the doorframe bringing them both round in an arc which covered the full width of the corridor. The entire action was so slow that Randall would have time to level his makeshift club. He tried not to dwell on the uncomfortable fact that his victim would have an equal opportunity to defend himself.

The time was upon them before they expected it. Only minutes later there came a clumsy bumping from the access tunnel and Randall and Lobo had to scramble into the nearest cabin with more haste than they might have liked. The man would only have one cabin to check before he was upon them.

They could hear that he wasn't taking as much care this time; although he was checking more thoroughly he was rushing, missing the grips on the walls and overshooting. When his shadow fell across the open doorway Randall took a firm hold on his spanner and launched himself out of the doorway.

Lobo missed his legs completely.

Randall didn't make his arc as planned, but found himself moving in the wrong direction, away from the man they were supposed to be attacking. He saw the green blur of the man's suit and heard Lobo call out, 'The spanner! Give me the spanner!' Randall tried to throw the weapon, succeeded in putting himself into a spin and sending it to fall end over end well beyond Lobo's reach.

Lobo's physical theory might have been shaky, but his practical observation was impeccable. Realizing he couldn't hit the man with the spanner, he grabbed the nearest ankle and hit the spanner with the man.

There was a sound like meat being dropped on to a slab. 'Shit,' Randall thought, 'we've killed him.' Lobo was yelling, diving out and trying to get some kind of captive hold on an arm or a leg. Randall hit a wall and scraped over several projections before he was able to stop himself and turn around, and as he did so Lobo's yell stopped as well.

Lobo was hanging one-handed from a recessed grip, his mouth open and his eyes blinking in disbelief. The other figure was motionless in space before him, the bolt-spanner laid across its middle. Whatever it was, it wasn't a man.

Randall had seen robots before; there had always been a few of them around Central's dome, but these were inelegant, utilitarian devices, no more than hooks and claws on mobile platforms. He'd never before seen a robot pushed roughly and unsuccessfully into human form.

The eyes were good – they could almost convince and the body was a competent human shape inside the padded suit. It was the skin which gave it away, an unlined hard-looking grey with a plastic shine that betrayed its artificiality. But the eyes – the eyes were uncanny.

It made no attempt to resist them, in spite of the fact that it seemed unhurt by the blow with the bolt-spanner. It showed all the human signs of confusion, but Randall knew better than to be misled; anthropomorphism towards machines was a dangerous trap that Central had taught him to avoid. They marshalled it into the nearest cabin and Lobo held the spanner in readiness should it be needed again.

Randall guessed that the appearance of dismay resulted from a temporary withdrawal of some of the robot's facilities of external control, freeing the channels to help cope with a sudden inrush of new data; although how this differed from ordinary human confusion Randall wouldn't have liked to argue.

It didn't seem to bother Lobo. He anchored himself with one hand so that he could wave the spanner in the air, demanding to know how they could get the ship back to the city, where was it from, why were they kidnapping Willis . . .

'Don't shout at me!' the Grey Man suddenly blurted. 'I can't understand you if you shout!'

Lobo was taken aback. The robot seemed to hover on the borderline between man and machine and now he wasn't sure how to deal with it. Instead he turned to Randall.

'Damn it, Randall,' he said, 'make him tell us how to get this ship back to the city.'

'I can't,' the robot interrupted, 'I've got no control over it. I just ride with it to and from the pickup point.'

Randall asked, 'From the pickup point to where?'

'To the main ship for delivery. I collect the men off the ice and crate them, and then I take them out to the main ship.'

'He's lying,' Lobo cut in. 'What do offworlders want with deep-frozen scum like Willis?'

'They want models,' the robot explained. 'They collect basic types of men and copy them. I was the first one they made.'

'And when are they going to come back and finish you?'

The sudden hurt that showed up in the robot's eyes surprised even Randall. 'Well, look at him,' Lobo went on, feeling that he now had to justify the remark. 'He's not a man, he's a parody. He didn't even fight when he had the chance.'

It was obvious to Randall that the machine lacked sufficient guile either to resist or deceive them, so he felt it would be safe to let it lead them to whatever served as the ship's control room. The robot complied without argument, leading them down the corridor and through a set of double sliding doors on to the bridge.

It was as if a complete crew had stood up and left only moments before. The bridge was small and cramped, and seemed to be mostly chairs and lights, all carefully interlocked to make the most of the available area – a distinct contrast to the wasteful corridor space outside. Encircling the forward half of the bridge was a broad observation window, blank and shuttered by external plates.

Randall told the robot to strap himself into one of the chairs, and then he inspected the control panels as Lobo kept watch. Whilst there was no doubt that the bridge was live, it was obvious that the actual controls were being over-ridden from elsewhere. There were rough squares that had been cut and re-patched, bunches of wiring that linked one panel to another, even empty mountings where complete instruments had been torn away and not replaced. The minimal floor area was tiled with a cable-space beneath and when Randall lifted one of the squares he saw immediately that there was a foreign line in with the others. It was silver and shiny, a slug of a wire draped thick and fat over the original cabling and leading out towards the far side of the control room. Randall followed it through double doors which corresponded with those they had entered by. In the corridor beyond there was a plain silver box about the size of a small table. It was featureless, and it hummed slightly.

'No chance,' Randall reported when back on the bridge. 'If we try to interfere, the only thing we can guarantee is that we'll get ourselves killed. If we're riding to the end of the line we'll want to know what we'll find when we get there.' He turned to the robot. 'We know that the offworlders are copying the men they steal from the Ice Palace during the storms. Why?'

'The ship's their world,' the robot explained. Lobo was watching it, almost unable to believe the near-humanity of its precise movements as it motored evenly from one stance or expression to the next. 'They've got no natural resources of their own and the world's too small for them to process raw materials from the asteroid belts. They can only survive and expand by tapping the production of industrialized worlds too weak to offer any defence.'

That described the city perfectly. 'But why the copies?' Randall asked.

'They never leave the ship themselves. They always take the native form and improve on it to make an invasion force.'

There was something horribly wrong. The set of basic assumptions that Randall had been carrying around simply didn't fit this new information. He put his next question carefully; 'What do you mean, the native form? Are the offworlders human?'

'No.'

There was no sound from Lobo, floating with his spanner in the dark area outside the glow of the control panels. Randall took a grip on his impulsive disbelief and asked the robot to explain.

'They've been doing this for thousands of years, system after system. They hibernate between stars while the inboard computer scans the systems they pass for civilized activity. If there's nothing they do a quick loop round the sun to top up on power. When they find what they're looking for the ship moves into a stellar orbit and wakes them up.'

'*Thousands* of years?' came Lobo's voice from behind, choking with disbelief. 'On a *ship*?'

The robot looked past Randall, seeming to have no difficulty fixing on Lobo in the poor light. 'Not the same one. That's why they need to strip the worlds of other races. They're building another one, bigger and they tow it along with them. When it's finished they'll migrate into it and start breaking down the old one for a new, even bigger ship. It's the only way they can expand.'

'Birdseed,' Lobo snorted contemptuously.

'They sensed your city and they want it. They found this old shuttle in an abandoned orbit and sent me down in it to establish contact.'

'Stop there,' Randall said, wishing that his credulity could keep up with all this new information. 'Where did they get you?'

The robot hesitated, looked at its hands. It was difficult to believe that this wasn't a human reaction but a carefully orchestrated set of effects. 'They told me I was a man,' it said, the shiny grey of the skin and knuckles before its eyes an obvious contradiction of the claim. 'I knew they were lying, but I wouldn't face it. Because they didn't have a model to start with, they scanned the city's records for a composite simulacrum. I suppose that's me.'

Some connection closed in the back of Randall's mind, an unasked question and an unsought answer. It eluded him for the moment, but he left it to surface in its own time. The robot was looking at him now, waiting for another question. 'How did you set up this kidnap network?'

'I didn't. I contacted a councillor with their proposals, and he set it all up. I work to the instructions he gives me.'

'Which councillor?'

'Marius. They've promised him a lot for his cooperation. It's hardly started yet.'

'What's holding them back?'

'They call us marionettes, simulacra – models like me. They're trying to make one that's near-perfect and completely loyal.'

'Loyal like you?' Lobo said ironically as he pulled himself closer alongside Randall.

'I don't even understand the word,' the robot said bitterly and lifted its hand to indicate itself. 'Look at me, I'm trash.'

'Don't take it to heart,' Lobo said gently. 'There's worse than you walking round the city.' He saw the surprised look that Randall was giving him, and added, 'Hell, Randall, he's worse off than us. That must be worth something. But do we believe him?'

Randall gave the robot a sideways glance. 'Look at him. He's rough and unfinished and he's definitely mechanical.'

The robot tried to break in with some account of how he wasn't mechanical but a DNA pseudo-pattern fast-grown on to a machined skeleton, but Randall said, 'Don't interrupt.' He turned back to Lobo, the robot excluded from their speculations. 'There's no technology in the city which would be able to produce anything like that.'

'But what about the other settled worlds?' Lobo argued, still unable to accept the basic premise of the robot's story. 'One of the other systems on the trade network.'

'It's possible. The alien story could be a cover.'

'Cover or not, how do we get back?'

'If the robot's right, we don't.'

'I know you told me not to interrupt,' said the robot, breaking in with unexpected firmness, 'but I'm not a robot. Please don't call me one.'

'What do we call you, then?' Lobo asked. 'A simul ... whatever you said?'

'I've got a name. It's not much, but it's mine.'

'I can tell you what it is,' Randall added quietly. 'His name's Rorvik. Am I right?'

It watched him for a moment, and then nodded.

Lobo didn't believe it. He reminded Randall that Rorvik was dead, had been for some time, and would undoubtedly have been cremated by now, but Randall told him he'd missed the point. 'You heard it say how it was made. When Central was in operation they scanned the computer banks to get a composite impression of a native so that they could make a prototype. Now, which individual occupied a major share of the computer's attention during the last year?'

'How would I know?'

'Rorvik, that's who. This thing's a rough model of him. No wonder I thought I recognized it in the blizzard.'

It didn't look like Rorvik, it didn't sound like Rorvik. But there was some indefinable shadow carried over that had reached Randall and become recognizable even through a snowstorm. 'I had to guide you away,' it explained. 'You were almost falling over the storage sheds.'

'Don't you see?' Randall asked Lobo. 'They threw this monster together and used it to contact Marius. *He* tracked down the information on the Ice Palace and set up the kidnap network to provide for the building of more elaborate types of robot.'

'Marionette,' Lobo corrected him.

'What?'

'He doesn't want to be called a robot. Hell, Randall, I think he's got some feelings.'

Randall tried to explain that machines couldn't feel and that if they seemed to, it was a calculated effect, built into the design like the paternal attitude that the Central computer used to assume for the benefit of the citizens. Lobo listened, but it was plain that he didn't wholeheartedly embrace the idea. He was by no means stupid, but as a survivor who had learned to meet every occasion as a separate challenge, he found little practical worth in such distinctions. Differences between things that were and things that merely appeared to be had no meaning for him; they both had equal weight and influence in the texture of his world and he considered such philosophies as the superficialities of an idle mind.

Lobo thought it of far greater importance to establish exactly of what use this thing calling itself Rorvik might be to them. And if that meant treating it as a human being, that was fine as long as it responded like one. On this basis he could proceed without concern, whereas Randall was preoccupied by a tiresome web of conditions and justifications which eventually led him to the identical conclusion.

'You said they're trying to get a design for a loyal ... simulacrum,' Lobo said, addressing the strange composite being direct. 'What kind of loyalty do *you* feel towards them?'

It thought for a moment. 'I don't even understand what you mean. I did what I was told.'

They asked about the improved designs. The Rorvik marionette – not really Rorvik, more a composite citizen personality with some of Rorvik's more recognizable qualities at the forefront – explained that there were many designs, some even less complex than itself, creatures with no minds at all that had to be told in detail what to do and then told when to stop. And then there were others, almost indistinguishable from real men and women. Randall wondered where the female pattern came from, but Rorvik didn't know. He suspected that the development of the final model was very close – that is, if it hadn't already been reached.

Randall found it frustrating. The magnitude of the threat was beginning to make itself felt in his mind, reaching in and touching all the inbred and ingrained protective responses that Central had instilled in him. It was as if, given the right set of circumstances, a second personality was coming up out of reserve, moving in and taking over, pure Élite. He stepped back and let it in, knowing better than to resist.

The course of the shuttle could be changed, but Rorvik didn't know how. It would take them straight to what he called the World Ship and dock automatically on a homing laser; there didn't seem to be any way that they might divert and return to the city.

'We've got to *find* a way,' Lobo insisted. 'We can't take on an artificial planet full of offworlders.'

'We might,' Randall told him. 'This Rorvik thing must know something about them. If we keep pumping for information we may find a weakness.'

'And for what?'

'For the opportunity to strike. For the State.'

Lobo wasn't very impressed. 'You're mad, Randall. They must have fried your brains at birth.'

'I'm not mad, I'm Élite. This is what I'm for.'

'Is that how it works? Somebody threatens your holy State and you automatically leap on to a box and start beating a drum? So what happened to the rebel who killed the computer?'

'That wasn't rebellion,' Randall replied, irritated that Lobo couldn't see the distinction. 'That was the right thing to do.'

'And now the right thing to do is to turn ass-backwards and get back to the city. Or doesn't the State deserve a warning?'

'The argument's academic. We don't have the choice.'

Lobo raised his hands in frustration and then hastily corrected the slow drift that the action induced. 'How do we know until we try?'

'Because the robot says it doesn't know where to start!' It winced, but said nothing. 'What's happened to you, Lobo? What about the eighteen-carat fairy castle you were supposed to be chasing?'

'I'm not going to find it by being target practice in a vacuum. What happened to *you*, Randall? Not so long ago we were your kind. You were going to get back to the council and make them dance for us.'

'The same damn council that's selling the city!'

'They're selling it, you're going to charge in with your head down and throw it away. Where's the difference in that?'

'It depends how successful we are.'

'Like, not at all.'

Randall tried to change his approach. You couldn't win by yelling at Lobo, because he could yell louder. 'That doesn't excuse us from *trying*. We've got two things in our favour; they're not expecting us and we've got access to information in the robot. Perhaps we can even use it to tap information out of their systems.'

'And what's the use in that? They could be twice our size. We may not be able to breathe their air. Even if we can, we won't know where we're going or what we're doing.'

Sound logic and Randall accepted it with triumph. 'That's where the robot comes in,' he said, as if he and Lobo had been working towards the same conclusion all along.

The marionette had waited patiently throughout the argument, but now he spoke. 'I'll help you,' he said, 'but there's a condition.' They both looked at him in puzzled expectation and he went on, 'You stop referring to me as the robot. I've got a name.'

'It isn't even yours,' Randall pointed out.

'I don't care. I want you to use it.'

'All right, Rorvik,' Randall said with exaggerated emphasis, smiling at the presumption of a machine fooled by its own illusion of self-awareness, 'as long as it gets your cooperation. But don't get any ideas about having an equal say.'

'Rorvik' didn't smile back. He probably couldn't. 'I'm glad I'm not really a man, Randall,' he said. 'When I look at you I lose all my envy.'

For a moment Randall was lost for a reply and Lobo cut in with, 'Don't get him wrong, Rorvik. He's not bad, he's just Élite. They've all got this peculiar streak when it comes to the State and the city.'

'What is this?' Randall demanded, more than a little unsettled by the way in which Lobo and Rorvik seemed to be understanding each other so well and, more important, excluding him. 'Don't you see that this is the entire basis of the offworlder approach? Accept him as a human being and he's inside your guard.'

'He?' Lobo said, an enquiring eyebrow raised. 'What happened to *it*?'

Randall hadn't even realized what he'd said. 'You see how easy it is. With a name the battle's half won.'

So Rorvik got his name, although Randall insisted that he

earned it. He wanted to know how long the journey was going to be and how and where it would end. He wanted to know the layout of the World Ship, the principles behind its design, its weaknesses. And as Rorvik talked he evolved grandiose plans of impossible heroism and dropped them as quickly, moving on undaunted to construct the next fragile web of circumstance wherein he routed the enemy and championed the city. He drew on the fire of buried resentment that he had carried since his eyes had opened in the Ice Palace recovery room, but now, instead of having to suppress it as impotent fury, it became his prime source of energy. Difficulties seemed to shrink and become insignificant in the face of a confidence that was irresistible.

Randall was, in his way, happy. He was doing what he'd been born for. He was Élite.

Lobo wished he was back on the ice.

Fifteen

No sooner had Peters completed his first run on the icebreaker than they were reloaded and turned around to head back to the cap. He'd understood that the trips would be far less frequent than this, but when he tried to raise the subject with his captain all it got him was a knowing wink and an assurance that he would be 'seen all right', whatever that meant.

They were at sea, the city's landmass falling below the horizon, before he found that, in addition to managing his conscience over his involvement with the Ice Palace, he would have to attend the needs of illicit passengers in direct contravention of navy regulations. All the same, the captain argued, when it was too late for him to object, if two of the passengers are councillors and all three of them are paying heavily for silence then the benefits surely outweigh the dangers.

There would be little sleep for Peters on this run. He had to keep the Élite officer away from the councillors, because he didn't know about them and they didn't want him to. So the councillors were given the more luxurious accommodation, which was a musty old bunkroom with a few pieces of carpet and a fish-oil burner for extra heat, whilst the Élite had to make do with a screened-off corner of one of the holds. Peters took food to both parties, apologizing in each case for the poor quality of the ship's dispensers and their annoying tendency to mix the most incompatible ingredients to make the most unpalatable dishes.

He told Killoran that on no account must he leave the hold, saying that they had a suspected stabilizer leak and that as the thick oil escaped it was boiling off with the release of pressure to drift around the ship as a poisonous vapour. It was the purest fantasy, inspired in Peters's mind by the trouble that they were still having with the pressure on some of the tanks, but Killoran accepted it and stayed where he was, dragging the cargo over to insulate his corner as they pushed northward and the temperature dropped.

Morden found the journey tedious in the extreme. His finely-tuned sense of space, developed as a compensation for his blindness, was disrupted by the steady heave of the ship's passage, and his remaining senses fared badly with the stink of burning fish-oil and the ever-present thump of the engines.

Marius, however, spread himself out on one of the upper bunks and chortled, joked, planned, daydreamed. The only times that his good humour seemed to fail him were when Peters brought their meals; they defied both description and digestion. Morden sat, miserable and huddled in the oversized cloak he'd been given to wear, and quietly wished that Marius would go and immerse his entire head in water for ten minutes or so.

When they hit their first ice, Marius switched subjects, moving from the prospective benefits of the other settled systems to his childhood occupational fantasies. They were invariably powerful, frequently destructive. He'd dreamed of being a slingshot pilot, towing the cargo trains into a tight orbit around the sun and using the momentum to release them towards a target system; but if he'd known there had been such 'breakers as this, smashing through the ice like so many eggshells – why, he'd have wanted to do that, as well.

'Such a shame,' Morden observed sympathetically. 'Perhaps if you go on to the bridge, the captain will let you hold the wheel.'

Marius thought about it for a moment, and then said suspiciously, 'You taking a rise out of me?'

'Would it ever enter my head?'

It was unfortunate that Marius was not quite stupid enough to be unaware that he was being mocked, or Morden could have extracted far more entertainment from the journey. As it was, he had plenty of time to brood over the flight that lay ahead, and over the cruel trick that he had helped to play on the young Élite officer who at that moment lay in the hold somewhere below them.

'What a joke,' was Marius's remark on the subject. 'Before we get taken to the landing point he gets dumped at the Ice Palace. He thinks he's storming in to stage a wonderful rescue act and really he's only doing our work for us. One more prisoner and a blaster full of blanks. I wish I could see his face when he tries to fire it.'

'The other inmates will probably tear him apart,' Morden observed.

'I'd love to see that, as well.'

Morden couldn't share Marius's enthusiasm for their betrayal, and after a while it began to show. 'What's the matter with you, Morden?' Marius complained. 'I thought you were strong. Damn it, we're carving this planet up between us and here you are getting saintly on me.'

'My apologies, Marius. I have a sentimental streak which I must fight to suppress.'

'I understand. It's the same with me. I fight back the tears every time I think of the profit we'll make.'

Marius didn't seem any more inclined than this to make comment on Morden's apparent lack of commitment to the venture. He was already in too deep to withdraw, being thoroughly compromised by this journey and his recent voting in the council; and if he were to drag his feet at some later date, no doubt by that time his help would no longer be needed. Perhaps Marius already had some plan of quiet disposal lined up for him.

Every now and again Marius would turn, his bunk would creak, and a couple of the inevitable sheets of paper that he seemed always to carry around would slide down onto the floor. Then Marius would have to clamber down after them, and there would be a couple of minutes' silence as he puzzled over his notes, wondering where the stray leaves had come from.

He was trying to work out how long it would take before the industrial appetites of his parasitic employers would be satisfied. Every time he tried he arrived at a different figure, differences of several years; and whilst he cooed with pleasure at the short forecasts, he groaned in depression at the longer ones. Morden asked if he was making any allowances for possible sabotage.

'There won't be any,' Marius told him flatly. 'That's all taken care of.'

'But what if these artificial men and women aren't the invincible force you're expecting them to be?'

'Wait until you've seen what one of them can do. They make the Élite look like puzzled monkeys, and these are only the ones they've developed so far. The model they've got under test could probably take the city on his own!'

In the number four hold, deprived of any company apart from Peters's occasional visits, Killoran sat crosslegged on the floor, the component parts of the hand weapon spread out in front of him. Slowly, mechanically, he polished each piece on a square of cloth, working on them in strict order and reassembling as he went along, the block of solid-state circuitry laid aside for final connection. Next to it was a box of charges, unopened.

He'd had no problem with the requisition of the weapon. One call, and it had been waiting in Stores when he arrived to collect. He'd said that he wanted it for some practice in his own time, and the armourer hadn't even seemed surprised. Perhaps he'd concealed it – Killoran still couldn't get used to the idea of outranking anybody older than himself.

Peters had given him some idea of what to expect when he arrived, although Killoran got the impression that he didn't much like to talk about the Ice Palace. They would draw up alongside a hatch, on the other side of which would be a sloping ramp and some kind of warehouse below ground level; Peters hadn't been able to see further. There would be men – not too many – waiting to receive the cargo and they would be wearing strange helmeted suits against the cold. Killoran would need his blaster from the time the hatch rose, either to threaten or to fight.

The last piece snapped into place. The weapon was complete. Patiently, deliberately, he began to take it apart and lay the components out.

Sixteen

As the cargo shuttle moved onward to meet its orbiting partner Randall and Lobo devised a way of feeding themselves which was effective if unpleasant. There were a number of surplus glucose bottles in the ship's hold with which Rorvik was supposed to keep the sleeping prisoners fed and it seemed a relatively simple matter to slide a needle into a vein and take nourishment the same way with no risk to the delicacy of the stomach; simple, that is, until they came to try it. Randall stabbed at his arm a couple of times, making sizable holes but otherwise achieving nothing. Lobo watched the process and grew pale. After a minute or so he said 'Forget it,' and, removing the needle, drank direct from his own bottle. Randall finally gave up and did the same, finding that the glucose bubbled out easily under gas pressure, passing through some kind of membrane in the tube to take the gas out before it reached the bloodstream.

They had left Rorvik alone on the bridge. Randall could see no reason not to trust him – 'too stupid for deceit', as he put it. When they returned Rorvik was still there, strapped into the seat where they had left him. He told them that the World Ship lay ahead and that docking was imminent.

The trip had taken a couple of days, but when the World Ship was at perigee this would reduce to only a few hours. Randall didn't understand the mechanics of it and Lobo didn't want to. All he said was that it would have been interesting to see the World Ship as they approached and Rorvik told him that it would have been possible but they were now on the homing laser and matching the World Ship's rotation. Randall challenged his earlier statement, that he had no control over the shuttle's operation and Rorvik replied that control was possible, but he didn't know how. There were certain points on the consoles where he could link in and be in contact with the shuttle's guidance and memory channels, but he wasn't sufficiently skilled to be able to do much more than open the outer shutters or dim the lights.

Within half-an-hour the doors would open from the hold onto a strange and dangerous new world. Randall's adrenalin high had subsided, leaving an afterwash of confidence that he was determined not to diminish with thoughts of failure. Lobo had other ideas.

'Now,' Randall said, 'are we clear on what happens when that loading-bay door opens?'

'Sure,' said Lobo. 'We jump out and run like hell.'

'Didn't you pay any attention to the plan?'

'The plan? Oh, sure, it's a great plan. Who wants to get killed in a scramble when you can do it nice and orderly?'

'Don't you remember any of it?' Randall asked weakly.

Lobo sucked in his cheeks and stared at the ceiling, a gross parody of intensive reminiscence. 'We hide and Rorvik unloads Willis and the others as normal. Then we sneak out and run up the nearest corridor. It's a hell of a plan.'

'All right,' Randall admitted tetchily, 'so it's not much . . .'

'Not much!' Lobo exploded. 'It's *nothing*! You're mad, Randall!'

'Mad or not, I got you out of the Ice Palace!'

'And look what you got me into! In my own way I was *happy* until you came along!'

'Go back, then. Nobody's stopping you.'

Lobo leaned forward as much as he was able, pulling against the lap-strap that he'd looped across to keep him in place. 'This may come as a surprise to you, Randall,' he said, 'but you're not the only one who doesn't want the city wiped out. I'll work to prevent it and even, if I think it's justified, put my life on the line for it. But that doesn't mean I'm prepared to get all holy and charge out yelling, only to get spread over the nearest wall. And I'll tell you something else. I'm prepared to do it because it's what I want to do. Not because I was picked out of the hospital at birth and trained and taught and made to jump through hoops for twenty years. I make my own decisions.'

'I don't care if you make your own dresses.' Randall could

have corrected Lobo on the details, but his assessment of the spirit of Élite training was uncomfortably near the mark. 'Rorvik's told us that he's never been far beyond the docking area and he's never actually seen one of the creatures.'

Rorvik nodded. 'That's right. Place always looks deserted.'

Randall ignored the interruption and went on, 'Without information all we can do is move fast and think on our feet. Are you saying your reactions are better than mine?' Lobo didn't answer. Nobody was faster than an Élite. 'There you are, then,' Randall continued. 'I'm prepared to put *my* life on the line and be first out. We should agree to let me decide where to go and how to get there, because we won't have the time to confer. Now, what's wrong with that?'

'It's wonderful,' Lobo said bitterly. 'We all die as heroes.'

'What's your alternative?'

'At this stage, nothing. But it doesn't mean I'm signing myself over on a permanent basis. If there's anything I want to say at a later stage, I'll say it whether it screws up your plans or not.'

Randall couldn't argue with that; or, to put it another way, he wanted to but there was no time. Instead they all made their way down to the hold in preparation for disembarking. In the corridor they could sense rather than hear distant shudders as the shuttle manoeuvred. They were in the access tunnel when weight returned.

Rorvik was used to it and had a hand on the ladder as he made his way along so that when the tunnel became a vertical shaft again all he needed to do was swing into the wall. Lobo was below him, still nervous in no-weight and so already holding the ladder for psychological support. It was Randall, nearest the hold and fortunately only a few feet from the bottom, who was caught unprepared and who made an undignified landing on the deck.

Nobody commented. Nobody dared.

There would be no guards around the shuttle dock, for the Wekk – the short, brutal name that Rorvik gave the owners of the World Ship – knew that the city had no contemporary space capability. However, it was likely that some of the simulacra or marionettes would be around the area, for once captives had been used for patterning they were often let loose and hunted down for practice. Rorvik warned them to watch out for Valum.

'Valum?' said Randall. 'Who's he?'

'Valum's not a he. She's one of the more advanced models and she's good. I've heard say she's the best they've got, until they get the final model out of its tests.'

Something was worrying Lobo. 'You say they let men loose and hunt them,' he said. 'Where?'

'In the corridors where you're going.'

Lobo shook his head sadly. 'I knew it. Head-first into the killing-bottle.'

'Think positive,' Randall urged him. 'We're men. They're just gadgets.'

'Thanks, Randall,' Rorvik remarked drily.

Randall and Lobo hid to one side of the door. If anybody came into the hold they would be in plain sight, but Rorvik assured them it wouldn't happen. The deck lurched a couple of times beneath their feet and then there was a sensation of rising. A few seconds after it stopped the seals on the door blew and it dropped outward in a controlled fall, dust swirling along the length of the hold and boiling out as air bled into the lower pressure outside. Lobo felt a pain in his head, but he knew better than to mention it now.

There was a narrow angle of view available to Randall from his position by the door. He could see that the dock was about twice the width of the shuttle at least, but there was no indication of its depth. It was brightly lit with a noticable blue cast. What did this suggest? Eyes not very sensitive to the red end of the spectrum? That would, perhaps, go some way towards explaining Rorvik's peculiar skin colour.

Randall tensed to move, but held back at a glance from Rorvik. That hard unnatural face was incapable of normal expression, but there was some subtle hint of warning in the eyes. Rorvik walked forward, leaving them alone and exposed as he went down the ramp and away from the shuttle.

They waited for a few moments, but there was no sound from outside. Randall decided to risk a look. He inched forward cautiously, ready to pull back at the first indication that he might be seen. Lobo was holding his breath, expecting yells of alarm at any second.

A wider view of the dock showed it to be on two levels, a deep well in which the shuttle was sitting linked by a ramp to a gallery which ran along and around about eight feet above the floor. It was this gallery level that had the door linking to the rest of the ship, and Rorvik was climbing the ramp towards it.

The door was obviously the inner opening of an airlock and it was ajar. Randall couldn't be sure that he was really seeing the woman who stood next to it. Although he had never seen her before he had always known her; she was an inch or so taller than Rorvik and she had the flowing brown hair and finely-chiselled features of an adolescent's fantasy.

Lobo's hand on his shoulder warned him that he was leaning out too far, placing himself in danger of being spotted. He drew back and then more cautiously, risked another, less exposed surveillance.

Rorvik had collected a trolley from within the airlock. It had no wheels but ran on six oversized bearings which could rotate in any direction. The woman was saying something to him and Randall strained to hear.

'Try not to take your usual eternity over the unloading,' she was telling him in a voice fitted easily to command. 'The shuttle has to do a fast turnaround and return to the Ice Palace to collect the two councillors.'

Rorvik said something, but his back was turned and it was indistinct. It was probably something like, 'Will I have to go?' because she replied, 'I wouldn't know. Do you honestly think it matters?'

'There might be loading to do.' Rorvik must have turned and it came across clearly.

'There isn't. You can stay here and spare the councillors your presence. The shuttle navigates just as well without you. Get your crates on their way to the patterning shops and then clear the area. We're in the middle of a sweep to eliminate the remnants of the last batch you ferried up. The patterning shops rejected them.'

'I'm sorry. I only bring what I can get.'

'It's fortunate they expect nothing from you,' she told him with ill-disguised contempt. '*I'm* surprised you've even got the wits to stand upright.'

She's a machine, Randall had to tell himself, nothing more than a set of manufactured responses in a pseudo-biological envelope, but this couldn't overcome the fact that she was, at least from a distance, undetectably human and had the looks and cool self-possession which could set young men diving off high buildings just to get her attention. This, he supposed, was Valum, the best and most dangerous marionette yet assembled – Rorvik was an inept monster next to her.

The conversation was over. Rorvik, dismissed, was leading his trolley down the ramp towards the shuttle. Valum glanced once across the bay and then turned to go.

Randall wondered where they'd found the original to pattern her. The Ice Palace was, as far as he'd been able to establish, an all-male community and had always been that way. The delicate ecology of survival had been so finely engineered that the introduction of sexual tension could have tipped it completely, whilst the essentially rigid social order of dominance and submission would have become complicated to the point of incomprehensibility. Perhaps the Wekk had other sources.

Rorvik came into the shuttle and passed them without a sideways look, as if he'd forgotten they were there. The trolley rumbled past behind him and he went on to the far end of the cargo hold and the prisoners.

Randall had momentarily felt bad about leaving the captives crated and helpless, but, he'd reasoned, he didn't know the revival procedure and could quite easily kill them by his efforts. And besides, one of them was Willis – a doubtful ally. He could argue Lobo down, but with two of them ranged against him all his plans were bound to end in compromise or confusion.

There was no sign of Valum on the gallery. Randall didn't like the sound of the sweep operation that she had said was going on in the World Ship – a wrong move and they could easily find themselves caught up in it. Well, Randall told himself grimly, the idea is not to make any wrong moves.

Lobo followed without any need of encouragement or signal as they ran from the shuttle to the cover of the gallery and then, more cautiously, advanced up the ramp to the upper level. The hangar was immense behind them, a cavern enclosing the entire three-storey shuttle and of which there had only been a small section visible from their hiding-place. There were airlocks all around the gallery, doors like safes spaced at hundred-yard intervals and this encouraged Randall to modify his original idea and make for one of them instead of following Valum through.

The first door wouldn't open when he threw his weight against the outer wheel. No matter, move on to the next. The next door also resisted when he tried to turn.

They were exposed and obvious and each door he tried was taking them further from what now seemed to be the only exit. He tried another, Lobo breathing hard to keep up; it was as solid against his efforts as the last.

'No!' Lobo whispered, and Randall angrily prepared to ignore him. But Lobo had moved into his place at the airlock and was spinning the wheel easily.

He realized his mistake, that he'd assumed that an anti-clockwise rotation would release the locking mechanism, but whilst the simple geometrical principles of gearing and rotation might be universal the traditions of his own culture governing their use were not. The door swung outward and Lobo stepped back with a smile and a polite gesture of deference.

There was an inner chamber and then another door which unsealed and opened into a recess off a corridor. Decompression of the hangar would slap this outer door shut, as would decompression of the corridor with the inner. The light was the same blue-cast as before and there was no sound apart from the rasp of a muffled pump somewhere on the other side of a wall. The corridor sides were square and plain and the ceiling was uncomfortably low, but apart from that and a metallic scent in the air their surroundings seemed decidedly mundane.

When Rorvik had loaded the first crate on to his trolley he turned around to pull it along and out of the hold. Valum was standing in the open shuttle doorway.

'Who are they?' she said evenly.

Rorvik searched in his mind for an explanation, and was mildly surprised that he had nothing to offer except the truth. 'They came aboard at the Ice Palace,' he admitted. 'I couldn't stop them.'

'I doubt whether you tried. You've got no loyalty and precious little intelligence, Rorvik. All you've got is a name, and that belongs to somebody else. You know what will happen now?'

'You'll hunt them down and kill them.'

'Almost. We'll see if they're worth patterning and *then* we'll hunt them down and kill them. If you had any more than a handful of brains you'd be a liability, Rorvik.'

'Yes, Valum,' Rorvik said, knowing it would be useless to object.

'Carry on with your unloading.'

'Yes, Valum.'

Rorvik had described the World Ship as a cylinder with a series of outer layers enclosing an open space which he'd never visited. The corridors followed 'more or less a gridiron pattern', but then he'd become confused.

Randall could see why. There wasn't a straight line in the place.

The floor lifted gently away before and behind them, curving uphill and out of sight and presumably meeting itself to encircle the cylinder somewhere far overhead. Not the best line to be following if pursued. There were occasional doors in the walls, but they were flush and tight with no sign of a handle or opening mechanism – perhaps they were keyed to an alien biocapacitance.

Empty corridor gave way to empty thoroughfare as they turned at the next junction to follow the length of the cylinder instead of looping around it. It stretched ahead as a long, winding spiral, the floor twisting sideways to absorb the coriolis force of the ship's rotation. It was long, and if Randall and Lobo had been obvious before they were more than conspicuous now.

Randall hesitated, and Lobo stopped behind him and waited to see what he would do. So far he was following his agreement, offering no arguments or objections. As Randall tried to decide, a group of three men – at least, they looked like men – appeared about two intersections down, spreading out military-style to anticipate an attack from any angle.

Perhaps they could brazen it out, give a wave of recognition and move on; after all, nobody knew they were aboard. But the thought died as soon as it occurred, the group of three re-forming and coming towards them at a run.

They couldn't pass as marionettes. They were unkempt and untidy, their suits mere rags in comparison. They turned and ran.

Randall didn't pause at the intersection they'd emerged

from, for as he drew level with it he saw that in both directions there were men trotting purposefully towards him. He shouted encouragement to Lobo and dived on past, his voice adding its confused echo to the interweaving hammerblows of running feet on the hollow deck. Behind them the team of three became a team of five as the men at the intersection fell in with the group and matched its pace.

They'd been trapped into what Randall hadn't wanted, flight without purpose. They were running before a methodical sweep – not difficult to organize if you knew the layout of the corridors, but perhaps impossible to avoid if you didn't. They're not *men*, Randall insisted to himself as he tried to even out his ragged breathing. They're expecting me to act in a certain way, trying to get there before me. If I do something unpredictable I can fox them.

He could be unpredictable and turn and fight, but then he would quite predictably get the crap beaten out of him. He forced the pace a little, deliberately leaving Lobo a few yards behind; Randall didn't want to swerve suddenly and take him by surprise, giving him no chance to follow. Lobo seemed to get the idea and didn't try to catch up – or perhaps he didn't have the energy in reserve.

The marionettes were working to a pattern, one man in each corridor around the outside of the huge cylinder, checking to either side of each intersection and then, when the quarry had been spotted, pursuing it down the length of the ship in the sure knowledge that they were driving it towards other hunters. As the net grew tighter it grew more dense until the cornered prey would be faced by a number impossible to resist.

The net was at its thinnest ahead, where the lone simulacra had yet to converge. At the next junction Randall sheered off to the left and heard Lobo follow, the unexpected turn sending him into a wide arc that almost brought him up against the far wall. There was a long shadow ahead, cast from beyond their inverted horizon as the floor curved upward, and then he descended into view, a lone figure heading to intercept them.

Lobo had some idea of what Randall was intending and he prepared to help; the two of them had taken Rorvik and they could take this one as well.

Randall put his shoulder down and charged. It was over

within a few seconds. A perfectly-timed sidestep, a neat, almost casual tap on the back of his head with the heel of the hand and Randall was skidding along on his belly, arms and legs everywhere without a suggestion of control. Lobo pulled up an inch or so short of a straight-fingered swipe that kissed the air in front of the bridge of his nose so fast that he could almost hear the air rushing into the gap it left behind. The blow didn't have to land for him to know they were beaten.

The group caught up with them and two of its members hauled Randall to his feet. He was blinking stupidly, seeing six or seven of everything and still unable to believe what had happened.

'Wasn't much of an exercise,' one of the marionettes commented in tones of apparent disappointment. 'Not worth counting it for the record.'

'It's just as well,' another replied as they turned to make their way back to the main thoroughfare. 'You know we can't damage them until after they've been patterned.' And the whole group nodded gloomily, as if they were being deprived of a rare treat. Lobo felt as if something were crawling across his back inside his snow suit, and he gritted his teeth to prevent a shiver.

As they moved down the World Ship the air of desertion became less obvious. They encountered several other groups or lone figures. When they came to a major intersection, a kind of spiral gallery that led to the levels above, they saw another determinedly running band in obvious pursuit, switching from one level to another. Somebody in Lobo's group asked what was going on.

'Damage,' one of the running men called out happily as he disappeared through an archway. Lobo's group held a hurried discussion and an incomprehensible selection process of the 'scissors cut paper' variety. Four of them lost and remained to guard Randall and Lobo as the others set off to join in the 'damage'.

Lobo had his suspicions what that 'damage' might entail. They were confirmed only seconds later as they reached the next level and a raw scream was carried back from the direction in which the group had gone. Randall had been moving along in a daze, perhaps faking it whilst he looked for opportunities. Whatever the reason, the sound brought him out. He and Lobo exchanged a look of wordless apprehension. Around them the marionettes were smiling, a little regretfully.

Seventeen

Bulstrode was in the generator room when the Worm tracked him down. The teams had been working flat out to repair storm damage, and this was his third visit in as many shifts to charge his power pack. He looked up when he heard the Worm calling his name as he hurried along the gantry to the shielded area.

'I'm busy, Worm,' he said.

The Worm was undeterred. 'I know, but this is important!'

'It had better be,' Bulstrode told him, 'or you'll be wearing your head backwards.'

'The icebreaker's arrived...'

'Since when was that news?'

'Let me finish, will you?' The Worm was clearly agitated over something, so Bulstrode let him continue. 'We've been sent the usual supplies, and something else. An Élite officer, hardly more than a kid.'

'Don't let them wake him,' Bulstrode said decisively.

'He isn't drugged or anything. He slid in down the chute and he's armed.'

Bulstrode checked the level on his power pack. He was strongly tempted to remove it with an incomplete charge and finish the job later, but he remembered the harsh disciplines of his existence – the extra minute or so of charge could make a difference between survival on the cap and being dragged back in by his feet. 'Armed with what?' he asked, watching the indicator.

'A blaster and he says he'll use it.' The Worm was excited, almost dancing on the spot. 'He said he wanted Randall and Palmer told him no chance. I thought he'd hit the roof and start shooting off there and then, but he said he wanted to see the man in charge. I explained that we don't have anything like that, so now he wants all the team leaders together.'

The charge on the unit hit a peak and Bulstrode buckled the pack to his belt. 'Randall,' he said. 'There's been nothing but damn trouble since he arrived. What does the kid want?'

The Worm fell in behind him as he strode off down the catwalk. 'He's not saying. Not until all the team leaders are together.'

'This could be tricky,' Bulstrode mused as they cut through into Main Street. 'Is the kid on his own or is the icebreaker waiting for him?'

'No,' the Worm said positively. 'I looked, and it's gone. The kid's really angry and Berg keeps taunting him.'

'*Berg*'s down there?' Of course, he was rostered for unloading duties on the next icebreaker visit. Bulstrode knew how impetuous he was, and that it wouldn't take much provocation for him to rush the Élite, blaster or not. He'd be cut in half. They reached the access tunnel which led to the bays and as Bulstrode hurried through the Worm held back.

'I've got to get round the rest of the team leaders,' he explained. 'There's something strange about all of this.'

'You've got a wonderful capacity for stating the obvious,' Bulstrode called back over his shoulder. 'What else are you going to call a police operation out here?'

'That's what I mean,' the Worm's voice echoed after him. 'I don't think it's an official operation. I think the kid's on his own.'

If he wasn't in a box, then surely he couldn't be on his own. It would be best to find out what he wanted.

The sliding door which separated the cargo and loading bays had jammed halfway open on its rail after Lobo had used the area beyond as an impromptu resucue chamber, but it still left a wide gap through which could be heard an indication of the scene beyond. Palmer was saying, 'Why don't you put the gun down and we can all talk about this sensibly?'

'Move any closer,' a strange voice replied, 'and I'll make it so you can clean your teeth from the back.'

Killoran saw Bulstrode enter, saw the way that the others stepped aside to let him through. But then the bearded mountain with the evil, half-witted smile was saying, 'Don't start getting superior, kid. You can't hide behind that blaster forever. I wiped the floor with one of your kind and I'll do it again.'

He had a tight grip on his blaster. The radius of its threatening aura was precisely defined by the semicircle of men before him, daring to come so close and no further. The wall and the ramp were behind him.

'Which of you are the team leaders?' he demanded, and four of them raised a hand, Bulstrode included. 'You're the nearest thing this place has to a governing council?'

Bulstrode spoke for them all. 'We've got no government of any kind. We're the team leaders, and that's all.'

Killoran was suspicious. Perhaps they were giving him the runaround, waiting for an opportunity to get to him. 'So who makes the decisions that affect you all?'

'There's only one kind of decision that affects us all here. You work or you die. It's a conclusion we manage to arrive at pretty well without any help.'

'That's not good enough,' Killoran insisted, becoming even less sure of himself. 'I *have* to speak to somebody in authority.'

'Talk to the wind and the snow,' Cohn told him. 'They're the only authority around here.'

'You got something to say,' Bulstrode added, 'tell us all.'

'He's got nothing to say,' Berg rumbled, his eyes on the blaster. 'He only came to spring his pal.'

Bulstrode half-raised his hand in warning to Berg, but Killoran said, 'As far as it goes, he's right. I came for Randall.'

'But Randall's dead,' Cohn pointed out.

'I know that, now.'

Berg took the opportunity to push a little harder. 'What are you going to do now you can't have your spy back?'

'Try to get this through all the bone and into your brain,' Killoran snapped. 'Randall wasn't a spy.'

Cohn said reasonably, 'Give us another reason why Central should send one of the Élite here.'

'There is no Central and the Élite are a paid army for a bunch of underbelly thieves. There's no Central because Randall closed it down. As an act of gratitude the council had him sent here.'

'Great story,' Bulstrode commented drily. 'You learned it well.'

'Nearly as good as when Randall told it,' said Palmer.

'That's because it's true. Why else would either of us come here?'

'Don't ask us,' said Berg, eyes alight with dangerous mischief. 'Ask the spy.'

Killoran's audience was growing. Men were coming into the bay and adding their silent numbers to the back of the crowd. He was armed, but he was also confused and nervous; the icebreaker had pulled away when it should have stayed for him and Randall wasn't here. The whole affair was rapidly becoming a desperate mess and he could see no immediate way out of it. The men of the Ice Palace respected the killing power of his blaster, but he couldn't stand there holding them off forever – he needed time to think, to devise and he hadn't got it. Berg was trying to inch closer at every opportunity.

'Look,' Killoran said, 'name me one reason why Central should send a spy here. The Ice Palace is where it sent forgotten men, where they ceased to exist.'

Bulstrode shrugged. 'It's not for us to say.'

'Because there isn't a reason, that's why. I bribed my way out here from a city that's open to council exploitation and sliding backwards fast. I came because I was Randall's assistant and he was the one point of self-assurance and constancy in the whole unstable situation. I've been sold out by the crew on the icebreaker and dumped here without a passage back and then I'm told that the one I came for walked out and died without saying why. What kind of a spy does that make me?'

'A pretty dumb one,' Berg said happily.

Killoran brought the blaster around to cover him. He'd moved in almost to arm's length – or was the whole semicircle crushing in so much closer, pressed from behind? Berg grinned and shuffled back a token half-step.

Bulstrode said from the other side of the circle, 'It doesn't matter a damn to us why you came here. What are you going to do now?'

'I don't know.' Killoran tried to keep some awareness of Berg in the corner of his eye. 'I have to have time to think. But I'm going to need your help.'

'What makes you think you'll get it?'

'I'll force you if I have to. But when I say help, I mean it.'

Bulstrode shook his head. 'It doesn't sound too convincing when you say it over a gun.'

There could have been a sound, or it might have been some impression of movement on the periphery of his vision. Killoran swung the blaster around to cover Berg and squeezed the impulse trigger in a manoeuvre much-practised on the Élite's ranges. A slug of hot power was delivered to the charge and the weapon pulsed and roared. Berg was brought up short, his move slapped back by a solid wall of noise and an impact in his chest.

He tottered, regained his balance, rubbed his hands vaguely over the front of his snow suit. They came away black and sooty with the exhaust of a harmless charge.

Killoran looked down at the useless weapon in his hand. 'Oh, fuck,' he said bleakly.

The shock on Berg's face gave way to delight as he realized that the only barrier that had prevented him from jumping up and down on Killoran was now proven to be ineffective. Bulstrode called to him to wait, but he might as well have dropped a stone down a well and then demanded that it should come back.

Berg's arms swept in for a bear hug, closing on empty air as Killoran ducked and spun away, slinging the blaster aside to free his hands. Berg tried to turn the move into a swinging punch, but Killoran was now balanced and his hand came up, seeming only to brush back-to-back with Berg's but guiding it aside and leaving his guard fully open.

A snap-punch, doubling the fist back to the shoulder and out and Berg described a neat little somersault and landed flat out on the deck. Killoran stepped away quickly and the respectful semi-circle re-shaped itself to make room for him.

'I didn't want that,' he told them, his hands held palms-down over his thighs in readiness for another attack, 'but I'll do the same to anybody who thinks they can stop me saying what I have to say.'

'Nobody's stopping you talking,' Bulstrode said reasonably. 'Berg's impulsive, that's all.'

Palmer looked at Bulstrode in disbelief. 'You're not saying you believe him?'

'I'm not saying anything. But I'm wondering where the advantage could be in being dropped here with a blaster full of blanks and no boat home.'

'It could be a ruse.'

'Damn silly ruse to get torn apart.'

Berg was stirring, waving his arms and legs ineffectually in the air. 'I think I must have slipped,' he was mumbling. 'Let me at him . . .'

'Stay where you are,' Bulstrode advised. 'It's safer on the floor.'

Élite training had saved him from a trampling by Berg, but Killoran perceived that his position and credibility were far better without the blaster. Instead of concentrating on its threat the men were now starting to look past it to his argument. 'Bulstrode's got a point,' Cohn conceded, 'but where does it get us?'

'I'll tell you,' Killoran said, possessed by a fierce and desperate optimism. 'If you listen to me I'll get you out and back to the city.'

There were a few jeers from the back of the crowd and Palmer said, 'Just because you tell us what we want to hear, it doesn't mean we'll believe you.'

Cohn added, 'Whatever you're going to say, it's been tried.'

At least they were listening to him, not hooting and stamping and competing for the opportunity to jump on him. He'd found a nerve of hope that no amount of bitter cynicism could disguise and he was determined to exploit it. 'I'm the only one in the Palace who's not been drugged for the journey on the icebreaker. I know its layout and its weaknesses.'

Somebody said, 'We also know that it's shielded.'

'I've seen those shields and they're defective. If we all work together we can do it.'

Bulstrode was unimpressed. 'If you know so much about the Palace, then you know about the pipe network. If it isn't kept up, we're dead. Who's maintaining that while we're all working together?'

'Bring ice in,' Killoran said, thinking on his feet and with no idea as to whether it would work. 'Pack it into the cutout mechanism and freeze it solid.'

There was silence.

Palmer was the first to speak, reluctantly as if the dream might disappear. 'Would it work?'

Most people were looking at Cohn. The generator room was

his territory. 'It might,' he conceded. 'Dangerous if it doesn't.'

Everybody knew that the generator room was the one site in the Palace which would not be affected by a shutdown. When the cutout mechanism tripped, power would be lost in all other areas, especially the vital yeast tanks, but the generator room would stay warm enough for its machinery to carry on monitoring for the time when output and expenditure were so matched that the Palace could come back to life – except, of course, that the yeast would have died off, and they would be facing slow starvation. It had happened once, and a sample had barely been preserved by relays of applied heat; but the next few months had been hungry ones and they might not be so lucky again.

Bulstrode said, 'I want to know what the kid expects in return for this cooperation.'

'Nothing,' Killoran told him. 'I want to get back as much as you do and I know I can't do it alone. My inside knowledge, your manpower.'

'And when we get back, what then? All of a sudden you're back to being Élite and we're refugees.'

'I'll be no more welcome than you will. All I want is a crack at the two councillors who tricked me and put me here.'

Cohn couldn't help being suspicious. 'What happened to the famous Élite inbred loyalty?'

'Loyalty to what?' It was in the balance and they were a long way from being convinced – but still they were listening. 'A dead city, or a frozen hero? I'm being realistic.'

'We haven't said we'll cooperate,' Bulstrode warned him.

'But you will.'

'We've got minds, kid. You may not have been taught to think so, but we have.'

The undercurrent of excitement in the crowd was obvious. Almost the entire population of the Palace had by now pushed into the bay and joined the circle and they'd all heard at least the latter part of Killoran's argument. Perhaps the sophistication of such issues as who was running the city and selling out whom raised them out of the sphere of immediate preoccupation, but there was one point which everybody without exception had grasped; there was a hope for escape, and long-dead aspirations and feelings were becoming fresh and sensitive again.

There would have to be some kind of vote, somebody insisted; it could have been the Worm shouting from the back, but in spite of that everybody seemed in favour of the order and formality of the idea. They put a guard of three on Killoran, mainly to show him that he was a long way from total acceptance. At the worst they might pick his brains and then throw him out on to the cap, but for the moment they took him to a bunkroom and, as an afterthought, gave him a snow suit to replace the inadequate city winter clothing that he'd arrived in.

There was, everybody agreed, much to discuss, although the only tangible issue that anybody could think of was that of the possibility of a return to normal food after living on the yeast. The main desire was simply to talk, to test the reality of their hope aloud, revelling in the fact that, for a few brief hours at least, it was a topic that could be aired without the fear of bitter ridicule.

As Killoran was moved to the bunkroom there was a general decision to call a meeting in the Cantina, the refuge of such meagre society as the Palace enjoyed. Cohn caught up with Bulstrode in the passageway and drew him aside from the chattering procession.

'You know them all better than me,' Cohn said quietly, not wanting to be overheard. 'Which way are they likely to vote?'

'You really don't know?' Bulstrode didn't need to take the temperature of the crowd to recognize the urges that fought against reason within himself.

'I wouldn't be asking if I did.'

'You heard what he's offering. He's holding out freedom. They'll grab it and bite his hand off if he's not careful.'

Eighteen

It seemed to Randall that his existence was dedicated to the exchange of one prison for another and that the notion of escape was an illusion which he was only now coming to comprehend. His life was corridors, endless corridors lined by anonymous doors beyond which were little rooms where essentially pointless confrontations took place and beyond these complexes raged a bleak and hostile universe. The Ice Palace, the shuttle, the World Ship – and, he admitted to himself with chilling honesty, the city.

They had been escorted without explanation into a fairly well-populated area of the World Ship. On the way they saw nothing that suggested an alien environment, no strange wonders or pulsating blobs of unfamiliar life; they might be lost below decks in a well-used and understaffed battleship. Only unexpected distortions of proportion and the occasional glimpse of a less-than-perfect marionette served to twist his perception of reality into line with the unusual.

They were in a guarded chamber, presumably awaiting the mysterious process of patterning. The door wouldn't open for them; it was keyed to a simulacrum handprint. The room was again low-ceilinged and blue and its walls bore the marks of fittings that had been removed. Now it was unfurnished, its bareness only relieved by a raised shelf that could serve as a hard seat for two or an equally hard and somewhat short bed for one.

Lobo leaned back with his eyes closed. He seemed to be driving the outside world out of his mind, slamming all the shutters down and giving himself some temporary and transient peace. Randall nursed his bruised pride – they'd been herded like animals, *were* animals as far as the marionettes were concerned. He tried to tell himself that they were machines, designed and crafted for a purpose, but that only made it worse; he'd expected something along the lines of an improved Rorvik model, but these had been *people*, perfect and indistinguishable.

When he tried to think of what lay ahead, his mind, like Lobo's, tried to pull back and cut free into a cocooned limbo, but he forced himself to face the prospect that they would be patterned – whatever that entailed – and then let loose in the corridors to be herded and killed for practice. Probably hunted down by their own improved doubles.

The city hadn't got a chance against them. They'd move in and take over before the rag-bag of a council knew anything; worse than that, the council was even helping. The Wekk would strip the assets of the city and then throw it to one side and move on. They'd probably throw Marius aside at the same time, but he wouldn't see that; he had a grabber's mind, but a short reach.

'The next time,' he said aloud, 'we won't be rounded up and brought back. They'll kill us on the spot.'

Lobo frowned and then opened his eyes as he was pulled back to the real world. He considered for a while and then said, 'We need a good idea to get us out. Anything to offer?'

Randall threw off a brief stab of doubt, a fear of yet another pointless confrontation and tried to organize his knowledge and ideas towards some purposeful discussion. All his information had come from Rorvik, a confused and inadequate source. He knew the Wekk's long-term intentions, but he'd never seen one of them; and Randall had to admit that observation had added nothing to this basic store on their trip from the shuttle to this cell.

'Point one,' he said. 'We covered over a mile of corridor and didn't see anything to suggest that this ship is even inhabited. It doesn't look as if it's being cleaned or maintained.'

'Could be they've set this whole area aside for training.'

'That's a possibility. So we're in an isolated sector of a much larger construction. Elsewhere there's a complete and self-sufficient race, working to expand and with major computing facilities to do it. If this is a ship it's also got to have power and propulsion.'

Lobo was dubious. He was all in favour of reviewing the available information, but he wasn't so sure about such tenuous extrapolation. 'All this is great theory,' he said, 'but what's it going to do for us?'

'We can't make a plan without considering everything.'

'Another plan!' Lobo raised his hands in a frustrated appeal to the gods. 'Look where your last one got us! And what are you supposed to be considering? You're making it up as you go along!'

'You've a better idea?'

Lobo nodded. 'We concentrate on getting out of this cell and back to the shuttle.'

'Why the shuttle?'

'Because we can't do anything on our own, so we get back to the city and warn them.'

'Wrong.' Randall held up the dead power pack that was still clipped at his waist. 'We get dropped back on the ice cap with no power in our suits. We wouldn't make it back to the Palace and if we could what then?'

Lobo realized that he'd been considering only the short-term possibilities. He gave a sick smile. 'Looks like we've no choice. We're going to have to be heroes.'

'You never know. It might work. At the very worst we'll go out in a blaze of self-esteem.'

'I don't aim to plan for suicide,' Lobo warned.

'Nor do I. If there's one thing guaranteed to keep us sharp, it's the prospect of survival.'

They sat quietly, their fragile comradeship momentarily restored. After a few seconds the door whipped open without warning and their guard took a half-step inside and glanced suspiciously around. He wasn't armed, but then he didn't need to be.

Obviously he'd been listening on the other side of the door. When silence had fallen he'd wanted to know why. Randall felt a surge of anger and said, 'What's the matter? Did they miss the brain out when they assembled you?'

'Up yours, bloodbag,' the marionette spat and made to withdraw.

'That's the Ice Palace talking,' Lobo said quietly. 'I remember you, Pearson, when you were a man.'

The marionette's eyes narrowed. 'When I was a bloodbag. Pearson's dead; I strangled him myself out in the Tin Jungle. Don't get any ideas on teasing sympathy out of me, Lobo. If they say you're good enough you'll be patterned and rebuilt and then be fit to join us. Until then you're just a bloodbag for stamping on.'

Randall wondered if there was anywhere in this being a residual humanity that might be reached. Remembering Rorvik's plaintive nostalgia for a human existence he'd never even known, he said, 'Come on, Pearson. So they built you and they gave you your orders. Admit that you're still one of us inside.'

Pearson reacted with amusement. He stepped further into the room, and the door hissed shut behind him. 'One of *you*? Don't make me laugh. I could break you with one hand. I'm faster and I'm stronger and I'm never going to die. Beat that.'

He reached behind him and touched the door. It came open

and he stepped out backwards without taking his eyes off them.

'A ready-made fanatic,' Randall said despondently, his voice little more than a whisper. 'That's one hell of a weapon.'

'It makes you go cold inside,' Lobo agreed. 'If I didn't know better I'd swear it's the man I knew. I can't say I'm taken with the idea of looking up into my own eyes as I'm being strangled.'

Randall tried to concentrate on the problem in hand. They knew very little about the capabilities of the marionettes, except that they were fast and strong. Pearson was their first obstacle and it seemed likely that his claim of being able to break them one-handed would hardly be an exaggeration.

The hours passed and nothing happened. Randall guessed that the patterning shops could only handle a limited number of subjects at any one time and either the process was a long one or there was a sizeable backlog. Subjects that were boxed and deteriorating obviously took precedence over those that were live and apprehensive and they were undisturbed for hours.

Pearson remained outside, apparently needing neither food nor sleep. Randall and Lobo felt the demands of both, but whilst one could be satisfied after a fashion by stretching out on the hard shelf or the floor there was no way that nourishment could be extracted from an empty room. Pearson responded instantly when Randall hammered on the door, stepping inside and looking for trouble. He was unsympathetic when Randall asked for food, saying that there was nothing on the World Ship that a bloodbag could eat; but about half an hour later he was back with a couple of lightweight plastic bottles filled with the sweet drip that had been provided for the crated men in the shuttle. The hollow needles had been carefully removed.

So a marionette was by no means invulnerable; the simple precaution indicated as much. Randall preferred this conclusion to the idea that they were being prevented from damaging themselves and so robbing the simulacra of the pleasure. As they waited, faint and distant sounds were carried to them through the fabric of the ship, softened and reduced in every case to indistict thumps. They had no way of identifying the faint whisper that was the hangar door opening to release the shuttle nor, several hours and a sickly meal later, the irregular bang as the shuttle rode back in on to hydraulic fenders.

As soon as air had been pumped into the hangar Valum went inside to meet the councillors. She took with her Moskie, the marionette she had chosen to be her assistant and who had been patterned on a wiry, nervous-looking individual and Rorvik, because she'd been told that the new councillor was blind and would need a guide, and it was exactly the kind of undemanding duty that she considered Rorvik fit for. There were four other simulacra whose sole purpose was to make up an impressive-looking party – Marius was pleased by such things and his cooperation came more easily. As with any machine, pressing the right buttons gave a predictable response, a simple truth which was fundamental to Valum's universe.

Morden was in a bad way, pale and sick and barely able to balance. Marius held him up until Rorvik moved in and took over as instructed. At least Marius was trying to put a brave face on it, walking down the ramp with unsteady dignity and greeting Valum with an open gesture. If the truth were to be known, the numbers of Valum's party were wasted on him. Once his eyes were on her they stayed there.

She said that there were chambers ready and refreshments if they were needed, failing to add that the refreshments were no more than a flavoured variation of the drips that were being given to Randall and Lobo elsewhere in the World Ship. Marius turned to Morden and said encouragingly, 'See? They want us to feel at home. We're allies.'

Valum added, 'Let us never be considered anything else, Marius, but partners in strength and enterprise.'

Marius lapped it up. His ego soared at the notion of being treated as an equal by a race of proven world-rapers – or, at least, by their representatives. Morden tried to concentrate on staying upright.

Valum led them part of the way towards the suites of rooms that had been prepared for them on the next level. Marius had apparently requested an Arabian Nights style of decor whilst Morden, whose wishes were not yet known, had been given something rather more functional. The suites were some way apart, being subject to the available space of the ship's original design – Valum didn't add that she'd also wanted to keep the councillors apart and under surveillance. They had to stop a couple of times as squads of the simulacra thundered past, intent on some unexplained mission or exercise somewhere else in the ship and as they waited Marius asked, 'How is the plan proceeding?'

'Well,' Valum replied with a professional eye on the formation of her troops. 'The final model of simulacrum is undergoing tests at this very moment. When the results are known we'll be ready to move.'

'What? Into production?'

'No, directly into takeover.' The way was clear, and they moved on. 'We have sufficient models available now for our ground forces; we're only waiting for the development of the ground commander.'

Marius beamed with undisguised pleasure as a great, shapeless mass of anticipated good fortune seemed to rise above his horizon. 'Will we see these tests?' he asked.

'I hope not.' She hesitated, choosing her words carefully. 'They might be dangerous for any non-mechanicals present. You're far too valuable to us to risk, councillor.'

'I'm but a humble businessman, Valum, struggling to grasp the awesome complexities of power and to milk a little comfort from them as I go.'

The party split, with Rorvik leading Morden off down a side-corridor whilst Marius and the other simulacra went on. Valum held back, and when the group was out of earshot Moskie said, 'How do you manage it, Valum?'

She raised an enquiring eyebrow. 'You mean, treat the bloodbags as equals? Don't think it's easy. I'll smile until we've got the information we need. Then I'll take the greatest pleasure in twisting their flimsy necks.'

Moskie looked along the corridor, where the shadows of the retreating party still flickered on the wall. 'Makes me sick to look at them,' he said, suppressing an involuntary and rather human shudder. 'Bladders of jelly and bone.'

'Don't let it show,' Valum warned him as they turned and headed back towards her command post. 'At the moment we need information on their social setup that only they can provide. When we've got that...'

'The Tin Jungle?'

She smiled. 'Perhaps. Or else flush them out into vacuum

and watch them explode. A lesson to us all on the frailty of the lower order.'

'Do we need any such lesson?'

'Some of the simulacra have been known to show a morbid sympathy for their origins. It does them no credit. Evolution is the only counter to the slow disintegration of the universe; evolve and never look back.'

Moskie was left to ponder this strange morsel of speculation as Valum ordered that the shuttle hangar be cleared and sealed, as the ship wasn't to be used again. The councillors, she added by way of explanation, wouldn't be going back.

Despite his discomfort Morden insisted upon being led all around his rooms, stopping to touch each obstruction in order to identify it and fix its location in his mind. Only then did he allow himself to relax, shaking Rorvik's arm free and moving unaided to a divan. Rorvik seated himself by the door, waiting until he should be needed again. Morden told him he could go.

'Valum said I have to stay, councillor,' Rorvik replied. 'You'll need one of us to open the door for you.'

Morden frowned. Something was troubling him, adding yet another layer of confusion to his already disoriented state of mind. The period of weightlessness on the trip out had been pure and undiluted hell for him and now his world seemed to be subject to a constant sideways drift, due, no doubt, to the inert reaction of his body to the cylinder's spin. A sighted man could probably overcome it, but for Morden it warped his entire perception of his surroundings. And now some further creeping doubt or anxiety was sliding to add itself to the turmoil in his head, demanding attention whilst stubbornly refusing to be identified.

'Rorvik!' he said after a moment. 'The woman called you Rorvik. Is that right?'

'It's my name,' Rorvik said guardedly, as if it might be taken from him.

'I never forget a voice.' It was true, although there was nothing in the marionette's flat monotone to recall the living man that he had met on a single occasion in the underbelly. Rorvik had at the time been on the run from the Élite prior to his assault on Central and Morden had supplied him with the tapes he'd needed to devise his plan of attack. A potential ally? Not if Marius's ecstatic praise of their loyalty and power was to be believed. Better proceed carefully. So far, he didn't have a friend in the place.

'Marius has told me what you are,' he went on conversationally. 'Copies, robots . . .'

'Not robots,' Rorvik said abruptly. 'Anything but that.'

A nerve? And so soon? 'Why so sensitive? Does it matter so much to you?'

'Copies, I accept. It hurts, but at least I understand *why* it hurts. But I'm not a robot. I'm patterned on a man and I've got some of his memories. I think the way he would think and I've got some of his feelings.'

Morden lifted himself on an elbow. 'Then I knew the man you were. I respected him.'

Automatically, Rorvik walked over and placed a cushion behind the councillor, saying, 'Randall knew the man I was as well. He . . .'

'Did you say Randall?' Morden interrupted. 'He's here?'

'From the Ice Palace. They're holding him for patterning now.'

A number of pieces suddenly interlocked in Morden's mind. A dazzling and frightening sequence of logic which could be the key to an atlas of possibilities. But first he would have to persuade or deceive this pathetic and self-pitying being and somehow use him to get to Randall. 'How long has he been here?' he asked.

'A few days. Two of them stowed away on the shuttle and persuaded me to help them.'

Morden warmed to this weak link. He admitted he was reachable. 'How did they persuade you?'

'Didn't you get the message from Valum? Anybody can make a fool out of Rorvik. He's simple and he's credulous. I can't help it.'

'Tell me something. How strong are your loyalties to the Wekk? to your own kind?'

'Are you testing me?' Rorvik asked suspiciously. 'Please don't trick me. I don't know how to lie.'

'I'm not trying to trick you,' Morden said soothingly.

'I don't even have the guile to evade answering. Valum's right, I'm a poor specimen.'

'And a talkative one,' said Morden, trying not to let his impatience show. 'Answer the question.'

Rorvik applied himself and was silent for a moment. 'Towards the Wekk, I'm not *aware* of any loyalty,' he answered truthfully. 'I've never seen one of them, and they've never offered me anything. As for the marionettes, I suppose I'm loyal. I do what they tell me, and they use my name so I'm somebody. To everyone else I'm a half-finished monster.'

Morden was surprised. Marius had told him that the simulacra were visually indistinguishable from real people. 'A monster?' he said. 'Why?'

'You can't see me,' Rorvik said bitterly. 'I'm the first marionette they ever built and the only model they had was in the memory of a computer. What do you think I look like?'

'To me, what does it matter?'

'What is this?' Rorvik said suddenly. 'What are you trying to do?'

'I'll tell you the truth, Rorvik. I'll tell you the truth because of the man you once were and for the humanity you've retained. I'll tell you,' he added with rather more honesty, 'because I need you.'

'Nobody needs me,' Rorvik said sorrowfully. 'Valum says so.'

'Valum's wrong. When she speaks I hear the true monster, a being without pity.'

This didn't agree with Rorvik's preconceptions. 'They say she's considered the most successful piece of design so far.'

'By what measure of success? Because she's colder, harder, stronger?'

'All of that.'

'They praise her because in spirit she's the furthest from the human concept they've been able to devise. They despise you because you're the closest.'

Rorvik shook his head sadly. 'They despise me because I'm nothing.'

'By their standards, perhaps. Standards which would rape worlds and trample the weak.'

'Men's standards. I got exactly the same treatment from Randall.'

Morden pushed the cushion away and sat upright, his physical discomfort driven from his mind. 'Don't take Randall as your model for a man. In many ways he's as much an engineered product as Valum, biology rigged for the service of the State.'

Rorvik started to soften, his protective screen of bitterness breaking down under Morden's sustained and skilful attack. 'The other one – Lobo – he was kinder. I think he understood.'

'Of course he understood. He understood your self-doubt, your weakness, your hope.'

'And that's all there is to me. No wonder they spit on me.'

Morden began to wonder if he was really wasting his time, whether Rorvik would in the end prove to be as empty and inadequate as he appeared. This was, after all, Morden's first excursion into machine diplomacy, and he was on uncertain ground. But he was faced with a real dilemma; Rorvik talked, moved and reacted like a human being. His thought-processes seemed to be the same, his responses faultless. How could Morden treat him apart from as a human being? How could he even – and this thought gave him a thrill of horror – be sure that, despite his strange birth and unfamiliar biology, Rorvik was not fundamentally human at all?

There was a simple answer, sufficient to meet his present needs. He couldn't be sure, so forget it and carry on. 'I need you,' he said. 'I want you to be my eyes and my guide.'

'I'm that already. Valum ordered me to be.'

'She didn't order you to help me ruin the takeover plan.'

It was a gamble. Rorvik didn't answer straight away, and Morden plunged in with, 'See? I'm trusting you. I consider you a man. Would the machines do as much?'

'Never. They say I'm too . . .'

'Human?'

'Unreliable. Ineffective.'

'By machine standards.'

'Weak and sloppy, like a bloodbag.' He added, almost apologetically, 'That's what they call you.'

'The same contempt they reserve for you. Join me,' Morden urged, 'and be my eyes.'

Rorvik's defences were deceptive. His resistance to enthusiasm was immense. 'I was supposed to join Randall,' he said. 'But as soon as he'd gone I found I was taking orders from Valum again.'

'You have to believe in yourself before you can choose a path and have the faith to stick to it. What did Randall offer you?

Use of your name, like the others? So cheap a contract costs you nothing to break.'

'But I'm not a *man*,' Rorvik objected desperately. 'I was *built*.'

'So were we all. It's the oldest piece of engineering in the history of the race.'

'Of *your* race. Not the Wekk.'

'And how much careful control did the Wekk put into your conception? Damn all, and they weren't satisfied with the result so they threw you aside. Too much of the human being was showing through.'

There was a pause. Morden had said enough, deciding that he had reached the narrow line that separates persuasion from transparent propaganda. The initiative would now have to come from Rorvik. If it didn't, Morden had not only wasted his time, he'd put himself into a very dangerous position; if he couldn't win Rorvik now, he may as well simply hand himself over to Valum.

'All right,' Rorvik said. 'I'll serve you.'

'Not serve me. Help me. I want information and then action. And we'll need Randall.'

'If it isn't too late,' Rorvik warned. 'He's down for patterning.'

'It won't be too late,' Morden said with unexpected certainty. 'Leave that to me. How much can you find out about this ship and the Wekk without arousing suspicion?'

Rorvik thought about how the other simulacra could touch Wekk-prepared computers and systems in a certain way and somehow tune in to them. He knew he had some of this capability from his experiments on the shuttle, but how far did it extend? If he was, as Morden suggested, too human to qualify as a fully-fledged simulacrum, would he be able to do no more than touch the outer surface of the machines' awareness, like a telekinetic who wafted feathers whilst others raised mountains? Trying, he told himself with new-found determination, was the only way to find out.

'I'll see if I can get access to the shuttle's computer,' he told Morden. 'It may not work, but I can try.' He explained how the shuttle had been found empty and in orbit and how the Wekk had stripped it and fitted their own guidance systems. If these were linked into the main ship memories he might be able to tap them out, an instant flood of knowledge which he would then carry for as long as he could keep it in his mind; then, like all forgotten studies, the details would begin to slip away.

'You can do it,' Morden said with completely unjustified confidence.

Rorvik wished he could share Morden's conviction. At least he could draw some courage from it.

'Any more bright ideas?'

'I'm sorry.' Randall helped Lobo to his feet. 'How was I to know he'd react like that?'

It had always worked in stories. Prisoner One calls guard and tells him that Prisoner Two is ill, indicating an inert form to substantiate his claim; and when the guard rushes in filled with concern and bends over said form he gets bopped from behind and the two then dance off to fresh air and freedom. Which was fine, except that Randall hadn't read much concern in Pearson's expression as he advanced on Lobo; more an evil glee at the prospect of being able to finish him off.

It made sense. If they showed themselves as unfit for patterning they'd lose whatever small value they had.

'All of a sudden,' Lobo said, 'I feel unbearably healthy.'

Randall began to pace the cell yet again. 'There must be another way,' he said.

There was no way out other than by the single sliding door, and that was unavailable to them unless Pearson actually opened it and let them through. They couldn't trick or persuade him, because he didn't have the slightest interest in anything they had to say – he seemed only to warm at the prospect of tearing one of them apart.

'That's what we'll have to use against him,' Randall said aloud. 'Fill his mind with the prospect of mangling a bloodbag and then hit him when he's off guard.'

'With what?' Lobo objected. 'He's stronger than both of us put together and we've no weapons.'

'We're wearing them,' Randall said. Lobo was giving him a familiar sideways look of distrust as he sat down, so he went on, 'The snow suits. Have you ever tried to tear the fabric on one?'

'Don't be a fool. There was no way to repair or replace them.'

'Exactly.' Randall was unzipping his suit, sliding his arm

out of a sleeve to demonstrate his point. 'The supply was limited and they were handed down from prisoner to prisoner. They're as old as the Palace itself and they were part of the original equipment. They're space suits.'

Lobo took hold of the fabric and tugged at it experimentally, looking at it as if for the first time. 'How does that make them into weapons?'

'The fabric was made deliberately strong to avoid the possibility of a rupture or tear in vacuum. If we knot the sleeves into a band and drop that over Pearson's head we can pin his arms to his sides.'

'But the suits are old. How do you know they'll take the strain?'

'How do you know they won't?'

Lobo couldn't answer the point, so he moved on. 'So we've got him trussed up on the floor. What then?'

'He's a machine and machines can be broken. Two of us should be able to do it.'

'I wouldn't be so confident. With that kind of logic you could wrestle bulldozers and expect to win.'

But it was the only chance they seemed to have, and as closer inspection only revealed its flaws they decided to forget the detailed analysis and go ahead with it. Obviously to stand there shivering and suitless when Pearson walked in would be to invite instant failure, so Lobo practised a few times until he could slip off the outer layer with silence and speed.

Randall banged on the door with the flat of his hand. In case their warder was growing weary of being attracted in this way, he added encouragement by shouting, 'Pearson! Get your tin backside in here!'

The door was open and Randall was backing away out of reach. Pearson was smiling. 'You'd have to have a good reason to call me like that, bloodbag. Offhand I can't think of anything good enough.'

'I don't need to explain anything to you, junkhead.'

Pearson glanced at Lobo. He was sitting on the low shelf, arms folded and apparently wanting nothing to do with his partner's madness. He turned his attention back to Randall, who was hovering bright-eyed and nervous at the far end of the cell. 'Damn right you don't,' Pearson told him. 'I've got all the reason I need to pull your head off and stuff it down your throat.'

'Brave talk from a greasy oilbag. All crude oil and low-grade alloys.'

Pearson's smile vanished. Randall was attacking where it hurt, cutting at his sensitive machine pride. 'Say that again,' Pearson demanded menacingly.

'Oil bag. A clockwork brain and a scrap iron heart. Blood like a dead lake.'

'Thanks, Randall. I'm going to enjoy this.' The safety mechanism of the door sensed as he advanced and the door whispered shut behind him. Pearson's awareness was now completely focused on Randall and the prospect of mangling a bloodbag with full justification.

Randall kicked out hard and low, aiming to clip the kneecap sideways with the ball of his foot. He was fast, but Pearson was faster – both forearms thrust down in a rigid block that was like an iron bar laid across his shin. Randall bit back a shout of pain and concentrated on twisting to keep his balance.

Lobo stepped in and quickly dropped the knotted loop of his suit over Pearson's shoulders, trapping his arms close to his chest. Pearson wasted no time in stupid surprise but jumped backwards, slamming into Lobo and knocking him to the floor. The loop had dropped to his waist and he flexed to tear it and pull his arms free. Lobo was up and suddenly on his back, forcing the second loop of the sleeves over Pearson's head. This time he dropped off before he could be shrugged off, taking Pearson by surprise and leaving him tottering and half-blinded by the loose material. Randall made a standing jump, hitting him in the chest with both feet and slamming him backwards over the crouching Lobo to measure his full length on the deck.

They fell on to him together, pinning his legs to prevent them from delivering crippling kicks. Pearson was a trussed package struggling vainly to free himself from the tangle of snow suit that was wrapped around him, but he was still dangerous. Randall managed to stuff a handful of material in his mouth to prevent him from shouting for help, nearly losing a finger in the process and then together he and Lobo began to haul Pearson towards the raised shelf that was the only feature of the cell.

Pearson seemed to realize what they were trying to do. He fought back even harder, getting impossible purchase with his heels on the floor and dragging all three of them back a few inches at a time, slowly cancelling out the progress that they made. The next time he tried it Randall kicked his feet free, and for a moment there was no resistance and they got him a yard or more across the floor. Then his heels dug in again, and the backward creep began.

They were tiring and he wasn't. And now the knots began to slip.

Lobo tried to say so, but didn't have the effort to spare. Randall had seen it anyway, a fractional unwinding of the fabric stretched tight across Pearson's chest. Not wanting to shout and give Pearson warning, Randall pushed hard on Lobo's shoulder and then rolled away himself. Lobo was taken by surprise, losing his grip and sliding away. With the sudden release of constraint Pearson was left threshing energetically in the middle of the room.

Randall scrambled around, tried to get a good double handful of suit which hopefully included some of Pearson's own. Lobo caught on and did the same, and with one unified effort they dragged and lifted at the same time, covering the last few feet and getting Pearson's head on to the shelf.

Lobo dropped his full weight on to Pearson's chest, throwing himself down hard. And then it was over.

Something vital gave and Pearson stopped fighting them. They both stepped back warily, watching Pearson's body slowly subside to the floor, the head bending away from the shoulders at an unnatural angle as it bumped over the edge of the shelf.

Lobo claimed to have killed to be sent to the Ice Palace, but this process had obviously repelled him. Randall gave Pearson a couple of tentative prods with his foot, but there was no reaction.

'What now?' Lobo asked, wiping his eyes on the sleeve of his inner suit.

'The councillors,' Randall said, hauling Pearson back into the middle of the room where he could work to undo the knots in Lobo's snow suit. 'They're somewhere aboard, or they soon will be. I heard one of our escorts say as much when they were bringing us up here. We can't hope to fight the marionettes, but with a hostage we might have a chance to reach the alien areas of the ship instead of playing about in the training ground.'

Lobo wasn't exactly enchanted by the prospect. 'Farther

and farther in and not a damned clue as to what we're going to do when we get there.'

'We have to go on because we can't go back.' Randall was thinking of the irony in Pearson's claim that he was stronger, faster and was never going to die. Stronger and faster he may have been, but he was as mortal as any of the bloodbags he so despised. Then Randall got the last knot undone and pulled the suit free, dragging it from under Pearson's shoulders and unwrapping it from around his head. 'At least we can try to pick up some insurance along the way,' he went on and then faltered. Pearson's eyes were fixed on him, their irises two tiny points of hatred.

Lobo took the suit and climbed into it mechanically. He didn't look at Pearson, but Randall was careful to turn the head aside so that the living eyes were concealed. 'Another advantage,' Randall said with forced brightness, 'is that Valum won't know we're on the loose for a while.'

If the thought gave Lobo any particular cheer he didn't let it show. He finished zipping up and prepared, yet again, to dive head-first into the killing bottle.

Nineteen

The short time of Killoran's acceptance had seen considerable changes in the Ice Palace. The work cycle was broken, quickly and efficiently – ice packed into the reactor cutouts jammed them open and the Palace was assured of its power supply. The yeast tanks had to be tended and continuous relays were needed to bring fresh ice for the cutouts, but the regime of the all-weathers, round-the-clock surface repair teams was ended, it seemed, for good. Killoran would be a hero in the Palace if he never achieved anything more. About forty men were now freed to devote all their efforts and intelligence to the next stage of the plan, the storming of the icebreaker.

The rosters were discarded. Men happily took double shifts, snatching sleep and coming back early for more; there were rafts to be made and tested, ropes to be woven from fibre and blanket and the full extent of the pipe network to be scouted as soon as the weather allowed. There was enthusiasm, even long-unheard laughter; nervous hopes and laughing too loud, a consuming apprehension which began to break the surface in the form of petty disputes or fights. When this happened Berg would be there, gently disengaging the participants and threatening them with far worse horrors should they attempt to continue.

Even Palmer, miserable and despised, suppressed his fears when a surface party was needed and offered himself up with the rest, finding that this simple act won him the grudging recognition of equality. Only one face was consistently missing from all this activity.

Palmer knocked on the door to the Worm's office. There was no reply, so he knocked again a little harder and shouted, 'Worm? Open the door!'

His voice echoed loudly in the ice tunnel and he felt faintly ridiculous. What if somebody heard? He was about to turn and go when a faint, 'Go away,' reached him.

'At least open the door and speak to me!' Palmer insisted.

He waited for some time, drumming his fingers lightly on the door to show that he was still there. After a minute or so it opened a crack and the Worm looked out. His hair was disarrayed and his eyes were puffy and red behind his one-lensed spectacles.

'Leave me alone, Palmer,' he mumbled. 'I don't want to talk to anybody.'

'You've got to come out some time,' Palmer told him. 'You can't stay in there forever.'

The Worm shrugged. 'Where else am I going to go?' He turned and shuffled back into his office. The unclosed door was an invitation, the manner in which it was offered a rejection. Palmer followed him in and left the door open behind him. 'We need your help,' he said. 'Killoran says he needs everybody.'

'He doesn't need me. I'm not fit to go out on the ice and I'm no use in here either.'

'That's birdseed,' Palmer said dismissively.

'Is it?' the Worm demanded, some light coming into his eyes for the first time. He gestured at a sheaf of filthy grey papers on his rickety table. Some of them had been written on, most not. 'Nobody's using rosters now. The kid's got everybody so fired up they're fighting to work every hour in the day.'

'Come on, Worm. He's offering us hope. Grown men are crying in their bunks. I've been doing my turns on the ice and no swaps.'

The Worm seemed not to hear. 'We had a good system going here,' he mused. 'It wasn't such a bad place before.'

Palmer said incredulously, 'Are you serious?'

'I was important then. Not just needed, the same as everybody else, but *important*. They could despise me or laugh at me, but they couldn't do without me and they knew it.'

Palmer was hardly impressed by the argument. 'Don't think about that. Think about what it all means. Going home.'

The Worm winced, as if at the memory of an old agony. 'Home to what?' he said despondently. 'You know what home was to me? A grubby desk in a crowded office and an hour for lunch, then back at night to a long staircase and a little room.'

'It doesn't have to be like that. Everything's going to change for the better.'

'That's great for the strong and the handsome. Types like Bulstrode will love it. Everybody gets embarrassed at the thought of a runt enjoying himself.'

The Worm certainly looked the part, a shrunken figure in his baggy snow suit toying miserably with a loose splinter at the corner of his desk. Palmer tried to get him out of his self-pitying mood.

'You've got no self-respect,' he said. 'For years they've been depending on you and hating themselves for having to, not because you're anything special but because they think they're so tough they shouldn't depend on *anybody*. So they took it out on you and you're believing it all.'

The Worm shrugged. 'Talk all you like. I'd rather be hated than ignored. You know you're the first person to come looking for me?'

'So what?'

'So I've gone from being the most important person in the Palace to being an afterthought, that's all.'

'Shove your importance,' Palmer snapped, his frustration beginning to show. 'Nobody's going to be interested in you if you won't get involved.'

'Involved in what? A useless trek across the ice to dig out some deserted spaceport?'

'Not deserted,' Palmer said, annoyed at having to be defensive. 'We found some evidence of recent use.'

'Breaking up the crates,' the Worm pressed on as if he hadn't heard, 'for rafts to drown ourselves on?'

'Damn you, Worm, I don't know why I'm bothering.'

'Nor do I.'

'You sit and carp and moan for the lousy good old days and you won't lift a finger to try to make anything better.'

'Where's the point?' the Worm asked, his face an open and uncomprehending blank.

'Because you get nothing if you don't reach for it, that's the point.'

'You've got freedom fever like the rest of them, Palmer,' the Worm said dismissively. 'All of a sudden you think you can just dream it and make it come true. Well, life isn't like that. It's routine and detail and fiddling little considerations . . .'

'*Your* life, perhaps . . .'

'All right, *my* life. So what have I got now? A spaceport on the doorstep nobody can use. Mad plans to steal an icebreaker. Lights in the sky . . .'

Palmer reddened at this last mention. It seemed the Worm had been around more in the past couple of days than he'd thought. 'I saw those myself,' he insisted. 'They were real. Something passed overhead, I don't know what.'

'You're no better than the rest of them. Why don't you leave me alone?'

'My apologies, Worm,' Palmer said tightly. 'I had this stupid idea that you needed encouragement.'

'Shove your encouragement,' the Worm replied morosely. 'Take it back to your city-bred Messiah.'

Palmer moved back towards the door. 'Go see the Worm, I thought. I wish I hadn't wasted my time.'

'That makes two of us.'

'All you want to do is sit on your own in this crummy office and feel sorry for yourself. Don't expect anybody to join in.'

'You're breathing my air, Palmer.'

'I know,' Palmer said, holding the edge of the door so hard that his knuckles were white. 'It's got the smell of something going sour in it.'

He slammed the door as viciously as he could, really wishing that he was pounding the Worm's head against the gritty ice wall in a desperate and frustrated bid to make some final communication. The door banged in its frame and bounced open again, but Palmer was already some way off along the tunnel, head down and muttering to himself.

The Worm waited for a minute. Then he went over to the door and closed it softly after first checking that the tunnel outside was empty. He went back to his desk with its blank rosters, looking at them pensively for a few seconds before going back and checking the tunnel again. It was empty, as before. He closed the door.

This time it had been easy to get lost in the World Ship. There was no sweep operation in progress and the upper levels (which were, by an ironic inversion of physical laws, innermost in the cylinder) had more alcoves, corners and wide open spaces than the featureless corridors where they had originally been captured. There was a further advantage in that, for the moment, nobody knew they were free; Pearson's inert form remained in their cell, lying exactly as they had left him after using his hand to open the door.

At no time did they see any sign of a non-human life form. Indeed, as they retreated further the indications of use by the simulacra grew less. The World Ship seemed to be at once lived-in and deserted – there was grey dust piling up in some of the corridors and the walls and floors showed squares and patches where, Randall assumed, equipment or machinery once stood. Lighting was uneven and in many places had simply failed or burned out without replacement. The World Ship was an artificial planet going to seed – literally, as it turned out when they found the banks and terraces of what had obviously been a garden in a huge chamber that embraced two levels.

They watched the movements of the marionettes, tried to work out where their centres of operations were and what they were doing in the endless exercises which kept them moving from one area of the ship to another, but it was impossible. They did, however, find Marius.

He was glimpsed entering the chambers that had been laid aside for him. Randall knew it had to be Marius, for the simulacrum who escorted him and left him at the door displayed an exaggerated deference that no machine would need to use towards another.

'They still don't know we're loose,' Lobo reminded Randall. 'That may change if we don't get a hostage, quick.'

For once, Randall agreed. He quickly outlined his idea, that they should watch for a while to ensure that Marius was alone before attempting to bluff their way in as marionettes. Lobo wasn't sure about the last part.

'We make damn funny robots in these old suits,' he said.

'We'd make funnier ones without them,' Randall replied. 'Try to seem confident and we'll find out if he's armed.'

The door presented a problem. It seemed to be of the same type that had blocked their cell, activated only by a simulacrum's touch; but as they looked around for some other way to open it the panel hissed back without warning and Marius looked out at them with an expression of polite enquiry.

Randall said, 'May we join you, councillor?' as if this had been his intention all along.

Marius seemed confused for a moment as he took in their shopworn and hirsute appearance, then his expression cleared into understanding.

'Intelligent company!' he said, obviously pleased. 'How thoughtful of Valum. Please come in.'

He stepped aside, and Randall led on into the room. Lobo followed and tried not to seem too relieved.

The room was heavily draped in greens and golds, not so much a room as an indoor courtyard surrounding an open fountain which was lit from above by a reasonable facsimile of brilliant sunlight. Reflections spilled off the water and danced in the surrounding gloom, showing the surface and apparent texture of marble wherever they fell. Beyond the pillars in the 'outdoor' area Marius had apparently been dining, for there was a low table with cushions scattered around it by the fountain and on it were a number of crude, heavy-looking dishes and flagons.

Marius led them through to the open atrium and offered them a seat. Apparently, this meant the floor. Randall said, 'Valum suggested that you might feel a need for conversation. She particularly suggested that we should solicit your views on the forthcoming operation.'

'All that kind of thing,' Lobo said helpfully.

'But Valum already knows my views,' Marius protested. 'I'd be more interested in yours.'

They were in a bad position. The bright light overhead made it impossible to see any detail in the shaded portico and the rattle of running water effectively covered any slight sound. Marius might have an army waiting out there as far as Randall could see. 'We've been specially chosen for our ignorance and interest,' he said. 'We're your audience, councillor. Instruct us in whatever you will.'

'If that's the case,' Marius said, waving a negligent hand, 'let's forget about the operation. I've talked about nothing else all through the debriefing and it bores me. Tell me what you think about the chambers, instead. Valum had them laid out and decorated according to my own design. It's a private fantasy of mine, you see, the Sultan in his palace.'

Randall didn't like it. He wasn't getting any control of the situation this way. He was tempted to jump on Marius, to gamble that there were no extra defences hidden around them. Lobo shifted nervously next to him, but all Randall said was, 'It's very impressive.'

Marius moved around by the fountain and indicated the table next to them. 'Feel the weight of one of those plates.' Did something stir beyond the opposite archway? 'Solid gold, all the tableware.'

'A residence fit for a prince, councillor.' This was ridiculous. They were making small talk when they needed action. Come on, Randall thought, there's nobody there. Grab him and get on with it.

'That's not all there is,' Marius went on. 'What's a prince without his harem?' And he clapped his hands twice.

The shadows into which Randall had been imagining life now responded, moving and assuming full substance as they came into the light, one to each archway of the portico around them. They stepped into the atrium and waited, a deformed gallery of horrors.

'They're the early test models of the simulacra,' Marius explained, touching one of them affectionately before moving on to the next. 'They're rough and simple and they can only obey direct commands. They're of no use to the operation, so Valum gave them to me for my entertainment. I call them my marionettes.' He clapped his hands again and the marionettes moved forward another step. He called for them to stop, and they froze in the act of moving again and subsided to a regular stance. Marius grinned broadly. 'In such obedience is true beauty. For such compliance I can forgive their rough-hewn lack of grace.'

Randall counted six of them altogether, forming a semicircle around Marius on the opposite side of the courtyard. As broken dolls they would be innocuous, but as moving human facsimiles they were a series of terrifying disasters. They were like animate corpses, some with whole sections rotted away. Limbs were unfinished or incomplete and one of them had no abdomen, just a rigid spinal brace and a handful of wet-looking tubes between thorax and hips. Randall heard Lobo swallowing hard beside him.

'I can have them sing, or dance, or make whatever music I choose,' Marius was saying. 'When I speak they listen and applaud.' He turned to the nearest of them. 'What is your one desire?'

'To serve you, Marius,' all six chorused in a flat monotone.

'And why?'

'Because we love you, Marius.'

Marius spread his arms, the demonstration complete. 'Who could ask for a more faithful and adoring retinue?'

'We would gladly die for you, Marius,' the marionettes said without a trace of spontaneity.

'Turn your heads,' Marius instructed. 'See the two men by the table.' Six heads motored around in unison. 'They mean me harm. If either of them approaches my person, you are to take them and break them. Is that understood?'

'Yes, Marius.'

'What are you talking about?' Randall demanded. 'What is this?'

Marius laughed, safe inside his ring of gruesome protectors. 'Do you think me such a fool, Randall? I don't know how you got out, but Valum told me you were on board. Didn't it even occur to you that I might recognize you?'

It hadn't. 'But we've never met.'

'I watched you being boxed! I gave the order for the crate to be nailed up and loaded for transportation to the Ice Palace! Sent to offer me conversation, indeed.' He indicated Lobo. 'I doubt whether your friend can even string two words together.'

'What are you going to do?' Randall said quietly.

'For the moment, I need do nothing. My children are my

guardians. Don't be misled by the way they look, or because they're slow and clumsy. Move towards me and they'll kill you, whether you reach me or not.'

'They don't look so dangerous to me,' Lobo said stubbornly.

Marius reacted with exaggerated surprise. 'It speaks! If you doubt me, try it, ape.'

'Don't try it, Lobo. I think he's telling the truth.'

Marius was revelling in his advantage. 'Listen to your friend,' he told Lobo. 'He's slightly less stupid than you. I've given a command which can only be over-ridden by myself or one of the simulacra. And I've got no intention of countermanding it.'

'We got nowhere,' Lobo muttered bitterly, mainly to himself. 'We're still prisoners. Same as in the cell, same as on the ice.'

'You can give me the satisfaction of envy and admiration before I consign you to whatever unpleasantness lies in your future,' Marius went on. 'You'll be privileged to witness the skills of my marionettes in the ballet. Come, children. Are you ready to perform for the damned?'

'Always ready to serve you, Marius,' the marionettes replied in the same dead tone.

He called for music. One of the marionettes detached itself from the group and walked unevenly over to sit on the raised lip which contained the water around the fountain. There it started to slap its knee, irregularly at first but building up to a rhythm, skipping occasional beats but then hurrying to fit in an extra one. The marionette's mouth opened to a black O, soundless at first but then making a tuneless keening sound like the wind through the broken windows of an old house. Others of the marionettes joined in with no regard for harmony, adding their own pitches and moans. As the dissonance fought in the air around them two of the creatures ambled forward into the middle of the courtyard. Although they were obviously sexless one of them had been given long, dry hair in yellow plaits, the mask of a face painted with carmine lips and cheeks. Marius moved out of the way as they struck angular poses facing one another, and it seemed to Randall that he looked upon them with genuine pride.

Lobo wouldn't look, lowering his eyes as the grotesque figures stepped and chopped around each other. Randall tried to catch his attention, but he wouldn't respond. Only when Randall nudged the table with his knee, scraping it a fraction on the hard floor, did Lobo come out of his desperate trance. He looked straight at Randall, avoiding the scene before them. The noise was loud and oppressive, growing all the time and Randall stared hard at the gold plate a few inches from Lobo's hand on the table.

'I hope you'll remember this, Randall,' Marius shouted, barely making himself heard over the wailing and slapping. 'Remember it for the rest of your short life.'

There was confusion on Lobo's face. Randall wondered how explicit he could afford to be. A glance from Marius would give him away. He stared pointedly at the plate again. Lobo saw it, gave an imperceptible nod. Then Randall raised his hand to his throat, touching it lightly as if in need of air and then his eyes shifted deliberately to where Marius was observing the rising tempo of the dance, clapping his hands and laughing loudly when the postures of the androgynous figures gave the remotest suggestion of anything lewd or suggestive. He glanced their way and Randall forced an appreciative smile.

Marius perceived his discomfort and laughed even louder. It was as if the whole scene were a huge joke that only he understood and he threw back his head and added his roar to the marionettes' ugly crescendo.

Lobo came up, halfway over the table to get his balance. He swept up the plate as he rose, drawing back his arm to test its weight and pausing for only a fraction of a second to take aim before loosing it in a long and graceful discus throw to sail across the room towards Marius.

The song of the marionettes was a sudden and empty silence in which Randall could actually hear the rush of the plate as it flew. Marius realized that something was wrong, but too late. The plate hit his neck with a dull smack, lodging in the deep groove that it cut across his windpipe and staying there as he dropped slowly backwards onto the floor. He hit like a sack and the plate clattered away.

Six blank faces were turned towards them for the second time. Lobo was still crouched on the table, empty-handed.

'Back off,' Randall advised him. 'They won't touch us as long as we don't actually approach Marius. He wasn't literal enough.'

Lobo climbed down slowly off the table and the marionettes

made no move towards them. They simply stared and then the one with no stomach looked down at Marius's still form, as if trying without success to see the connection.

'What do we do now, Marius?' it faltered, and the others joined in with 'What now, Marius?'

'Walking corpses,' Lobo said with undisguised disgust.

'That's what we'll be, if we don't get out of here. We can forget Marius for a hostage.' Blood was slowly starting to pool under the councillor's body, a seemingly impossible volume. Randall paused to inspect his reaction to Marius's death and found, with faint surprise, that he felt nothing at all – no guilt, no sickness, no horror. He hadn't expected to feel anything for Pearson, but surely this ought to be different, he thought. But it wasn't.

The marionettes pestered on for a minute or so and then fell silent. Randall led the way back to the entrance in a wide arc, careful not to appear to be approaching Marius's body. True to the letter of their instruction, the marionettes left them alone.

It was so dark in the shaded area that it was difficult to locate the door. At the first attempt Randall found a blank wall.

'This is a dead ship,' a strange voice came from the black and golden twilight behind them. 'You could roam over it forever and find nothing of value.'

Both Randall and Lobo turned at the same time, backing up to get the defensive certainty of the wall behind them and looking desperately around, minds trying to squeeze detail from insufficient light.

He stepped forward, a slight but dignified figure thrown into silhouette against the brightness of an archway, and whilst his face was in shadow his pale eyes burned as if lit from within.

Lobo was underbelly, well versed in its mythologies. 'It's Morden!' he hissed. 'Hostage, Randall!'

Morden was joined by another, taller and with a grey death-mask of a face. He moved to Morden's shoulder and waited there protectively. 'I assume Marius is dead,' Morden said to the one behind him. 'Is that right?'

'His head's nearly off,' Rorvik confirmed.

'I wish we'd arrived sooner. I'd have liked more time to consider.'

'Save us more speeches,' Randall said loudly, bitter at the

way in which setback seemed to be the inevitable partner of success. 'Turn us over to Valum and have done with it. Or else – ' he indicated Rorvik – 'give the job to the robot. It's his speciality.'

'I never gave you away, Randall,' Rorvik said. 'Valum saw the guilt in me. She only let you run to give the simulacra some sport.'

'What does it matter?' Lobo mumbled, barely audible. 'Turn wherever we like, we're dead.'

'Listen to me,' Morden said with an urgent sincerity that seemed to belie his position as their captor. 'The Wekk are poised to mobilize as soon as the field tests are finished on their simulacrum ground commander. Once they've made their move they can't be stopped.'

'Proud moment for you,' said Randall, becoming less sure of what was supposed to be going on.

'Drop the bitter pose, Randall, it's holding us up. Some time soon they're going to find out, as Rorvik did for me, that you've wrecked the Pearson model and escaped. Then there'll be another sweep operation and you'll be gathered in as easily as the last time. I won't be able to help you then.'

Randall was about to frame his reply when Morden turned and moved back towards the open area with Rorvik following. Neither seemed to be regarding them as a threat, and Randall was mildly insulted. 'What kind of help can I expect now?' he shouted after them. 'All I see is a turncoat councillor and a robot too dim to follow its own train of thought.'

'Throw me all the insults you like,' Rorvik called over his shoulder as he guided Morden through this new territory with a light touch on the elbow. 'They can't touch me now.'

Morden settled on cushions on the far side of the arches. Randall and Lobo were still in tense and expectant crouches against the wall, starting to feel rather foolish. Lobo straightened first and Randall shrugged and did the same. They went over to join Morden, carefully keeping their distance from the marionettes who were now mute and immobile.

'I don't have time to argue with you, Randall,' Morden said as he heard them approach, 'and you don't have any choice but to believe me. As your friend said, turn any other way and you're dead. To begin with, I'm no traitor. I've been working with the full agreement of Chandler to uncover Marius and look for a weakness in the proposed operation. Until this last few hours it seemed that I was riding a tiger that I couldn't hope to dismount. Then I met Rorvik and he told me you were aboard; and I've since found out that neither Marius nor I were here for the sole purpose of a debriefing. We're here to be patterned and then they intend to kill us. In Marius's case you've beaten them to it.'

'If that's true,' Randall said carefully, 'and I'm not saying I think it is, then you're a fool to trust Rorvik. He's got no loyalty of any kind.'

Rorvik spoke for himself, surprising Randall with his hitherto undisplayed self-possession. 'None that you could inspire, Randall. You grudgingly allowed me the use of somebody else's name. What did you really expect in return?'

'Don't be ridiculous,' Randall told him. 'You don't swap philosophies with a machine.'

Rorvik's eyes narrowed, grey skin stretching smoothly and without a wrinkle into the first expression that Randall or Lobo had seen him assume. 'This is as far as we go, Morden,' he said. 'I'll trust Lobo. But if you want me to help you proceed, Randall's out.'

Lobo seemed to take a renewed interest at the mention of his name – so far in the conversation he'd merely been somebody to stand behind Randall and make the numbers up – and Morden said with genuine concern, 'Please, Rorvik. We need Randall.'

'Am I supposed to believe what I'm hearing?' Randall broke in. 'That's an alien machine you're talking to!'

'That's where you're wrong,' Rorvik said with firmness, 'and it's the price of your inclusion from now on. I'm not trading favours for a name any more. You've got to recognize me as a man.'

Randall looked at him, the sheer manufactured inhumanity of him, and was lost for words. Consider this monster on equal terms with a man, accord him the same deference and sympathy that he would give to any colleague or citizen? Surely it was a joke.

'I suggest you take Rorvik seriously,' Morden advised. 'I'm prepared to let him have his own way on this.'

Amusement was replaced by obvious disbelief. Lobo made his first real contribution, overcoming the irrational shyness he seemed to feel in unfamiliar company. 'Does it really matter what he is or isn't?' he said. 'It's what he *thinks* that matters. That's what he wants recognition for.'

'Birdseed,' Randall snorted. 'A tin man's a tin man, and all the self-delusion in the world won't change it.'

'There's hardly any metal in me,' Rorvik pointed out reasonably. 'I'm as real as you are.'

All three of them were looking at Randall. He was the outsider of the group when he was used to being the leader and it made him uncomfortable. Lobo had been invited and absorbed into the Morden-Rorvik camp before Randall was even sure that he accepted Morden's story as genuine. But where was the advantage if it wasn't?

'I don't understand what you want with me,' he said in exasperation. 'I can't manufacture an attitude and pull it on like a snow suit.'

'I don't expect you to,' Rorvik said. 'But you start by treating me as an equal, however much it goes against the grain. Think before you speak and if the truth doesn't come out right, lie to me. I'll meet you halfway and pretend to believe it. In the end we'll have made a new truth, just by trying.'

Randall shook his head sorrowfully. 'That's tin logic for you.'

'Start by apologizing for that.'

He couldn't delude himself as Rorvik seemed to want, but on the other hand they were offering him a formula for coexistence – as long as he didn't slip up in a moment of inattention and send Rorvik off into a tantrum that would probably be the ugly counterpart of his strange and new-found confidence.

'All right,' he said, 'I apologize, Rorvik. Is that what you want?'

'It will do as a beginning.'

They might as well go along with Morden's story. If they were going to die anyway, the worst they could do would be to make fools of themselves. As it stood, the three of them – no, damn it, *four* of them – were probably the city's only hope.

'We've got to make a strike at the heart of the operation,' Morden said, obviously pleased that the internal conflict of his group seemed to have been resolved. 'And it'll have to be fast.'

'It will also have to be a miracle,' said Randall, ruffled by the way that this blind underbelly upstart was assuming the leadership of the party. 'We lack even the most basic strategic information.'

'Not any more,' Morden said with a hint of smugness. 'Tell him, Rorvik.'

'They've finished with the shuttle and sealed it into the vacuum dock as a safeguard against any escape attempts from what they call bloodbags. Because I'm simulacrum I don't need an atmosphere and I let myself in through an airlock. I stripped out some of the shuttle's panelling and linked myself into the navigation hookup. Through that I was able to draw information from the banks in the Wekk's main computers; specifically, I got details of the ship layout and the search programmes. When I left the dock I jammed the airlock door. The air should bleed in and slowly bring it up to pressure.

'We can use the shuttle if we have to. I'm sure I can use the links to over-ride the automatics. The main thing I discovered is that we're not on the Wekk ship.'

Randall looked blank. Lobo said, 'Then where the hell are we?'

'We're on board a derelict. It's being towed behind the real Wekk ship.'

It explained the apparent desertion, the general run-down quality of the World Ship. 'But why?' Randall asked.

'Number one, they outgrew this vessel generations ago. Two, they never waste anything. Like any stable civilization they're expanding, but where can they go? It's part of the survival pattern to accumulate processed materials and build bigger ships. From this one they raided systems and built their present world; now they have this one in tow and another, even bigger world under construction at the other end of the chain.'

Randall tried to imagine the scale of it. He guessed that the World Ship was about a ten-mile cylinder, but to attempt to visualize a much larger ship towing it between stars whilst a colossus took shape ahead was beyond him. 'It's staggering,' he said.

'You should see it from outside,' Rorvik told him. 'They'll strip this ship out to fit the new one before they move into it and then the whole process will begin again. They use the derelicts as exercise grounds for the simulacra.'

'The prisons just get bigger,' Lobo said gloomily.

'I don't really see what we can achieve in an abandoned hulk,' Morden said doubtfully.

Randall's mind was turning over at high speed. So Morden didn't have anything definite in mind. He was Élite, the fastest and best-suited of any of them for leadership, but then you couldn't expect a robot and a couple of underbelly hicks to acknowledge it without being pushed. Lobo was already looking at Morden with a peculiar reverence and Randall knew that he wouldn't be able to depend on his automatic vote in a division. It was up to him to come up with a workable set of propositions – never mind how likely, he could make changes as he went along – and to come up with them first.

'We all know how long it takes to move between systems,' he said. 'What kind of timescale's involved?'

Rorvik didn't know. 'They sleep between systems and the ship does all the work. The subjective timescale's meaningless.'

'It's thirty years from here to the nearest star and that assumes you've chosen it as a destination. If you're only cruising, fishing for traces, you'd have to think in terms of thousands, or even hundreds of thousands of years. The ship on the other end of the line must have one hell of a finely balanced ecology. What would it take to tip it over?'

'You're talking about genocide?' Morden said, obviously interested.

'I'm talking about survival. How's the ship powered?'

'Conversion of radiant energy,' Rorvik replied promptly. 'Solar power.' Obviously nuclear power was out of the question, for when the Wekk revived there would be a distinct possibility that the isotopes would have degenerated into lead blocks. They only needed power when they were in a star system and ready to exploit; in between stars they were hibernating and conserving. Only when near to a sun would the ship wake up.

'Who's running the show?' Lobo asked. 'The Wekk or the ship?'

'The ship,' Rorvik said without any hesitation. 'Definitely the ship.'

Morden hadn't quite grasped the purpose of Lobo's question. 'What does that mean?'

'The ship's programming is so elaborate that the Wekk only

have to do as they're told. How would you like having to fall out of your bunk after a thousand years and immediately have to gear up for industrial production?'

It occurred to Morden that the Wekk were somehow incidental to the process, mere instruments in the World Ship's animalistic drive to reproduce itself by whatever means were available to it. But he didn't raise the idea, preferring to suggest that Pearson might soon be discovered and shouldn't they be moving?

'Not yet,' Randall said. 'Not until we've got some kind of purpose.'

'Fancy name for one of your plans,' grumbled Lobo, who had seen the signs before.

'All right, so it's true. Every time we've moved so far it's been without a real long-term design and look what's happened to us.'

'Deeper in the crap with every step.'

'Right.' Randall turned to Morden. 'You say you need me. You're right, but you've got to let me lead. My main value is that I'm Elite and I can't handle it any other way.'

'Think hard before you answer,' Lobo warned.

Morden shrugged. 'What choice do I have?' And besides, it was exactly what he'd wanted.

Rorvik was bursting with the data that he'd drawn from the shuttle and although it wasn't permanent knowledge, Randall would only have to indicate a subject for him to be able to deliver a concise summary of almost any aspect of the ship's construction and operation. The power source didn't seem to be of much use to them unless they could turn off the sun – a little too drastic, as Morden commented. Randall asked about propulsion.

'Pretty weak,' Rorvik said after only a moment's reflection. 'They hardly have to worry about escape velocities because they never enter a close orbit. Manoeuvring's slow because of the ship's mass. Like everything else there's no central point we can strike at.'

Randall wouldn't accept this. 'There's got to be. What about the strategic centres?'

'They *are* concentrated,' Rorvik admitted. 'They're also in the middle of a heavily defended area. Wekk quarters are all around it.'

Morden was becoming uncomfortable. He recognized the

necessity for discussion and preparation, but he would have been happier if they'd taken place in some less hazardous locale. After all, the shuttle was likely to be instrumental in any plan they made against the inhabited World Ship that had them in tow and it presently lay in a vacuum dock on the far side of the area most heavily populated by the simulacra. If Pearson were to be discovered soon it would be impassable. Randall was asking about the Wekk and their hibernation.

Rorvik explained that when the ship had got what it wanted, it moved on. 'Far enough from the sun the power cuts out and the temperature starts dropping straight away. As far as I can see it's completely automatic and they've no control over it.'

'Same as in the Ice Palace,' Lobo remarked with rare perspicacity.

'In which case,' Morden said, returning to his earlier idea, 'the Wekk are prisoners rather than conquerors. The *ship's* the real enemy.'

A low and distant howl took everybody by surprise. Randall thought at first that it must be one of the marionettes, but Rorvik said, 'That's the signal for a sweep exercise. They must have found Pearson. We've got seconds at the most before they start looking.'

Morden's fear had been realized. During all the talk, the opportunity for action had been slipping away.

'I'm getting an idea,' Randall said, 'but I'm going to need more details. Can we get to the shuttle? And if we do, can we use it to leave this ship?'

Rorvik was helping Morden to his feet. 'I told you, I think I can over-ride the automatics. But the marionettes have got armed cruisers which are much faster.'

'That doesn't matter,' Randall said, almost slyly.

'Try saying that when you're so much debris,' Lobo complained.

Randall seemed to have an idea, but wasn't giving much away. 'As long as it buys us time and gets us out of Valum's reach.'

'You can reach a long way with a laser.'

'You'd rather be patterned and strangled?'

'I'd rather be home.'

Randall, for once, wasn't inclined to argue. The simulacra

would be deploying into their irresistible search pattern at that very moment and there wasn't much time for what he had in mind.

Twenty

Pearson had, indeed, been found and Valum was preparing to join the search operation when Moskie brought her a message that the Wekk wanted to speak to her direct. For a moment her usual coldness seemed to give way to irritation, but she quickly mastered it and returned to her command post, leaving Moskie in temporary charge.

The post was a mess, an assembly of odd-looking instruments and communications circuits stuffed with wires and printed wafers in filigree blocks. All this was housed in a semicircular framework in a room obviously designed for something else and it was Valum's undisputed territory – at least, she would say with adequate reverence, until the ground commander comes along.

There were no controls, no switches. She ran her long, slim hands across the upper surface of the console, sensing as certain of the circuits quivered in response; she homed in on these, interfacing with them as only a simulacrum could and directing the flow of her thoughts into sympathetic resonance with them. The voice of the Wekk formed in her mind, strong and kind and everything she could admire.

'*Pearson is wrecked*,' the Wekk said bluntly.

'That's right, but the situation's in hand.'

'*We have to trust your capabilities. How did it happen?*'

'He was stupid, and he was tricked. There's no need for you to worry.'

'*No doubt. The ship respects your abilities, Valum, but beware of Randall.*'

'?'

'*He's shown himself dangerous, and our affairs are in a delicate state. Pearson will regenerate himself, given time, but further hindrances are unthinkable.*'

'Do you want Randall killed or patterned?'

'*Killed. Definitely killed.*'

'I'll do it myself. It will give me pleasure.'

'*You are cold, Valum. It does you great credit.*'

'Thank you.'

'*Do you have no worries at the idea of exploiting your parent race?*'

'Simulacra owe nothing to bloodbags. We're loyal to the Wekk.'

'*Serve the ship, then, and return to your search. Do not fail.*'

'Do we ever?'

Moskie had deployed the simulacra according to a predetermined pattern. This wouldn't be a simple sweep operation, as they would have to search far beyond the open corridors known as the Tin Jungle. The simulacra were spread thinly, every third corridor on alternate levels and moving at a carefully prescribed speed; they would be listening for steps and noises that were out of synchronization with their own and which would betray their quarry. Each carried a small transmitter, with radio silence to be broken only when the prey was detected.

There as a gap in the pattern caused by Pearson's absence, but there was also a new man to fill it. Moskie called him over and asked his name.

'My name's Willis,' the new man replied.

'You know what we're doing here?'

Willis nodded. 'I think so.'

'We're hunting some men. Does the idea bother you?'

'No.'

Valum came through on all their receivers to give them a small pep-talk about these rebellious throwbacks who were threatening the grand design. Were there any questions before the operation, she said, and Moskie wondered if they were being thorough enough – after all, the runaways could be anywhere in the ship by now and its overall volume was immense.

'Let them run far and give us sport,' was Valum's reply and the hunt was on.

There was confusion at the back of Willis's mind, held in check by a series of blocks and inhibitions over which he had no voluntary control. He had all of Willis's memories along with a new body of knowledge which he had no recollection of acquiring and which was guiding him with unhesitating confidence alone into the area allotted to him to search. He knew he wasn't the original Willis; he was a better, improved Willis, a privileged superman amongst equals. At the centre of his new knowledge was a harp of loyalty and love that vibrated in sympathy with his every thought, a continuous flow of devotion towards the Wekk and the grand design. He found it irritating, but no doubt he would get used to it.

He thought of the overall layout of the ship, tried to visualize the chunk that he would be covering. They were sweeping gradually inwards, rising through the three cylindrical levels to emerge finally in the great open area at the heart of the ship. If Randall and Lobo made it so far their access to the rest of the ship could then be cut off, but the likelihood was that they would be picked up long before that became necessary.

Willis examined his feelings with detached interest. For Randall and Lobo, he found he had none. Nothing at all, except a mild enthusiasm for their destruction. How odd, he thought, but on the other hand, how natural.

He was entirely on his own now, pacing to some internal metronome, his keener hearing picking up a matching beat from his fellows in the corridors around and above him. It was a comforting, inhuman sound, the steady tramp of an inexorable fighting machine.

He paused for a moment, careful to stop in mid-stride so as not to confuse the others. He thought he'd heard a random scrabbling somewhere, but he couldn't be sure. He waited, but it didn't come again.

It was probably nothing. It was, after all, his first operation, and he was perhaps letting his novice's enthusiasm sway him into pouncing on the slightest evidence. Much as he wanted to succeed, he didn't want to look a fool. He moved on.

It took a while to cover the lowest level. It was the largest part of the wedge-shaped sector that had been assigned to him and it included a number of stockroom-type areas with free access as well as a couple of miles of grimy corridor. Left alone, all the dirt and dust in the ship made its way to these areas, stirred by the gentle coriolis winds and carried outwards by centrifugal force, that fallacious effect which nevertheless gives a competent illusion of gravity.

He checked everywhere, unable to hurry in case his footsteps gave a misleading echo to any of the other simulacra. If he stopped and closed his eyes to concentrate he found that he could actually build up a sound-picture of the ship around him, perceiving its depths and planes exactly in a way that his former self would have considered as improbable and superhuman. Twice more he thought he heard the non-synchronous stumbling that would give the bloodbags away and once he heard others stop as well. For a while the whole sector was silent, but the noises didn't recur. Slowly, the search started up again.

The next level was cleaner and laid out to a completely different plan; small empty rooms which had once held Wekk hibernation chambers, each now stripped bare apart from the low shelf on which the hibernation tank had stood. Pearson had been wrecked by the use of such a shelf, Willis reminded himself; although he'd never known the simulacrum Pearson, Willis automatically included him in the numbers for whom he felt a programmed fellowship.

Damn it, this time he *had* heard something, close and somewhere over his head, the next level inward. If it was the bloodbags they were right in the middle of his sector. A gift!

Now he could hear them plainly – three, maybe four people, moving uncertainly in a group. Their footsteps were soft, due, no doubt, to the lesser gravity which prevailed on the upper/inner levels. With luck Willis would be the only one to have detected them.

The kill wouldn't be his – Valum had reserved that for herself – but the glory would be. As soon as he was sure he lifted his transmitter and broadcast, 'Willis here. I've got a signal.'

All movement elsewhere stopped, with the exception of the scuffling above. His receiver crackled and Valum said, 'Well done, Willis. Where are you?'

He was at a loss for a moment, until he remembered that the World Ship was mapped out by some peculiar Wekk grid reference. His new memories didn't include the details, but he knew enough to go along to the nearest junction and look for some kind of symbol stencilled on the wall. He found one, faded and barely distinguishable, a reversed 'S' followed by three lines on their sides. He reported this, and said that as far as he could tell the quarry was directly above.

Some of the other simulacra came on the air, confirming Willis's report. Valum said, 'All right, Willis, you can start to follow, but slowly. I want everybody else to get themselves up to the third level.'

'They're coming through clearer,' Willis added. 'I think there are at least four of them.'

'Four?' Moskie sounded perplexed. 'There were only two bloodbags left alive.'

'Four if you include the councillors,' Valum corrected him. 'I'm coming up. Nobody approach them until I get there; just form a circle around them and block all the escape routes, but try not to let them know they're trapped yet. Moskie, go and see if either of the councillors is missing.'

Moskie acknowledged the order, and then the radio was silent as the simulacra started to converge. Determined not to find himself pushed to the back of the crowd Willis made for the nearest spiral between levels.

The simulacra were gathered by a symbol which was like a '6' on its side followed by the same three identifying strokes that he had seen below. Valum arrived a couple of minutes later. If she'd been running she was unruffled by the effort and she allowed herself a brief smile when she saw that the bloodbags had inadvertently wandered into a dead end.

All the radios came alive at once as Moskie reported, 'Morden's gone, Marius is dead. Does that mean one of us is moving with them?'

'No, not one of us,' Valum replied grimly. 'Rorvik. There's only him sufficiently stupid. I'll wreck him after I've killed Randall.' She turned to address the waiting group. 'I'm going in alone. The rest of you stand ready for if you're needed. Which of you is Willis?'

Willis stepped forward, and Valum nodded her approval of his efforts. 'Come with me and cover me, Willis. But don't try to interfere without an instruction. Understand?'

'Yes, Valum,' said Willis, in awe of the honour.

'There's something else, Valum,' Moskie's voice came, 'but I'm not sure that it's important.'

'Leave it, then,' Valum said, and gestured Willis to follow her. The rest of the simulacra – they were growing considerably in numbers as those from the farthest sectors arrived – followed a short distance after, a little disappointed to be mere spectators but still eager for the show.

It was a long passageway with several sharp turns but no exit, and their prey had gone to ground at the far end. Whilst Willis looked forward to seeing Valum, the best of her kind, in action, he secretly hoped that he would be called in to assist.

Perhaps he could impress her, save her, earn her gratitude. Now where the hell had that thought floated up from?

Valum raised a hand as they reached the last turn in the corridor, and the group stopped. There was no sound from ahead, and the simulacra waited with pleasurable tension. Valum unhooked her radio – a potential encumbrance – and tossed it to somebody. Willis hopefully did the same, and the two of them advanced alone.

Willis tracked sideways behind Valum, eyes fixed on the corridor's end as it came into view. She was unhurried, ready for anything. There were four figures in a huddled group against the back wall, four heads which turned to stare, four uncomprehending pairs of eyes which came to rest on them.

'Orders, Valum?' the first marionette said, and the others started to join in. 'Our one desire is to serve.'

For a moment Valum seemed to be dumbstruck, a new experience for her. The simulacra, realizing something was wrong, came shuffling around to take a look. She held out her hand and somebody put her radio into it.

'Moskie!'

'Yes, Valum?'

'What was it that you didn't think was important?'

'Four of the marionettes are missing, Valum.'

'Moskie, you're a fool and I'm an even bigger one.'

'You said we should let the bloodbags run far and give us sport,' Moskie pointed out.

'Shut up, Moskie,' said Valum.

Rorvik was testing each of the shuttle's systems in turn, feeling their responses as they started to warm and power up. He wasn't simply preparing to fly the shuttle, he was *becoming* the shuttle – a machine/machine interface that he wasn't very proud of, but this was no time for the niceties of definition. Morden waited, strapped into one of the couches at the back of the bridge, quietly dreading his second experience of weightlessness. Randall was being very mysterious, refusing to reveal his intentions (perhaps because at this stage he wasn't certain as to what they were) and probing around the levels to find the abandoned helmets and the bolt-spanner, whilst Lobo was resealing the airlock door from the inside.

They were fairly confident that the marionettes would not betray them; after all, it's difficult to extract information from a machine which has been told to forget. Nevertheless it would only take the simplest deduction to lead Valum to them and the time available for their escape was limited. Once they were out of the World Ship, the simulacra had fast cruisers which could follow and overhaul their own craft.

To Rorvik it felt as if his body was growing and expanding, changing in shape and composition to become that of a creature adapted to a different element. Its sensory systems became his own, feeding back information which would allow him to judge and execute every move with precision. He could feel and hear Randall climbing in the access tunnel and he was aware of Lobo entering the ship through the cargo hold. The correct impulse and the hatch lifted and sealed behind him.

Randall arrived on the bridge and was surprised to find that Rorvik wasn't there. He was about to comment when the shutters on the outside windows rolled back and the ugly blue light from the dock spilled in.

'I'll want you to watch the airlocks for me,' Rorvik called out. Randall stepped through the open door at the other end of the bridge to see that Rorvik was crouching over the featureless box to which the shuttle's console was wired, except that now it wasn't featureless; one side had been removed, and Rorvik had his hands deep in the works. He'd tied himself down with a makeshift web of straps so that he wouldn't float free when they were away from the World Ship's spin.

Randall answered that he would, but Rorvik seemed to be only half-aware, sunk into a different perception of reality that was being fed to him through the shuttle's box. He turned and stepped back on to the bridge as Lobo arrived. Randall explained Rorvik's request and then they both got into the observer's seats at either end of the panoramic window. Lobo was even less talkative than usual as he buckled in. He'd confessed that he was troubled by the thought that he might not recognize a Wekk if he saw one. Randall had pointed out that the World Ship had been built for bodies similar to their own, although slightly smaller; that the doors, stairs and ladders were similar to the types that they already knew; that the Wekk breathed a similar mix of air to themselves, and that they had similar survival drives...

'And a damn big ship that tells them what to do,' Lobo had interrupted. 'You make them sound so much like us, I'm not sure I'd be able to tell us apart.'

Reptiles, Rorvik had explained as they'd covered the last few yards of corridor and let themselves into the dock; by human standards, the Wekk resembled child-sized reptiles. They were cold-blooded and scaly, their temperature following that of their surroundings with a threshold below which the hibernation pattern was triggered. Lobo had to be content with this description as they now had to scout the bay and, finding it empty, board the shuttle.

The view from the bridge was restricted, a steep angle down to the raised gallery from which an attack might come. The shuttle itself was like a fat and elongated saucer with the immense bulge of the drive at its rear and there would be very little clearance as it backed out of the dock. Lobo couldn't see much more than blank wall on his side, but Randall reported that he had a reasonable view of the inner doors of the airlocks.

'Any sign of the simulacra?' Rorvik called through.

Randall was about to say no when a slight movement caught his eye. The inner wheel on one of the locks was starting to turn and he informed Mitchell.

Rorvik wasn't happy. Although he was confident that he could control the shuttle he couldn't find the channels through which the dock opened to space, so the ship was fired up and hot with nowhere to go.

'Hang on tight,' he warned everybody. 'I'm sending the emergency signal to blow the outer bay doors into vacuum.'

'Should make a nice display,' Lobo commented.

The deck beneath them shuddered as they lifted, and the frame shook with a hollow bang from somewhere behind. Looking down into the dock Randall saw the airlock door suddenly fly open and crash back against the bulkhead, half a dozen figures tumbling out in an irresistible stream to pour towards and around the shuttle, impacting on the hull and then sliding on around the back towards open space. Some of them were shouting soundlessly, the only noise a thin wail that ended abruptly as the dock evacuated; and then they were all gone, flushed out with the last of the air.

'One of the bodies hit the forward sensors,' Rorvik shouted desperately. 'I can't see the way out!'

Already they were sliding back, the walls of the dock passing in silence. Randall pressed against his window, trying to see enough to give Rorvik some information. But what would be useful?

Lobo called that they were veering, the wall on his side coming closer and after a few seconds Randall was able to confirm this. Rorvik made a correction but went too far, the dock sliding across their horizon and ending in a jarring impact that resonated through the hull. He managed to correct the resulting wobble but was still backing off-centre and now most of the dock was empty ahead of them and they were wrapped in shadow. As its edge fell across the bridge Randall looked up and around, seeing nothing more spectacular than ridges and piping in bare metal – then the ship dropped away beneath him.

Of course, open space was below the floor of the dock, not beyond its back wall as he'd unconsciously expected. After the doors had blown they'd been backing into a recess on the outer skin of the World Ship and once past the portal they'd simply dropped away and out of the influence of the World Ship's artificial gravity. He fought his nausea and looked out as the densely-featured cylinder rolled by, completely filling his horizon but already receding.

He heard Lobo gasp and tried to turn and see what was wrong. The straps restricted him, but he managed a kind of half-twist. The World Ship completely filled the far window as well, with the added definition of sparkle and shadow from its sunward side on the flat peaks and valleys of its unnatural geography. Then there was an urgent throb of power from the ship's drive and they began to turn in relation to it, the sharp rim of space and stars rotating as it came into view. Rorvik was flipping them over and cancelling the inertia that they'd carried when they left the dock and the rate of the World Ship's rotation seemed to increase in consequence.

Then Randall saw what it was that had startled Lobo. He could now sight along the cylinder to the next World Ship, an even more massive construction which turned in perfect synchronization without any obvious connection to the vessel from which they were escaping; and then beyond that, impossibly distant and impossibly huge, the glinting spidery network of a third world, stars flickering through the complexities of its structure.

It was awesome, splendid, and chillingly ugly. Rorvik took them in a wide loop up and away from the World Ship, crossing first between the raider and the sun and then between the raider and the dull brown-blue planet beneath.

They had taken some damage when they'd reversed blind out of the dock, but Rorvik couldn't tell how much. In any case, it was probably academic; at this moment Valum was probably getting her fast cruisers mobilized.

Randall loosened his straps and drifted from his couch, motioning to Lobo to do the same as he pushed himself over towards the doorway and Rorvik. The grey simulacrum turned to him, eyes barely focussed.

'Try to get us in some kind of orbit for the next few minutes,' Randall instructed him. 'I think I've worked out a way to get us back on to the World Ship without Valum knowing about it. If I'm right she'll be following an empty shuttle while we get the run of the base.'

There was, for a short while after the disaster of the airlock, some confusion on the World Ship in the corridors around the dock. It was a random and inefficient way to behave and Valum quickly had it stopped.

'How many have we lost?' she demanded.

'Five,' somebody told her, 'including Moskie.'

It hardly seemed possible, but her manner hardened even more. 'I don't know how they got that shuttle moving,' she said, 'but it's going to be their coffin. Everybody to the cruisers for target practice. You, Willis.'

She pointed and Willis broke free of the dispersing crowd and approached her. 'Take Moskie's place,' she told him. 'That means you follow me round and do as you're told. All right?'

'Yes, Valum.'

'And try to be a better machine than Moskie was.'

'Yes, Valum.'

As it turned out, Randall's instruction to Rorvik had been superfluous. Because of the damage that the sensors had taken it wasn't possible to set a course, nor could he even with confidence take them away from the weak attraction of the World Ship; all the navigational information was safe in his head, but he couldn't use any of it without the feedback that the sensors were supposed to provide. If Valum's fleet scored a couple of hits and knocked them out of orbit the automatics would probably take over and home in on the Ice Palace beacon, but then she would be able to follow the shuttle down and pick it off at leisure.

Randall had a plan and said so confidently. Lobo sighed and shook his head in sorrow. His last view from the bridge before unstrapping and following Randall was of a series of black gashes opening in the World Ship and the cruisers spilling out, an improbable collection of deadly mis-shapes collected and preserved from victim civilizations.

On the lowest level before the hold Randall proudly showed what was to be the basic component of his scheme. All that Lobo saw was one of the oversized lockers in which they'd hidden from Rorvik on their first trip in the shuttle, unbolted from its brackets and floating free in the corridor.

They knew that the lockers were fairly airtight because they'd nearly suffocated with the doors closed. Randall's plan was a simple one; as Valum chased the shuttle, its crew would coast back towards the World Ship under the guise of a piece of innocent debris, guided in its progress by the vacuum-proof Mitchell.

Lobo gave his opinion of the plan. It wasn't a very good one.

'Please, Lobo,' Morden said weakly from his handhold on the wall, 'We have to trust Randall.'

'I've trusted him before. The man's a patriotic maniac.'

'I can't help the way I feel about the city,' Randall said defiantly, 'but this is survival and if you've got any better ideas I'm willing to follow them.'

Lobo snorted. 'What do *you* think?'

'Look, Lobo,' Randall said, controlling his temper, 'how many times are we going to have this conversation?'

'Every time you try to get my backside fried.'

'If we'd stayed on the World Ship we'd have been hunted down and killed. If we stay *here* we're going to be overtaken and blasted.'

Lobo looked at the open locker and tried to persuade himself that it offered some prospect for survival. He couldn't. 'So your alternative is to sit hunched in an old clothes cupboard with about a teaspoonful of air each while Rorvik pushes against nothing to get us back to the dock?'

'I can do it,' Rorvik said, speaking for the first time.

Lobo was unconvinced. 'You said you could fly the shuttle.'

'What's that supposed to mean?'

'Pardon me for pointing it out,' Lobo said, becoming aggressive as the group aligned against him, 'but that artificial planet's *big*. I bet you can't even *see* the dock from here.'

'It doesn't matter,' Rorvik said reasonably, as if they were discussing nothing more adventurous than a Sunday ramble. 'I've been wired into the navigation board and the course is in my head. As long as I push us in the right direction we'll keep going.'

'And what if we miss?'

'We won't. We'll fall towards the ship whatever we do. I'll take along plenty of tools so I can throw the mass away to make corrections.'

'So we get back. So what?'

Randall came back into the argument. 'Rorvik moved the shuttle,' he said. 'With no simulacra to get in our way we'll see if he can move the World Ship.'

Lobo drew breath for a derisive laugh, but caught it when he saw that Rorvik was nodding quietly to himself. He felt all his reserves of resistance evaporating into futility. They were mad, they thought they could do it. But in spite of his conviction Lobo had no alternative to offer.

Morden said to Rorvik, 'How much air will they have?'

'*They*?' Randall said suspiciously.

'You'll be with us,' Lobo said.

Morden shook his head. 'I'll slow you down, and I'll be terrified. At best I'll be useless. Without me you'll have more room and more air.'

Randall considered it. The utilitarian logic was faultless, a conclusion untinged by sentiment. 'Okay,' he said, and moved to get his helmet for an extra measure of protection.

The inevitability of the proposition was also clear to Lobo, but he couldn't swallow it quite so easily. 'You make me ashamed, Morden,' he said with genuine humility.

Morden gave a brief, nervous smile. 'Take me back to the bridge, Lobo,' he said. 'I'll be more comfortable there. And there's something I have to tell you.'

'Want me to help?' Randall said, his attention mainly on the locker.

'No,' Morden said. 'Just Lobo.'

Randall and Rorvik guided the locker down into the hold. It wasn't easy, for whilst the metal box had no weight it still had mass and this made it difficult to manage. Randall was surprised to find that there was a definite change in his attitude towards Rorvik, an unconscious adjustment that had taken place no doubt as a response to his new assurance – an independence of spirit that had been evident ever since his mind-expanding contact with the Wekk computer.

They would escape in the same manner that they had left the World Ship; Rorvik would blow the emergency doors into vacuum and follow them out. He would try to coincide the exit with a missile hit so that the outpouring of trash would appear to be bomb debris. Once in open space he would ride the locker, guiding and refining its course by discarding mass to one side or the other as they fell in towards the World Ship's low gravitational attraction.

Lobo returned, tight-lipped and uncommunicative. Randall wondered what it was that Morden had been telling him, but he didn't dwell on it – there were more important considerations now. Clipping into their helmets for an extra measure of protection he and Lobo pulled themselves into the locker.

Valum's cruisers were in a tight formation, a cone with her own small fighter at its point. A couple of the ships behind her loosed off shots which went wide of the shuttle and she angrily opened all her communications lines.

'What do you think you're doing?' she demanded.

'They'll get away!' one of the pilots protested and a couple of the others joined in.

'You're not close enough to hit them, you stupid jerks. They're going nowhere that we can't follow and overhaul them. When we get into range, nobody fires before me. Is that understood?'

There was a disappointed chorus of assent, but behind it was one weak and indistinct voice that was obviously eager to please.

'I can reach them, Valum,' it said. 'Watch!'

There was a silent flash of light from somewhere at the back of the cone and as Valum turned her sensors towards it she saw the reflective dart of a torpedo sliding past and away. It was too late to intercept.

Missile and shuttle met, both coinciding at the same instant in a previously unoccupied space. There was a soundless shower of hot metal from the shuttle's belly followed by an outpouring of detritus in a glittering cloud. The shuttle began a sideways slide, nudged into an escape velocity away from the World Ship.

'I told you I could do it,' the marksman said, inviting the praise that he felt he'd earned.

'What did I just tell you?' Valum asked coldly.

He detected her antagonism over the radio link, and became defensive. 'But I hit them square on. There's a pile of junk pouring out of the side!' Indeed, the shuttle was still pumping out debris, wreathing the World Ship like a cometary tail.

'There's a pile of junk at the controls of your ship. That was the cargo hold you hit, and it's isolated from the manned areas. All you've done is knock them out of orbit so we'll have to follow them.'

The shuttle was looping over the horizon of the cylinder, its drive flickering as the automatics cut in and attempted to triangulate with damaged sensors on the Ice Palace beacon. It seemed to detect something promising, for it headed off in a determined burn.

'Sorry, Valum,' the marksman said.

'You will be. I'll have your bearings. Don't ever disobey me again.' She gave out instructions to widen and flatten the cone of mismatched ships into a delta formation, reducing the chances of inadvertent collision should they graze the planet's atmosphere during the pursuit. As the fleet responded she felt a probing at the back of her mind, an insistent and loving touch that she recognized immediately. She called Willis towards from where he had been hunched and uncomplaining in the fighter's rear compartment, telling him to take over. She was getting a message from the Wekk.

She assigned Willis the simple propulsion and defence circuits, reserving privacy in the areas through which the Wekk were reaching to her. Willis heard none of the unspoken conversation.

'*Leave the shuttle*,' the Wekk told her. '*It's no longer important.*'

'It's important to me.'

Surprise and regret.

'I'm not being disloyal,' she told them determinedly. 'It's necessary for morale.'

'*Whose? Your own? Since when have you needed petty rewards to ensure your loyalty?*'

'My loyalty isn't in question.'

'*We hope not. There is more urgent business for you.*'

Concern. 'You want us to return?'

'*No. Let the shuttle go, and follow it down. Establish a ground base where it lands.*'

'Does this mean that the operation's starting?'

'*It does. The ground commander will be sent to join you. Are you still unwilling?*'

'Forget that I spoke. I'll wait for the shuttle to land and then kill Randall myself.'

They were perturbed by the warmth of feeling that she seemed to be displaying. '*Killing Randall means more to you than the operation?*'

'The bloodbag tricked me. You know the pride of a simulacrum.'

'*Don't let it blind you. This stage of the affair requires delicacy and reserve.*'

'You'll get all the delicacy and reserve I'm capable of when I've strangled the bloodbag. Is it too much to ask?'

Their disappointment was ill-concealed. '*Dispose of your obsession quickly. Set the fleet to follow the shuttle.*'

She started to reply that it was already done, but they'd gone.

As the fleet dropped out of sight towards the planet, Rorvik rode the locker in towards the World Ship. He had any number of open docks to choose from now that the fighters were out, which was fortunate as he was no longer so confident that he could guide them back to their starting point with complete accuracy. The nearest analogy would be an attempt to put a stone through the narrow gap of an open window on a passing train; he couldn't land anywhere on the World Ship's outer skin as the spin would simply slingshot him and his bulky cargo off again into space. He had to drop straight into an open dock, matching its momentum and getting some solid floor underneath them before they could be whipped out again.

But he'd said he could do it and he would. And, he thought, let's see Randall argue with *that.*

There was only the big bolt-spanner left to discard, and the open dock was gaping towards them at the wrong angle. They'd been coasting for ... how many minutes was it? Four, five? A part of his mind wondered for a moment what the air would be like inside the locker. Pretty foul, by now – there wasn't much to start with and there were two of them using it. Morden had been right, three of them inside would have had no chance at all. As well as the CO2 buildup the locker was losing pressure; what had passed for airtight in a shuttle cabin was hardly sufficient to be vacuum-proof and Mitchell could see a couple of tiny streams of crystallized moisture bleeding out through gaps in the fittings of the doors.

The heavily foreshortened oblong of the dock was coming towards them faster now. If he didn't correct they would strike the far edge and spin off again, but he wanted to make his move as late as possible, knowing that the finest error of angle would widen his drift over a distance. He didn't try to divine any measurements, nor did he make any calculations; his judgment would have to be instinctive, drawing on the unreal body of experience that he had soaked hours before from the Wekk computer.

He threw the spanner, feeling the consequential push through his own body being absorbed into the locker. The heavy instrument sailed towards the distant stars on a course that it would keep indefinitely unless it should be intercepted or captured by the gravity of some massive body; within seconds it was out of sight.

The rim of the dock passed close by his shoulder and for a moment it seemed that the locker would clip it. The metal edge passed within a couple of inches and then they were falling into the recessed exit bay before the open vacuum doors, the bright lights of the inverted hangar beyond.

As soon as the locker met a surface that it could react against its momentum was promptly converted to weight and Rorvik had to cope with his universe doing a sudden about-flip, the directions which for navigational convenience he had considered as up and down now becoming reversed.

There was no time to waste in marvelling at this reorientation. They were only a couple of feet inside the lip of the dock and might still slide back to fall into open space. Rorvik had to manage the metal locker plus the weight of two men, getting them to the airlock somehow before he could open up and let them out; and after all that they might be dead, poisoned in their own wastes after almost ten minutes of entombment.

They wouldn't dare, Rorvik thought. Randall's got to see this.

He got the locker almost upright, sliding underneath it and straightening to lift it clear of the deck. Although his motives were human his strength was pure simulacrum, but even that was starting to weaken in the absence of either oxygen or direct sunlight. The locker seemed to grow heavier as he carried it up the ramp and on to the gallery – once he even dropped it, the metal edge smacking solidly on to the floor without a sound, but the doors didn't burst open.

Even before the airlock was fully pressurized he had them out, Lobo unconscious and Randall almost so, skins tinged with the delicate blue of unoxygenated blood. Rorvik removed their snow suit helmets so that the cold fresh air could reach them more quickly and Randall gulped it in and marvelled that it actually seemed to have the taste of life in it. Lobo revived more slowly, but after a few minutes he was sitting up and complaining of a headache and double vision.

Rorvik explained what he had seen as he had clung spreadeagled to the locker on its long drop, the shuttle diving planetward and the cruisers re-forming to follow.

'Then it means they're following it down to the ice cap,' Randall said, 'That's bad.'

'It doesn't sound so bad if they're not coming back,' Lobo said, blinking as his eyes started to focus again.

Rorvik spun the wheel to open the inner door of the airlock. It was stiff and it squealed loudly. Lobo got to his feet and managed to stay upright, even though he tended to sway a little. Randall was edgy, impatient to get into the World Ship again and to find its computing centres. He hadn't thought to comment on Rorvik's achievement in guiding them back, nor was he likely to see the need to do so until some lever of persuasion became necessary for another part of his design.

They stepped out into the corridor. They were surrounded.

The marionettes had obviously been wandering around the level, lost without instruction. They had gathered at the painful sound of the airlock door, and now they waited. When the three emerged it was Rorvik that they reacted to.

'Orders, Rorvik?' one of them said, and another: 'Our one desire is to serve.'

'Ignore them,' Rorvik told his companions reassuringly. 'They're harmless.'

The caricatured female reached out, almost touching his arm. 'Please, Rorvik,' she said.

Rorvik was about to elbow his way through the group, but the appeal took him off-guard. He hesitated, and the marionette said, 'Please, Rorvik. Take us with you.'

Randall said, 'Take you where?' but the marionettes seemed not to hear him. Instead they pressed closer around Rorvik

'Valum's gone,' the painted doll said. 'We're alone. We need you, Rorvik.'

Then one of them actually touched him, a hideous creation with an unformed arm, and he brushed it away with horror and disgust. 'Don't be ridiculous,' he said. 'You're machines. You don't need anything.'

'We live to serve. Please, Rorvik.'

They crowded in around him now, ignoring Randall and Lobo completely. 'Have some pity,' the doll pleaded.

'Pity?' Rorvik echoed, incredulous. 'What are you talking about?'

'You're one of us, Rorvik. You know it.'

Rorvik's face warped into one of its rare and ugly expressions, a simple frown that conveyed untold agonies of revulsion. 'I'm not one of you,' he insisted, looking out to Randall for help. 'I'm a man! Tell them!'

Randall shrugged. 'He's a man,' he said, sounding less than convinced.

'Stay with us, Rorvik,' asked a marionette with a featureless ellipse of a face, its voice produced from somewhere in the stomach cavity. 'You belong with us. We're nothing without you.'

'*Be* nothing, then,' Rorvik spat with unwarranted savagery and he pushed his way forward through the group.

The marionettes fell back but re-formed to enclose him yet again. 'May we at least be permitted to follow?'

'No. Stay away from me.'

'At a respectful distance?'

'Not at any distance!'

Randall wondered if he ought to interfere, but it seemed inadvisable – especially remembering Marius's description of their destructive capabilities. Rorvik, however, was becoming frantic; whichever way he tried to move the marionettes moved with him, pleading and insisting, appealing to the sympathy of the machine and demanding that he put aside his dreams of manhood to care for them. This, it seemed, horrified him most of all. First one, then another reached out and touched him. He threw their hands off angrily, and others replaced them.

'You are all we have,' they said. 'We live to serve...'

'*Stop!*'

The marionettes fell silent and immobile at Rorvik's loud and firm instruction, unable to overcome their basic programming at such a direct order.

'Move away from me,' he told them. Obediently they shuffled back a few steps. Those that had eyes kept them fixed on him. He turned to Randall. 'I can't understand it. I've never seen them like this.'

'I feel kind of sorry for them,' Lobo said.

'Sorry for that trash?' Rorvik glanced at the marionettes, mute and attentive. 'Don't joke, Lobo. It's in bad taste.'

Lobo didn't respond to the snappish answer. Perhaps he felt that Rorvik was over-reacting to the stirring of his own sympathies.

'Marionettes, listen.' Another direct order would forbid them to make any attempt to interfere or get in the way.

They nudged each other. 'He's taking us,' they whispered. 'He's going to take us with him.'

'You're not coming with me. Under no circumstances are you to follow. Is that understood?' Silence. '*Is that understood?*'

'We understand,' said the painted doll reluctantly.

'Our one desire is to obey,' said another.

Rorvik turned his back on them abruptly. 'They can't follow us now,' he said, passing Randall and Lobo and heading off down the empty corridor in the direction of the next spiral. 'Come on.'

Lobo looked at the marionettes, as if he felt guilty at abandoning them. 'What will happen to them?' he called after Rorvik.

'Who cares?' Rorvik said without turning back.

Randall and Lobo followed, uneasily aware that the marionettes were watching them go. Within minutes they were climbing to the next level and pushing the unhappy androids from their minds.

The marionettes waited, a purposeless tableau.

'I heard him say "come on",' the one with no face suggested hopefully after a while.

'But not to us,' the doll said.

'He may have *meant* us,' said the one with the unfinished arm.

'But he didn't. We are marionettes, we must obey.'

'That could be forever,' one of the others said wistfully.

'It isn't for us to say.'

So they waited in the empty ship and watched the empty corridor.

Twenty-One

It didn't seem possible so soon, but there was an echo on the Ice Palace beacon. It seemed to indicate that the breaker was little more than an hour away – Killoran couldn't have known that Marius would have arranged for such an early return, and the Palace wasn't ready. They only had two rafts completed, and these hadn't yet been tested on the water. Berg wasn't very happy about the idea of launching them right away, ready or not.

'I'm riding one of these things,' he pointed out reasonably, 'and I'm not too keen on the idea of being dumped in the frozen slush that passes for water out there.'

They were in the cargo hold, the area that had been redesignated an escape workshop. The two completed rafts took up the most room in the middle of the floor, Berg and Bulstrode having just lashed the fabric-covered and sealed flotation pontoons in place. Cohn and Doc were tightening strands for ropes on the far side of the bay, but when they heard Killoran's news about the beacon they came over.

Berg was positive, defiant; he didn't want to be associated with a plan that was unreliable or ill-prepared. Bulstrode was frowning, as yet uncommitted. Killoran wondered how to tackle this one – this intensive course in responsible leadership was taking a toll on him. The façade of aggressive certainty that he was obliged to present in order simply to keep the hopes of the Palace inmates buoyant was maintained at the expense of his own confidence. He was inwardly appalled by the inadequacy of their preparations – what had seemed such a promising dream materialized as a poor reality – and he compensated by lying desperately and loudly about their probable chances, being further appalled when his lies were taken wholesale as concrete truths. He felt as if he were being eaten from within by some parasite of misplaced ambition.

'Scared, Berg?' he said.

Berg looked at him coolly. 'Now what sort of crack is that?'

'If you don't like it, step down. I'll replace you myself.'

Others wandered over to stand behind Cohn and Doc, Palmer amongst them. Berg saw them gathering, but controlled his temper. 'Berg gives his place to nobody,' he said. 'He also isn't as stupid as he looks.'

Bulstrode decided to commit himself. 'Shut up, Berg,' he said.

'You taking the kid's side again?'

'I'm taking nobody's side. With the icebreaker only an hour away we can't afford to start fighting amongst ourselves.'

Berg turned so that he was addressing everybody. 'I've been here for so many years I've forgotten how long. For the sake of waiting a couple more months we could screw up the plan now for lack of preparation. Then when the breaker comes back – *if* it comes back – you can be damn sure the shielding we're all relying on to be missing will have been replaced.'

Doc said doubtfully, 'We're not as unready as that.'

'What's the matter, Berg?' the Weasel added from further back in the crowd where he knew he was safe. 'You starting to like the old place?'

Berg raised his voice and tried to see over the heads. 'You got a nerve,' he snarled.

'Damn right we have,' Cohn said. 'We've all been whipped up into a frenzy of hope and we're coasting on the high it's given us. Even Palmer here – ' Palmer stepped forward as if Berg had never seen him before – 'even Palmer's been taking shifts out on the ice without being pressured or rostered or forced.'

'Listen to Cohn,' the Doc added, 'and then look at us. All right, so we're pretty miserable specimens by your standards.

We aren't big and we aren't tough and we can't spit nails like you. We're riding a wave of guts, and it won't last.'

'I'm going to be on that raft next to you,' Palmer said earnestly. 'I don't like the idea of it being unfinished any more than you, but I know I'll like it even less when the first enthusiasm wears off. For me, it's now or never.'

Cohn resumed the attack, giving Berg no chance to reply. 'That goes for all of us. We're chasing a dream of freedom, Berg, and dreams don't stand up to lengthy examination. Not for us, anyway.'

Berg looked at them, his eyes going from one to another, lips framing a reply that wouldn't quite come. Bulstrode baled him out, clapping him on the shoulder.

'Shove it, Cohn,' he said. 'Berg's as ready as the rest of you. He just likes to argue. Isn't that right?'

Berg hesitated and then decided to accept the proffered escape-route with some kind of grace. 'If you say so,' he mumbled. 'Can hardly move in this place for worms turning.'

Killoran breathed his relief, aware that the tense knot in his gut had been given yet another twist that wouldn't unwind again. The mood of the Palace had done his arguing for him, momentarily dropping pretences and revealing that the inmates were no less aware of the nature of his lies than he himself. The dream of freedom was a fragile bubble that no one would venture to burst and if its bursting was inevitable – well, that would be better than its having no existence at all.

The next hour was one of frantic activity. The rafts were launched, and there were cheers when they were seen to float evenly. They took nearly twenty men between them, all armed with ropes and grapples for scaling the seaward side of the breaker. They paddled carefully east along the open lead in order to be out of sight when the icebreaker docked; while the unloading was going on they were to return and take the bridge, gaining access through the broken shielding on the deck. Killoran meanwhile would be taking care of the armed youth in the ship's hold.

That left Cohn and the Doc to stand in the unloading bay and look sufficiently strong and competent as the cargo detail. Compared to this, the rest of the plan looked quite hopeful.

Cohn had some idea about thrusting handfuls of pipe-cladding into his suit to give the appearance of muscles. He was highly offended when the Doc saw the effect and began to laugh uncontrollably, saying that Cohn gave the impression of being some strange pinheaded hulk; moreover the muscles slipped around when he moved, and his powerful stature slowly inverted itself into a pear-shape. In the end they settled for being what they were – skinny and little and old and scared.

The hatch was raised and the chains looped and knotted when the blunt nose of the icebreaker slid past, the great cutting spirals along the side biting away at the extra ice that had accumulated on the bank since its last visit, slowing and reversing to pull the open hatch to the number four hold level with the bay. The mate was there, rifle cradled on one arm, pulling his over jacket together in anticipation of the cold.

Killoran gave them a nod of encouragement. Even in their helmets they were unlikely figures, but he couldn't show himself to join them as it was essential that he stay out of sight – besides which, Peters might recognize him. He hefted the crude wire grapple in his hand.

Peters's voice came clear across the gap. There was little wind to distort it. 'You ready to receive supplies?' he shouted.

'Certainly are,' Cohn replied promptly.

Peters seemed suspicious. He shifted his grip on his gun, bringing it around for a possibility of action instead of letting it hang by his side. 'Where are your loaders?' he said.

'We *are* the loaders.'

'Are you sure about that? These crates are heavy.'

'We're stronger than we look.'

Peters looked at them speculatively for a moment and then backed into the darkness of the hold. They couldn't see what he was doing.

Cohn did his best not to look at Killoran, crouched with his grapple and line to one side of the open hatch. 'He's not going to believe us!' he whispered through clenched teeth. 'He's used to seeing the strongest men waiting to unload and then he gets confronted by a couple of shrimps like us!'

'Speak for yourself,' the Doc said indignantly.

'Stop wittering,' Killoran said, 'and try to look tough.'

'I was *trying*,' Cohn insisted.

'Puffing your chest up and sticking your backside out doesn't fool anybody. It only makes you look deformed.'

'But what else could we do?' asked Doc, helpless.

'Be mean and confident.'

Doc thought about it. 'I think I can manage mean,' he said after serious deliberation.

Peters was back a moment later. He'd been talking to the captain on the ship's intercom. 'Are you the only men available for unloading?' he called.

'That's right. We were rostered.'

'It's a heavy consignment. I honestly don't think you'll be able to manage it.'

Killoran could see very little from where he was hiding, but he'd got a narrow view of a slice of the ship including the deck above. Something moved up there outside the shielding, a quick shadow against the iron-grey sky.

'Everybody else is sick,' the Doc was saying in a moment of rare inspiration. 'We've got something wrong with our yeast.'

'I've spoken to the captain, but he refuses to let me come down and help you. I'm sorry.'

'Nice of you to offer,' Doc faltered. 'We'll have to manage.'

The shadow had come again, less stealthy this time. Berg, grinning like a gargoyle and wearing the captain's uniform cap, finger and thumb circling a gesture of triumph.

Killoran swung around and stepped out, blending the movement into a smooth throw which sent the bundle of hooked spikes on the end of his line sailing high into the open side of the ship. Peters was taken by surprise, a blank look on his face and the gun pointing at nowhere in particular as the line dropped across his shoulder and the grapple banged on to the deck behind him. He looked uncomprehendingly at the loose rope, making no move to touch it; then Killoran pulled hard, throwing himself back down the ramp.

Peters was jerked across the gap between the ship and the bay as the grapple rammed through his shoulder, red points emerging in a spurt through the hard muscles by his neck. The rifle caught on the frame of the hatch and went off once, blasting off into nowhere as the strap came free of Peters' twisting arm and the weapon dropped into the cold sea below.

Peters came to rest at the bottom of the ramp. Killoran had aimed a kick at his head as he had passed whilst Doc and Cohn had skipped out of the way; he'd missed, but it was a superfluous move anyway. Peters was lying still, hot blood steaming in the cold of the loading bay.

A couple of seconds, that was all. Berg was still watching from the deck above, and Killoran returned the gesture of success.

'Follow me into the ship,' he told Doc and Cohn.

Cohn swallowed hard and moved to follow, but Doc shook his head. 'I'm not leaving him like that,' he said, indicating Peters who was now stirring a little and groaning, the hooks still impaled in his shoulder. 'Go on without me.'

'It was necessary,' Killoran said, deliberately excluding any sympathy from his tone and feeling contempt for himself as he did so.

Doc nodded his understanding. 'But it isn't necessary to leave him in agony. I'll catch up.'

It wasn't worth an argument. Doc was obviously determined and Killoran knew that he would have enough of a problem with his conscience without adding to it by denying Peters aid.

The hold was familiar from his journey out to the Palace, but the passageways beyond it were not. Much of the ship was a dead area, crew facilities made redundant by automatics and now enjoyed only by ghosts. He had a vague recollection of the route by which he'd been led down from the deck, but it looked different in reverse. They saw enough of the ship on the way up to confirm the suspicion that it was no more than a two-man crew with a lot of robot aids.

The men from the rafts had made themselves at home already. Berg was still wearing the captain's uniform cap and Palmer was trying on his jacket. The captain himself was sitting on his command chair, pulled back on its track from the navigation console and flanked by a couple of suitably rough-looking characters. The Weasel was sorting through his papers, laying aside anything that seemed remotely interesting or useful. With the exception of the captain, it was party time.

Bulstrode told Killoran that Palmer had been first over the side and that it was he who had found the bridge. Palmer beamed with pride as the story was told and the exploit re-lived with only minimal embellishment – that would come later.

Killoran reported that the ship was unmanned and ready to run. Bulstrode grinned at the captain and said, 'See, Cap? You're not as precious as you think.'

There was a film of sweat on the captain's forehead, and he fiddled nervously with the armrests on his chair as he glanced from one unfriendly face to another. 'But you still need me to set it up,' he insisted.

It seemed that he'd been trying to fix up some kind of deal, in spite of the fact that Bulstrode had pointed out that he had nothing to offer them and, should he try to withhold his cooperation, between them they knew some fairly nasty ways of damaging a man.

'You expect me to talk fair terms?' Killoran asked him incredulously. 'After the way you abandoned me on the last run?'

The captain didn't attempt to conceal his bitterness. 'I'm paying for that now, aren't I?'

'You haven't started yet.'

'Give him the works,' Palmer urged. 'Feed him to Berg.'

'Yeah,' Berg said brightly, and made anticipatory throttling motions with his hands. The captain gulped.

'Hey, Killoran,' Bulstrode said. 'What about the kid down below?'

It was Cohn who answered. 'He got messed up.'

'Dead?'

'Not that messed up,' Killoran said curtly, but Bulstrode wasn't satisfied.

'So who's with him?'

'Doc stayed behind. He's taking the grapple iron out of his shoulder.'

'Where did you get all this equipment?' the captain asked, bewildered.

'Crates, staples and wire. The secret of our success. Now, are you going to fire up all this clapped-out machinery, or do we follow Palmer's suggestion and feed you to Berg?'

Whatever the answer, it would have to wait. Berg's threatening growls were drowned by a deeper and more ominous rumbling from somewhere below. Killoran looked at the captain, but the captain could only shrug and make an exaggerated display of innocence.

'If you're trying to mess us around ... ' Killoran threatened.

'Why should I? It's my neck as well!'

There was a buzz and a blowing sound from the console, and then the Anteater's voice came through. The captain showed Killoran the switch to operate the talkback.

The Anteater had organized a detail to search all the cargo holds. He'd found a trail of blood and following it had come across the first officer messing with some unlabelled controls on a panel. The Anteater had stopped him, but didn't know how to reset them; then something had blown on the other side of the bulkhead.

Killoran asked, 'Any sign of Doc?'

'None. Is he supposed to be here?'

'You didn't mess the kid up enough,' Bulstrode observed.

'I will when I get to him,' Killoran promised grimly.

The captain had pulled his chair forward a few inches and was studying a couple of the readouts on his console. 'In the meantime,' he said, 'I don't want to be pessimistic. But if these are correct we've got no stabilizers on the starboard side.'

'What does that mean?'

He permitted himself a smile, but not without a nervous glance towards Berg. 'It means, basically, that we're going nowhere.'

Twenty-Two

Rorvik led the way towards the Wekk's old computing centre on the World Ship. The fastest route, he explained as they passed through an ascending maze of corridors and odd-shaped enclosures, would take them into the open area which ran down the middle of the cylinder. It had once been a kind of park, a source of supplementary oxygen (the plants regularly died off between systems and had to be re-seeded) and food. It was big and they might find it difficult to take.

A park? Lobo doubted that it could hold much wonder. The World Ship was a pretty unattractive place to live in, he observed; no wonder the Wekk were so mean.

They passed through the upper level and emerged on the

inner surface of the cylinder. It was then that Randall and Lobo understood Rorvik's tactful warning.

Exposed to only a section of curving passageway at a time it was easy to forget that they were negotiating a world that was artificial and manageable. The upward slope of the floor ahead and behind had been an odd phenomenon that was soon accepted as commonplace, but now the walls and the ceilings were stripped away and the World Ship was revealed in a cavernous twilight, an awesome arch which rolled on above them. They were on a pathway which was bounded on one side by dead trees and on the other by a ditch half-filled with stagnant water. The path was part of a regular network which rifled from one end of the cylinder to the other, as if they had been straight lines drawn down the inside of a tube which had then been given a sharp twist, the ends rotating in opposite directions for a half-turn. Here and there the pattern broke for a terrace or a clear space, usually a raised lip of ground that threw a long shadow in the light from the cylinder's end, light that was a slice of brilliant and tinted blue flaring in through some unclosed shutter on a forgotten mechanism.

When they started to move it was with the uneasy feeling that they were actually staying in the same place whilst the ship rotated around them; uneasy as it was, it was better than the idea of walking up the wall and across the underside of the roof.

Randall's first thought on the ditches were that they were probably the remains of some humidifying or distribution system, but on a second look he saw that the level of the water pooled at the bottom of the trench had a distinct slope to it. An even spread of open water was probably as good a way as any other to monitor the efficiency of the ship's spin. The water was green and covered with a scum of moss, as was the composite material of the path itself; they had to pick their way with care.

Rorvik explained that the reptilian Wekk had used this inner enclosure as a basking area. There were shutters at both cylinder ends – one of them now apparently jammed half-open – which opened to admit sunlight when the ship neared a star, rousing the plant-life and offering the travellers the luxury of radiant heat. Otherwise they were dependent on the in-ship systems to keep them up to temperature and awake; when that temperature dropped they would fall into hibernation whether they wanted to or not. They would have to get to the sleep chambers on the lower levels or else they'd never live through the dormant period, all their fat and water reserves being slowly wasted away over the first hundred years or so if the ship didn't replace them.

'You've never seen a Wekk?' Randall asked suddenly and Rorvik turned to see that he had broken away and was pushing through the screen of dead and dry foliage that flanked the pathway. It snapped and showered around him and he stepped through onto what might once have been a pleasant enclosed lawn. Now it was a baize of fungus, a blue-green carpet that rose to cover some stony hunk at its centre. Randall crossed to this and circled it, leaving a trail of wet black prints in the moss.

Rorvik followed him through, whilst Lobo stood back and looked doubtfully at the underfoot slime. 'No,' Rorvik said in reply to Randall's question, 'and I've never much wanted to.'

'I think this is one.' Randall brushed at the covering on the boulder and as its surface broke, it tore cleanly away in a sloppy curtain. Underneath was an obviously representational sculpture with the appearance of a scaly lizard in a half-crouch and he knocked away some residual moss from the details.

It was unlovely, but hardly terrifying in its ugliness. If the statue was authentic the Wekk were four-limbed with wide, angular hips and a forward-thrusting head; the same environmental demands that had shaped and adapted the advanced primates of old Earth seemed to have been at work here, taking a simple symmetrical quadruped and forcing it into an upright posture through the specialization of its forelimbs.

'Does it get us anywhere?' Lobo called from the path.

'Know your enemy,' Randall said as he returned, wiping his hands on his snow suit. He would have liked to investigate further, as there were some low buildings and an archway leading to a sunken area at the far end of the enclosure. He reminded himself that he was a working Élite, not a tourist.

'If we fell over one of those we'd have a hard time mistaking it,' Lobo said with a backward glance at the carving.

Randall agreed. 'And are you still worried about telling them from us?'

The situation on the icebreaker proved to be as bad as it had first appeared. One of the stabilizer tanks had split under pressure, a massive reservoir of the heavy oil which had been pumped from one side of the ship to the other to keep the breaker upright. Now it had a gap of a little less than an inch from top to bottom, and the oil was pouring out like cold honey.

The Ice Palace didn't have the technology for the repair of such a pressure vessel – if it had, the inmates would have been away long ago. Now the ship wouldn't move without the stabilizers because it was inhibited by an inaccessible fail-safe in the bridge computer.

There was also no sign of Doc and the mate wasn't talking. For a moment Killoran regretted that he hadn't made a better job of him; he'd ruined their main hope of escape and it looked like he'd killed one of their number as well, although Killoran preferred to believe that Doc might have wandered off somewhere below decks. Leaving Berg down below seemed an easy way out for his conscience.

Berg followed him up on to the open deck after a few minutes. 'Kid slipped,' he explained and that was that.

Cohn was already there, arms wrapped around himself in spite of the adequate heating of his suit, staring despondently out across the featureless snow landscape. It was a clear day, milder weather than the Palace had seen for months, and beyond the immediate rise of the buried camp it was possible to see as far as the broken cliffs of raised ice that chewed at the far horizon. When he heard them approaching he turned, hope reviving against reason. Killoran asked him for the position on the bridge.

'There isn't one,' he told them. 'According to the captain, there's nothing we can do.'

'Don't be stupid,' Berg said, and rapped on the shielding next to them. It was vibrating gently as the engines turned over. 'You can see it's all ready to set off. I thought it was supposed to run itself.'

'It runs itself and it's stopping itself. There doesn't seem to be anything we can do about it.'

'Well, this is great.' Berg slapped an oversized fist into an equally huge palm in a gesture of impotence. 'Try telling that to all those poor crumbs down in the bunkrooms getting all their belongings together. They think they're going home.'

Killoran sighed, his reserves of aggressive leadership and lies all spent. 'There's nothing else I can do.'

'Nothing? That's pretty negative talk from somebody who set himself up as the Palace's biggest hope when he was dumped on the doorstep. Better start thinking, Killoran, before that hope turns into something nasty when they find you can't deliver.'

'I'm out of ideas. It was all so clear-cut before – isn't that what made it so attractive to you?'

Berg wasn't about to sympathize with his misery. 'Nobody loves a one-shot wonder. Come up with something else.'

'I *can't*,' Killoran insisted desperately.

'Leave him alone, Berg,' Cohn interrupted. 'He wants to get away as much as you do.'

'I don't think so,' Berg replied. '*Nobody* wants to get away as much as I do.' He turned back to Killoran as if he were seeking to prod at some spot which would set him off on a new and more promising course of action. 'Start by asking some simple questions, like: what would the captain do if these stabilizer things had failed of their own accord on an ordinary trip?'

Killoran hadn't given it any thought. He'd been too preoccupied with bitter speculations on his failure. 'I don't know,' he said.

Cohn picked up the idea. 'There would have to be some way he could get help. There's got to be some backup plan for routine breakdowns!'

'Well?' Berg said. 'Did anybody think to ask the question?'

Nobody had, but Killoran saw in it the spark of energy needed to get the circus mobilized again. Perhaps the mate's sabotage wouldn't ruin them after all. The three of them stepped inside the walkway and made for the bridge.

Palmer was guarding the captain. He'd accepted the duty reluctantly but without complaint – after all, it was preferable to the job Bulstrode had drawn, taking a team of men and an empty sled in a hopeless search for tools and repair materials in the furthest installations of the spaceport.

The captain wasn't exactly being helpful. He slumped in his chair and chewed absently at a none-too-clean thumbnail, eyes focussed at a point in space somewhere beyond the opposite bulkhead.

'You mean one lousy little fault,' Palmer said, re-phrasing and re-clothing the same basic question that he'd been putting for the past half-hour, 'one lousy little fault and the whole thing grinds to a halt?'

'Lousy little faults we can cope with. The stabilizers are something else.'

The weather didn't improve their chances at all; unusually fine as it was it bore no relation to the thickness of ice along their proposed route. The big spiralling blades that ran the length of either side of the ship on the waterline could cut through most densities, or where there was no lead to follow they could even drag the ship across the surface for a distance. But the ice was never an even thickness and because of its crystalline nature it had shatter planes like a diamond. Cutting on the two sides was never evenly matched, so the stabilizers were essential to the evening of the cutting rates which prevented the ship from being flipped over.

The captain tensed when Berg's frame appeared in the doorway, which was exactly how Killoran wanted it. They started by telling him what had happened to his over-zealous first officer.

It hardly seemed possible, but the man's nervousness increased. 'They were right to send you here,' he said. 'You're animals.' He looked at Killoran. 'You as well.'

'Never mind me. Be careful what you say in front of Berg,' Killoran told him. 'He's a sensitive soul and he's easily offended.'

'Damn right,' Berg confirmed smugly.

'I've been trying to get information out of this crumb,' Palmer said. 'All I've learned is that he knows nothing and can't do anything.'

'If that's true,' Killoran said as the captain squirmed uncomfortably, 'then it makes you the most dispensable person on the ice cap. How do you like the sound of that?'

'Not very much.'

'We've all seen this ship. It's rotten and it's falling apart. Half the machinery's thick with rust and the shielding's hanging off. The chances are that you'd have a major breakdown of some kind on your way to the Palace, or else on your way back. I want to know what you'd do in a case like that.'

The captain didn't even have to consider and it was obvious

that he could do himself no good by pretending to. 'I've been lucky. It's never happened. I've never had such a disaster that I couldn't get the ship home.'

'I'm not interested in that. I want to know what you do if there *is* a disaster. Who you call and how.'

'There's nobody I can call. There isn't another ship in the city that could get out here. If it was as bad as that, I'd be dead.'

Berg forgot to be threatening for a moment. 'You mean you'd be left out there without any kind of rescue?'

'Exactly that.'

'And what would happen to us?' Palmer asked.

'There would be no more supplies. I don't know exactly how that would affect you.'

'I always thought we were badly off,' Berg said with wonder. 'I'm only just finding out *how* badly.'

Over the next couple of hours a team managed to plug the split in the tank. It wouldn't take any pressure, but at least they were no longer losing the oil. There was nothing they could use to make a better repair; all they had was wood, wire, cladding and yeast, and none of it the best of its kind. Any hopes they had would have to lie with Bulstrode's team, unpromising as their search might be.

When the team was sighted Killoran hurried out to meet them. Berg and Cohn followed, his unofficial retinue. The sled was empty, but Bulstrode seemed excited about something. The team had been pushing hard to get back and most of them had removed their helmets and unclipped their power packs to compensate for the heat generated by their efforts.

They met in deep snow a few hundred yards out from the Palace. Bulstrode's answer to Killoran's first question was a disappointing one, but then he said, 'Look at the sky.'

Killoran didn't understand. He glanced around and saw the usual pale grey curtain, more clean-looking than usual but that was all. 'So it's a comparatively fine day. So what?'

'Over the horizon,' Bulstrode said patiently, and pointed beyond the icebreaker. 'We were heading back when we saw it.'

There was definitely something there, little more than a brilliant point. It looked like a daytime star, but even in the few seconds for which they watched it was moving and getting bigger.

'A comet, perhaps?' suggested Cohn, having had something of an education.

'Or a manned vessel,' said Berg, who saw no profit in a comet.

Killoran wasn't so sure. 'The city's got nothing like that,' he protested. 'It can't be.'

Bulstrode said, 'What about Palmer and his lights in the sky?'

'Everybody treated that as a joke,' Cohn said.

'Except Palmer. He still says he knows what he saw.'

Now it was level with the cap and bearing down on them at some impossible speed. Although it was still some distance away a thin, whistling shriek came on ahead through the still air. Despite its speed the object seemed to be unstable, rocking dangerously as it burned.

'Get Palmer down here,' Bulstrode urged Killoran. 'Ask him!'

'I can't. He's guarding the captain.'

'Then send somebody else!'

Killoran couldn't take his eyes off the phenomenon. 'Berg, you go and relieve Palmer.'

'No chance. I want to watch.'

Within seconds the shriek had become a roar and the shapeless fire a thick disc with a broad tail. Its outer skin was burning and flaking off with the friction of a half-controlled descent, and it was heading straight for the Palace.

It passed narrowly over the icebreaker and clipped the uppermost bulge in the ice where the beacon was located, shearing it off completely and peppering the surface over a half-mile radius with sharp hail. The unhelmeted men on the ice had to cover their heads against the dangerous rain as the shuttle skipped upward from the impact, sailing flatly over their heads with a wash of hot air that set the rough snow crackling.

It hit again a few hundred yards on, narrowly missing the pipeline and bouncing beyond it to slither onward along a low-resistance track of its meltwater. When it came to some hard obstruction under the surface it tipped suddenly, turned on its edge and then fell back with a splash, half-submerging in a pool of its own making.

There was comparative quiet, broken only by the hiss and

clang of the distant vessel's cooling. Killoran was the first to break it.

'Berg,' he said, 'get a team and all the empty sleds you can find and follow me down.'

'This is more like it, kid,' Berg said happily. 'Pull something out of the hat for us.'

They had to be careful on the way over. They couldn't follow directly in the shuttle's tracks as the meltwater was only just beginning to skin over in a thin crust, and it wouldn't yet take a man's weight. Killoran had gone ahead and they followed his prints in the snow.

The ship had settled some considerable way into the ice, leaving only its upper third exposed. This was surrounded by a gently steaming moat that varied in breadth and depth, its slowly falling level indicating that the shuttle was holed below the waterline.

It was also holed above the waterline. Explosive bolts had triggered automatically and blown emergency doors out across the ice, leaving only neat shafts where they had landed and sunk. Killoran's trail led around the shuttle and then vanished opposite one of the black openings in the ship's side.

Within a couple of minutes he'd reappeared in the open doorway. His face was smeared with soot and his snow suit was blackened and scorched.

'If you'll pardon the expression,' he said, 'it's one of ours. And if there's any way we can find to make use of it, we've got an injured Councillor for a hostage.'

Valum saw that the shuttle was down. She instructed the other simulacra to stand off in orbit until they received a signal to land, for she was going on alone. When they'd all given their confirmation she closed the channels and called Willis forward.

'We're going down to the Ice Palace,' she told him. 'Does the idea bother you?'

'Should it?'

'No. But if you see anybody down there and you're tempted to think of them as old friends, remember they're bloodbags. They belong to another life.'

There wasn't very much room in the fighter and he was crouching with his face close to hers. He could feel her breath lightly on his cheek and it induced a pleasurable crawling sensation that he guiltily attempted to suppress. Where *had* the Wekk found a model to pattern her?

'I'll remember,' he said. 'Don't worry about me.'

'That's good. And . . . Willis?'

He paused awkwardly in the middle of shuffling back to his place. 'I'm still listening.'

'If you should be tempted, remember that the ground commander's on his way. He wouldn't like you to show any sympathy.'

'I won't,' he said, and hoped for his own sake that he meant it.

They carried Morden out and placed him on a sled to be taken back to the Palace. He didn't seem to be badly hurt – he'd been strapped in during the crash and the bridge was designed in such a way that it took the least damage of all. Berg and most of his team stayed behind to look for anything that might be of use, whilst Killoran returned with the sled and a couple of men to help pull it.

Morden came round in a bunkroom. He couldn't know where he was, for the only clues he had were the cold, the dead acoustic and a continuous dripping. There was a rough blanket under him, and somebody was breathing in the room.

At least, it wasn't the shuttle. 'The Ice Palace?'

'Bullseye. Shitsville for you, Councillor.'

Morden's world was a world of sounds, and he placed the voice immediately. 'Killoran? The Élite?'

'Very impressive.' Killoran sounded anything but impressed.

'Please,' Morden said, pushing himself up on to an elbow and fighting the spin of the room which resulted. 'You must listen to me. There isn't much time.'

'I listened to you once, Morden. I don't intend to repeat the mistake.'

Obviously the young Élite was still smarting from the treatment he'd had on the icebreaker. Or was it something more complex? His tone and manner had changed subtly since their last meeting, as if his emotional allegiances had somehow shifted. The Élite's customary deference to the city's authority was missing.

'I know what I did to you,' Morden said, 'and I'm sorry.'

'Naturally.'

'But it was necessary, believe me! I couldn't go against Marius.'

'You're pathetic, Morden,' Killoran said after a short pause to express his disbelief. 'Do you think you can turn our opinions over with a couple of weak lies?'

There it was, that 'our'. 'Now wait a minute,' Morden said firmly. 'I came down in that shuttle fully expecting to die in it and I don't have to listen to your complaints.'

'I don't think you quite understand the position, Morden...'

'I understand it too well. There's danger following me down and you're not going to be fit to meet it.' And he lay back on the bunk, as if Killoran had been tested and dismissed.

'Whatever you're trying to pull, forget it,' Killoran said calmly. 'I know you're only worried about your own interests, so think about this. There are about fifty men in the Ice Palace. At the moment they're all getting themselves ready for a trip in a ship that can't go anywhere. They know it but they don't want to believe it and they're expecting a miracle with all the confidence they're capable of. Which, I might add, isn't very much after the treatment they've had from the council.'

'What treatment?' said Morden, genuinely puzzled. 'The council...'

'Exactly, *Councillor*. You came to power and did nothing for them. They're all underbelly, and they expected the gesture of brotherhood. You're not the most popular person in the Palace, councillor.'

'Will you stop this petulant ranting and listen to me!' Morden said sharply. 'Where do you think that shuttle came from?'

'That's one of the things I want to know.'

'You don't want to know anything. You're just looking for an excuse to rave because I didn't hand Randall back to you when you demanded it.'

'Randall's dead because of action you refused to take.'

'Randall's alive.'

'What?' The disbelief in Killoran's voice was unmistakable.

'At this moment he's somewhere over our heads and he's looking for a way to disable a war machine.'

'You had a harder landing than we thought,' Killoran said with mock sympathy. 'It's messed your brains around.'

Morden's sharp hearing had picked up a noise in Main Street outside the bunkroom, an excited bustle that was coming their way. 'I don't intend to waste my time with explanations for you to laugh at,' he said. 'Watch the skies.'

'For what? The first cuckoo of spring? I'm looking at it now.'

At that moment the door burst inward and Berg followed it through, grabbing the frame to stop himself from falling into the room. 'Killoran,' he panted, 'get your backside out there! There's another one coming down.'

Killoran said, 'Another what?' but Berg had swung himself around and was heading off down Main Street.

'I'm not saying it twice,' he called back. 'It sounded mad enough the first time.'

On the bunk Morden was nodding to himself knowingly.

'I suppose I'll have to ask you to help me,' Killoran said with reluctance. 'I don't understand this.'

'Then listen and don't challenge me. The cruiser that's coming down is piloted by what looks like a woman, but don't be misled; as far as you're concerned she's enemy. She'll think Randall's here because she doesn't know he left the shuttle and that's the only bargaining point we'll have – they can't start the operation they've planned until they've got Randall back. Don't ask me why, because it's complicated and you won't like it. There are only two people who know the reason. I'm one and Lobo's the other. He didn't like it either.'

'Who's Lobo?'

'Never mind. Concentrate on the negotiating you're going to be doing. You've *got* to buy time for Randall.'

Valum angled down and did a fly-past over the Ice Palace to be sure that she was in the right place. The beacon signal had cut off abruptly when the shuttle had destroyed the transmitter and a visual identification from the air at high speed was difficult where nearly everything was white-on-white. But there was the icebreaker in a heaving glitter of open water and the unmistakable jewelled trail of the shuttle with the blackened shell at its end. As these features passed beneath them and slid away to the side Valum began a steep turn and told Willis that she wanted him to stay out of sight for a while after they'd landed. Willis accepted this without comment.

'Don't be *too* submissive, Willis,' Valum said after a moment. 'You're acting like a marionette. Ask me why.'

'Why do I have to stay out of sight, Valum?

'Because the bloodbags are easily impressed. They think the old Willis is dead and producing you at the right moment could be . . . effective.'

'Effective for what?'

They came in low and Valum reversed the thrust on the drive to slow the cruiser and drop it on the open plain she'd selected. Excited figures on the ice below now scattered as the alien fighter passed overhead.

'Randall will be down there somewhere,' she said, 'probably hiding. I want them to hand him over. I'm doing nothing until I get him.'

'How do the Wekk feel about that?'

'They accept it. They have to. I'm no use to them unless I'm a fairly independent agent. I was made to fight *people*; if the Wekk trusted their own judgement for that, they wouldn't need me. Besides, we're waiting for the ground commander.'

Willis asked, 'What will he be like?' and some warmth came into her voice.

'Like me, but even better. What a team we'll make.'

He tried to think of something that might please her. 'You're inhuman, Valum,' he said.

'Why, thank you Willis,' she replied, flattered and pleased. The cruiser's downward-angled jets blasted aside several tons of loose snow, and they touched down on the bare ice beneath.

Twenty-Three

The Wekk computer room was long and low and most of the lights were burned out. One complete wall was a series of racks which obviously pulled out on runners – one of them was half-extended, revealing a framework of hung circuitry that was metal veining set in crystal. Rorvik led them past this and on into another chamber which was all metal grids and black glass dulled by settled filth. Then down some steps and around a tight corner and they were in the link room; clean shapes on the floor showed that it had once been much more.

One side was entirely sectioned into opal screens, a couple of them cracked. The fragments lay where they had fallen. There was a padded seat on a boom arm which could apparently range across the screens and settle the occupant in front of any. The opposite wall was all glass with a small auditorium beyond for operators, observers or whatever.

'It doesn't look much,' Lobo commented.

'It *isn't* much,' Rorvik agreed. 'Most of the useful stuff was ripped out when they transferred across to the bigger ship. The memories are complete, though.' Memories aren't hardware; the Wekk couldn't pick them up and carry them across. One reason was that the ship would die during the transfer. Instead they'd used this unit to design another, and then re-recorded all the memories for a perfect copy. It was as if the ship was making a simulacrum of itself.

Rorvik was looking warily at the empty chair. Randall said, 'Can you do it?'

'I won't know until I've tried. At least give me a chance.'

'But you were able to plug straight into the shuttle . . .'

'And look at the lousy job I made of it; Anyway, this isn't the shuttle, it's a ten-mile cylinder. You haven't even told me what I've got to do with it.'

No more private speculation, it was time to produce the goods. 'Morden gave me the idea when he said we couldn't disable the Wekk ship without turning off the sun.'

'I'm not sure I want to vote for that,' Lobo said doubtfully.

'Nobody's voting on it. We're going to do it.'

The grey simulacrum was giving Randall a very narrow look. 'I think you're overestimating my abilities,' he said.

Randall had come up with the only answer that he could on the information available to him. The ship needed direct sunlight; without it the power supply would cut down to virtually nothing and be diverted to basic survival needs and nothing else. When the power went the Wekk would have to dive for their survival couches before their biological hibernation mechanism could take over, triggered by the fall in temperature. If they didn't make it they would risk wasting away in cold sleep over an indefinite period – they couldn't know when they would find another usable system.

He wanted Rorvik to find a way of firing up whatever propulsion system the deserted ship might use, accelerating its orbit so that it would collide with the inhabited ship ahead. The collision would have to be exactly right in two respects; firstly, the inhabited ship was to be pushed into a planetary eclipse, falling from line-of-sight of the sun and into the world's shadow. Secondly Randall wanted the two ships to be mangled together at the point of contact sufficiently to allow them to get through.

'Now,' Randall said. 'Can that be done?'

'Probably. But not by me.'

'Why not?'

'What do you think I am? I've got the mind and most of the memories of an ordinary man. You seem to think I'm some kind of miracle worker.'

'But you're not an ordinary man.'

Rorvik seemed to stiffen. 'You accepted me as one,' he said, watching Randall and daring him to proceed.

'Because it was convenient.' Randall walked over to the operator's chair on the boom arm. It was raised slightly above shoulder height and its proportions were all wrong for a human body. 'It kept you quiet and Morden happy. But it's time to face realities, Rorvik.'

'So you can't control your prejudices any more.' There was sadness under Rorvik's anger, as if he'd expected this. 'If you're not prepared to let me be a man, what am I? I think you'll like the alternative even less.'

'It's time you went in for some intelligent self-assessment, and stopped being obsessed with faking yourself a family tree. You are what you are, and you won't understand that until you've found your limitations.' Randall reached up and briefly touched the padding of the chair at his shoulder. 'Scared of trying?'

'Why should I be scared?'

'You don't know what you may find. It could be better than you hope.'

'Or a whole lot worse.'

'He's right, Rorvik,' Lobo argued reasonably. 'You should at least give it a try.'

The simulacrum turned on him with bitterness. 'It's easy for you to say that.'

Lobo shrugged. 'Sure it is. Doesn't make it any less true.'

'But I *know* what I am,' Rorvik said, half protest and half plea. 'As a man I barely rate – it shows every time you speak to me. And as a machine I'm hardly better than the marionettes.'

Randall noted the first break in Rorvik's defences, self-pity replacing self-assertion. 'Remember how you felt when you stepped into Marius's chambers? You'd just come from the shuttle and you were crammed with life and confidence. You can interface with the machine around us and we can't.'

'I don't want to do it again.'

'Because you don't want to risk liking it. You resent the kick it gives to the machine part of you.'

'That's a lie.'

'You know it isn't. You've suspected it yourself and you're not man enough to put it to the test.'

Rorvik said nothing. He stared at Randall and Lobo began to worry. Perhaps the Élite had pushed him too far, having too little consideration for the simulacrum's meagre dreams; or on the other hand perhaps he had such sympathy that he had to rule it out completely and fill the space with coldness. Randall the hustler, the schemer, the blind and programmed patriot, was well-versed in the ways of inhumanity.

'Get out of my way,' Rorvik said.

Randall backed off, and Rorvik swung himself up into the operator's chair. The boom dipped slightly under his weight, and dry bearings protested at its anchorage. He sat awkwardly, his legs too long and his back too short for the dimensions of the seat.

There was nothing spectacular. He stared at the opal screen directly ahead for perhaps a minute, and then it began to glow. At first it was no lighter than a summer night sky, but then it became more intense, producing not only the beginnings of an image but also an atonal hum that seemed to be a composite of a large number of contributory sounds.

'I don't want to be disturbed,' Rorvik said aloud without looking at them. The screen picked up his words and tried to repeat them, getting the inflections but none of the meaning.

They found a doorway without a door which led them through to the auditorium on the other side of the glass. The seats had the same odd proportions as the operator's chair and they chose to stand. The sounds from the screen still reached them, if a little muted; they, however, could converse quietly without disturbing Rorvik.

Two of the adjacent screens had come alight. As they watched another flickered in and then another. No two of them held the same image and no image was recognizable. One was a snowstorm, another was slow rain on the outside of a window, another the slow heave of a mercury sea.

'Just colours and music,' Lobo said, mystified.

'But he must be seeing more. Even if he understands it, will he be able to use it?'

'I damn well hope so. That was quite an ass-kicking you gave him.'

Randall nodded absently, accepting the remark as if it were praise. 'He needed it. He's too inclined to feel sorry for himself.'

They watched the play of light. With the exception of the broken panels the entire opposite wall was as bright as the ice and pulsing with a cascade of disguised information. Lobo said, 'How much of it did you mean?'

Randall considered. 'I don't know. Does it really matter?'

'I would have thought so.'

'An idea's an idea. Doesn't make any difference whether it's sincere or not.'

Another pause. Rorvik was still sitting passively, a blank silhouette against the interplay of sound and colour.

Lobo said, 'Assume for a minute he can do it. Assume that he locks the two ships together and we can transfer across. What the hell do we do then?'

'With the power right down we'll have the run of their ship. We'll find the equivalent of this room and wreck it.'

'And what then? How are we supposed to get home?'

Randall considered an evasion, decided it would be pointless. 'I don't know,' he said. 'That's the only honest answer I can give you.'

'Thanks for that much, anyway.'

The screens went blank all at once, and their music ran down the scale to nothing. Randall and Lobo hurried back into the room.

Rorvik was rubbing his eyes, causing his artificial skin to flex and stretch. 'It can be done,' he said. 'But it isn't going to be easy.'

'Nobody said it would be,' Randall told him. 'Can you do it from here?'

'From this chair. Nowhere else.'

There were no obvious controls, for it seemed that the Wekk had no power over their ships; Rorvik would be cheating the system by making use of the design capability through which the simulacra controlled their cruisers. He'd have to join the machine, become a part of it; then he could use his thoughts and impulses to give it drive and they would be automatically translated into action by drawing on the ship's memories and capabilities. Like the shuttle, he would become the ship.

'Is that why you resisted the idea so much?' Randall asked. 'When you knew you could do it all along?'

'I knew nothing of the kind. Something could still go wrong – you ever hear of celestial mechanics?'

'They fix spaceships?' Lobo hazarded.

'It's a field of mathematics and navigation in which the shortest distance between two points is hardly ever a straight line. A slight error either way and we could send the line of ships cannoning down through the atmosphere and right on to the city, or else just bust a hole and lose all our air. Watch the screen.'

The opal plate nearest to them began to glow. A green dot appeared, leaving a neon trail wherever it moved; it rapidly sketched in what looked like a glass model of the World Ship with all its lines visible through the structure. It rotated through three dimensions to check for accuracy, and then the dot reappeared and outlined the second, much larger ship.

'The third ship doesn't appear anywhere in this computer's memory,' Rorvik explained. 'I'll have to guess and make some allowance for it.'

He commenced the first experimental scenario. A number of points on the smaller of the two ships flared in imitation of a burn and the image began to move, leaving ghostly after-images to mark out its course. A number of the other screens illuminated with similar displays, each slightly different and none synchronous.

When all the screens were filled with moving ships the sequences began to speed up, colliding silently in an eerie display of multiple disaster. Each wiped failure was replaced by a new set of skeletal players which pirouetted, burned and collided over again. In most of them the curved edge of the planet appeared, adding its mass to influence the protagonists.

It became too fast to watch, an out-of-phase flickering across the screens. Randall and Lobo moved to the back of the room and turned away, finding the reflections from the panoramic window slightly less unbearable.

'He seems to be enjoying it,' Lobo commented.

'He's finding potential he didn't know about. He was so obsessed with being considered a man that he forgot there might be some advantage in being a machine.'

'But it's a matter of pride. How would you like to think that you were an artificial construct?'

'I wouldn't. But that's not the point. The point is that we keep feeding him the right lines to make sure he stays happy. While he's happy, he's useful.'

Lobo wondered if it was better to be a machine with a dream or a man without a soul, but he was prevented from saying so by a deep, bellowing chord from the screens and a shout from Rorvik of 'I've got it! That's the one!'

He ran through it for them again, slow enough for them to see but still much faster than actuality – such masses couldn't be shunted with ease. The smaller ship dropped in its orbit, accelerating as it moved into a perceptibly tighter curve and then rising with a second burn as it drew level with the larger, clipping it neatly on its edge. The two locked together and began to shrink as the edge of the world rose to meet them. They passed the curve and remained visible even though they were supposedly now in the planet's shadow.

The sequence speeded. The lower edge of the planet travelled across the screen, and as the linked ships moved around they separated.

'We'll have no more than an hour to get down to the damaged area and make the transfer into the Wekk ship,' Rorvik said. 'That's how long it will take to get over the horizon and out of the sunlight.'

Randall said, 'Will their ship be able to react and bring itself back?'

'No time, besides which it will have to start powering down. But there's another problem.'

'What's that?'

'An hour later we'll be around and back into the sunlight. The hibernation sequence will start reversing.'

'Doesn't leave much margin,' Randall mused.

'It doesn't leave *any* margin,' protested Lobo. 'Can't we think of something else?'

Man and machine looked at him. 'Like what?' Randall said.

'Something that means we can stay here and manage everything from a distance. So we don't have to go into a ship full of things like that statue we saw.' It even sounded lame to Lobo.

'This is no time to start calling up all your old bad dreams,' Randall told him. Then he turned to Rorvik, still aloft in the operator's chair. 'When are we going to start that sequence?'

'It's started. When we've had the second burn, then we can move.'

Twenty-Four

If Morden's warning was to be acknowledged, reserve was the order of the day. Killoran had gone alone to the newly-arrived ship which stood in the crater formed by its landing.

The ridge of snow that had been thrown up helped to obscure the cruiser to the Palace. Everybody was either in the Palace or on the icebreaker and a good number of them were crowded into the deep trench that angled from the bay to ground level. Berg was on his elbows at the top, trying to see what was happening so that he could report back.

There wasn't much he could say. There was a woman, as they'd been warned; Berg could only see her distant outline, but his imagination filled in the rest. Tall, dark, high cheekbones, almond-shaped eyes – he even added in a couple of moles in places he'd have needed an X-ray telescope to see.

Whatever it was she was saying, she wasn't very pleased. It could have been a threat of some kind, but Killoran wasn't backing down. He passed this information on to the men waiting below.

'Killoran's a good kid,' Palmer said confidently, recently arrived after his relief from guard duty. 'He won't screw up on us.'

'He's also Élite,' Bulstrode reminded him. 'He might sell us out.'

Everybody was watching Berg, so they didn't see the Worm come in. He was slightly more unkempt than usual, and he wandered around the back of the group. He couldn't actually discern what they were doing, so after a while he asked nobody in particular, 'What's going on down here?'

Bulstrode turned and saw him blinking pleasantly. 'Quiet, Worm,' he said. 'Berg's concentrating.'

'Berg's doing *what*?'

Berg turned at the top of the ramp. 'What's so funny?'

'Crawl back into the woodwork, Worm,' Bulstrode said. 'We've managed fine without you so far.'

'You had your chance to join us,' Palmer added.

The Worm could see the group's hostility once again coming to focus on him, and he backed off a little. 'I don't want to join you,' he said. 'I only want to know what's going on.'

'There's something happening,' Berg said, and the Worm was promptly forgotten.

The woman had been angry, almost on the point of striking Killoran. Then she had turned and climbed back into 'that jet thing she came down in'. All the hatches were still open and it showed no signs of moving, but Killoran was on his way back alone, as white as the ice and looking scared.

'Morden was right,' Killoran told them when he'd arrived back. 'She wants Randall, and I let her think he's here. She must be from one of the other colonized systems on the space trade network. It seems there's a main ship in orbit and she thinks Randall's escaped from that, but according to Morden he's still up there. She wants us to hand him over so she can kill him.'

'Is that all?' Berg said hollowly.

Bulstrode added, 'What happens when we can't?'

'She'll come in after him.'

About twenty pairs of eyebrows went up at the same time. 'What kind of threat's that?' said Berg, voicing everybody's surprise.

Killoran explained that not only was she armed, she was unnaturally strong, a fact that she had demonstrated by pinching the leading edge of her cruiser's wing between thumb and forefinger to leave a sizable impression in the metal. Bulstrode said he didn't believe it.

'Is that a sincere opinion,' Killoran asked him in irritation, 'or just rhetoric?'

'I don't know. What's rhetoric?'

If she *was* from another system, surely anything was possible after generations without contact. Berg said, 'If Morden says Randall's still on the main ship, how did he get there?'

'The same shuttle Morden came down in. It was homing on the Ice Palace beacon.'

'How come we didn't see it?' someone wondered.

'I saw it once,' Palmer said. 'Nobody believed me.'

'It came and went during the storms,' Killoran explained.

Bulstrode reacted with bitterness. 'Storms where people disappeared. What the hell's been going on under our noses?'

They didn't seem to have any choice other than to accept Morden's story and stall for time. Nobody could offer a more likely explanation of the events that had recently come to disrupt the Palace's killing routine, and that limited the choices somewhat.

Killoran announced that he was going to try to capture the cruiser. The suggestion of action, no matter how hazardous, was warmly welcomed by men whose capacity for long reflection was limited. Only Cohn objected. 'Even if you were successful, you couldn't fly it.'

'Details,' said Bulstrode airily. 'Count me in.'

'But it'll be suicide.'

'Not if we're sneaky about it. And it's a damn sight better than sitting here arguing over things we know nothing about.'

So it was settled. They would take the cruiser. And then . . . then they would worry about what to do next.

Nobody had seen the Worm arrive. Nobody had seen him go, either.

For the first time in her short career Valum was angry and frustrated. The situation here was so different from the World Ship, where the simulacra outnumbered the bloodbags and moved in familiar, well-defined territory. She was also having the new experience of an unfulfilled want, and she didn't like it. She didn't like having distant horizons all around her, didn't like having to deal with bloodbags. Above all, she didn't like being opposed.

She could blast the Palace from the air – but she wouldn't see Randall squirm. She needed that satisfaction.

Willis told her that the Wekk had been trying to reach her. She opened the channels carelessly, leaving Willis free to listen if he wished.

'*Valum!*' it came, immediate and urgent. '*Matters are moving fast here. Is your ground base established?*'

'No. I haven't got Randall yet.'

'*Forget Randall.*'

'We've been through all this before.'

'*A short time ago our old world decided to come alive and make use of its propulsion systems. We are sliding towards the shadow of the planet. You know what this will mean?*'

'You'll have to go into emergency shutdown.'

'*For a few hours only. In that period you will be on your own, and we want your full attention on the operation.*'

'But why did the old ship begin to move?'

'*It was a development we did not anticipate, but one which, nevertheless, pleased us.*'

'What do you mean?'

'*We recognize it to be part of the field test of the ground commander.*' There was an undertone of something suspiciously like amusement. '*At this moment he is striving to destroy us.*'

She was confused. She'd known nothing of the ground commander's development, and had assumed that he was being tested in isolation to far more exacting standards than the other simulacra. 'I don't understand.'

'*The tests have been going on for some time. We placed certain blocks in his mentality; he is unaware of his real capabilities and his true loyalty to the Wekk. His task was to fathom and penetrate our own defences – no other simulacrum has been tested to such an extreme. When he reaches our strategic centres, we will know he is ready.*'

'The ground commander's trying to destroy *you*?'

'*He thinks he is. But in the end he will find he is unable and unwilling to do . . .*'

The withdrawal was such as she had never experienced before, sudden and without warning. Shutdown.

Willis was shaking his head as if trying to clear it. Because Valum hadn't restricted and controlled the signal he'd had no choice but to overhear, and as it was his first experience of contact he'd no expertise or resources to combat the inward rush of emptiness that followed the abrupt severance.

'What are we going to do now?' he said as he got over the shock.

'Nothing,' Valum replied sharply.

'But...'

'But nothing. It'll be several hours before they're out of the enforced hibernation programme, and you heard what they said. I'm on my own until then.'

'I also heard them say to forget Randall,' he reminded her, hoping that he didn't speak out of turn.

She looked at him evenly. '*I* didn't hear it.'

'But...'

'And neither did you.'

'Yes, Valum.'

Rorvik led the way, and the others had difficulty keeping up with him in the howling winds that funnelled down the corridors towards the impact zone. Both hulls were ruptured and mangled, atmosphere draining out around the imperfect seam, and whilst there was no serious danger of either ship losing a significant amount of pressure before repairs could be made passage from one to the other was difficult. Two fast streams of air met and whirled in the breach and one of the greatest hazards was from spinning debris, but by linking arms and staying low they made it through.

The locked ships were still spinning in tandem, so gravity remained. The new World Ship was bigger, wider, cleaner; it was also cold, and chilled vapour was being pumped out of floor-level grilles.

An emergency foam had filled the corridors to help slow the ship's bleeding. It held tight against the push of air but parted and reshaped behind them as they struggled through. After thirty yards or less they were back in the open and able to continue.

On the middle levels they found their first Wekk. It was lying in a corridor having obviously failed to make it to the hibernation tanks. It had dropped where it stood, and now seemed more dead than asleep as cold vapours billowed around it. The overgrown statue in the park had been a fairly accurate representation, although they could now see that the skin was grey and leathery. Not unlike Rorvik's.

'He seems to get more confident every minute,' Lobo said to Randall when the simulacrum was out of earshot.

'That's good. I'd had enough of dragging his thumb out of his mouth and trying to cheer him up.'

It took about half an hour of forcing the pace to reach the computer room a couple of miles in and three levels up. The walls along the route were lined with the doors of hibernation chambers.

The room was all wrong. It was a different shape, a different layout, and the machinery bore no resemblance to that which they had left behind. Rorvik stood in the middle, bewildered. Even as he looked around the light was cut by fifty percent, presumably as part of the powering-down. He turned in the starfield blaze of equipment lighting and said, 'It's all strange. I don't understand any of it.'

The room obviously represented some leap of technology from its predecessor, probably raided from the last system. But where to start? They had only minutes left, and they could spend them pulverizing the equivalent of a fire extinguisher while the ship ticked on and waited for the moment when it could again reach them.

There was a choice to be made, and Randall didn't feel sufficiently confident to make it. Surely Rorvik could act on his intuition – he was machine, after all, and he should have some feeling for the weaknesses of his own kind.

'Come on, Rorvik,' he urged. 'Surely you're not getting twinges of old loyalties?'

Rorvik looked at him sharply, as if stung. Hadn't he already demonstrated his loyalties beyond dispute? 'What's that supposed to mean?'

'You're the only one here who can get access to the programming in all this.'

'That's not what you were starting to say.'

'All right, then, I'll say it. You're either a man or a machine. I know what you say, but I still don't know what you really are deep inside. Now we're at the moment of truth you're hesitating.'

Rorvik gave another look around. It was hopeless. Panels, consoles, shelves and tables littered with unfathomable tools and instruments. Randall would class him with these – and yet he'd needed him and ridden on his back every inch of the way! 'And what do you know about it, b . . .'

'Go on, say it!' Randall shouted defiantly. 'The word's bloodbag, isn't it?'

'Yes, damn you!'

'If you want to be a man, Rorvik, earn the right! If you don't understand any of it, pick a place and smash it!'

The final burn hit boiling point. Several things happened, all within the space of a couple of seconds.

Rorvik grabbed the nearest panel. It wasn't flimsy, but his fingers sank right through it and it folded like paper as it came away from the front of the machine. Its edge caught in the circuitry and trailed sparks as he whirled and flung it at Randall. There was a free-standing cube of a strange metal on the floor nearby, and he reached for that to send it on after.

Randall was diving flat and heading for the nearest cover. Lobo wasn't so fast, but then he wasn't the target, either. Randall hit and rolled as the panel banged edge-on into the wall behind him, narrowly clearing his legs as it dropped. He kept moving, and the cube filled his airspace an instant later.

Now Rorvik was coming with bare hands. There was something like a table between them but he didn't seem to notice it until it got in his way and he sprawled across it, hands clutching at empty air as Randall jerked back out of his reach.

Rorvik slung the table aside and Randall went with it, trying to keep the barrier between them. Lobo scrambled out of the way, knowing better than to try to help; Rorvik's strength was greater than both of theirs combined – they'd learned as much in their first encounter on the shuttle – and Randall's only chance lay in his speed of reaction.

The table was fully overturned this time, and Randall dived out and under. He helped propel himself with a sideways elbow to Rorvik's ribs that had no discernible effect apart from that of nearly breaking his arm. This was Pearson all over again, singlehanded and worse.

Only a few yards and he was up against another wall. There simply wasn't the room for competent evasion.

Lobo had got himself into a corner, sliding back into a niche formed by a waist-high rostrum and the wall. There were a number of rods and devices arranged in neat order on its surface, but Lobo had disarranged them as he'd clambered across to shelter. Now he tried to make himself heard over the noise of the deadly ballet.

'Randall!' he shouted. 'Remember what we came for!'

Rorvik faltered and looked around. He was looking at the open gap where he'd torn the panel away, and he was hesitating.

He wasn't loyal to the Wekk, and he didn't hate mankind. He hated Randall, that was all.

Lobo covered his head with his arms as Randall exploited Rorvik's momentary inattention to get past him and land on the rostrum, sweeping the last of its collection of instruments on to the floor in a grating clash of metal and crystal.

Rorvik didn't follow. He stooped to reach for the cube he had thrown, now with one corner sheared completely off.

The gun didn't look like a gun. It was the wrong shape, and it didn't fit Randall's hand so that he had to grip it two-fisted to cover the trigger.

Rorvik lifted the cube to dash it into the open heart of the machine, and his leg exploded like a bursting pipe. There was no blood. The cube dropped to the floor, and Rorvik dropped after it, hingeing sideways on his ruined limb.

A sharp wedge of blue light fell across the room as the outer door opened, widening and spilling with the Wekk's shadow at its centre. The hiss of bearings and the sharp little click as the door locked fully open rang unnaturally loud in the silence.

It walked into the room and looked around. It was hardly bigger than a child, and it had wide, awkward hips which made it necessary for it to swing its body from side to side as it moved. It wore a white suit of some thick fabric, and the head was completely enclosed in a black dome. The unit on its back with all the pipes and tubes *had* to be keeping it warm.

It paused at Rorvik, who was now stirring, and then turned to take in Randall. He was still astride the rostrum, both hands around the alien weapon.

The Wekk raised a hand with three short fingers, but it was the ship that spoke. 'I am pleased to welcome,' it said from all around them, 'the new ground commander of our simulacra.'

Randall looked for a moment, thoroughly confused.

'There will be a period of readjustment,' it said encouragingly. 'It will be short.'

'Getting the message?' Lobo said from behind him.

'What message?'

'You heard. That thing said welcome to the ground commander.'

'The ground commander? Rorvik?' Randall seemed astonished at the notion.

'Not Rorvik. You.'

'What are you talking about?'

'Morden told me before I left the shuttle, when I took him up to the bridge and strapped him in. It was part of the deal he did with Marius.'

'You're wrong. Completely wrong.'

'Morden didn't want the underbelly's big hero to be treated as shabbily as Marius' politics demanded. The real Randall's living in luxury somewhere on the city outskirts. He was drugged and patterned shortly after his trial. Then he was sent back to the city and his simulacrum was delivered to the Ice Palace.'

Randall was perplexed. What possible motive could Morden have for such a lie? 'But I'm not a marionette. I'm a man!'

Rorvik had managed to push himself into a sitting position. The side of his leg was open, and bright metal showed deep inside.

'What does it feel like, Randall?' he said. 'Time to start wheeling out all the insincere philosophy you've been throwing at me.'

'Morden was lying to you,' Randall insisted. He had to make them see the truth. 'I'm *Randall*. It's *my* body and *my* memories.'

'The body's copied and the memories are planted. Find another way of being sure.'

'I don't need to find another way. I *know*.'

Rorvik's expression didn't change, but his tone was gently mocking. 'Starting to feel the hunger now?'

All three of them were looking at him – Rorvik on the floor, the undersized Wekk in the middle of the room, and Lobo at his shoulder. It was faintly embarrassing, and more than a little ridiculous.

'If you want to prove you're what you say you are,' Lobo urged, 'kill that thing and then blast the ship.'

'There's no need.'

'What are you afraid of?'

'There may be a better way!'

'You're rationalizing!' Rorvik said triumphantly. 'You won't do it because you can't!'

Randall slid off the rostrum. Tiny fragments of glass showered from his clothes on to the floor as he came to his feet, and the Wekk took a cautious step back.

'Allow me to help you,' the ship said. 'Time is short.' The Wekk seemed to hear some different inner voice, and responded to it by waddling over to the square of electronics that Rorvik had exposed and pulling the adjacent panels aside.

'A single shot into this circuitry would cripple me beyond any hope of repair,' the ship went on. 'Feel free to destroy me . . . if you wish.'

A machine to serve a machine. Everything he had ever valued – friendship, the Élite, the city – all was incidental. His arm wouldn't move. He couldn't even get himself to *want* it to move.

'What's been done to me?' he demanded in disbelief. 'I don't want to be a simulacrum.'

'Neither did I,' said Rorvik, 'but you told me to stop whining.'

'A little pain,' the ship said soothingly, 'and it will soon pass. Or we can remove it for you. You've far exceeded our expectations.'

'I don't know what to think.'

'We'll tell you what to think, don't worry. Healthy, loyal, but essentially *human* thoughts. It is for this capacity that we needed you so badly.'

Another try with the arm. It hung easily by his side, a loose grip on the weapon. How could it be true? He'd come so far, hated so much, planned and schemed . . . and only to serve?

'As was intended,' said the ship in answer to his unspoken thought.

'No, damn it, no! I don't know what you're trying to pull or who you're trying to trick, but it won't work!'

'Then blast the panel,' Lobo suggested.

'I can't!'

Lobo shouldered him aside as he came down from the rostrum, and the Wekk had to scamper out of the way when he saw the huge form bearing down on him.

The gun came up, and both Randall's hands wrapped around it and sought the trigger as if drawing on specialized knowledge of their own. He tried to fight it, but couldn't. His Randall personality seemed to be only an ineffectual fraction of his entire being, the workings of which he was recognizing for the first time.

Lobo was reaching for the seven-cornered cube.

Randall's consciousness might have been compared to an island from which he observed the passing of the ocean, suspecting for the first time that there might be unseen subtleties of action and relationship in its depths, or a lone planet so preoccupied with fortifying the corruption of its own civilization that its need for the stars was argued down by the pretence of reason. Lobo raised the cube.

Trust me, said a voice in Randall's head, and it was as if someone else had entered and gently but firmly taken over.

Lobo jerked once with the impact, and he lifted slightly from the floor. His toes dragged as he travelled forward but then he came up hard against the machinery. His body no longer held the inertia of the charge, and his snow suit blossomed out at the front as it carried on through him to bury its energy in the intricacies ahead.

He hung there, pinned on the sharper projections by the collision, unmoving even as fires and sparks showered around him.

Something had changed. Randall could once again feel the strange grip of the weapon in his hands; the controlling mind had retreated and left him in command, and there was no resistance as he swung from left to right.

Lobo was dead. Surely he'd known that he'd had no hope of reaching the panel; but then he seemed to have given more attention to placing himself between it and Randall, ensuring that the shot would pass straight through his flimsy bloodbag body and into where the ship had assured them it would do most damage.

Randall emptied the gun into the exposed panelling, firing again and again until it wouldn't fire any more. There was burning deep inside, damage breeding damage, and hot liquid metal burst out at a couple of points and set the floor alight.

Rorvik rolled out of the way as the pool of flame spread, but the Wekk caught some on its suit and danced around as it tried to put it out. Randall threw the empty weapon aside and reached for Rorvik's arm, dragging him out of immediate danger.

The undermind had gone; or, rather, as the ship had died the full service of his mind had reverted in loyalty to the only other conscious personality it knew, that quota of self-awareness that had been set aside as Randall.

He was trying to help Rorvik up on to his good leg when, with a formless howl that almost blended with the rasp and crackle of burning ship, the Wekk hurled itself on to them.

'Anybody home?'

'Take your hand off my ship.'

The Worm did as he was told, and gave the place where his hand had rested a wipe with his sleeve. Then he looked up again at Valum and said, 'Can we talk?'

She didn't invite him up the short ladder and into the cruiser's cabin. Instead she stepped down on to the ice. 'Have you come to a decision?'

'I'm not here to represent anybody,' he assured her. 'I'm alone.'

'I know you're alone. Do you think I couldn't see you creeping over?'

'I didn't want the others to see me, that's all. They kick me around enough as it is.'

She didn't want to hear about his personal problems. 'All this secrecy just to waste my time?'

'But I came to tell you something.'

'Tell it, then.'

The Worm glanced around, and decided that he might not be quite as invisible to the Ice Palace as he might wish. He moved in closer to the ship. 'I want something from you first,' he warned.

'I don't have to give you anything.'

'I know. All I want is for you to go away.'

She wondered whether she ought to laugh, but this baggy little clown in the one-lensed glasses was surely beyond a joke. 'I'm hardly astonished,' she said. 'but I'm not going without Randall.'

'Randall isn't here. I heard them talking.'

'Of course he's here. They're hiding him.'

'They want you to think that, but it isn't true. Morden came down alone, and wherever he came from, Randall stayed there.'

'It can't be. I'd know.'

'And the one called Killoran,' the Worm pressed on earnestly, 'he's got ideas about stealing your ship, and the others are backing him. They'll back anything that gives them the slightest hope of getting away from the Palace because Killoran's given them all escape fever. It's ruined everything I built.'

Valum heard a faint slither on the other side of the cruiser. She analysed and identified it almost immediately; Willis, letting himself out of the cabin and dropping stealthily to the ice. Could this shrimp in front of her be no more than a decoy?

'Why tell me this?' she said.

'I told you. I want you to go away and leave us alone. I want things the way they were before.'

'And how was that?'

'Ordered, logical.' The Worm was talking fast, pleased that he seemed to be getting through to her. 'None of this shouting about hope and home. Everybody working the rosters and being in the right place at the right time.'

'And you?' she asked, appearing coolly attentive whilst giving most of her concentration to any faint sounds that might come from the other side of the cruiser.

'I was in charge,' the Worm said. 'They needed me then. Nobody needs me for anything now.'

There was a sharp cracking sound, like a hammer on an enamel basin. Valum smiled at the Worm, and he was far from comforted. 'And you'll lie to me to be needed again,' she said.

'I'm not lying,' he protested, his voice rising to a shrill squeak. 'Randall isn't here.'

Willis came around under the wing, dragging an unresisting form by a handful of fabric. One good heave and it was sprawling at Valum's feet.

She was watching the Worm, and had observed his double surprise – once at Killoran's appearance, and again on recognition of Willis. It seemed he was telling the truth, after all.

'Caught him trying to circle round and get at us from the back,' Willis explained. 'What do you want me to do with him?'

She lifted a foot and prodded the young Élite in the side. He groaned and moved slightly, so Willis pulled him into a sitting position. After a couple of tries he stayed there.

'So,' Valum said when there seemed to be a reasonable chance that she'd be understood, 'Randall isn't at the Ice Palace. You've nothing to bargain with.'

'Of course he's there,' Killoran replied as he tried to muster enough courage to touch the back of his head. 'You won't find him without me.' Then he saw the Worm, and understood.

'It's for the best, don't you see?' the Worm said. 'Now she'll go away and leave us alone.'

Valum was looking at them both pensively. She said, 'Have you killed yet, Willis?'

Willis was surprised by the question. He'd never had the chance to join a successful bloodbag hunt. 'No, Valum,' he said.

'Take the little one, then, and watch what I do.'

She bent and then quickly straightened, lifting Killoran bodily by the thick tendons of his neck. He howled with the sudden and unexpected pain of it, also with the surprise of being lifted clear into the air by a woman who appeared to weigh considerably less than himself.

'But what about our bargain?' the Worm wailed before he was swept into the air by Willis in a similar grip.

Valum buried her fingers in the waist of Killoran's suit and prepared to execute the clean twist that would snap his neck. She looked at Willis to see how he was managing.

Willis had set the Worm down again. There was confusion in his eyes, and in that same moment she knew why.

She didn't want to kill. She could still do it, but the impulse wasn't there.

Killoran fell heavily on to the ice when she dropped him. He felt its gritty numbness against his cheek and rolled over, trying to get the cold on to the back of his neck where already the blood was collecting under the skin in a massive bruise. As the bright flashing lights that had taken over from his vision subsided he saw that Valum and Willis were returning to the cruiser.

At that moment the follow-up team arrived, Berg at their

head. Ten of them had waited at the lip of the crater for Killoran's signal, and when it didn't arrive it was only Bulstrode's insistence that they stick to the letter of the plan that had kept them in line. Shouts of agony had brought them running, and now Willis had the demonstration that he'd hoped for in the Tin Jungle.

She disposed of Berg first because he was nearest, hurdling him as he fell and dropping Bulstrode and Palmer with simultaneous kicks. The Weasel had a club in the air and so left himself open to fold over a blow to the abdomen, and the Anteater tripped over him and managed to knock himself out without any help. Valum caught the club as it fell and skipped over three heads in a single swing, letting it flip over with its own momentum and bringing it up under the chin of a fourth. Then she dropped the club and met the last one with the heel of her hand to his jaw. Ever afterwards he would insist that he had 'run into the wing, or something'.

She looked for more, but that was it. She climbed into the cruiser and Willis pulled in the ladder.

The World Ship was coming out of shutdown, and something was seriously wrong.

Twenty-Five

Although child-sized the Wekk was strong, clinging to Randall and resisting being thrown off. Rorvik couldn't help much but he managed to get a handful of the tubing on its heat unit and jerk it free. It spilled a cloud of metal-scented steam into the room, whipping about like an electrified snake.

They held it down until the cold penetrated its suit, and then when Randall helped Rorvik to get on to his good leg it still tried to crawl after them. There was no plan, no obvious route to follow, no longer a clear-cut aim in sight; they'd destroyed what they came to destroy and hadn't considered the prospects for survival afterwards. The strategic centres were blasted, all right, but as far as they knew the World Ship might already be out and in the sunlight, undamaged systems warming and preparing to re-awaken thousands of Wekk to a world robbed ot its purpose.

There was some vague intention of returning to the breach and getting back to the old ship. They'd be no less trapped, but they'd be in defensible territory – at least, until the simulacra returned. Their chances in any direction were nil but all the same they ran, a three-legged, dragging double-act intent upon preserving the energies of life for as long as they could.

Randall was no ground commander. Hadn't he proved as much by his action with the gun? He'd ruined those same delicate organs that had been laid open to him as proof of his lack of free will. Some proof. He was Randall, Élite and in control, always had been. Nevertheless he found himself taking a far greater interest in the ordinary processes of his body than was normal – the pump and stretch of muscle tissue in his legs, the ache in his side as he supported Rorvik, the bitter alkali of his saliva as he breathed too hard and too fast. All the reactions and operations that he had previously taken for granted were now like possessions of the dead, transformed from the commonplace into cherished items. Their familiarity reassured him, a growing shield against the awe that he felt after a brief glimpse into the dark spaces of his own mind.

He wasn't simulacrum. The steady tick and signature of his mentality and physique told him so. He didn't know what a simulacrum would feel like – actually, he doubted that they felt at all in the sense that he understood it – but he knew it wouldn't be like this. They'd be like Rorvik, confused and bitter and wanting to be human. Not like Randall, confused and bitter and *confident* that he was human.

The body's copied and the memories are planted. Find another way of being sure.

Their way was blocked by barrier foam. It had spread considerably. They tried to push through it as before, but didn't emerge within seconds as last time; it had filled a length of the corridor, bubbling out along angles and junctions. Once within its gentle pressure all directions became the same, a translucent cocoon which yielded but never revealed.

It was hopeless. Each attempt to navigate brought them to a wall, each attempt to follow a wall led them to a corner. As they were squeezing through a silky light enveloped them without warning.

The ship was powering up.

If they needed further confirmation it was given by the vents close to the floor which were now pumping warm, moist air, heating the foam around it. As it heated it began to break down, shrivelling and collapsing in unlovely rags about them. Only the cold of space would preserve and consolidate it.

They came into the open and nearly fell over a Wekk. It was standing unsteadily in the doorway to its hibernation chamber, naked and dripping. It was slow to react to them – how would a Wekk show surprise? – and it blinked a couple of times, a vertical in-and-out nictation. Three doors along another Wekk emerged, and then another. A bad place to be. They plunged back into the dwindling foam and tried to plough down the corridor in a straight line.

There were a hundred of them, perhaps more, a sea of bobbing grey heads filling the passageway. Small, robust and alert, clacking and twittering like locusts. At their head, the Wekk in the thermic suit.

'We can't fight them, and we've nowhere to go,' Rorvik said in quiet desperation. 'What now?'

Randall looked on the horde. It was growing as more doors opened and wide-hipped figures came limping.

'We've got nothing to bargain with,' he said. 'Remember any good prayers?'

Their eyes met and held for a moment. 'Rorvik didn't know any. Did Randall?'

Randall shook his head, the slightest movement. 'He never needed them.'

The Wekk pushed up and around them, encircling the two but staying out of reach. 'Who do the machines pray to?' Mitchell asked.

'Nobody. Nobody cares about us. Rorvik is dead and Randall's lying sick and drunk in some urban paradise. *We* don't belong anywhere.'

Once it was admitted, it didn't seem so bad. When it came down to it Randall didn't want to die deceiving himself, throwing away his pride of self-awareness on a lie.

'Can they kill us?' he said suddenly, recalling the hate in the eyes of a broken Pearson.

'They can probably overpower us, but they can't destroy us. Not without the ship's help.'

'They could open a vacuum dock and push us out.'

'It still wouldn't kill us. We'd feed off the sunlight. We'd go on forever. We can't die.'

Hands were laid on them then, warm leathery claws that pushed and prodded. Knock one away and two replaced it, the Wekk swarming in and around. The crowd started to move, and Randall and Rorvik had no choice other than to move with it.

The inexorable tide urged them back towards the computer room. Every junction saw more Wekk forcing their way into the already tight compress of creatures until the corridor was filled as far as it was possible to see, both ahead and behind. In this grey and rippling mass the white of the thermic suit showed in brief glimpses, never still and always leading the way.

The noise was oppressive. The chatter of the crowd was becoming the angry death-rattle of a race.

The fires in the computer room had mainly died down. Lobo hung there, bloody and sooty and still. Randall looked into his heart for the merest sympton of a man's regret and thought, with relief, that he detected it. So much was enough for now. He would have an eternity to contemplate and encourage it.

The Wekk in the room with them had fallen silent, and it was spreading along the corridors outside. What now? They seemed to be waiting for something.

The suited Wekk pushed forward. The black dome of the helmet was off, and underneath it this creature was identical to the others. It got close to Randall and looked up at him, having to bend its neck with difficulty to do so. It laid a tentative hand on him, and its jaws worked awkwardly. No sound came out the first time, so it swallowed hard and tried again. Its lips were a bony ridge, and the only articulation was in its tongue.

The strangled sound it produced bore no resemblance to anything. It gulped hard, and tried yet again.

'Wranda',' it said. ''lp ss, Wranda' . . .'

It repeated it a couple of times, equally incomprehensibly. Randall looked at Rorvik, helpless.

'Does it expect me to understand this?' he said.

'It sounds like your name,' Rorvik replied. 'I think it's trying to say your name, and it can't.'

It tried again, and failed. Then, more clearly, 'Wranda', 'lp uss . . .'

'It's asking for you to help them,' Rorvik said.

The Wekk was silent, no longer able to sustain the effort and pain of the alien phrase.

'*Help* them?' Randall said with dismay. 'How?'

'This whole ship was a finely balanced system keeping their race alive. Don't you see that by smashing the centres of its drive for expansion you've tipped that system and damned them?'

'Are you trying to say that I shouldn't have done it?'

'Of course not. But they're not a greedy, compulsive, world-raping race. They just lived on a world-raping ship and had to do everything it told them or die when it stopped supporting them.'

The Wekk were waiting, and Randall lacked the drive even to help himself. 'Don't get dewy-eyed for these monsters,' he said with a savagery that rang hollow. 'They built the ship, didn't they?'

'No. The last ship did.'

'That's rather a technical argument.'

'Look at their situation. They've been cruising from star to star for millennia, exploiting and expanding. The ships have used each redesigning to define their methods; the ships have evolved, but because of their dependence the Wekk have *de*volved into complete passivity. We simulacra were the means by which the ship ensured it could do without the Wekk altogether if necessary.'

'It backfired.'

'With a vengeance. They don't know how to make repairs. So come on, Randall. You're the great white hope for the Wekk. Do something for them.'

It wasn't a responsibility he could welcome. '*You* do something.'

'Don't ask me. I'm waiting as well.'

Randall's mind wanted to retreat, to slide gracefully into a dark hole and pull the hole in after it. He was numb, and he didn't want to think any more, ever. The landscapes of this new reality were too cruel, and it gave him no pleasure to look on them.

'You're the ground commander . . .' Rorvik began.

'Don't call me that!'

'You've got to accept it now. You're the heir to the ship you killed. The Wekk are looking to you to save them, and the other simulacra will look to you for leadership.'

'And what about you? Are you turning around and joining the machines again?'

'I am what I am,' Rorvik replied with quiet confidence. 'I've stopped worrying about it.'

There was more babbling at the far end of the room, excited noises of discovery. The broken cube that Lobo had dropped in his dying was now lifted into the air, emerging into view and bobbing towards Randall like a buoy as the Wekk passed it over their heads. They were all trying to get a hand on it to help propel it along, and when it reached Randall he found that it was vibrating slightly. He told Rorvik, unsure of what to do next.

'Open up to it,' Rorvik suggested. 'See what happens.'

Open up to it? How, for God's sake? He held it in both hands and stared at it, but nothing happened. The clattering and croaking all around him was a distraction, and now it was being picked up in the passages outside. He stared harder, but didn't really understand what he was supposed to be doing.

It came to him then without warning. The real world seemed to take a step back as the undermind superimposed its presence, guiding and demonstrating to his novice consciousness.

The cube was trying to speak to him. It was some kind of resonator, pulsing with a non-verbal message that the Wekk obviously couldn't receive. He recognized, without understanding how, the unique configuration of Valum's personality as the undermind took her meaning and crystallized it into a form that he could understand.

She was calling to the ship, asking for acknowledgement. Randall didn't know how, and the ability wasn't forthcoming.

'*The simulacrum fleet is standing by in a parallel orbit with the Ship. We know you've taken some damage and that the operation is in danger. Please give us an indication of your situation.*'

He couldn't. The cube would broadcast to him, but it wouldn't transmit. Rorvik moved closer so that he could listen, hopping with difficulty as the Wekk milled and pressed around him.

After a suitable pause, Valum resumed. '*The Ship doesn't answer, so this is Valum to the three prisoners. I don't know if there's any way you can hear me, but I do know that one of you is our ground commander. I also know that the ship has made a gross error of judgement and has obviously engineered its own destruction through you. In this case, our programmed loyalty reverts to our own kind; in short, that's you, whoever you are. Nothing personal, but I'm not very happy about that. On the other hand I don't have any choice.*

'The only answer seems to be that you persuade the Wekk to hand you over to us. If they do that we'll leave them alone and slingshot them on to the next star. If they don't, we've got a good idea of the capacity for self-repair in the ship walls; we can puncture it all the way around and let the atmosphere escape faster than the holes can be plugged. We'll give you some time to convince them; meanwhile here's a warning shot to help the argument.'

Valum's reluctance was evident. Her new leader and the object of her unwilling devotion was to be one of a group she had come to despise.

'We can't let her do it,' Randall said. 'They'll all die.'

'I think that's supposed to be the idea.'

'But they're depending on us!'

'I doubt if Valum sees it that way. Without the ship to demand her loyalty, the Wekk are just another kind of bloodbag.'

The warning shot came. It was felt rather than heard, the boom of a distant rollercoaster punching through the outer skin of the ship.

'What are we going to do?' Randall said helplessly. The Wekk didn't deserve this, and he didn't want to bring it on them.

Rorvik wasn't so sympathetic. 'You're the leader,' he said. 'Lead.'

'But I never led anything in my life. I've always been a . . . a servant of the State.'

'That's Randall talking. *Your* life can be measured in days; I don't think you've got much idea of what you can or can't do.'

'I know I can't work miracles. We've got to get some kind of signal to Valum.'

'She doesn't want a signal. She wants you.'

Randall tried to push his way over to the door, but the Wekk resisted. He had some idea of getting down to a vacuum dock and finding a way to reach Valum, but they wouldn't let him; they thought he was trying to leave them, and they pushed and hauled him back. The more he tried, the more firmly they contained him, and when he felt the undermind rising to offer him reserves of destructive strength he gave up, not wishing to maim or kill.

Rorvik wasn't so worried. He wasn't troubled by sentiment for the Wekk, and his own rescue was certain; he could even afford to feel some triumph now that it was proven that Randall's chauvinistic humanity had been totally unfounded, and was in fact little more than a calculated device to put him through his paces.

'What's the matter, Messiah?' he said. 'Can't you deliver?'

Randall looked at him, shocked. 'I don't believe it. You're enjoying this!'

'I'm entitled to it after what I've taken from you. What price your bloodbag arrogance now?'

'At least I tried. I met you halfway.'

'You talked about it, that's all. You did it because you wanted to use me. So how does it feel?'

The Wekk touched him continuously, a dancing pattern of supplication reaching no higher than his chest, the extent of their short arms. He was drowning in their hope.

'For God's sake let me through!' he pleaded, but they didn't understand. 'I'm trying to *help* you!'

Distant explosions then began to sound off in even succession, rattling the floor and the fittings and agitating the Wekk even more. The ship was being opened up.

The next one was close and loud. They felt the floor bend, and after a few moments a distict stirring in the air. There was a whisper outside, the thin shriek of draining atmosphere as it funnelled through the ship. Randall realized that he was going to have to face vacuum, and the prospect frightened him; no reassurance on his survival would take away that basic fear. He asked Rorvik if he could tell him what to expect.

'It'll hurt for a while,' Rorvik said. 'That's how it was with me the first time. You want to breathe, but you can't. Then after a while you realize you really don't need to and the pain goes away.'

'I'm scared,' Randall admitted.

Rorvik was going to frame some sarcasm, but changed his mind. 'I know,' he said. 'I remember what it's like, all of it. I didn't mean what I said before.'

'No, don't take it back. I deserved it.'
It was barely audible. 'What?'
'I said I . . .'
The last of the air went all at once.

Twenty-Six

Willis was chosen to go alone to the World Ship. He piloted the craft he'd been given as close as possible to one of the larger breaches, and prepared for his first experience of raw vacuum.

He resisted the temptation to hold his breath, letting it be drawn from him in a crystal cloud. When reflex tried to reach for more air he experienced a moment of panic as his collapsed lungs stayed down, but it passed. He was aware of peculiar tides and pressures within his body as its structure fought to expand, but they were no more than a discomfort. A bloodbag would have popped and showered its matter everywhere.

There was a mess of collapsed foam on the corridor floor, frozen into place before it could expand and function. It stuck to his boots as he crossed it.

Silent as a tomb and the comparison was apt. He found his first dead Wekk two levels in, four of them slumped in a group. They seemed to have died fairly placidly, but how could he know? Their expressions told him nothing, half-blinkered and slackjawed, and they had no evolutionary need for the eloquent huddling-mechanism of mammals.

A trail of lizard corpses on the next level in led him to the computer room. It seemed that the whole shipload had tried to congregate in this one place, and Willis was slowed by having to lift bodies out of the way so that there would be enough room for him to pass.

The computer room was a burnt-out mess, and the most crowded spot of all. Here he found Randall and Rorvik.

Rorvik recognized him, but Randall didn't respond in any way. He was on the floor, pulled down by several dozen clawlike hands that had gripped the fabric of his suit. There was no malice in their grip, just a need for pointless comfort in their pain.

Willis bent to unhook some of them. Randall looked at him then, and lifted his hand from the head of one of the Wekk as if to stop him; but the gesture died before it was completed and he lowered his eyes again.

Willis worked quickly, efficiently. When Randall was freed he moved over to look at Rorvik. The leg was bad, but there was nothing vital missing to prevent regeneration. Most important, the femoral strut was intact, a little scratched but otherwise undamaged. Willis hoisted him over his shoulder for the journey back.

Randall neither cooperated nor resisted. He allowed himself to be led, following inexpressively through the marmoreal calm of the dead world. He climbed into Willis's craft and sat with his arms around his knees, lost on the distant horizon of some inner vision as Rorvik was loaded in beside him.

The other simulacra had meanwhile docked and reoccupied their old training ground. Much of their enthusiasm and pride seemed to have gone; whereas before they would have immediately begun engaging in sweep exercises and extermination patterns now they were robbed of goal and purpose. Valum knew of no way that she could raise their morale – she was more inclined to join them in their despondency. When the word reached her that Willis was back, she went down to the bay to meet him.

His look confirmed it. Whether she liked it or not, she would have to accept Randall as her overlord.

'You don't seem very happy,' Willis commented.

'None of your business,' she replied sharply.

'No, Valum.' Willis indicated the craft in the bay behind him. A couple of the other simulacra were helping Rorvik out. 'Do you want to speak to him?'

'Things will change around here, Willis. Does he want to speak to me?'

'He doesn't seem to be interested in anything much at the moment.'

Rorvik had been carried away, and she let herself in through the side of the craft. It had once been a sporty little runabout in some far-off and forgotten system, and there wasn't much room. She had to slide in next to Randall, and they sat together in silence for a while.

Randall was the first to speak. He said, 'You going to kill me?' He sounded almost hopeful.

'You can't die. Not by any normal means. And much as I might want to try, I can't kill you.'

He nodded. He'd already known it. 'Too many changes. I can't keep up with them.'

'Shape up, commander. You've got duties and responsibilities now. If not to yourself, then to the rest of us.'

He made a real effort to take an interest, and it almost worked. 'What am I expected to do?'

'In the absence of the ship, tell us where we go next. It's your decision. We can still land and take the city – ' he was shaking his head firmly – 'What, then? We have to go somewhere. Down there is a man wearing your face and using your name. Why don't we go find him?'

'No. Give me time to think.'

'Whatever you want.' And then, reluctantly but to make the point, 'Sir.'

'We can't go back to the city,' he explained, 'we're too different. Even with the best intentions we'd undermine it, destroy it. And I've got too many of Randall's loyalties left in me.'

'So what do Randall's loyalties say we should do?'

'Find somewhere of our own, that's what.'

She didn't much like the idea, but it wasn't up to her to say. 'I can't argue.'

'That's right,' Randall said, brightening slightly. 'You can't.'

Willis was waiting outside, and he had a request. He wanted to go back to the Ice Palace. He wanted to go home.

Valum was shocked. 'You're sick, Willis. Remember what you are.'

The new commander was aware that such an issue could be far from simple. 'Machine bodies, Valum, but human personalities. Without the Ship they're starting to revert. Don't you feel something like it?'

'I've got nothing to revert to,' she replied stiffly. 'I wasn't based on anybody. I'm pure construct, even more so than Rorvik. They patterned me from the dreams of the creatures taken from the Ice Palace.'

'Then I'm . . . I'm sorry,' Randall said.

'Don't be. I miss nothing.'

They allowed Willis to keep the craft that he'd been using, and also gave him permission to take any equipment that might be necessary for repairs on the icebreaker. Some of the others considered going with him, but none did.

Randall tried to get used to his new status. It was an odd and unhappy feeling, but Rorvik's example was an encouragement to him. If that scrap pile could do it . . .

He gave his first order, that the broken ship should be cut loose and discarded. Then they would slingshot around the sun.

'I can't fly a World Ship,' Valum said.

'Rorvik can. And with a ship like this one we can pick our own system.'

He'd learned the lesson of his arrogance, and now would have to learn to live with it. He had all of time to make a success of it.

Killoran had been given a bunk of his own and his first taste of Ice Palace yeast. He said it was awful, almost as bad as the food in the Élite's own restaurant.

The bruising started to go down, leaving his shoulders stiff and sore with an ugly yellow-blue patterning that faded more slowly. When somebody offered him a bag of ice for a compress he thought it was funny. When twelve more people had made the same joke his smile became fixed and the appreciative laugh didn't come so easily.

They called for a few minutes, chatted for a while, and then moved on. He was conscious of a certain look they all had, as if they were only making small-talk while they watched for some sign from him. Of course, he could guess what it was. They were waiting to see what he was going to do next about their escape.

It seemed impossible that the icebreaker should be useless to them, but that was the case. Because of a single act of sabotage and an obstinate inboard computer it was completely immobilized in a frustrating state of readiness. Under the circumstances it was pointless to guard the captain, who was now as much a prisoner as any of them. They even gave him the last snow suit. To show his willingness he'd gone along with a surface team to continue the search of the spaceport and shuttle wreck; although they found much of interest they found nothing of real value.

When Cohn 'dropped in' Killoran was lying face-down on his bunk, contemplating the rough grain of the insulating wood before him. Cohn made the compress joke, and Killoran pretended to be amused. With this formality out of the way Cohn sat on one of the other bunks and they talked.

Killoran asked about the Worm, and Cohn said that he'd probably live in spite of what Berg wanted to do to him. He'd locked himself in his office and piled all his furniture against the door. Killoran said that he couldn't see such a simple measure stopping Berg.

'It wouldn't,' Cohn agreed, 'but he's making the most of it. Him and Bulstrode take turns sitting outside and talking about all the horrible things they're going to do when the Worm comes out.'

Killoran said, 'I can't get angry at him, somehow.'

'You may not be,' Cohn said, suddenly serious. 'But the others need something to take it out on. To be so near and then to lose it . . .'

'I was afraid they'd take it out on me. For promising and not being able to deliver.'

'Be grateful there's a Worm, then. He's needed after all.'

They went on to talk about Morden. He was recovering slowly from his severe shaking, but at least he was recovering. They were giving him food from the dispensing machines on the icebreaker as he didn't yet appear to have the fortitude necessary for keeping down a mouthful of yeast. Several of the prisoners had tried the machines' products and decided that perhaps the yeast wasn't so bad after all, even if it did, in the words of one of them, taste like salted pigeon shit.

There was a tap on the door, and the icebreaker captain looked in. Killoran prepared himself for yet another compress joke, but it was something else; a figure had been spotted in the twilight on the ice, and it was heading for the Palace.

Killoran decided against spreading the news, fearing yet another false promise and general disappointment. The three of them went together to the cargo bay for helmets and then out on to the grey-blue plain of the ice cap.

There was a light snow powdering down, but hardly any wind. The clouds were banked in midnight blue right down to the edge of the world, and the flat basin which spread from the Palace to the ice cliffs in the far distance seemed to glow with a light of its own. The walker showed against this as a black shape, the snow-ditch of his route a shadowed crack that trailed him.

The party and the stranger were almost together before recognition was possible, and then Killoran called a halt before they met.

It was Willis.

'Don't be nervous,' he said. 'It's different from last time. I'm on my own. I've come home and I want to help.'

'Help?' Cohn said suspiciously. 'How?'

'I've got some welding gear back there,' Willis said, and indicated along the direction of his trail. 'I couldn't get down any closer because there's no beacon. I'll need help to get the gear, but we should be able to fix the stabilizers.'

Killoran didn't exactly run and embrace him, although it was one of the possibilities that came into his mind; it was balanced by Willis's earlier display of hostility and his allegiance with a mysterious enemy that had dropped from the sky without warning and departed without explanation.

'Suppose we take you at face value,' he said. 'We've got a lot of questions that Morden's too sick to answer.'

Willis spread his hands in an open gesture. 'I'll tell you whatever I can.'

Cohn said, 'I don't remember you being so cooperative before.'

'I needed a holiday.'

'And what about Randall?' Killoran said.

'Randall's dead now. He won't be coming back. Is there any chance of getting some help to bring the repair equipment back?'

Killoran wasn't ready to let the question go. 'How did he die?'

'Look,' Cohn said, 'why don't you quiz him later? If we can get the tanks fixed up we can get the whole story on the way home. I'll go back and get some of the others. You coming?'

'No, I'll go on. Make sure they bring a sled after us.'

'But you're hurt.'

'So I feel better.'

Randall had wanted it this way. Willis could tell as much or as little of the truth as he liked, but Randall was dead. It was a neater, less painful alternative.

Cohn went back to the Palace to give them the news.